IN FOR
THE
KILL

IN FOR THE KILL

SHANNON McKENNA

KENSINGTON BOOKS
www.kensingtonbooks.com

KENSINGTON BOOKS are published by

Kensington Publishing Corp.
119 West 40th Street
New York, NY 10018

All Kensington titles, imprints, and distributed lines are available at special quantity discounts for bulk purchases for sales promotion, premiums, fund-raising, educational, or institutional use.

Special book excerpts or customized printings can also be created to fit specific needs. For details, write or phone the office of the Kensington Special Sales Manager: Kensington Publishing Corp., 119 West 40th Street, New York, NY 10018. Attn. Special Sales Department. Phone: 1-800-221-2647.

Kensington and the K logo Reg. U.S. Pat. & TM Off.

eISBN-13: 978-1-61773-858-6
eISBN-10: 1-61773-858-1
First Kensington Electronic Edition: February 2015

ISBN-13: 978-0-7582-7351-2
ISBN-10: 0-7582-7351-7
First Kensington Trade Paperback Printing: February 2015

10 9 8 7 6 5 4 3 2 1

Printed in the United States of America

PROLOGUE

Rome, Italy

Josef picked at his nails with his knife, stupefied with boredom. Despite all his contacts, his skills with explosives, interrogation, and small arms, he was still forced to babysit the vor's worthless son.

Sasha Cherchenko was engrossed in his tablet, sunken face eerily lit by the screen's glare. Mute, pathetic, junkie waste of skin. Heir to an empire worth billions. His very existence offended Josef, who had fought for every bite of food and breath of air he took, for his entire fucking life.

The silence grated. Josef got up to stretch, and circled Sasha from behind. He was watching a lecture on the tablet. A pretty young woman was talking. Josef abruptly recognized her and froze, startled.

That was Svetlana Ardova, daughter of that hellbitch Sonia, who had fucked Josef over. He had not seen pictures of the girl in years. Abducted at twelve, doomed for death by organ harvesting.

The camera zoomed close. Big, tilted hazel eyes, lush mouth, glossy hair. A sweet treat. The media had glommed on to that avidly after her spectacular rescue years ago. She was prettier now. He licked his lips.

Svetlana indicated a screen, where a photo was projected. Sonia's striking face stared out. Words, scribbled on the picture, in Cyrillic. Josef lunged for Sasha's tablet, yanking the headphones off him, ignoring Sasha's startled yelp of protest. He hit the volume, maxed it.

". . . book will be dedicated to my parents' memory," Svetlana's voice blared. Josef dragged the cursor, let the last few seconds of video run again. He froze the frame when Sonia's image appeared.

The scribble read, The Sword of Cain. The rest was trimmed away but for a couple of numbers. His ears roared. After six years, a place to begin the search again. Someone to squeeze, until she popped.

Sasha croaked, in his hoarse, halting voice, trying to tug the tablet back. Josef struck him, sending him sprawling across the coffee table. He ignored the young man's scratchy whimpering as he dialed his boss.

"Yes," drawled Pavel Cherchenko's gravelly voice.

"We have a lead." Josef's voice shook with excitement. He waited a beat to calm it. "The Sword of Cain, written on one of Sonia's photos. Svetlana displayed a slide, in a lecture online. I can fly to Portland today."

The vor grunted. "And my sons? Who watches them?"

Sasha whimpered. Josef smacked the back of his head. "They have Andrei and Aleksei to guard them."

A long, teeth-grinding pause ensued. "Go to Portland," the vor said.

The video was playing again. ". . . only one heart is healed, only one life saved, it will have been worth it. Thank you."

The room erupted in applause. Svetlana stood in the spotlight, challenging him with her eyes. Such a delicate thing. Ripe to be conquered, ravaged. Punished, for all of Sonia's sins.

Oh, yes. Let the pretty little daughter pay and pay.

CHAPTER 1

Sam Petrie leaned against the wall, arms folded. He stared into the dance floor, careful not to meet anyone's eyes. He wasn't here for chitchat. Against every last lingering instinct for self-preservation, he was at another no-holds-barred McCloud Crowd wedding, trolling for a chance to scope out the elusive Svetlana Ardova. She of the big, tragic eyes, the high, pointed tits. And the obscure, inexplicable prejudice against him.

It was almost two years since that kiss in Bruno's studio. But that event had transformed his schoolboy crush into a full-out obsession.

Which was why he'd snookered himself into accepting the invitation to Aaro and Nina's wedding. Nina's pregnancy had derailed it last year, but their twins, Julia and Oksana, were six months old now, so wedding plans had finally gone forward, and the gang was all there. Great food and booze and music. Squealing kids. Everyone dancing, having a good time, being curious about shit that was not their business. While he lurked in the corner, hot-eyed. Staring at Sveti like a panting perv-weasel. It was humbling. He'd locked up many specimens of the kind of obsessed asshole he was now, and rejoiced to see them off the streets.

Sveti was talking to a bevy of hotties in evening gowns, all holding stringed instruments. The Venus Ensemble, aka the eye candy orchestra. Trafficked from Eastern European conservatories, lured by promises of green cards, subsequently embroiled in a deadly scheme involving mind-control drugs and other crazy shit that Sam still didn't quite believe. Kev McCloud had saved them from an unspeakable fate, and the news coverage had given the group awesome publicity. They'd formed a hot string ensemble and were making money hand over fist.

Hurray. Chalk one up for the good guys.

The Venus Ensemble were stunners, yes, but Sveti blew them away. She was the smallest, even in killer heels, but so perfect. Vivid, in that crimson dress. His eyes hurt from the hyperstimulation. Tilted hazel eyes over Slavic cheekbones. Full, soft red lips calculated to invoke impure thoughts, and a regal attitude that instantly rebuked said impure thoughts. High, perfect tits. Taut nipples. The sight made his hands tingle. Her hair was twisted into a complicated knot. It looked great, but he liked it better loose. His fingers clenched, remembering that silken floss. He wanted to kiss the heart-shaped port-wine birthmark on her neck. Trace its borders. Study it like a map.

He sidled closer. She was talking in Russian or some dialect thereof. It turned him on, hearing her speak her native language. Then again, it turned him on to hear her talk at all, period.

Aw, fuck it. Even her sullen silences turned him on.

He wrenched his gaze away and stared out at swaying couples. There was Sveti's date, Josh Cattrell—tall, prosperous, and flushed with champagne. Might or might not be the reason Sveti blew off Sam's phone calls, texts, e-mails. Any comparisons between Josh and Sam would not be in Sam's favor at the moment. He'd been too lazy and rebellious to cut his hair lately, and had resorted to yanking his brown mane into a ponytail. He'd shaved last week, for the psych eval, but the shrink's conclusion had pissed him off so much, he hadn't bothered since. And he was too thin for his suit, everywhere but the shoulders, which strained at the seams as a result of obsessive workouts. His face looked grim and sunken when he caught it reflected in glass.

Nah, he didn't stack up well next to Cattrell's stylish haircut, fresh shave, charming dimples, fake tan. The perfectly cut suit.

Empty-headed dickface. Sam hated him on sight.

Sveti had known Cattrell since she was thirteen. He'd briefly shared her imprisonment, before they'd been rescued from the organ thieves. Most episodes involving McClouds and their pals had an off-the-charts weird factor. Weird usually turned him off, but not when Sveti was involved. It was wrist-thick iron cables, yanking him in.

Josh Cattrell was an ass-bite, flashing his overly whitened teeth at every babe he saw. Sam watched him punch the number of one of the catering staff into his smartphone, whisper in her ear, pat her ass.

This piece of shit was his competition?

The guy turned without missing a beat and held out his arms to Sveti. He pulled her onto the dance floor and dropped his hand to her hip, like he hadn't just been fondling another woman's booty. The singer crooned a slow tune as the hand crept lower.

Fuck this shit. Fuck it into lightless oblivion.

The feeling built like steam, hot and dangerous. He didn't recognize it, or have a strategy for dealing with it. He played it cool with the ladies, as a long string of disgruntled would-be girlfriends would attest. He'd heard plenty about his "commitment issues" over the years. "Man slut" was another phrase they tossed around.

Out, out, out. Get your deranged, unhinged ass out before you do something pointless and stupid. Just fuck off. NOW.

Sveti was too young for him, anyway. Josh was closer to her in age. Not a lot closer, though. Maybe five years younger than Sam's thirty-three. Maybe only four. Four fucking measly years. *Four.*

He barreled into someone on his way to the coatroom and mumbled an apology, but the person grabbed his arm. "Hey, Sam."

It took a few moments to place the guy. Tall, tanned, closely shorn dark hair. It was the nose that finally pegged him. "Oh. Miles."

The man partly responsible for derailing Sam's career as homicide detective. Not that he held any grudges. Miles had just been trying to keep himself and his girlfriend alive. But Sam's involvement in Miles' bizarre adventures, however slight, had not helped his career prospects.

"I've, uh, been meaning to talk to you," Miles said.

Not. Miles had been busy rolling around on sugar sand beaches with his adoring bride on their protracted, well-deserved honeymoon.

The weirdness of their tale had made the higher-ups nervous and uncomfortable. Which made people want to blame someone. Punish someone. Step right up, Sam. At the ready.

The woo-woo factor had sealed his doom. They'd put him away. Using the excuse of last year's gunshot wound and the psych evaluations that followed. PTSD, the shrinks said, but that was bullshit. His symptoms weren't that bad. Sure, he was twitchy and depressed, but so were a lot of people who were out there working. That diagnosis had far more to do with some discreet phone calls from his father to various local politicians who were tight with the police commissioner.

He pushed on past the guy. "Gotta go, Miles. See you around."

Miles grabbed his arm. "Wait. I just wanted to say, uh, that I appreciate your giving me that heads-up, back when I was fighting for our lives. I haven't said that to you directly, being out of town so long, and I've been wanting to. And you, uh . . . weren't at our wedding."

"Yeah." He'd been in the hospital. Gut shot. Miles looked just too fucking relaxed, tanned, and sexually fulfilled. Choffing all those ripe mangoes, boinking his true love on all those beaches. It stuck in Sam's craw. "Where have you guys been?" he asked, just to torture himself.

Miles had the grace to look sheepish. "Bali, most recently. We rented this tree house, in a banyan jungle."

"Sweet," Petrie said.

"Pretty much. We only came back because Lara, well . . . we're expecting." His large Adam's apple bobbed nervously. "So we wanted to settle into the house. Get ready for the new arrival."

"Great." Sam coughed it out like a hair ball. "Congratulations."

"Thanks," Miles said. "We're really excited. But if there was anyone I could talk to, you know, to explain how things really went—"

"God, no. Thanks, but no," he said hastily.

"Okay." Miles looked downcast. "Just wish I could help. So what are you doing with yourself these days, anyhow? Still on medical leave?"

Wow, where to begin. Loafing like a slob, when he wasn't sprinting through the park as if flesh-eating zombies were chasing him. Day trading. Reading Sveti's anti-trafficking blog. Watching the flesh-crawling adventures she sometimes live-streamed on her viral v-log, following every peep of her Twitter feed. Watching her TED talk, about her own personal journey into anti-trafficking activism. On his computer, tablet, smartphone. Obsessively. Or staring at her Facebook photo gallery. Not that she'd friended him. He'd hacked her account.

"I've been evaluating my options," he hedged.

"I hear you're getting pressure to join the family business. Some big hedge fund, right?"

Sam was startled. He'd mentioned it in passing to Kev, weeks back. Now here was Miles spouting it back at him. He hadn't thought they were so interested in his life. Hell, he himself wasn't that interested in his life. "Yeah, some," he admitted. "I'd rather slit my own throat."

Miles' eyebrow went up. "Why? Do you suck at it?"

"No, I'm good at it. But just because you're good at something doesn't mean you should be doing it." He'd gotten dangerously skilled lately at high-tech stalking, for instance.

"I hear you. I've got a few unspeakable skills myself these days."

Miles sounded like he was veering toward the issue of his purported psychic powers, about which Sam really did not want to hear. He turned to go, then jerked back into the niche in the hall that led to the bathrooms. A phalanx of blood-chilling femininity was advancing down the corridor. Tam and Becca were frogmarching a struggling, squawking Sveti straight toward them.

"You . . . shut . . . *up!*" Tam snarled. "I'm not letting you do this!"

"I have shut up for years! I am done shutting up!" Sveti lapsed into some Slavic language or other, her voice shrilly impassioned.

"No, you are not," Becca said in response to Sveti's tirade. "He would kill you if you did that. Calm down, Sveti. Keep it together."

"I will not be gagged, not again! I am *sick* of this. . . ."

Her voice swelled in volume and then faded as the three women proceeded past the niche without noticing them.

Miles peered around the corner. "Weird," he said, in a wondering voice. "I've never seen Sveti freak out. Wonder what set her off."

He took off in pursuit, and after a second, Sam did, too. Anything that could drive Sveti into a hot frenzy had something to teach him.

It didn't take investigative skills to find the door. Sveti and Tam were bellowing at each other, Becca in between, bleating desperate entreaties to calm down. The two men slunk into the parlor. Nina and Aaro had rented a lavish nineteenth-century timber baron's mansion for their reception, and Tam flipped on a wall sconce fashioned of stained glass that lit the ornately decorated room with a dim glow like firelight.

". . . expect me to be silent while that man smirks in my face? He did business with Zhoglo! And heroin dealers, and meth cooks, and the filthy scum who traffic women and children for slave labor and organs and sex! And I'm supposed to sip my champagne and make nice?"

"I expect you to keep your head!" Tam yelled back. "Why this overwhelming need to attract attention from people who would kill you for an insult? You've already gotten death threats! What more do you—"

"Death threats?" Sam's voice was sharp. "From whom?"

The three women swiveled their heads to glare at the intruders.

"Piss off, Sam," Tam said, with a flap of her hand. "We're busy, and we didn't ask for your input. The man is everything that you say, of course. He's also the groom's father, so you have no business—"

"They were fools to invite me to an event where a piece of filthy mafiya scum is on the guest list!"

"They didn't invite him!" Becca yelled. "He crashed, Sveti, with four big, armed thugs escorting him! So unless you want this party, full of your friends and their young children, to turn into a dangerous brawl at best and a shootout at worst, you will stick a fucking sock in it!"

Sveti hid her face. He saw a flash of her shaking mouth, painted slut red. The gloss had worn off, but the matte stain lingered.

She caught his glance. "What are you looking at?" she snapped.

"Nothing," he said. "So Oleg Arbatov crashed the wedding? That's special." And typical. This crowd liked to keep things interesting.

"He walked in twenty minutes ago," Becca said. "Nick about had a heart attack. Aaro's trying to psi-bully him into leaving. Nina's working the charm angle. He wants to spend quality time with the twins. He's sick of being put off. Benevolent old Grandpa Oleg."

Sveti shot Sam a look that was bright with challenge. "You're a cop," she said. "Arrest the corrupt old goat. Throw him in jail."

"I'm not currently representing the law," Sam pointed out.

"Can't you do a citizen's arrest?" Miles asked innocently.

"You know how the system works," Sam said. "If I don't have evidence that's admissible in court, what's the point? If you want to provoke him into cutting your throat in front of witnesses, that would work. I could arrest him then. Your move, man. Feel free."

"Shut up, Petrie." Sveti's voice quivered. "You're useless."

"Call me Sam. And what's this about death threats?"

"None of your goddamn business!"

Sam turned his gaze on Tam. "Death threats from whom?"

Tam rolled her eyes. "If she wants you to know, she'll tell you. Otherwise, fuck off."

"Mama?"

They turned at the small voice. Rachel, Tam's adopted daughter. She held Becca's little girl Sofia by the hand. Rachel was tall, pretty, a mop of black curls. Starting to bud.

"Is Sveti okay?" Sofia piped up.

Sveti gave the girls a tremulous smile. "Of course, sweetheart."

Sofia ran and flung her arms around Sveti's waist. Sveti hugged the little girl back, fiercely.

"You're sure?" Rachel looked unconvinced. "You were yelling. You never yell. Did that old man do something bad to you?"

"No, he didn't. Everything's fine, baby." Tam clapped her hands. "Rachel, come with me to find Daddy. Sofia, you come, too. Becca, monitor the situation in the ballroom." She fixed her piercing topaz gaze on Miles and Sam. "You two stay here with Sveti. Do not under any circumstances let her go back into the ballroom. She has enough problems without getting her name on Oleg Arbatov's hit list."

Tam clicked past them and seized the young girls by the hand. Becca followed, adding her own glare to reinforce Tam's directive. The door clicked closed. The silence that followed was profound.

Miles' glance darted from Sveti, who had hidden her face behind her hands again, to Sam. He gulped. "I, uh . . . need to go find Lara," he said to Sam. "Can you handle this okay on your own?"

His heart gave a sharp, percussive thud, like a jackhammer. Oh, *fuck* yeah, he could so handle this on his own. "I'm good," he said.

"I do not need to be *handled!*" Sveti flared. Her mascara had run, smudging into a sexy, wild-girl raccoon mask.

Miles backed toward the door. "'Course you don't. Good, then. So, later, dude." Miles sidled out. "All yours." The door clicked shut.

All yours. The fantasy head rush was swiftly quenched when she lunged for the door. He blocked her path. "No way."

Her golden eyes widened, shocked. "You don't think you're keeping me in here, do you? You're not serious!"

"You heard Tam," Sam replied. "You leave this room, and she comes after my balls with the bolt cutters."

Sveti's chest heaved, which highlighted her excellent nipple hard-on. "What Tam might do to you is nothing compared to what I will do to you if you try to stop me from walking out that door."

Sam reached and flicked the knob lock. "I'll take my chances."

She crossed her arms over the nipple jut. "Wrong answer."

"Yeah? What are you going to do to me? You got a pair of bolt cutters under your skirt, too?"

She snorted. "Most guys seem to think so."

He admired the hot flush staining her cheekbones. "I don't."

"Good for you. Congratulations. You're very brave. Now get out of my way. I can't stand being confined. Not after what happened to me."

He waved that away. "Don't play the captive-waif-in-the-dungeon pity card with me. It's old and tired. Move on."

Her jaw sagged in utter shock. "You *asshole!*"

"Yeah, sure," he agreed. "I have nothing to lose. You already think I'm a dickhead. Why not say whatever I damn well please?"

Curling wisps of hair swayed around her chin as she shook her head. "I have bigger problems than your unrequited crush, Petrie!"

"Burrrrrnnn," he murmured. "Tell me about those big problems, since we're shut in here together. You can start with the death threats."

Her eyes slid away. "I do not want to discuss that."

"Too bad. I say we do."

A tense silence followed that statement. She flicked him a wary glance from under those long lashes. "You can't bully me," she said.

"You think not?" he said. "Let's see about that. Spit it out. Who, what, where, and when. Was it that sweatshop bust, six months ago? Those piece-of-shit snakeheads Helen Wong and Him Goh?"

Her eyes went wide and startled. "How do you know about them?"

"I watch the news, Sveti," he said patiently. "I'm a cop. I have friends. I hear things. Plus, you live-streamed, blogged, and tweeted the whole thing to a hundred and twenty thousand followers."

"And you are one of them now? Spying on me?"

He plowed right on past that one, there being no point. "Sneaking into that place with a live video camera on you was suicidal. You should have just passed the tip on to the police and let them deal with it."

Her chin tilted up. "There were thirty-four trafficked Chinese nationals locked in there, slaving eighteen hours a day! I saw my chance and took it! People have to see for themselves. It's the only thing that makes it real for them. That's what pulls in the donations!"

"You can't help anyone if you're dead," he pointed out. "But never mind that now. Just tell me about the death threats."

"It was just a letter," she said, defensive. "Hand-delivered. It said they were going to kill me. That's all. Nothing came of it."

"When?"

She shook it off. "Months ago, now."

"So why aren't you guarded twenty-four/seven?" he snarled.

"I was! For months! Finally, I put my foot down, because it was absurd, Sam. I can't live my life like that. Don't worry! It's covered!"

Covered, his ass. But he knew a dead-end conversation when he heard one. He had lots of practice. Those were a Petrie family hobby.

"Fine," he said. "On to the next item that's not my business."

Her eyes dilated. He wished he had the super-senses they said Miles had now. His heart pounded too hard to hear hers, certainly at that distance. He started to close that distance, and she skittered back a pace. It took all his willpower to stay motionless, leaving none to hold back the incredibly ill-advised question. "If you don't want to talk about death threats, then tell me about your love life."

Her mouth tightened. "I would rather not."

"Tell me about lover boy. How long have you been seeing him?"

"You mean Josh? I've known him ever since Nick rescued me from Zhoglo. He's a good friend."

"Define 'friend,'" he said. "Does it mean, free to fondle your ass?"

Her chin tilted up a notch. "You're being invasive."

"Yeah? Would you feel invaded to learn that he's hitting on two girls on the catering staff, in between groping slow dances with you?"

Her gaze dropped, but she did not look as startled or upset about that revelation as she ought to. "You have no right to judge."

"Wrong," he informed her. "That ten minutes in Ranieri's home office two years ago. No matter how long ago, no matter how you've ignored me since then, that ten minutes gives me the right to give a shit. Tell me about Cattrell. Are you fucking him?"

"No!" The denial popped out, vehement and breathless.

"Planning to?" he persisted. If this was going to be the definitive crotch kick of reality, then bring it on.

Sveti's gaze dropped. He waited.

"You're not involved with him at all," he said.

"I told you," she said. "We're good friends."

"And it doesn't bug you that he was fondling the waitstaff."

"No, not anymore," she said softly. "I've known for a long time that he doesn't have the feelings for me that I'd, um, hoped."

Hoped? Sveti had hoped, and the guy hadn't delivered the goods? God, Cattrell must be brain damaged not to hit on that.

"He was touching you as if you were lovers," he said. "But you're not an ass-grab kind of girl. You asked him to do that for my benefit. He was a safe date, in case I came to smoke you out. Your human shield."

Her color rose. "Wow, Petrie. You may be surprised to learn this, but you are not, in fact, the center of all my thoughts."

"Tell me if I'm right," he persisted, though he was already sure.

"Get out of my way!" She tried to push past him, toward the door.

He grabbed her. He knew he shouldn't, but the part of him that knew had no say. The rest of him clamped on to her, nerves jangling at the sweet shock of contact. Laced up into that tight cage of crimson satin, her heat and scent overwhelmed his senses. She strained away from him. Provoking a dangerous, animal urge to drag her close. Pin her down.

"Let me go, Petrie," she said. "Or I'll start to scream."

"You treat me like I'm a criminal lowlife, out to rape and pillage," he said. "I'm one of the good guys, Sveti."

"Hah," she muttered. "There are no good guys."

"We're all bad, then? You lump me in with Arbatov? Zhoglo?"

The mention of the two mafiya vors energized her struggle. He clamped her tighter against his body. Her heartbeat was so frantic and birdlike. She felt so fragile. But she wasn't.

"I can't believe we're talking about my love life when that monster is in the ballroom with my friends and their kids, eating tempura-dipped zucchini flowers! He's committed horrible crimes against innocents!"

"You're not the only one who tries to protect the innocent."

She sniffed. "Yes, of course. The police are so very noble."

He waited for a moment. "Not fair," he said quietly. "We try."

She looked down, abashed. "That is true, and I apologize," she said. "This is silly, Sam. I promise, I won't be rude to the criminals. I won't get myself or anyone else killed. Let go. Please. I'll be good."

Now she was trying sweet reason. Who cared. She might have gotten a handle on her self-control, but he most definitely had not.

His grip did not slacken as he put words to the thought forming in his head. "You know what your problem is, Sveti?"

She tilted a winged dark brow. "I imagine you're going to tell me?"

"Your love life, the thing with Josh. Me. It's the same issue. You think sex is frivolous. The real deal is the big bad story of your life. Ogres trying to cut your heart out and sell it. The last-minute rescue from a grisly death. The hell you went through gives your life purpose. It defines you. The rest is fluff. It doesn't deserve your full attention."

"And you think you deserve my full attention, Sam?"

"Yeah," he said baldly. "And you deserve mine. My full, undivided attention, all over every inch of your body, for a prolonged period of uninterrupted time."

She shrank away. "I don't have time for games."

"Yeah, getting buried in a concrete bridge piling, that's Svetlana Ardova's idea of a good time. You must be a lot of fun at parties, babe."

"Fuck you, Petrie!"

Ooh, hostile. "You have to let the past go," he told her.

"Do I?" She shook with a bitter jolt of laughter. "Really! Wow, Sam, thanks for the insight! Like it's that easy! You have no idea."

"You've still got to let go," he repeated stubbornly. "The evil vor, the dungeon, the whole fucking horrible mess. You survived. It's over. The end. Stop dragging that ten-ton weight around."

"You don't know shit about it! You can't say that to me!"

"Of course, nobody can say that to you. That's why your love life is so hot and happening. All those unsayable things start to choke a guy after about ten minutes."

"Let go of me, goddamnit!" She flailed furiously.

"But I can say the unsayable. You already think I'm scum. I don't have to pretend to be anything but a dickhead. Ahhh. Freedom."

"I never said you were a dickhead," she whispered.

Happy news, but he wasn't getting cocky about it just yet.

"Where do you get courage to say unsayable things?" she asked. "All the men I meet are afraid of me. So what makes you so brave?"

He shrugged. "I don't know. Just dumb that way, I guess."

There was a floor-length mirror. He tugged her across the floor until they were reflected in it, right down to the pointy toes peeping out beneath the hem of her skirt. She made a distressed sound and fought her arm free to fumble for a tissue, with which she tried to wipe mascara.

"I scare you to death," he said.

She somehow managed to look haughty while mopping up her nose with a tissue. "No, you do not. But you are very intense."

"Just with you. Usually, I'm Mr. Mellow."

"Oh, please. Mellow men do not become homicide detectives, Petrie. They become botanists, bicycle repairmen, mathematicians, mindfulness bloggers. Organic gardeners. Zen monks."

"Call me Sam." He bent to smell her hair and she arched away, a tremor rippling through her body. "You don't have to be afraid of me."

Laughter vibrated through her. She mouthed the word. *Bullshit.*

His hand slid over her warm curves, shadowy dips and hollows. He wanted to eat up her delicate scent. Devour it in one breath. Miles could break down those pheromones into their chemical components and list their molecular formulas. But for Sam, it wasn't chemistry.

It was magic. Crazy, balls-deep enthrallment.

"You just won't give me a break," he murmured against her throat. "And I know why. You want to know my theory about you?"

She flinched away as he cupped her jaw, letting her delicate, wispy ringlets tickle his wrist. Insubstantial as a puff of breath.

"No, Petrie," she said. "To be honest, not really."

"I'm telling you anyway." He nuzzled the whorl of hair below her ear and dragged his lips over the edge of that crimson birthmark. "That day in Bruno's studio. It was too good for you."

A burst of laughter shook her. "Really?"

"It made you forget," he insisted. "For a little while, it was just you and me in the room. No evil vor, no organ pirates. No past. No future."

"Marco was there. In his crib," she corrected, primly.

"Whatever. You're so wound up in this scary story of almost getting your heart ripped out. It defines you. It freaks you out, to be cut loose from that. It makes you feel lost. Scared."

"Petrie, do everyone a favor, and don't take up psychology."

"You lost yourself," he persisted. "I could help you find it again."

The frown line between her brows deepened. "You're so arrogant."

"That day when I touched you. You came so hard. I dream about it at night. Wake up shaking. Drenched in sweat. So fucking hard."

She shook her head. "Please," she whispered.

He rubbed his cheek against that loose, gleaming topknot. "It scared you, baby. You thought you were going to die. But you won't. I'll take care of you. You won't fall to pieces. Or if you do, it'll only be for a few seconds, and I'll hold you all together. I'll hold you so tight. I'll keep you so safe." He tasted her, trailing his lips down to her collarbone.

"Sam," she breathed out. "Please."

"I'll make it so good. I'll get you off like that, over and over. I won't be rough. I won't scare you, and I won't hurt you. Just . . . trust me."

She looked up to meet his eyes. He went very still. The raw pain blazing out of them jolted him right out of his seduction schtick.

"I don't know how to trust like that," she said. "I just . . . can't. I'm really not playing hard to get. You tempt me, yes. But I hold back because I just don't have what you want. It's not there, Sam."

"What makes you think so?" he asked gently.

She shook her head, eyes squeezed shut. "That mechanism, it doesn't work, in me. I don't mean to be a tease, or cruel, or . . . or disdainful. I never wanted to be a frigid bitch. It's sad and it's awful, but it's the truth. It's my reality, and I'm sorry if I . . . I'm just so sorry."

He processed that. "So we'll work on it," he offered. "I felt a lot of potential, back there in Bruno's office. We'll fix it. No biggie."

"No biggie, he says." Her voice was strangled. "Don't try to rescue me from my past. You'll just hurt yourself. It's bigger than you are."

"How would you know how big I am?"

She shot him a glance and snorted, reddening.

"I didn't say it," he crowed, delighted. "It was you."

"English is not my first language," she said haughtily. "Don't try to trap me in word games. I will never get the joke."

She wasn't pulling away. He stroked her shoulders, encountered the straps that held up the cups of gathered fabric that her perfect tits were nestled in. He flicked the ribbons down. Her eyes widened as the fabric slid down—catching on her nipples. She jerked her hands up—

Or tried to. He caught them up short, staring into her eyes as the cups slid down to dangle over the shell of the bustier.

She didn't fight, didn't flail. Just stood there, breath stuttering rapidly in and out. Her high, beautiful breasts bared to him.

"You are so beautiful," he whispered. "I've lain awake nights staring at the ceiling, imagining you exactly like this."

He felt his way, slowly. Using those secret senses that jolted to life only when she was near. Eyes and ears that opened only for her. He strained for more. He wanted inside her hidden depths, to take possession. He waited, savoring the tension, until he dared to risk sliding his hands up to cup her breasts, with fingers that trembled.

A ripple went through her, then a sighing, barely audible moan. He caressed her, tender, spiraling whorls over and around her taut, deep pink nipples, the soft, plump under-curve, the tender fullness. So perfect. Springy, luscious. Suckable. But not now, because she'd rested her head on his shoulders, and the slight, warm weight of her head upon him was such a miracle in itself, he didn't dare mess with it.

He inhaled her scent. Warm and spicy and sweet. Her hair had come unpinned, and the thick horsetail draped over his arm, making him wish his arm was bare. His sleeve blocked out the live heft of that heavy silken rope. His fingers buzzed. She was actually letting him touch her. It put him in a state of trembling, worshipful awe.

She twisted around and looked up. Lips in reach.

That was it, just like the last time. Conscious control vanished.

She melted into him, arms twined around his neck. Oh, God, that sweet, tender inside flavor, the impossible softness of her lips. A swift glance yielded scant possibilities for taking this tryst horizontal. The floor was gleaming oak. Spindly legged chairs, tables with runners, antique breakables. No couches or lounges. So it was the wall again. He could deal with gravity. What was upper-body strength for, after all.

He scooped her up. A few steps, and he pinned her to the closest bare spot of wallpaper, fiercely intent upon tasting, touching, knowing more. He leaned to kiss her breasts, and she moaned, rib cage heaving, fingers twining in his hair. He lifted armfuls of skirt, slid his hand up her thigh. Hot, smooth. Stretchy lace, soft skin, filmy silk stretched over tender girl parts, the moisture seeping through. The heat, the wet. He couldn't wait to taste it. Lick it. Get inside. Deep inside. Oh, God, now. The wanting was a huge, feral beast inside him, clawing to get out.

Her thighs trembled. He slid his finger under the elastic, into silky folds that yielded sweetly, pressing deeper into a hot, slick paradise—

Rap, rap, rap. "Sveti? Sveti! Petrie? You in there?"

Rap, rap rap rap rap, louder and sharper. Tam's voice. A brief pause and then again, rattling at the locked door. *Rap, rap, rap.* "Sveti? Goddamnit, answer me!" Her voice was sharp with alarm.

Fuck. What, was he under some kind of a curse?

Sveti struggled out of his grip, batting his hands away. She smoothed her hair, shoehorned her tits back into the satin cups, wiping her mouth, all to no avail. She still looked like a woman who'd just been madly making out. Tousled, flushed, damp, dazed, blurred. Fuckable.

"Just a second!" she called, her voice shaking. "Coming!"

Oh, how he wished. It wouldn't have taken long to get her off, and explosively. She'd been almost there. It was so goddamn cruel.

Sveti jerked her chin toward the door. "Open it for them."

He did so reluctantly, as it rattled on its hinges.

"Sveti, open this goddamn door or I will break it down!"

Oh, man. Nick Ward's voice. He was meat. He snapped the lock and leaped swiftly back as the door flew open. Nick, Tam, and Val burst through. They stared at Sveti. Color streaked her cheekbones. Her makeup was a blotchy mask. Their accusing gaze swiveled to Sam.

"What the fuck is going on?" Nick demanded.

"Where's Miles?" Tam asked.

Sam shrugged. "He had some urgent stuff to do."

"Did he?" Tam's gaze dropped to Sam's crotch, which was still not quite presentable, despite the stressful and disappointing situation. Her mouth tightened. "I'm going to have a talk with him about that."

"Don't bother," Sveti said. "Sam was just keeping me company. I seem to remember you bullying and threatening him to do so."

"I didn't tell him to get whisker burn all over your tits," Tam said.

"Oh, shut up," Sveti flared.

There was an awkward silence. Val spoke, his voice modulated to soothe. "Go on out, Sveti. Our uninvited guest has left the premises."

"Um, who's that?" Sveti kept compulsively smoothing her hair.

Tam rolled her eyes. "Who, she asks? You were having a seizure about Oleg fifteen minutes ago." She gave Sam an appraising glance. "Never thought I'd say this, cop, but it appears you're good. Who knew?"

He didn't dare reply. Acknowledging that dangerous compliment could be his definitive bolt-cutter moment.

Sveti tossed her hair back. "Good, then. I'm glad he's gone."

"So are we all," Tam said. "Time for you to call it a night. I've told Josh to get your coat. He'll—"

"I'll give her a ride home," Sam said.

"No!" Everyone in the room, including Sveti, said it in unison.

Sam sighed. "Or not." Fuck him. Whatever.

Cattrell strode in. "I couldn't find her jacket. Tell me which—"

"No, you stay here," Sveti said. "I'll go alone."

"Alone?" Cattrell looked confused. "They said you needed a ride!"

"I'll get home by myself," she said. "Give the ride to the lucky girl from the catering staff. Whichever one you pick for the night."

Cattrell looked huffy. "We've been through this. I told you that I'm not interested in—"

"She knows," Tam cut in. "Don't flatter yourself. Puppy."

"Stop interfering, Tam!" Sveti snapped. "It's okay, Josh. I appreciate the thought, but I can call my own car." Her eyes flicked to Sam. "Thank you all for a truly memorable evening." She swept out.

Shit. The point of coming here had just walked out. The point of staying away was arrayed before him, between him and the door.

Josh Cattrell whistled softly. "Jeez. What's up with her?"

Tam pointed at Sam. "Him," she said. "He's up with her."

"Him?" The guy's eyes got round. "You mean, you're the cop?" His fists clenched. "You were supposed to scare me off, right?"

"Didn't work very well," Nick observed.

"Sure didn't," Sam agreed. "The human shield here was too busy playing grab-ass with the catering staff to do his fucking job."

"You sound like you are blaming him." Val's faintly accented voice sounded amused. "It was lucky for you that he failed, no?"

"No, love." The sweetness in Tam's voice made his neck prickle. "He's not feeling lucky. Maybe if we'd arrived five minutes later."

He would have made it last longer than five minutes, but this hardly seemed the time or the company for that particular assertion.

"What the hell are you doing, Sam?" Nick's voice was menacing.

"Minding my business," Sam said, from behind clenched teeth.

"Sveti is our business," Tam told him.

"Sveti's an adult." He barreled through them, promptly disgusted at himself for stating it, which implied that it needed to be stated.

"I'm not comfortable with this," Nick growled.

"Nobody asked you to be." Sam struggled not to cringe as he

brushed past Tam, who could poison him with an earring post. Tam's exclusive jewelry line was named Deadly Beauty. Costly bling loaded with blades, explosives, or poisons. Sam wished he didn't know about it. Not that he currently represented the law, but ignorance was bliss, if you could maintain it with any sort of credibility.

He slunk out of the place like a whipped hound and drove one-handed, to keep the hand that had gotten inside Sveti's sweet body right under his nose. He would have licked it clean, but then her heady scent would be gone from his finger too soon.

And that kind of waste was criminal.

CHAPTER 2

Rome, Italy

Sasha peered out from behind the recycling bin at the pastry bar across the street. Tables were out beneath the striped awning, but it was too cold to sit out there. The guy was now ten minutes late.

He could still change his mind, and run like hell.

It scared him shitless, to choose the meeting place. Too much responsibility. He had no faith in his own wits. He'd failed to cover his tracks before. Sonia had trusted him, believed in him, and made him believe in himself. She'd shown him a way out of this black hole—and he had let her down. Let her die. He'd been paralyzed ever since. Afraid to move a muscle, or even think a thought for himself.

But it was Sveti in danger now. Careless, brainless idiot that he was, to have watched her online lecture with Josef in the room. He was so used to pretending he was alone while they guarded him. So used to being ignored. He tried to bore his guards into a coma, and mostly he succeeded. Being guarded upstairs was far preferable to being locked in the hole downstairs. More air. He'd been watching Sveti on the tablet on autopilot, just to look at the face of another human being who did not despise him. Just to listen to her soft, musical voice. It soothed him.

But Sveti just had to choose that particular photograph of Sonia to project in that lecture. And in all the time she'd spoken, Josef just happened to look over Sasha's shoulder at that precise, disastrous moment. Now doom was crashing down on one of the last people on earth Sasha still dared to care about. All his fault. As usual.

Ironically, it was only because Josef had gone hunting Sveti that Sasha had escaped. Josef was the smartest of his father's men, of the ones in Rome, at least. The cruelest, too. Aleksei and Andrei and the others were stupid and lazy by comparison.

He had tried to be careful and methodical in his planning. Witnesses would make it harder for his father's men to slaughter them outright, but there could not be too many, so as to minimize the carnage if things went bad. The bar was in a business district, but it was early for the breakfast rush. If the man arrived at all. Lives at stake, and the guy was twelve fucking minutes late.

Sasha's life was over at this point, that was certain. Circling down the drain. It was a familiar feeling, that vertiginous swirl, the hollow gurgle. Down he went, lower than dirt. A piece of meat to be chopped up and sold by the pound. He ached to shoot some blessed peace into his veins and let the stabbing pain smooth out. But his stash was all gone, after months of captivity in the Rome house. He was clean. Horribly lucid. His nerves were raw, his belly a black hole, a cigarette burn.

And he had a job to do. He wouldn't have to wait long for it to end. They would find him soon enough, and put a vicious end to him. Unless he beat them to it, of course. He'd dragged his heels on that, for Misha's sake, but his continued existence did Misha no favors. It forced his brother to choose sides. Choosing against their father was bad for Misha's health. It would be best for everyone if Sasha erased himself.

But not today. All his limited courage was focused on blowing this secret open. If the world knew, there would be no point in hurting Sveti. His father and his crew would have far more urgent things to do.

There. Mauro Mongelli, strolling up the street. Sasha recognized him from the photo on his column. Terror turned his legs floppy and boneless. The journalist seated himself at one of the outside tables and called for a barista. He looked ill at ease, eyes darting

around. Sasha had been clear about the dangers, but no true journalist could resist a career-changing scoop like this one, no matter
the risk.

Sasha clutched the envelope holding the documentation he'd
gathered: Sonia's photos and videos, the computer files, the e-mails
and screenshots. Proving what he'd found the courage to do, six
years ago. He had almost won his freedom. Almost.

He fought to control his bowels as he shuffled forward. A heavy
wind of fear blew him back. The Taurus revolver he had stolen
from Aleksei was tucked into the small of his back. His body heat,
such as it was, could not warm it. The metal against his clammy
skin made him shudder. He'd been forced to tighten his belt to
hold the hateful thing in place, he was so skeletally thin. Food
sickened him.

The man caught sight of him and half rose from the table. *"Lei è
Alexsandr Cherchenko?"*

Sasha coughed but could not get the words out. He nodded.

Mongelli was a sharp Italian guy, well groomed. His deep, even
tan was set off by discreet glints of man jewelry. He looked politely
repelled, as well he might. Sasha knew he looked like a walking
corpse.

The barista came out, bearing a tray. A cappuccino, a cornetto.
He glanced at Sasha. *"Qualcosa per lei?"* he asked, almost fearfully.

"Niente." Nothing. Sasha mouthed the word but couldn't voice it.

The barista fled. Mongelli sank back down to his chair, indicating
the chair opposite, but Sasha hesitated, not sure if he could tolerate
such close proximity to Mongelli's rich, buttery cornetto without
disgracing himself. Nausea churned inside him.

"Sta bene?" Mongelli asked. Are you well?

Sasha suppressed a cackle of hysterical laughter and nodded.

The man's eyes dropped to the envelope he clutched to his
chest. "That's the photographic evidence?"

"Sí," Sasha forced out. He tried to say more, coughed, sighed
out the tension, concentrated. Nothing coming out. *Fuck.* He
pulled out the pen and pad he kept in his pocket and scribbled the
words down.

*Take the police to the location I wrote in the e-mail, immediately.
The proof is there. I brought the pictures to demonstrate that it is
worth your while to do so.*

He ripped the note off. Handed it to the journalist.

Mongelli studied it. "Why not just go to the police directly
yourself?" His eyes were beady and suspicious.

Sasha closed his eyes, his jaw twitching, and put the pen to the
pad again.

*I tried, before. People died. This must be made public, as fast and
loud as possible. Do you understand the danger?*

Mongelli read the note and nodded, but Sasha could tell by his
glittering eyes that he was thinking about career advancement, not
danger. "You have photos of these thermonuclear generators?"

Sasha shook his head and scribbled.

*I have photos of their shielded containers. The cylinders have been
pulverized for easy bomb construction. Strontium-90. If I had
opened the container to photograph the contents, I would have died
very quickly.*

The man's eyes slitted as he read. "And this deadly radioactive
material has been hidden out behind Torre Sant' Orsola for six
years? And no one ever found it? It seems improbable."

Sasha nodded, wearily, and wrote.

Indeed, that was the point.

Then it happened, and so fast, but time warped in his head so
that it seemed hideously slow. His body felt locked in tar as the silver Mercedes gunned its engine and jumped the curb, but he
must have leaped backward. He glimpsed Aleksei at the wheel as
the car barreled up onto the sidewalk.

Mongelli could barely turn and gasp before it mowed him
down, smashing into the glass-topped tables.

From where Sasha lay on the street, he saw table and chair legs stuck out at crazy angles. Mongelli lay beneath them on his belly, the Mercedes' front wheel crushing his back. Blood trickled from his mouth. His eyes were wide, accusing.

There was the pop of a car door, but the pole holding up the awning had been knocked down, and a curtain of heavy canvas fabric had fallen over the vehicle, blocking the door.

Someone screamed from inside the bar. Shrill, continuous. Aleksei cursed, kicking at the car door against the weight of the thick canvas awning, like a chick trying to hatch from a big striped egg.

The grace of that fallen awning, those extra seconds, was what saved him. Sasha ran, passing people before they knew what they had seen. Just a ghoul flashing by, feet pounding, trying to escape from hell.

But hell was too big. Its boundaries kept expanding, infinitely.

He finally collapsed on a park bench and realized that he had dropped the envelope.

All his precious proof. Collected at such great danger and cost. The photographic prints Sonia had entrusted to him. All that remained of her great sacrifice, her courage. He did not have the JPEGs, nor had he ever dared to scan or copy the prints. He had been watched so closely, for so long. There had been no chance to do it. Ever.

The only proof that the lab had ever existed, the only clues at all to this horrible cruelty—and he had fucking *dropped* them.

He hunched down, shivering. Too exhausted even to sob. There was no way to save Sveti now. This had been his one big chance, and he had blown it. He'd killed poor Mongelli for nothing. No, less than nothing. He was infinitely worse off now. And so was Sveti. He had to warn her. Find a place with an Internet connection, get access to some device or other, with what cash he had left. If only he could just call, but he couldn't shove words out over a phone. Not even to Misha.

He could not crawl out of this hole. No matter how he tried.

No matter how they died.

Portland, OR

Sveti stared out of the taxi window. Her eyes were dry, hot. Knots in her throat and belly burned like points of fire. The tangle of freeway bridges swooped and swerved around her. She'd lost all sense of orientation, except for in relation to Sam, of course.

A needle inside her body pointed straight at Sam, night or day.

She shouldn't have gone to the wedding. She'd known perfectly well that he would show up, after all those e-mails that she could not seem to delete, all those texts on her phone. Those sweet, hot, sexy things he said. Things that made her want to fall to her knees and beg.

The phone beeped in her evening bag. She jerked it out and scrolled down the arriving e-mail on the screen of her smartphone.

> **Dear Ms. Ardova:**
> **We're so pleased you'll be joining us in Italy for the conference, and in London next week! A driver will pick you up at Fiumicino on Friday and bring you to San Anselmo. Attached is your e-ticket, as discussed.**
> **Have a great flight. I look forward to meeting you. Please don't hesitate to call me with any problems or questions.**
> **Til Friday, all my best,**
> **Nadine Muller, Executive Assistant**
> **Illuxit Transnational, Inc.**

Sveti stared down at the message and the attachment below it. Where was the euphoria, the triumph? She'd been called to Italy as an expert consultant to speak at the Tran-Global Business Organization against Human Trafficking. She was being awarded the Solkin Prize for her contribution to the fight against modern slavery. After that, it was off to London. Illuxit Transnational, a multi-billion-dollar contract research organization, had recruited her to consult for their new corporate anti-trafficking initiative and their Victims Fund. It was a coup for someone as young as she. Excellent money, too, most of which she would save to fund her own budding nonprofit, Soul Rescue. She regretted putting Soul Rescue on hold for the length of the two-year contract, but this was worth it. She'd nailed it, crushed it. She should be proud, full of hope for the future, riding waves of giddy energy.

And all she wanted was for that message to have been from Sam.

She clicked on the e-ticket attachment. First class, when she had specifically told them she preferred economy. It was annoying. Wasteful.

She hugged her bare, goose-bumped shoulders. She'd flounced out of the reception without her jacket. Showing great maturity and sense.

This night was so fucked up. Why couldn't she just be normal? Just be attracted to a great guy and go with it. Have him become her boyfriend. Have fun with him, then have it lead someplace wonderful and permanent. Ahhh. The normal girl's dream. Classic. Romantic.

But she was not normal. Reliving that kiss in Bruno's office always ended with her huddled in bed, hot face shoved into her pillow, following one of her many erotic Sam fantasies that always led to orgasms like thunderclaps. Knowing perfectly well what came next. Feeling so stupid for inflicting it upon herself, again and again.

Her punishment was always swift and brutal. If she saw Sam, or fantasized about him, it unleashed her worst nightmares, and often stress flashbacks during the day as well. It was like a cruel spell, to crave him so much when giving in to the craving was so self-destructive. Their hot tryst in Bruno's office had touched off a period of waking flashbacks so violent and awful, she'd considered checking herself into a mental facility. Same thing, after Sam had gotten shot last year, and she'd spent all those nights in Intensive Care. She'd paid for that. During the day, she saw Yuri, her captor from the days of her imprisonment, leering at her everywhere. He was at the DMV, behind the counter at Starbucks, foaming her latte, pumping her gas at the 7-Eleven. At night, it was nightmares from the bad old days. She was naked, chained to a table. They were coming at her, raising the sacrificial knife, and she woke screaming as it was about to plunge into her chest. Or the other classic, where she was making love to Sam, and it was marvelous, and suddenly, he morphed into Yuri. That one was particularly hideous.

It wasn't fair. Sam deserved someone less fucked up than she was, even if she weren't leaving the country. Even if he didn't have checkmarks next to every characteristic she could not possibly accept in a lover. He was a homicide detective, like her father. He was addicted to danger, he liked bourbon, he had multiple bullet scars.

That, she did not need, on top of her other complicated shit. Thanks, but no. It would be like painting a target on her chest that said, *Yes, hurt me, please. Go ahead. I was genetically engineered for it.*

Hell with that. She wasn't going to play out that sad, sick drama. No matter how deeply she'd been programmed to do so.

Maybe she'd just skip sleep from now on. Maybe she could just stay awake forever. She ran her fingers through her hair. Found two pins that clung to the remnants of her updo and twisted the thick rope up again. A temporary measure. It would tumble down soon enough.

Sam never gave up, never lost interest. His laser focus was unnerving. A normal man would have written her off by now. His focused intensity cut through her defenses, to secret places she'd forgotten were there. But she was not that terrified twelve-year-old, locked in stinking darkness. She did not appreciate being forced to feel like that again. Remembering it was painful. The way the little ones had clung to her. Needing her to be strong, needing her to love them. She'd hated herself for lying to them, even as she soothed or reassured them.

But she had, by God, learned how to put on a good show.

Sam brought those feelings back. No defenses. Back to the wall.

Not that Sam was cruel or frightening. On the contrary. It was the rawness she could not endure. It hurt, to be so bare. Buzzing with lethal voltage. She couldn't breathe, think, function in this condition. She would melt down, go nuts, totally lose it. Not even during her long, historic crush on Josh had she felt like that, but she'd been too clueless and innocent at the time to know the difference.

She'd drawn some conclusions about sex, pre-Sam, after her hopes for Josh had come to nothing and her college dating adventures had gone nowhere. What she'd taken away from it all in the end was that there were far more important things in life to fuss about.

It made her squirm, to hear Sam echo that private conviction back to her. Who gave him the right to know something so intimate about her when she'd barely articulated it for herself? She couldn't let someone so deep inside her head. She'd watched that dynamic play out between her parents. It had not been pleasant watching, even before Zhoglo's revenge, her abduction, her father's murder.

Even finding her daughter alive had not saved Sveti's mother. She'd become unbalanced and paranoid. Had begun making bizarre claims about mass graves. People being murdered in illicit experiments.

No proof of her claims was ever found, and eventually, they had locked her in a mental hospital. Sveti had been fortunate to have a safe place to be with her friends in America for that awful interval.

But even after she was released a few years later, Sveti had not gotten her mother back. Sonia had promptly run off to Italy and taken a new lover. Some rich, pampered, hateful Italian guy. Ick.

And then, without warning or a good-bye, she'd killed herself.

Sveti had been finishing high school in Cray's Cove at the time, living at Tam and Val's. Mama's last letter had been to tell Sveti to cancel her plans to come to Italy to spend Christmas together.

Visit another time, she'd said. Right before she threw herself off a bridge.

Stupid, to think about this stuff at all. Old pain, dredged up to no good purpose. Her mother had seemed so strong, but it was all show. Like her own show, with the kids in the traffickers' dungeon. Bombast and theater, and behind it, the ugly truth. Weakness, despair. Loss of hope.

And a long fall through the dark.

Love did that to a person. Grief drowned you. Or it ripped out your guts, as Zhoglo had done to her father. Or ripped out your heart, as Zhoglo had almost done to her. Call them life lessons or call them dysfunctional hang-ups, it hardly mattered. They were part of her now, like her bones or her blood. And speaking of dysfunctional hang-ups.

She pulled her phone out and logged in to the account she used to communicate with her best friend, Sasha, who had shared her ordeal. Sasha was the son of one of Zhoglo's henchmen, Pavel Cherchenko. The man had fallen out of the vor's favor, and Zhoglo had punished him by selling the man's young son to the organ traffickers.

She and Sasha had been together from the very beginning. They had bonded in their captivity, although Sasha had stopped speaking, even to her, after a few months. The other children had been too small to talk. Several had been developmentally disabled as well. It had been so lonely. Sveti had almost forgotten how to talk herself, by the end.

Sasha had his own struggles these days. Depression, heroin addiction, and his extremely dangerous father. Pavel Cherchenko had taken over Zhoglo's empire after he'd killed the old vor, and he was, if anything, more ruthless and cruel than Zhoglo had been. Tricky, with her calling in life, to have the son of a mafiya vor for a best friend. But who got to choose?

There were no messages from Sasha in the drafts folder. Just the ones she had sent to him, still unanswered. She opened a message document, and typed.

You still in Rome? Did you see my talk? Coming to Italy next week. Can't wait to see you. Sveti.

She saved the message in the file without sending it, hoping that he was all right. Poor, hunted Sasha. She did not blame him for his addiction, knowing what he struggled with, but it drove her mad with anxiety. She'd lost so many people. She couldn't bear to lose Sasha to that awful black hole, too.

She hadn't had the courage to tell her friends about the Illuxit job yet. She cringed from the thought of telling Rachel, but there would be visits, and Skype. Her friends had saved her and sheltered her, and she loved them for it, but they continued to see her as a vulnerable child. They'd never understand that she was an adult until she broke away.

The Illuxit job was a bolt from the sky. It knocked her a few spaces ahead on the playing board, the game being to stop the filthy scum who kidnapped vulnerable people, used them, and tossed them. She would pound those bastards into powder. Rinse them down the drain with a high-pressure hose. She wasn't afraid of death threats.

Truth to tell, she was more afraid of Sam's kisses.

You don't have to be afraid of me. Right. She squeezed her legs together around the buzzy throb of arousal. She'd been off balance since the day she met the guy, years ago. He'd been trolling for info with a stack of grisly photos, intent upon his task of finding killers and bringing them to justice. At which, from all accounts, he was very talented. Intuitive, relentless. A good detective, like her father had been.

She'd tried so hard to hate him for it. It just wasn't working.

Her phone rang. Her heart thumped as she jerked it out.

No. Not Sam. Hazlett, her benefactor, boss, and brand-new friend. The one who had pushed through the nomination for the Solkin Prize. He was an attractive man, who was showing all the telltale signs of being interested in her. Like she needed any more of that right now.

She was half-dizzy with disappointment, but she put on her game face and hit 'talk.' "Good evening, Mr. Hazlett."

"I've begged you to call me Michael," Hazlett replied, his deep voice jovial. "Is this your subtle way of keeping me at a distance?"

Um, yes, actually. "No, it isn't. I got Nadine's e-mail, with the ticket. I told you that economy class would be fine, remember?"

"Allow me to treat you, Svetlana. You deserve it."

"That's not the issue," she said. "Donate the difference in price to an anti-trafficking nonprofit, if you want to make me happy."

"I do want to make you happy. And I will donate that money to the nonprofits, many hundreds of times over, I promise. And guess what—I'll still put you in first class, given the opportunity. Sorry."

She gritted her teeth. "But I don't need—"

"That's the freshness of youth talking," Hazlett said with a chuckle. "In twenty years, you'll treasure that leg room, believe me."

She exhaled. "Michael," she said slowly. "Don't condescend."

"Oh, never. Just joking. And I'm so glad you're calling me Michael. So, how was the wedding?"

Incendiary. Mind blowing. Outrageous. Orgasmic. "Ah . . . lovely."

"I wish you had been with me here in New Delhi," Hazlett said wistfully. "These pompous blowhards at the seminar could have used a dose of distilled reality about human trafficking like only you can give. It's so satisfying, seeing people's faces change when you do your magic."

"I wish I could have gone, too, but I—"

"Certainly you couldn't. I understand completely. A friend's wedding takes precedence. I stand rebuked."

"I'm not rebuking you!" she protested, flustered.

"Of course not. I'm glad to know that you have your ticket. Forgive me for insisting on first class, but I can't help myself. I can't wait to see you in San Anselmo. Bon voyage, Svetlana."

She got through the rest of the pleasantries somehow and closed the call, red-faced and smarting. Feeling clumsy and stupid.

Sam shoved her off balance, too. He rattled her cage, melted her into hot, mindless froth. But he never made her feel stiff or humorless.

The cab was almost home. Soon, she'd peel off that dress and all the fantasies that went with it. She'd bought it for the gala in Italy, and decided at the last minute to wear it to the wedding, too. The rum breezers brought over by her upstairs neighbor Paul last night were also partly to blame. It was so easy to rationalize, with alcohol in her system. A single girl had no business not looking her best, Paul had sternly lectured her. She should look smoking hot at all times, particularly at a wedding.

And Sam would be there, looking at her. She'd been so busy not allowing herself to think that thought, it had filled her consciousness.

The minute he'd actually seen her, she'd wanted to run and find a blanket to wrap herself in. The piercing intensity of his eyes, the vast heat blazing out of him. It crept insidiously into her secret places from across the room, making her shiver and melt. And yield.

Sam looked different, with his hair yanked angrily back, his face so tense and thin. His jaw shadowed with beard scruff a shade darker than his hair. He looked grim, focused. Hard. But no less gorgeous.

For God's sake, why? This was a guaranteed disaster. Of course, her improbable friends had pulled it off. Even the more problematic ones, like Tam and Nick and Aaro, and the McClouds, too. All of them were beating the odds somehow. Happy, in their own weird, particular ways.

But she was Svetlana Ardova, with a rattling crowd of skeletons in her closet. There was no more room in there. She was at capacity.

Josef rifled through the silky undergarments that lay on top of Svetlana Ardova's open suitcase. The place had been stripped to nothing, furniture sold, books and pictures boxed up.

He'd rifled through her boxes with latex-gloved hands and had found nothing of interest. No computers, tablets, or external drives. No photographs. Her electronics must be at Cray's Cove, where she'd been holed up for days, to his jaw-cracking frustration. No matter. Tonight, he would extract everything she knew. He was a very good interrogator.

Jason Kang, one of the Triad snakehead thugs he'd hired for this special job, was peering out the window. Cretin.

"Taxi at the curb," Kang said. "She's getting out."

"Get your head out of the fucking window!" Josef snarled.

Kang jerked his head down out of sight, his thick face sullen and clouded. He was not especially bright, nor was his colleague Chan Yun, waiting downstairs in the van. Both men were fresh out of prison and very much out of favor with their previous employer. But Josef couldn't complain about their incompetence, since he'd specifically gone shopping for Triad-connected thugs who were expendable. Men whose former employers would be genuinely glad to see the last of them.

Neither man would live out the night, once he had spread prints and genetic materials all over Svetlana's apartment, and inside her lovely body. He had paid a hefty fee for this arrangement, but the men would die happy, he thought, philosophically. Out on a high note.

And Svetlana had made it so easy, getting in everyone's face, being a naughty, inconvenient girl who never knew when to shut her mouth. There would be so many fingers to point when she disappeared.

And not a one of them would point at Josef or his boss. Seamless.

He picked up a framed picture of her from the topmost box. Bikini-clad, on a beach, holding a laughing baby girl, her arm around a mop-haired child of ten or so. Beautiful smile. So like Sonia, but dewy and fresh. He indulged in a brief, vivid fantasy of sparing her life and running away with her. Of her, showing her gratitude for his mercy on her knees, with his cock in her mouth. Anxiously sucking. Mmmm.

He shut the fantasy regretfully down. There could be no turning back. Too much money at stake, and women more beautiful than Ardova could be bought by the truckload at a fraction of the cost.

The cab slowed at the renovated Victorian house where Sveti had rented an apartment for the past couple of years. A strange, clawing desperation rose up inside her as she fumbled for the fare. Something precious was coming to an end. Her Sam fantasies, entering a new phase. Shifting from glowing possibility to bittersweet memory.

She wasn't ready for the shift. It pressed her chest, hurt her heart. The driver accepted his fare and tip. The cab pulled away.

"*Stop!*"

The car lurched to a startled halt.

Sveti reeled, swaying on the sidewalk. Shocked at the enormous sound that had just emerged from her body. Not a yell. Not a screech.

No, that had been a wake-the-dead bellow, like a maddened bull.

He shifted into reverse and backed to where she stood. She jolted into movement, wrenched open the car's back door.

"Did you forget something, miss?" he asked.

"Yes." She slid inside before she could chicken out. "I forgot where I was going. Will you take me to 233 Hauser Street?"

The driver looked perplexed. "It'll have to be a new fare. I already zeroed out the meter."

"That's fine." The vehicle surged forward. Her heart was bruising her ribs from the inside. Oh, God, oh God. She was about to smash herself full-on into a brick wall. Just to see how it felt. For the pure, bloody, messy, masochistic fun of it.

What the hell. She was no stranger to pain.

Amazingly, Kang dared to peer out the window again, tempting Josef to kill him now before he fucked things up any further. "I told you, get *down!*"

"She won't see me," Kang said, his voice defensive. "She's in the cab again, turning the corner. So's the van. Chan Yun's following."

Josef bolted for the window. *Fuck.* He seized the walkie-talkie. "Chan Yun!" he barked. "You're following her cab?"

"Yes," Yun replied. "They're a block ahead and heading north."

"Keep on them," he snarled. He'd been so primed to touch her.

His cell vibrated. His boss. Micromanaging, as always. "Yes?"

"Have you questioned her yet?" the vor demanded.

"Not yet. She arrived, but got back in her taxi and left again without coming upstairs."

Cherchenko was silent for a beat. "So. You lost her. Again."

"No, sir. I have never lost her. Chan Yun is following the—"

"And you trust that snakehead filth?"

Josef's nostrils flared. "He's competent enough to follow a cab."

"Can it really be so difficult to subdue a little doe-eyed hundred-and-ten-pound cunt, Josef? Have you lost your touch?"

"She was up all last night with her upstairs neighbor, packing and trying on clothes," Josef said through his teeth. "The night before, the landlord had a barbecue on his lawn and half the neighborhood was there until dawn. Before that, she was up at Steele and Janos's residence on the Washington coast, and I could not risk—"

"There's a great deal you do not risk, Josef. Because I am the one who carries the risk. I took a risk on you when you brokered that deal with the Georgians for the generators, remember? I risked twenty-eight million euros, and where is it? Have I seen it? I am the one fronting the fee for your snakehead patsies, too, so do not talk to me about risk."

"I will earn back that money for you ten times over," Josef said.

"Yes? And while you hypothetically multiply my cash, my sons are left unguarded. Sasha got away, Josef. He went straight to the press."

"The press?" Josef was aghast. "But Aleksei and Andrei—"

"Are fucking fools. Aleksei barely caught him in time. He was with a journalist. We recovered an envelope. Full of photographs that would have ruined us all, including you, my risk-averse friend. He knows exactly where The Sword of Cain is hidden, that lying piece of shit. Six years, he's fucked me over. My own flesh and blood."

Josef was startled. Sasha? He would never have thought that frail, wasted bag of bones would have the nerve. "Is he dead?"

"No, unfortunately," the vor growled. "The journalist, yes, but Sasha is still at large. Aleksei lost him. You must come back. Hurry up with this job, Josef. It is getting less important by the minute."

"Yes, Vor," he said stoically. "I will take her tonight and return."

"Get your answers however you must; but afterward, I want your snakehead goons to chew up what is left of her and spit out the bones."

Josef relaxed. "Of course. They specialize in that very thing."

"Film it," Cherchenko ordered. "Record every moment. With good light. Every detail. Every scream. Every cut. Make it ugly. Make it last."

Josef paused, mouth dangling. "Ah . . . Vor, documenting the event in that way would be extremely risky—"

"It is an absolutely necessary risk. Sasha must watch. I will set the footage to loop endlessly, tape him to a chair, and lock him in a room with it. Then he will understand the price of disappointing me."

The implied threat hung heavy in the air after the boss hung up on him. Josef stared into space, feeling a muscle in his cheek twitch.

He had fully intended to let the snakehead thugs do the honors, both men being stupid and self-destructive enough to fill the girl's orifices with their genetic material with no thought of consequences.

But he might have to join the fun. A soft, squealing target upon which to channel his rage would ease the sting of the conversation he'd just had. Until he could make his very favorite fantasy a reality.

The fantasy that starred Pavel Cherchenko, spread-eagled, staked out. Alive, moaning . . . with all his skin removed.

CHAPTER 3

The light was on in Sam's living room.

Sveti stood in the shadows of the shaggy rhododendron bushes that flanked the porch of his bungalow, feeling the seconds tick by. She could call another car, and stand shivering in the dark waiting for it, but why? The bellow that had risen up from inside her outside her apartment would just start to howl again.

She had to throw it a chunk of meat, or it would rip her to pieces.

At least he hadn't gone out drinking, or to another woman's house. He couldn't have been back for more than a half hour. Not enough time for a booty call. She propelled herself up the steps. Poised her finger over the bell. Froze, without pressing. Her finger shook.

Oh, God, this was stupid. She'd known that if Sam got her alone in a room, he would seduce her. She'd taken deliberate steps to prevent it while desperately hoping it would happen anyway. It was so confusing, so messed up. Rocks and hard places, wherever she turned.

A shadow flickered behind the curtain. The door jerked open.

Sam had changed into sweat pants and a frayed, shabby T-shirt decorated with a faded stencil of Mt. Hood. His big, thickly muscled body looked as formidable in sleep rags as it had in the elegant suit.

He looked blank. Seconds ticked by as she floundered for something to say. Her English had deserted her. It happened when she was scared. Which was to say, mostly when Sam Petrie was around.

Sam's thick, winging brows drew together. "What the fuck?"

"I . . . I . . ." She licked her very dry lips. "Can I come in?"

His eyes narrowed. "Are you here to put me out of my misery?"

She tried to parse that. "Ah . . . in what sense? I'm not sure if—"

"If you walk through this door, the only way out goes through my bed." He paused, waited. Prompted when she didn't reply. "So?"

She goosed herself into action and floated past him into his house. Excitement clenched her lungs, her thighs, her toes. She was in a tunnel that led to his bed. Tunnels were simple. Simple was good. There were no right or left turns in a tunnel. No turning back. All decisions were already made. She could not get lost in a tunnel.

Sam slammed the deadbolt shut and turned his scorching gaze upon her.

She opened and closed her mouth, and blurted it out. "I'm leaving Portland," she said. "I'm going to Europe in a couple of days. I got a consulting job. Helping big corporations do their bit to combat slavery and trafficking. I'll be based in London, for the next couple of years. After that, who knows."

His face was a mask. "I see."

"I'm flying to Rome," she babbled. "There's a conference on modern slavery in San Anselmo this weekend. I'm speaking on the panels, as an expert consultant. They're giving me an award. For what I did last year, and the follow-up fund-raising and crowd-sourcing."

"That would be the adventure that earned you the death threat?"

She could not meet his eyes. "Ah, yes. The very one."

He nodded. "Congratulations. Sounds like a dream job. I know San Anselmo. Spent time there when I was a kid, with family. Beautiful place, right on the coast. When did you say you were leaving?"

"Thursday," she said. "I'm speaking on Saturday."

His gaze was unwavering. "Okay. Help me out, Sveti. Explain why you're here. You're not here to put me out of my misery. You're here to ratchet it up as much as you humanly can, right?"

She forced air out of her chest. "No." Her voice was a breathless squeak. "But if it's too awful to endure, you can just throw me out."

He was shaking his head before she finished. "Too late for that," he said. "Just tell me what's expected of me. You don't want a boyfriend. That's crystal clear. So what do you want? A sex toy?"

She winced. "No, I want . . . I want . . ." She floundered for words. "I want a friend who . . . who—"

"Who fucks you," he finished. "You want my fucking services just for the night? Or do you want them extended until Thursday? My calendar's clear. I can fuck you nonstop until Thursday, no problem. Or is that too long term? Is a forty-eight-hour fuck commitment too scary?"

She lunged for the door. "Never mind, if you're so disgusted—"

"Oh, no." He seized her from behind and startled warmth jolted her body. She'd been primed to shove his arms away, but instead, her fingernails dug hungrily into the thick muscles of his forearms.

As if she were punishing him. Or claiming him.

"You're not going." His voice rasped against her throat. "Your fate is sealed. Just tell me what you want. Help me not to screw this up."

She inhaled, hungrily. Aftershave, soap, cologne, beer, the faint, salty tang of his sweat. "I want more of what happened today," she said. "More of what happened in Bruno's office. I thought you wanted it, too."

His arms tightened. "Sure I do. But what happened today was me trying to seduce you into being my girlfriend, and hopefully more in the future. That was me going out on a limb. If you don't want that, the vibe changes. I can no longer afford to really give a shit. You get me?"

"Yes," she said. "But you don't . . . want me to go?"

"No, I don't want you to go." He pulled her closer, his breath warming her neck. "You're cold. Where the hell's your jacket?"

"I'm okay," she whispered.

"Can I get you a beer?"

She didn't care for beer, but a drink might relax her. She nodded and followed him into the kitchen. Which was clean, for a single guy.

He pulled out a longneck bottle, popped the cap, and handed it to her. She put it to her lips, trying not to grimace at the sour taste.

He gave her a wry smile. "That good, huh? You prefer a lighter beer? I think I've got a lager in there somewhere. A Corona, maybe."

"I'm not much of a beer person," she said. "But it's fine."

That smile activated the long, sexy grooves that flanked his mouth. She'd found an actual printed picture of him once, in a pack that had documented Edie and Kev's son Jon as he learned to walk. Jon was toddling adorably in the foreground while Sam grinned down at him, beer in hand, sexy eye crinkles on full display. Oh, God, that smile.

She'd stolen the picture. Sneaked it home, to pore over, like a brainless schoolgirl. To say nothing of the insanely large collection of Sam JPEGs on her cell phone. If he only knew how many there were, he would probably be afraid of her. And justly so. The crazy, obsessed girl.

Sam took a swallow of his beer, his gaze traveling over her body with the slow deliberation of a man who had every right to examine.

"A beer looks wrong with that dress," he commented. "You should have a champagne flute, or a martini glass. You want some brandy?"

She gulped another mouthful of beer, nervously. "This is fine."

He reached to pull out the pins that anchored her hair, and unraveled it, spreading it over her shoulders. "That's better," he said. "I've been wanting to do that for years."

He reached out with the hand that held his beer bottle, and with his extended pinkie, he hooked the shoulder strap and tugged it down.

They stared at her bare shoulder and the dangling strap. She couldn't breathe. He raised the bottle, condensation dripping down the brown glass, and touched her chest with it, right over her breastbone.

She dragged in a breath. "Cold," she whispered.

"Yeah," Sam said. "You've been so cold. But check this out." He trailed the edge of the bottle over her cleavage. A merciless smile curved his mouth as she shivered. "Look what it does to your nipple. The contradictory effect of all that coldness. That's how it's been for me." He gently tugged until the soft fabric snagged on her taut nipple.

"Please," she said raggedly. "It's too cold."

"Don't worry." His voice was suede soft. "My mouth is hot. I'll fix it. Suffer a little first. God knows, I have." He seized her hand. Kissed her palm, her knuckles. "Pull the dress down. Show me your tits again." His deep, raspy voice sparked shivers along the surface of her skin.

She shut her eyes. "Don't turn this into a weird power game," she begged. "I'm already so self-conscious—"

"Show me you're serious," he said, his voice implacable. "Call it a statement of intent. I deserve one, after the way you've treated me."

He stepped back. Lifted his beer to his lips, eyes challenging her.

Her face blazed as she pulled the straps down and worked her arms loose, extricating herself awkwardly. The bustier was skintight. She pushed the cups down over her breasts and looked up defiantly, heart thudding. Breasts bared. "Do I look serious enough to you?"

He stared at her for a long moment and then set down his beer on the counter behind her. "Yeah," he said. "I'm convinced."

He seized her hand, never taking his eyes from her body, and kissed it again, then drew her fingertip into his mouth.

The shocking sensation of suckling heat made her drop her beer. His hand flashed out and caught it. He set it on the counter and cupped her breast, rolling the pad of his thumb around her tight nipple. The contrast of his large, darker hand against the swell of her pale breast made her breathing ragged. Those long, graceful fingers.

"Why me?" he demanded.

She was startled by the abrupt question. It seemed so incredibly obvious. "What do you mean? Why not you? Who *but* you?"

He snorted. "Why not me, she says. I've done nothing but bug you since the moment you laid eyes on me. You bust my balls whenever I get close enough to talk to you, which is almost never. Do you subject every guy to that kind of treatment?"

"Ah, no, actually," she admitted, abashed.

"Of course not. I knew I was special. So why me? Why not some guy you like better? That ass-bite Cattrell, for instance?"

"Josh?" She shook with a helpless giggle. "Josh is not an ass-bite!"

"They say you had a thing for him," Sam said. "He's good look-ing, he has a job, he's obviously straight and has a functioning li-bido. Any guy with a pulse could perform for you, Sveti."

She shook her head. Her disillusionment about Josh had seeped in so slowly, she'd never needed to verbalize it. "It would never work," she said. "Not for me, and not for him. I'm too far behind. I always miss the beat, and people have to explain the punch line of jokes to me, because I never laugh in time, and then when I get it, it isn't funny anymore. Josh likes with-it girls who get his jokes. I'm sure if I begged him, he'd oblige me. But I don't want a mercy fuck."

He let out a harsh bark of laughter. "Not a term I would put in the same sentence with you, Sveti."

"I would, since we're being brutally honest," she said. "You said it yourself. How I'm so heavy and serious, dragging my ten-ton weight around, killing everybody's buzz. I'm no fun at parties, I'm boring to—"

"You're the farthest thing from boring that I've ever met," Sam cut in. "You rocked that party for me. First, you attack a mafiya vor. Ten minutes later, you're bare-breasted and lubing all over my hand. You're a fucking force of nature."

"Don't. Don't make this into a joke. I'm trying to get this out, and you're not helping." Her voice quivered with frustration. She'd tried so hard to keep her boring insecurities at arm's length, so as not to jinx this moment, but so much for that. "Men are afraid of me, just like you said. Afraid of the bolt cutters under my skirt, or afraid to say the wrong thing and make me hate them for being shallow, or else they feel guilty because their parents are still alive and they never experienced bad things like I have. They're all waiting for me to start twitching and frothing. I always know when a guy finds out about my past. I can see it in his face. It's a huge turn-off."

"Sveti, it's not—"

"But it never seemed to be one to you," she rushed on. She had to get the thought completely out, or it would burn a hole in her head. "You're not afraid to say the wrong thing to me. You love setting me off. The more upset I get, the more you like it. You sick, twisted bastard."

He whistled, softly. "Wow. Intense."

"Yes, it is," she barged on. "That's why you, Sam. I chose you for that special, unique quality. Since you insisted on knowing." She braced herself, for him to be angry, or disgusted, or offended.

Her gasp choked off as he yanked her into a swift, hard kiss.

His mouth tasted of beer. Sex, hunger, hot, unbridled fulfilment. His tight, fierce grip, hot skin on skin, his hardness and solidity and musky male scent. His thick erection, prodding her belly. She clenched her lower body around the shivery, melting sensation. Knees gone soft.

After a moment, he pulled back, his breathing unsteady. His eyes glittered in the dimness. His pants tented out to an alarming degree.

"Unless you want this to happen on the kitchen counter, I suggest we take it upstairs," he said. "That's where I have the condoms."

She nodded. He engulfed her hand in his and led her out of the kitchen. She stumbled as she tottered up the staircase. He slid his arm around her waist to steady her.

It felt good. So warm, and strong.

Sam bypassed the light switch by the door, leading her into the dark bedroom. That light was too bright, too harsh. It would spook her. He had to keep this cool, keep it mellow, whatever "it" turned out to be.

This development totally blew his mind, which sharply compromised its function. It was years now that he'd been mentally rehearsing getting Sveti into his bedroom. She was finally here.

And he was almost paralyzed with terror.

It should be simple, straightforward. She wanted a sex toy. A guy who was not freaked by her tragic past, or intimidated by the gorgeous, charismatic, practically supernatural being that she was. But she had a mistaken impression of him. He was scared shitless. This was worlds away from all his man-slut experience. Svetlana

Ardova was a creature of myth and legend. The stakes were way higher when you seduced a goddess. A guy could get fried by lightning. Turned into a pig.

He flipped on a bedside lamp. Sveti waved at the light, shielding her eyes. "Turn it off," she said. "Too much."

He was dismayed. "I want to see you. You're so goddamn beautiful. It would be such a waste to just grope around in the dark."

"Too much," she repeated desperately. "Please."

He thought furiously. "Wait a minute." He turned to a stack of boxes against the wall and flipped one open, rummaging through it.

"What's with the boxes?" she asked. "Did you just move in?"

"Couple years ago. I'm lazy. Haven't gotten all the furniture yet. Ah, yeah. Here it is." He held up a large pink candle, wrapped in cellophane. Hearts were stenciled on it. "I got this a couple of Christmases ago," he told her. "A gag gift from some women I worked with. It's an aromatherapy love candle. I've been saving it for a special occasion. Can't imagine one more special than this."

She vibrated with quiet, nervous laughter. "I don't need props."

"Never meant to suggest you did," he said smoothly. "But it could solve our lighting problem. Can you deal with candlelight?"

She gave him a tiny nod. Sam tore off the cellophane and tossed it on a pile of folded jeans and shirts. He wished the place wasn't such a mess. Piles of boxes. Stacks of folded clothing. It was fucking immature, not to just go out and buy himself bedroom furniture, but back when he was working, he was too busy and couldn't be bothered, and now that he wasn't working, he hadn't been able to bring himself to give a shit.

It was a shock to the system. Giving a shit, so suddenly.

He placed the fat pink candle beside the bed and lit it. The pink cylinder glowed as the flame took hold. Shadows wavered and danced on the wall. "Work for you?" he asked.

"It's good," she whispered.

He studied her, still cowering by the door, shivering. "You look tense," he said. "How about mood music? I've got speakers in here."

"No, it would feel forced," she murmured. "I'd feel silly."

"Okay, we'll be all grim and focused, and do it in charged silence." He leaned, sniffing at the fragrant candle. "Mmm. Smells nice."

"Honeysuckle and vanilla," Sveti said. "And essence of rose."

"You can smell that all the way over by the door? You look like you're ready to bolt."

"I'm not going to bolt," she said. "And I wouldn't get far in these heels if I did. They're four inches. I'm so damned short."

"Yeah, five foot three. I love it. You're perfect. Like a little jewel."

"Oh, please." She turned her head, hiding behind the swinging curtain of hair. "I'm hardly perfect. You're the first to remind me." She reached thoughtlessly, pulling her dress up over her breasts.

"No," he said sharply. "Leave it, Sveti."

She dropped it, startled. She held herself so straight, tits out proudly, but her lips quivered with the strain of looking nonchalant. Too bad. She got no quarter. She'd asked for it, and she was getting it. Like she'd never gotten it before, or would again. It was a holy vow.

"I wouldn't let you run away in any kind of shoes," he said. "It's too late for that. In case you were considering it."

Her chin lifted. "I'm not considering it."

He sidled around her, placing himself between her and the door. Closing it, before herding her into the room, closer to the bed. Slowly.

"About those four-inch heels," he said. "Show me."

It had seemed like a nonthreatening way to start the process of disrobing her. Then she lifted the frilled hem over her ankles.

Whoa. He started to sweat, and he wasn't even a foot guy. He'd never paid much attention to feet, other than the occasional under-the-table sex game. But those shoes, Jesus. They were a message arrowing straight to his core. He understood it like the silent, wordless language of kisses. The arched delicacy of her feet propped onto teetering heels, the aggressive, pointy toes, the fierce ruby shine, the sexy slave-girl tangle of complicated ankle straps, the brash rhinestone buckle. The shoes told him how she longed to be taller, sharper, tougher. Powerful and sexy. How she wanted to be wanted. It made his chest twist and his cock ache. "Wow," he said. "Ruby slippers. Very cruel."

She licked her dry lips. "I'm not cruel."

"No? Take them off, then."

She laughed, silently. "I'll get a sore neck, looking up at you."

"Should have picked a short guy for your boy toy."

She winced. So did he. Fuck. The words had just fallen out.

He seized her upper arms, tugged her closer. "I don't mean to be an asshole, but I have to remind myself of what this thing is, and what it isn't. That way I won't get into a bad place about it. Get me?"

Her throat bobbed. She nodded and then let out a barely audible squeak as he sank to his knees, like a supplicant. He hiked her skirt up, pressing handfuls of it against her clenched, shaking fists.

"Lift it," he prompted. "Show me more."

She got on with it, dragging the skirt up, a slow, intensely erotic reveal, all the sexier for how clumsy she was. Her exposed ankles made his cock twitch in his pants. Likewise the shapely calves, the narrow, slender knees. She faltered, halfway up her graceful silk-and lace-clad thighs. Her arms were full of swags of soft crimson fabric.

"Chickening out?" he asked.

She tossed her hair back. Jerked the skirt up. A frilled band of black lace, trimmed with crimson rosettes, contrasted starkly with the pale perfection of her upper thighs.

He pushed her hands higher, to look at the panties. Black lace, stretched over the trimmed-up swatch of muff. His heart thundered.

"Beautiful," he muttered. "Did you wear this stuff for me?"

She murmured incoherently and nodded. And he believed her. She'd gone to the wedding with Ass-bite, but the lingerie was for him. The shoes, the dress, the shimmering body glitter, the scented lotion. That perfect little fastidiously groomed muff. "I love it." He pressed his face against her mound and inhaled her intoxicating woman scent.

Each heaving lungful made him gasp for more.

She moaned, twisting his hair as he scattered lingering, pleading kisses over that festive swirl of ringlets at the top of her cleft.

He wanted to insinuate his tongue into that vortex. Taste the sweet girl juice.

Rein it in, dickhead. He had to set the bar so high, it'd ruin the sex she'd have with other guys forever. Spiteful of him, yeah, but too bad. It was his only revenge for how badly this was going to fuck him up. The slower he went, the sweeter the torment. Hours of kissing, playing with her tits. Then when she was naked and spread out, he'd tongue-lash that beautiful muff until she'd forgotten who she was.

Then he'd mount up and go for a long, slow, juicy ride. On her final climax, he'd have her pussy clamped around his cock. Feeling every flutter, every squeeze, every pulse. His reward.

And his punishment.

His hands cupped her ass, struggling for control. He could do this. He could be a sex toy. Just service her, blow her mind, fuck her brains out, and walk away, sanity intact. He could.

"A thong," he muttered. "My God. Your ass is so perfect."

"I had to wear one," she confessed. "Panty lines."

"Of course. Can't have that." He hooked his fingers in the elastic and stopped as tension gripped her. He looked up into her face.

"I like the stockings," he said. "But the rest of it comes off."

Her breathing was ragged, her soft mouth slightly open. Eyes dazed. She still had not unbuckled her shoes. Her knees quivered.

Sam pried her fingers loose from her grip on the scarlet fabric. Her skirt tumbled over his shoulder, whisper soft, warm, scented. He seized her hand, pressed it against his shoulder, to steady her. Her fingers were chilly. Her nails dug into his skin. He loved their sharp bite.

He pressed his face against her mound. Slowly, gently, breathing her in, nuzzling her. Hanging on to his self-control by a fucking thread.

When he felt her lean in, he started unbuckling her shoes.

He stood up when she stepped out of them, towering over her. The top of her head fit under his chin. She let her head fall back into his cupped hand with a shuddering sigh. He reached for her zipper.

She put her hand on his. "No, you take something off first."

He whipped his shirt off and tossed it behind him.

•

She stared at his torso and laughed. "Oh, please!"

He was taken aback. True, he got strong reactions from the ladies when he undressed, but ridicule was generally not one of them.

"What?" he asked. "What's wrong?"

She gestured at his body. "Is that for real? Do you work out all day and eat nothing but protein powder and egg whites?"

"I've had a lot of time on my hands lately." He felt ridiculously defensive. "I'm bored out of my fucking mind on medical leave. But I'm not a gym rat. It just happened."

She rolled her eyes. "Nobody gets that ripped by accident."

Fuck it. He stood there stoically, letting her look her fill at the freak show. He was just a sex toy, after all. Sex toys were supposed to be vain and shallow, and eat protein and muscle-enhancing mineral supplements, and buy lots of tight microfiber gigolo clothing.

If it comforted her to think he was that guy, who cared?

She poked at his abs with a fascinated finger, tracing a vein that snaked across his belly. "You have no fat on you at all," she said. "Just stone-hard muscle. It's unreal."

He rolled his eyes and sighed. "So shoot me."

Her eyes darted to his scars. "Somebody's already done that."

Her fingers slid up to the scar on his chest. A bullet had perforated his lung in the showdown in New Jersey, right after she'd met him, when Bruno had been fighting for his and Lily's lives. She touched the newer scar, which was still an angry red, low on his abdomen. He'd been gut shot in the line of duty ten months ago. The injury that had stalled his career. The brush of her fingers had its predictable effect on his cock.

"This one happened last year," he told her.

"Oh, I know."

"You heard about that?"

She frowned. "Of course I heard about it! We all heard about it! Everyone was worried about you."

Of course. Collective, friendly, fraternal concern, from everyone. Nothing specific. Nothing personal.

"I dreamed about you, in there," he blurted. "When I was in Intensive Care. I used to wake up feeling like you'd been there."

She looked away, reddening. He was embarrassed at himself.

Her fingers trailed over the scar, and he grabbed her fingertips, pulled them down. Tucked them inside the waistband of his pants.

Out of nowhere, Sveti started snorting with nervous giggles.

"I'm so glad that my grotesquely overdeveloped body is such a source of amusement to you," he said. "I live to entertain." He shoved his sweatpants off his hips.

That stopped her laughter dead. She stared, transfixed. Her gaze skittered away from his cock, which rose proudly from its bush of pubes, extended toward her. "Public service announcement," he said. "Laughing uncontrollably at a guy's tool is considered to be bad form."

Another explosion of helpless laughter rocked her. "Petrie, you bastard," she said, voice muffled. "Stop it."

"Call me Sam. It's inappropriate to call a naked man by his surname. And you're behind."

She dragged her gaze back up to his face. "Behind in what?"

"In the striptease. I have nothing left to give. Lose the dress, if you want it to survive this encounter."

Her chin went up. "Do not threaten this dress," she said. "I paid more than I could afford for this dress, and I need it for the gala party in Italy, after the conference. If you hurt my dress, you reimburse me."

"The dress is safe if you hurry."

She had a hell of a time with the zipper, but the corset bodice finally fell open, like a shell, and she dragged the skirt down over her hips.

She stepped out of it, naked in her glory. Holding herself so straight. The queen of everything.

Oh, shit. His eyes were fogging. He covered his ass, just barely, by picking up her dress, inhaling her scent. Tears soaked into the fabric. Maybe it would stain, like sea spray did. He draped it over the chair as soon as he dared. Reverently, as if it were a ceremonial vestment.

Let her wear his tear stains at her swank party in fucking Italy. That seemed appropriate. Though he'd die before he would admit it.

CHAPTER 4

Sveti threw her shoulders back and held herself as tall as she could. Which wasn't very.

Relax, relax, relax, was the directive blaring frantically in her mind, but how? He'd said it himself, she was a ten-ton weight, and he'd get sick to death of it soon enough. Any man with a functioning brain would. Probably before the night was out.

But before he realized the trouble he was getting himself into, she would goddamn well get. Some. Of. That. If it worked at all, of course, when they did the deed. It was already miraculous that she functioned as well as she did, with her baggage. But functional, as she defined it, did not include sexual function. Her bar was set somewhat lower.

To her, functional meant that she got through her days, she slept a few ragged hours at night, between nightmares and erotic Sam dreams. She worked, she had friends, she had her beloved adopted family. She was committed to her crusade, but she did not attract undue attention—that is, no breakdowns, freak-outs, or stints in the psych ward. Death threats from snakehead scum did not count.

She'd struggled with depression for a while, after Mama's suicide, but she wasn't an addict, like Sasha, nor did she dream of suicide herself. Suicide would mean that the scum-suckers had won, and she would never concede that victory to them. Never.

She had goals, dreams, ambitions. She learned fast, she worked hard. She had a lot to contribute. She did okay. She really did.

But fun? Hah. Fun was too much to ask.

She had high hopes for pleasure, though, after that tryst at the wedding. The charged encounter in Bruno's home office was almost two years ago, but she remembered every detail. Only Sam had ever given her a clue what sexual pleasure could be. It would have been kinder if she'd never known at all, but now she did, so whatever. No going back.

She wanted more. At least a taste, which was all she could ever have, with the demons that stalked her. Considering the price she knew she was going to pay for this, it had better rock her world.

"I'm sorry I'm so . . ." Her voice trailed off. So what? So stiff, so tense, so shrinking? So clueless?

"Don't be." He pulled her hands to his lips and kissed them. His lips felt so hot, so soft. "You're perfect. My personal ultimate wet dream." He pressed her hands against his chest, over his heart. Her fingertips brushed the thickened skin of his scar. She could feel the quick, heavy throb of his heart, the crisp rasp of chest hair. A sheen of sweat. His nipples were taut against her palms. She wanted to nuzzle them, lick them. His hot, salty male scent filled her nose.

She cleared her throat, groping for words. Her English flitted away like a hummingbird in times of stress. "What . . . ah . . . do we do now?"

What a stupid question. They had sex. Duh. What else would they do, in this context? Play a game of fucking chess?

But he didn't laugh at her. He kissed her hands again. "We touch." His voice was a low, caressing stroke of deep harmonics across her shivering nerves. "I touch you. You touch me. We kiss, for as long as you want. We take our time. Let things happen like they want to happen. We let it unfold. You don't have to be nervous."

"I'm not," she lied.

"Come here." He sat on the bed and drew her onto his lap, arranging his cock so it pressed stiffly upright against her hip. So hard, and hot, burning against her. His legs felt strong, ropy and corded.

He cupped her breast. "This works great. I can lean over . . . and do this." He pressed his mouth to her breast, and the hot, hungry swirl of his tongue brought on a huge wave of emotion, sensation. He was drawing pleasure and sweetness from some magic well she never knew she had inside her, and it ran so deep. Below the bedrock.

She clutched his shoulders. Buried her nose in his thick, tousled hair, twisted her fingers into it, inhaling the scent of his scalp. Her fingers shook with strain as he licked and loved her breasts, bringing the tips of her tight nipples to throbbing points of bright awareness.

The sensation was sweet to the point of pain. A keening ache of longing. She was smothering him, clutching at his head, but the sound that rumbled through his chest felt like a growl of pleasure.

"So soft," he muttered, fluttering his tongue across her nipple, then drawing it in deep once again. She arched and squirmed in his lap.

"Am I smothering you?" she asked.

"Fuck, no. Cling to me. Grab any part. Squeeze it until I explode."

She hid her face against his hair. "You sounded like you couldn't get any air."

"Who gives a shit about air? I'm so turned on by your perfect tits, I can't breathe anyhow."

She smiled against his hair. They were very normal breasts, but if he wanted to exalt them, she wasn't going to complain. They certainly felt exalted, under his magic treatment.

"You're the one with the perfect body." She ran her fingertips over the taut muscles covering his back. "These lats. They're absurd."

He looked aggrieved. "I thought girls liked lots of cut muscle. I might have known you'd be the exception, and take me for a steroid-popping dickhead. Of all things for a guy to feel self-conscious about."

She gave him a stern look. "I am not one of your hordes of

girls," she said. "And I'll always give you a hard time. I can't help myself."

"You know, Sveti, it's amazing how having your naked tits at mouth level really takes the sting off that remark."

She shook with silent giggles as he pressed his face to her chest.

It felt so good. Shivering torment, his slow, sensual kisses, trailing tenderly over and under and around her breasts. The energy that charged her body was building into something frightening, unknown in scope. She squeezed her legs around the hot, unstable glow.

He pulled her hand down and wrapped her fingers around his cock. "Pet me," he said hoarsely. "Get acquainted."

She did so, exploring him timidly. He was so thick. Taut and hot. His pulse thrummed against her palm. The skin of his cock was so tender, a velvet sheath over that rigid core, flushed and reddened.

"Relax," he said gently.

His voice jolted her back to awareness of herself. "Hmmm?"

"Your legs. They're clamped shut. Like a vise. Try to relax."

"Oh." It was true. Her thighs trembled with strain. She was squeezing that sweet glow deep inside, keeping it armored by muscular tension. Keeping it hidden and secret. Safe from harm.

But that was for lying in bed reading sexy novels, not for going to bed with a real man. She would have to open up. God, so much could go wrong, she couldn't even imagine how it ever could go right.

But she kept petting him, with greedy fascination. Following her instincts, following his rough gasps and shudders and groans.

His calluses rasped against her inner thigh, catching on the thin nylon of her stocking. He clasped the top of her thigh, just resting his hand, letting her feel his heat, his strength. His immense patience.

That patience made it possible to relax. Open her legs for him.

He sighed against her chest, and his hand ventured between her thighs, stroking her mound as if it were a shy kitten. His fingers tangled tenderly into her muff, petting gently without penetrating. Every faintest, glancing touch moved her, melted her.

His hand ventured deeper, and her thighs clenched around it, re-flexively. His hand remained wedged between them, and he smiled at her as his long forefinger lazily stroked up and down the length of her labia. Up . . . down. Slow and gentle. Teasing, promising, reassuring.

"You're so wet." His voice sounded gravelly.

Oh, thank God for that. At least one part of the mechanism was in working order. She clutched his shoulders, clenched around his delving, stroking, clever fingers, gasping. Everywhere he touched or stroked or kissed came magically to life, blooming into bright-ness, full color, and it was a train barreling toward her now, certain annihilation, but it was too late to turn back, it was . . . *oh.*

It tore through her, shattering the world.

When she came back from that other, mindless, other-worldly place, her eyes fluttered open. She felt empty. Light and soft, dif-fuse. She could float on a breeze, like goose down. Dandelion fluff.

"So sweet," he murmured against her throat. His tongue rasped tenderly up the tendon in her neck, licking her sweat as if it were some magic substance that he craved. "God, that was good."

Then he cupped her breast again, and his arms slid around her, clasping her as he suckled her nipples again.

Sweet? Not sweet. It was total obliteration of self. But here she was, same old Sveti. Fears and problems and hang-ups fully intact.

"Ready to open up a little more?" His voice was low and care-ful, as if she were an easily spooked horse.

It embarrassed her to be so twitchy, which put the edge in her voice. "I have to, right? For this to work?"

His eyebrow tilted up. "I wasn't the one who engineered the design of human sexuality," he said. "It's not my fault I'm the one with the dick, so don't even try to make me feel guilty about it."

Stellar. Perfect. Very smooth. "I'm not," she said. "I'm just tense."

"Hard to believe, after an orgasm like that."

A lot of her life could be summed up like that. Hard to believe.

Sam scooped her into his arms and laid her gently in the middle of the bed. He reached to grab a string of condoms from the bed-stand.

God. His body was shockingly beautiful. Muscular contours, sharp angles, and ridges of bone. His fierce, driving personality. So seductive, to have all that seething energy focused entirely upon her.

Of course, his fascination was just the product of his own fantasies, which he was projecting onto her. He didn't really know her at all. When he did, he would run, without looking back.

So what? This was her chance. No mood-killing thoughts allowed.

Fortunately, she couldn't really think a straight thought while touching him, mood-killing or otherwise.

He jerked her into a ravenous, breath-stealing kiss, cupping her face as if it were something precious and fragile, raining hot kisses down on her. It was that oncoming train, but not just her body. Everywhere. She was melting into his kisses and happy to be lost. He wasn't grabbing or demanding. His lips just pleaded, softly, seductively, relentlessly, for her to soften for him. Open to him.

She did so, astonished. Opening like a flower to that sweet dance of lips and tongue, the sweet taste of him. She couldn't resist.

Even though she sensed doom in the air, like snow on the wind.

He lifted his face. There was just enough flickering light to see the soft look of wonder in his eyes. It scared her to death. She waved it away. "Stop," she said nervously. "Please. Don't look at me that way."

"I'm memorizing you like this," he said. "This moment makes the cut for deathbed memories. So I have to pay attention."

She flinched. "Don't say that!"

"We've all got to die someday. Would you begrudge me the memory of your sweet kisses to comfort me in my final moments?"

"Don't joke about that." Her voice shook with intensity. "Don't invoke death. It's never far away. It doesn't need to be invoked. It's bad luck. So please, stop. Stop staring at me like you . . . like you're . . ."

Like you're in love with me.

That was it. The weight of impending doom snapped her nerve. She scrambled off the bed. "I can't do this. I'm sorry, but I—oof!"

She was lifted, turned. She landed, disoriented and bouncing in the middle of the bed. Sam straddled her, legs and arms caging her in.

"You're not bailing on me now," he said.

She blinked up into his face. "Sam, I—"

"I don't care." His voice was savage. "You are seeing this through. No matter how long it takes us."

"Don't dictate to me!" She shoved at his chest.

He trapped her wrists in his big hand. "Don't be scared," he said. "I won't force you. But I won't let you run, either. Not gonna happen."

She bucked and squirmed. Something battered inside her chest, desperate to get out. Every move made her feel more frantic, in a frenzy of panicked excitement. He stared intently into her eyes.

"Is this what you need, to get through the wall?" he asked. "Do you need to fight me?"

That question was too dangerous and outrageous to answer, but the energy surged wildly inside her at his words, and he felt it. She thrashed and writhed, furiously. "Goddamnit, Sam! Let go!"

"No, just tell me," he demanded. "And don't be embarrassed. I'll give you that, if that's what works for you. But it's not the kind of thing I want to get wrong, so be very clear. Is that what you want?"

One last convulsive heave of her entire body and she subsided, panting. She had barely jolted his bulk. "I don't know," she snapped.

His eyes slitted. "Figure it out fast. The choice is about to be taken out of your hands. I'm counting down from five. Say 'stop' if you don't want this to happen. Okay? Five. Four. Three. Two—"

"You son of a bitch!"

"If that's what you need me to be," he said evenly. "One. Time's up. Fight as much as you want. It's my call now."

She exploded into frantic movement again, but he countered every move she made, gazing intently to monitor her reaction.

He kissed her again, but it was very different now. Not pleading, not asking, but demanding. His kiss commanded and impelled.

She couldn't stop struggling. It stoked the panicked, frantic energy like some crazy feedback loop. But he was incredibly strong. He steadily nudged her body into the position he wanted, flailing legs splayed, flopping arms pinned, chest heaving against his weight. Somehow immobilizing her without crushing her.

He let go of her arms, ignoring her slapping and flailing, and nestled his stiff cock against the folds of her labia. Slowly, rhythmically sliding it up and down, so that his cock stroked her in a long, gliding, oblique caress. His cockhead popped triumphantly out over the hood of her clit, gleaming from her lube—and disappeared again for a slow, voluptuous drag downward. She stared down, panting. His pulsing club of flesh was so thick, so hot and shiny. He caressed her clit with his cockhead. Circling, just enough pressure to madden her.

"Now," he said. "Fight me now."

The challenge in his eyes set her off, like the starting gun of a race, but he'd positioned her cleverly so that every writhing, heaving move she made just rubbed his thick shaft deliciously over and around her clit. Every desperate jerk and twist just made it worse. Or better. Tension clutched her throat. Her muscles were clenched and trembling.

Too much input, emotion, sensation. She was overloading.

He stopped, shifting his body so that he was no longer grinding against her, but poised and motionless, muscles clenched. Eyes closed.

She squirmed furiously in his grip. "Sam? What the hell are you doing? Why did you stop?"

"Stop moving," he rasped. "Stay still, just for a second."

"Still, my ass!" she snapped. "You were the one who got me all worked up. Don't you dare play games with me, or I'll kill you!"

"Just stop moving, or I'll come all over you," he begged. "Damn it, Sveti! Give me a second to breathe it down!"

"That is your problem, not mine! Move, goddamnit!"

His grin flashed. "Demanding bitch," he muttered, but he resumed his rhythmic pulsing.

Sveti worked herself against his body, her movements frenzied, her gaze locked with his. He held her so tight, keeping her safe as the whole universe heaved up beneath her and turned inside out.

When her eyes fluttered open, he was on his knees, intent upon rolling a condom over himself. He caught her gaze, and his smile flashed. "You game to go all the way?" he asked. "You up for that?"

"I'm up for anything." Her throat was cracked and dry.

"We never talked safe sex," he said. "Or contraception. Just so you know, I've been tested recently. No STDs. No sex since then."

"Me neither. And I have a contraceptive implant."

"Good." He didn't look at her as he smoothed latex over his thick shaft, stroking it from root to head. "I'm using a condom anyway, of course. Just because that's what you do, when it's a one-off."

"Ah, yes," she managed inanely. "Of course."

He rolled on top of her. "Got any fight left?" He gripped her wrists. "Because I have plenty left for you."

"For you, Sam, always."

He laughed as he jerked her into position, letting go of her hands to lift her thighs and spread them wide. He hissed with pleasure as she shoved against his chest, her nails digging into him.

"Cat claws," he muttered, as he nudged his cock against her. "Go ahead. Hit me, scratch me. I won't care."

"We'll see," she panted back, swatting him. "I hit hard."

"Do your worst, babe." He thrust, a sharp, hard lunge.

She cried out, tightening against the sharp, awful pain.

Sam froze. His face went blank. He stared at her for a long moment. "Holy shit," he whispered. "Oh, Sveti. No fucking way."

She didn't move, or speak. It hurt too much. Sam seemed likewise frozen. Seconds ticked by.

"You're a *virgin?*" His voice cracked.

There was no point in answering. It was painfully obvious. She tugged at her trapped hands. He let go immediately.

"You didn't tell me?" He sounded furious. "That's insane!"

"Don't yell," she retorted. "I didn't know it was required, to tell you everything about my sexual—"

"I would never have been that rough! Did you set me up for this? On purpose? That is so fucked up!"

She jerked onto her elbows. "No!" she protested. "I didn't know it would . . . *oh*." Her voice choked off as Sam withdrew, staring down.

He sucked in a sharp breath. "Oh, Jesus," he muttered, and lunged for a box of tissues by the bed. He grabbed a handful.

"What?" She struggled to sit up.

"You're bleeding," he snarled. "Here, take these."

Sveti stared blankly at the wad of tissues in his outstretched hand. After a moment, he made a harsh, impatient sound and pressed them between her thighs himself. "Squeeze your legs together, hard."

She did so, but her face burned, and her privates stung. She was mortified. "Is it so much? How much is, ah . . . I mean, have you ever—"

"Had sex with virgins? A couple times. Once in high school, once in college. They didn't bleed as much as you. One hardly at all. But I didn't go in that hard, either! Because they fucking told me first, Sveti!"

"I'm sorry," she whispered, helplessly. "Really."

He slid off the bed and slapped the door of the adjoining bathroom open with a smack of his elbow. The thud made her jump.

She stared at the patch of blood on the sheets. She hadn't expected that. Or for it to hurt so much. Not from what her friends said about their first times. It hadn't been such a big deal for them.

Though it didn't surprise her. Many things that were no big deal for other people were fraught with peril and embarrassment for her.

It was, after all, the goddamn story of her life.

CHAPTER 5

Sam stared in horrified fascination at blood going down the drain, swirling around his toes. He should have known. In retrospect, it was so clear, but he'd been distracted by his clamoring dick, and the statistical improbability of a woman that beautiful managing to stay untouched for so long. And a contraceptive implant? What the fuck was that about?

God. He wanted to slam his head into a door.

Her shadow flickered behind the shower curtain. Rings rasped, as the curtain slid aside. She waited. He couldn't bear to turn and look.

She laid a hand on his wet shoulder. "Sam—"

"Not fair, Sveti." He pushed her aside so he could step onto the mat and dried himself, careful not to meet her eyes. "You've been busting my balls since we met. But this? Is all this carefully scripted to make me feel like shit? If so, congratulations. It's working."

"I'm sorry," she repeated. "I didn't know—"

"That your hymen was intact? Seriously?"

"No! I mean, I didn't know it would be like . . . that. My girl-friends said . . . well, it was different for them. Not so dramatic. I was actually hoping you wouldn't notice, to tell the truth. I didn't want you to know."

With that, he did look at her, uncomprehending. "Why not?"

She hesitated. "I was ashamed," she admitted, her voice halting.

That left him floundering. "You lost me, Sveti."

She pressed her hands to her face. "It seemed silly. So childish. I didn't want to seem like . . . a loser."

"Everybody's a virgin at some point," he said. "There's no stigma."

"Oh, come on!" she snapped. "It's embarrassing! That I could never manage to . . . that no one ever wanted to . . . oh, bah, I don't know. To be twenty-four, to have gone to high school and college, and all that time, I never managed to get laid. It felt kind of . . . pathetic."

His jaw was sagging. "You?" He stared down at her body, which was such an astonishment to his senses, he could barely formulate a thought. "You, the goddess on high? The princess on the pedestal? You, pathetic? That's pretty goddamn funny, Sveti."

"It's strange, Sam, but I'm not laughing," she said.

"You know you're drop-dead gorgeous, right? You know that any man who looks at you wants to fuck you. Tell me you know that."

She winced. "That's a ridiculous overstatement. I'm glad that you think it's so, but I don't feel it. I look in the mirror and I just see plain old me, nothing so earthshaking. But, ah, thanks."

Plain old me. Hah. He gestured at his own erection, which had revved up to full length. "Check me out. Even after being traumatized, my banner's still on high. I never thought I'd be so heavy into pain. I'm discovering all kinds of dark, scary stuff about myself."

"Dark, scary stuff is my specialty." She grabbed him from behind and gave him a tight, awkward hug, and then fled for the bedroom.

He lunged for her, clamped his arms over her belly, and hid his face against her hair. "All I wanted was to please you," he muttered.

She leaned back against him, with a jerky, shuddering sigh. "I know," she assured him. "Really. And you did. You do."

"Why do you make it so fucking hard?"

"I don't know." Her voice shook. "I swear. I would stop if I knew how, but I don't expect it'll get any better with time. I'm a mess, when it comes to . . . this kind of stuff. Probably not worth the trouble."

It was precisely what he'd been telling himself ever since he met the girl, but his arms clamped tighter, squeezing out what air might have been in her lungs. "Trouble like my wildest dreams," he muttered.

He was such a masochist, whispering sweet nothings to this girl, but she was leaning back, accepting the comfort of his body, and he was strung out on the sweet buzz that vibrated in his skin whenever they touched. It was a fleeting moment of grace before the next door slammed in his face, and he would, by God, exploit it to the bitter end.

He was just made that way. He never learned.

She wiggled in his grip, turning to press her face against his chest. She tasted the salt of dried sweat on his skin. The little flash of warm pink tongue acted like accelerant tossed onto a fire.

Then she reached down and gripped his cock.

Whoa. Sam's breath froze. His shaft twitched and throbbed. She stroked, squeezed, from root to tip. For a virgin, she had some great instinctive moves. But no way. Not now, after what just happened.

He tugged her hand away. "Time out, Sveti. Take a moment. Clean up, chill out. Here's a towel for you." He passed her a towel from the stack and marched out without looking back at her.

He regretted it, the instant the door clicked shut behind him.

He turned on the bedside lamp, but the splotch of red on the sheet horrified him all over again, so he switched it back off. The candle was more forgiving. He got to work stripping the bed. Sveti came out as he was wrestling a fresh contour sheet over the mattress.

She moved to help, but he waved her away. "I've got it," he said. "Just let me get this sheet someplace where I don't have to look at it."

"It wasn't your fault," she said.

He scooped up the linens. "I'm the one with the dick," he said. "Technically, that makes it my fault." He hauled them into the spare bedroom that functioned as his catch-all and laundry room, and found her bent over the bed, tucking and straightening when he got back. The angle showcased her ass, painting it tenderly with candlelight and shadows. He wanted to drop to his knees, shove her thighs apart, and tongue-kiss the shadowy recesses of her pussy. It made him dizzy.

"I said I'd take care of it," he grumbled.

She straightened up, turned. "I didn't set you up to make you feel bad," she blurted. "I would never, ever do that to you."

He nodded. "Okay."

She cleared her throat. "I thought men liked to be the first one."

Sam tossed the comforter up and let it drift down onto the bed. "There could be some sort of Stone Age ego rush to it," he admitted. "Presupposing the girl tells you, so you can adjust your technique and not ruin her first time. Jesus, Sveti. What were you thinking?"

"Stop scolding. You've scolded enough. Nothing was ruined." She straightened the comforter until it rested on the bed with mathematical precision. "Please, don't feel bad. I'm fine. It was amazing. You can have your Stone Age ego rush, if you want. You're entitled to it. I never knew how good messing around could feel, until that day in Bruno's studio. Ever since then, I've been wondering if I was building it up in my mind. If it could possibly be as awesome as I remembered."

He waited until his head was about to explode. "And? Was it?"

"Better," she confessed. "Infinitely better. Right up to the part that wasn't your fault."

Sam blew out a sharp sigh and shoved the shaggy hair off his face. "I'd be happier about that if it was our wedding night."

Leaden silence followed that manipulative, childish, jerk-off pronouncement, but fuck it, why even bother with restraint? What was the point in all that effort? He'd get no return on his investment.

"Oh, Sam," she whispered. "That's not fair."

"Sure isn't." He folded the comforter back and sat on the bed, his head in his hands.

"I've messed this up." Sveti's small voice sounded as miserable as he felt. "The last thing I wanted was to hurt you. Shall I call a car?"

He startled them both with his swift lunge and grab. He jerked her jealously close. "Oh, no. I haven't suffered anywhere near enough tonight," he said. "Lay it on me, Sveti. Let me see what else you've got."

She gazed down with that sad, soulful look, the one that made him ache to make her laugh. Slid her fingers into his hair. The heels of her cool hands petted tenderly over the brush of stubble on his jaw.

"I never wanted to hurt you," she whispered.

He cupped her ass, his long fingers gripping her hungrily. "I never wanted to hurt you, either. I wanted to make you come until you fainted."

She sank to her knees, seized his cock. His body jerked back in startled alarm. "No way!"

"Why not?" She kissed the top of his thigh and rubbed her soft cheek against the grain of his body hair.

"After what just happened? Are you fucking *kidding* me?" He choked off a moan as she did one of those world-class twist-'n'-swirl moves. "Not comfortable with this," he gasped. "Jesus, Sveti!"

Her smile was mysterious. "My goal is not to make you comfortable. My goal is to make you come until you faint."

He shook with laughter, his hands clamped over his dick, holding her hands still. "You don't have to do this."

"But I've wanted to. For years." Her tongue darted out to lick the flushed, gleaming tip of his cockhead, the only part poking out of his fists.

"I can't," he told her. "I'm traumatized."

Another teasing lick and swirl. "This part of you doesn't seem traumatized at all," she said.

"That part of me talks all kinds of trash. Don't listen to him."

Her eyebrow tilted up. "Do you need to fight me, Sam? Is that what you need to get through the wall? Because I can give you that."

He doubled over in silent laughter. Oh, shit. She was winning. He was toast. He looked up, opened his mouth, and abruptly forgot whatever he'd wanted to say. He just stared at her face. Soft with laughter. Her smile, so wide and relaxed. Shining. Bonfire bright.

"What?" she demanded.

"Your smile," he said, helplessly. "Oh, my God, Sveti. Your smile is so goddamn beautiful, I can't even breathe."

It was that look in his eyes, again. It scared her to death. "Don't," she blurted. "Don't be silly and melodramatic. I can't take it."

"Oh, no!" he said, in mock distress. "It's gone! I chased it away! Come back, please! Come back!"

She swatted his thigh. "Stop it!"

He stroked her cheek. "I've never seen that smile. You look so different. I don't see it enough. The whole world doesn't see it enough."

Well, shit. It was the world's own damn fault for being so fucked up and crazy. But that was a bitchy thing to even think, let alone say.

Sam cupped her face and kissed her, delicately at first, but it bloomed instantly, from something tender and holy into something blazing and carnal. It felt so natural, inevitable, to bend down and take him in her mouth. She'd never gone down on anyone, nor had she been inclined to, until she'd seen Sam. At which point, a lot of things that had sounded distasteful to her had suddenly made sense.

He tasted wonderful, felt wonderful. She loved the vital throb of his heartbeat against her tongue, the velvet soft skin sheathing that thick, steely club, his salty scent. She cradled his heavy, pendulant balls in her hand, sucking him deep, swirling her tongue.

Sam clutched her shoulders, leaning over her. His muscles were rigid, like steel cables. "Have you ever done this before?" he asked.

She took the opportunity to rest her somewhat overextended jaw and drag in some deeper breaths. "No. Am I doing it wrong?"

"Fuck, no. It's amazing. Can I come in your mouth? Not that I'll have much choice, if you keep on like you're doing."

A flush heated her face. "I'm fine with that."

She leaned down to get back to it, but Sam cupped her chin and gazed down into her face. "I'm getting my Stone Age ego rush now," he told her. "I like being your first. I like it so much, it scares me."

"I'm glad that it's you, too." She bent to the task once again.

He hunched over her, his breath deep, rasping pants. She deepened the long, tight, suckling strokes.

He shuddered, shouting hoarsely as the hot jets of salty come spurted inside her mouth. Almost too much for her to hold.

She rested her burning cheek on his thigh, cradling his cock in her hand. Only slightly softer. Still gleaming. He hunched, still panting.

She wiped her mouth and sat back on her heels, but as soon as she met his eyes, she wished that she hadn't.

She could give him pleasure, but it wouldn't make him happy for more than a fleeting moment. He wanted so much more.

His stark gaze pierced her like a needle. It made her want to die.

He got up and stumbled into the bathroom. Water ran. He came out holding out a glass. She nodded her thanks and drank.

"Your turn," he said.

She was almost afraid to ask. "Ah . . . for what?"

He took the glass and tossed off the last gulp himself. "Cunnilingus," he said matter-of-factly. "Let's get down to it."

She laughed, startled. "This is not a game where we score points!"

"The hell it's not." He set the glass down on the bedstand. "I love going down, and I have been told that I am reasonably good at it. I've been dreaming for years about putting my face between your legs. So let's get on with it, before you get sick of my whining bullshit and blow me off definitively." He gripped her hips, dragged her across the mattress. Her torso fell backward.

She struggled up onto her elbows. "Wow! Smooth lead-in, Sam!"

"Yeah, I know. I'm actually a civilized guy, under normal circumstances," he said. "But you're not normal circumstances. Rude stuff just falls out of my mouth with you. I'd apologize, if my basic socialization skills were functioning, but they're not. Filter failure."

He was holding her thighs open with his big, hot hands. She tried, without success, to pry them off. "I'm glad you have filter failure," she said. "I prefer the truth. Even when it makes me angry."

"That's fortunate," he said, pushing her legs wider. His gaze narrowed at her resistance. "Relax, Sveti."

She kept her back straight, her chin high, her gaze steady. "I don't take orders well," she said. "You sound angry and controlling, and that does not make me want to open my legs."

Sam ran his fingers through his wild mane of hair. "Goddamnit, Sveti," he snarled. "Just let me fulfil my function as a disposable sex toy, okay? Just let me make up for hurting you! Give me that, at least!"

"You're not a disposable toy. And you sound so grim about it!"

"Sorry I'm not in a more playful mood, but there's nothing in the world I'd rather do right now than put my face between your legs."

His raw tone unnerved her. "But you're so angry."

"Yeah," he admitted. "Angry at myself for wanting you, angry at myself for hurting you—"

"I'm not hurt, goddamnit!"

"Angry that you're leaving," he went on, as if she had not spoken. "Fucking furious that you waited until now to give it up to me. You needed a plane ticket to Europe in your hand before you dared to touch me. A ready escape route, right? Just in case you actually liked it."

She wrapped her arms over her chest, shivering. "That's not true."

"Face it," he said. "I suck as a casual sex toy, at least for you. I can't help it and I can't hide it. I'm angry that you want so goddamn little from me. And now I've got no place to put all the rest of it."

She closed her eyes against the pain in his voice. There was no skating over it now. There it was, out on the table.

"It may seem little to you," she whispered. "But it's huge to me."

He seized her, pinned her down onto the bed. She fought him, even though she didn't want to. She ached for him, craved him, but the convulsive resistance was a pre-programmed reflex. It made her jittery and crazy and confused. But he did not relent. He pinned her straining, heaving body down, and slid down the length of her, his big hands clamped on her inner thighs. Staring hot-eyed at her pussy.

"Wait." She was racked by spasms of unreasonable panic. "Don't."

"I won't hurt you," he assured her. A quick jerk scooted her body to the edge of the bed, so he could fold her legs up and kneel there. "I swear, I won't touch the sore part. I'll concentrate on your clit. Okay?"

Hah. Sam Petrie licking between her legs was not an event that could be described as "okay." But that and all other thoughts fizzed into vapor the instant his mouth touched her.

Too much, at first. His tongue slid between her sensitive folds, provoking a jittery explosion that made her cry out. But her body adjusted, reframing the sensation into a lovely swirl of liquid heat.

She rose to meet his caressing tongue. She glowed like moonlight on water, crested like sea waves, surged like froth and foam. Sam followed every cue before she even gave it, lavishing long, lingering licks and swirls over her shivering pussy. He suckled and flirted, teased her with maddening flicks and trills, building the charge with masterful slowness, to a screaming point of intensity—and then letting it drift gently down. Again, and again. Until she was desperate.

When she pitched over the edge, each pulse of the wrenching explosion jolted her deeper into that place inside where she could feel it all. The infinite depths, the heart-breaking sweetness. A fleeting, whirling glimpse of all that ever was beautiful and true, or ever could be.

Her eyes fluttered open sometime later. She blinked at the ceiling. Her eyes were wet. She struggled to remember even who she was. She did not recognize this self, these sensations. She was not even remotely familiar with the place from which she'd just drifted so softly down.

The blankness lasted just long enough to feel a stab of anxiety about it. Then everything came rushing back.

Sam sat cross-legged next to her. His hand cupped her muff, cradling it as if it belonged to him. "You're incredible when you let go."

She was abashed. "Did I yell?"

"Mmmm." He scooped her legs up and nudged until she scooted over to make room for him. He twitched the comforter up. It settled over them, soft as a cloud. His body was so long, hot. A bulwark against the night. He pulled her close against him, chest-to-chest, legs entangled.

They stared at each other. The silence felt heavy, and dangerous. Charged with all the things that they didn't dare to say. Afraid to spoil the fragile sweetness of the moment. It made her throat ache.

He smoothed a lock of hair back off her forehead. "You taste amazing," he said. "I could lick you forever. I think I could live on that alone. Just sweet, juicy Sveti lube. My magical elixir."

She shook with laughter that could just as quickly turn to tears. Tears lurked around every corner, ready to ambush her. It was very strange. She was not a person who cried easily. Or at all, really.

He was erect again. His penis pressed against her belly. She grasped him. He went rigid, with a sharp, silent gasp. She cupped his balls. His penis jumped and twitched in her hand.

"Jesus," he muttered. "That wasn't enough for you?"

"You don't seem to need rest," she observed.

"You do." He pried her hands off, pinning them against her chest.

She stroked him, long and slow and tight. "Make love to me."

His eyes narrowed, and he shook his head. "I'm on to you now, babe," he said. "You want me to fuck all coherent thought out of your head again, right? Felt good, didn't it? To take a little break from the weight of the world, even if it's only a few seconds?"

She yanked at her trapped hands. "I did not expect you to—"

"You don't want any uncomfortable silences, either," he went on. "You might actually have to talk to me. Oh, the horror."

"Let go!" She yanked harder. "Now you're just being an ass-hole!"

"Oh, for fuck's sake, let me have my little tantrum," he growled.

"It's a problem when the person throwing the tantrum is naked and lying on top of you!"

He rolled his eyes. "You know I would never hurt you."

Her laugh was bitter. "There's all sorts of different kinds of pain."

"I guess you'd know, Sveti. You're the big expert."

Oh, that *bastard*. She struggled, but Sam pinned her flat and kissed her again. He could seduce her so swiftly into a quivering mess, despite his complicated mood. Everything he did made her hot and crazy. He lifted his mouth. She gasped for some badly needed air.

"Make me come again," he said.

"You're confusing me," she said. "I thought you just said no."

"To regular fucking, yes," he said. "Jack me off."

That blunt directive made her want to slap him. The arrogant bastard. It also made her want to do exactly as he asked. She only had tonight. No time for pride. No need to worry about establishing dangerous precedents. She still hesitated. "I might not do it right."

"I'll show you how I like it. Get your hands wet first."

She gazed at him, perplexed.

He made an impatient sound. "With your lube. Best stuff ever." He flicked the cover back. Slid his hand up her thigh. "Put your hand in your pussy." He leaned forward, inhaling hungrily. "Show me the secret pink girl parts. Let me smell you. God, you're so fucking hot and yum."

Even an hour before, such a thing would have been unthinkable, but his mysterious alchemy had burned away her self-consciousness.

She splayed her legs and slipped her fingers inside herself. The only sound in the dim room was the wet sound of her hands moving on herself. He sat next to her, stroking his cock as he stared intently at the spectacle. She stared at the way he touched himself, too. Aroused by his thick, swollen shaft, the tracery of dark, pulsing veins.

The pleasure that burst from her depths startled her. A shuddering flush of heat pumped up through her chest, down her legs, her arm, all the way to her fingers and toes. Even her face tingled.

"Beautiful," he muttered. "Wow. Bonus orgasm." He grabbed her slippery hand and squeezed it around the head of his cock. His slick precome and her own lube blended into a perfect, slippery fluid.

He guided her hand into a tight, twisting yank, up and down the length of his pulsing shaft. "You do that . . . while I do this." He slid a finger delicately inside her pussy and circled with his fingertip. Her body convulsed, shuddering.

"Does that hurt?" He pulsed it tenderly inside her, finding some mysteriously perfect spot in there that was soft, glowing with molten heat. It did hurt, just a little, but she'd die if he stopped, so she shook her head, unable to speak. Her throat was locked and trembling.

He guided her hand. She clenched and squirmed around his caressing fingers. Their pants turned to gasps. They were a taut, straining knot, making low, guttural sounds. His fingers probed deeper. Her strokes on his cock quickened. They fought their way toward that burning inevitability that beckoned and lured.

Sveti reached it first, pulsing around his hand with a shocked wail. Sam tightened his fist over hers, jerking it over his cock with frenzied intensity. He shouted as he spurted hot jets of creamy white come all over her belly, her breasts.

They stared at each other, drenched and limp, for a long moment.

"It's just so fucking good with you," Sam muttered. "Why did it have to be so good?"

She responded to the note of accusation in his voice. "I'm sorry."

"Don't be. It's my own fault, for getting all intense."

Sam got up and headed to the bathroom. He came back with a hot wet washcloth, with which he proceeded to wipe the sticky fluid off her body. The slow rasp of hot, wet terrycloth over her belly and her sensitized breasts felt like a big, caressing tongue against her skin. She stretched voluptuously to give him better access. She'd never felt this relaxed, limp, soft. Empty, floating. Strange. Soothing.

It couldn't last. As soon as she realized how much she liked it, it was ending. The heavy cold dragged at the bottom of her insides again.

Sam felt it, human antennae that he was, and the hot towel stopped moving. "Really?" he said, incredulous. "You're sad again? That's all the relief you get? That's one hell of a narrow window, babe."

"I know," she admitted. "It really is."

"Maybe it's a good thing you're leaving the continent," he said. "Managing your moods with sex would probably kill me."

She forced herself to smile. "Lucky you. Narrow escape."

He tossed the washcloth through the bathroom door, where it landed with a wet plop in the sink. He stretched out beside her again, pulling her into his arms, and hugged her, fiercely. Defiantly.

To her utter shock, she dissolved into tears.

"Oh, God. What, Sveti?" He shook her gently. "Did I hurt you?"

She shook her head, hiding her face against his chest.

"Okay, whatever." He grabbed the tissues, put the box by her pillow.

She groped for them and mopped up the mess. She'd known this would happen. That the sex would knock down barriers that held in a huge mess of inconvenient, inappropriate, dangerous feelings.

Sam held her quietly, kissing the top of her head. So sexy, that he was unfazed by geysers of nonspecific grief. Of course, he'd get sick of it eventually. And it was good that he wouldn't get the chance.

It had to be this way. Because she had oceans of grief inside her.

She might never plumb those depths.

CHAPTER 6

Sam stared up at the ceiling after Sveti's tears eased off, his jaw clenched so hard, it ached. He rarely allowed himself to descend to this nadir of suck-ass misery. Under normal circumstances, he had a whole arsenal of tricks for jumping tracks, taking his mind elsewhere. He'd gotten good at it, way back, while Mom was dying. He was very deft.

Investigative work had been his drug of choice since he'd discovered it by accident back in college. The games he played with money helped. When that failed, there were video games, excessive exercise, alcohol.

Sex was a favorite, too, but not in this case. Oh, no.

But he was barred from work, and he couldn't pump iron or suck down bourbon with Sveti's perfect body draped over his. Her head rested in the crook of his shoulder, her hand splayed on his chest. Not asleep, barely dozing. Her body was so slim, but charged with power. Lithe and flexible, every curve and hollow a miracle of nature. He sought out the delicate throb of her pulse.

That strong, stubborn heart. Almost stolen. Rescued in the nick of time. His mysterious maiden, with all her tragic airs.

Hell, no one was as entitled as Sveti to put on tragic airs.

It occurred to him that if someone had tried to steal his heart literally right out of his chest, he might guard it a little harder than a normal person, metaphorically speaking. It made sense that she was armored, alarmed, with infrared and motion detectors and chain-link and razor-wire and control towers. Who could blame her.

A virgin, for the love of God. He should have known. She kept the whole world at arm's length. And he'd never been able to resist a challenge. He was hardwired to leap for them, like a trout for a bug.

And he was still ready to mount right up and pound away all night long, staring down into her big, startled eyes. She'd seemed so surprised by pleasure. God, what a rush, those hot, clutching pulses around his finger, pressed to his mouth. If only it had been his cock.

He'd get her comfortable with multiple orgasms. He'd make them her nightly norm. Morning, noon, evening, whenever. It was masochistic, to fantasize about it. She'd have none of it.

Sveti sensed emotion roiling inside him, and stirred, lifting her head. "What's wrong?"

Why even start? There was no finishing that conversation. He'd be haranguing her back as she walked up the Jetway, desperately glad to be rid of him. He shook his head.

She propped herself up onto her elbow and laid her hand over his heart. "You asked before if I wanted to be with you for the two days that I have, until I leave," she said. "And I do want that. If you still do."

So he'd passed the audition. The fuck-buddy-til-Thursday scenario. His cock hardened, and his face went red.

"Don't go," he blurted.

Her hair swung down like a curtain. The long seconds of silence gave him her answer even before she spoke. "I have to go," she said quietly. "It's what I've dreamed of doing. It's an incredible opportunity."

"So do it. Just not in London. There's evil to fight wherever you turn. You don't have to fly to another continent to find it. Join a task force, join the police bureau, start a foundation. Whatever."

She shook her head. "Don't start, Sam."

He could not shut up. "Give us a chance, before you run away!"

"Give what a chance? You don't even know me! You've hardly ever talked to me, in all these years!"

"You never gave me a fucking opportunity! Give me one now!"

Her back stayed turned. "My decision is made. I won't unmake it because of a one-time hookup."

Hookup? He sucked in air. He couldn't even speak, for the rock in his throat.

"So," she said, still not looking at him. "Do you want to spend the next two days with me or not?"

Two days. Mornings, afternoons, evenings. Every quality of light falling on her naked body. Breakfasts, lunches, dinners, showers. His mind was all over that idea, like a pack of starving wolves. Two days of Sveti Ardova, naked and whimpering beneath him. Oh, *hell*, yeah.

And then? When she walked through the security line? When he drove home from the airport alone? Two days of frantic fucking would not make that easier. It would seal his doom. He was dangerously far from his right mind already, after just hours of Sveti-style sexual mind-melt. Two days of it, and he could totally lose his shit.

He forced the words out, like jagged rocks. "I can't do it."

There was an awful silence, and she slid to the edge of the bed. "I see," she said quietly. "This was a mistake. I'm so sorry. I'll just go."

He pulled her back, flung his leg over hers. Not. Fucking. Yet.

She wiggled. "You're confusing me, Sam. What are you doing?"

His arms tightened. "Making a huge mistake. I'm just not quite done making it yet. Give me til morning. Don't rush me."

The cutoff point was still an hour or so out. He could do all kinds of catastrophic damage to himself before then.

Sveti laid her hands over his arms, which were still clamped over her chest, and stroked them, very gently. "Until dawn, then?"

He nodded against her neck.

She twisted around to face him. "Make it worth my while, then. Make love to me."

Fresh lust flooded him. "No," he said. "It's too soon."

"I want to feel that, with you," she said. "If we had more time, I'd say sure, let's wait a day. But as it is, we can't."

"No," he resisted stubbornly. "You're sore. It'll hurt you."

She shrugged. "Big deal. I'm used to things hurting me."

Her offhand attitude about pain pissed him off. "I don't want to be the one who hurts you! Don't set me up for that ever again!"

"Shhh." She pressed her silk-and-velvet-textured, honey-scented self against him. "It's not pain I want. It's pleasure. You flood me with it. You fill me with it. Here, feel me." She took his hand and pressed it against the slick seam of her pussy, gasping as his fingers slipped inside. She was drenched. Plush and soft and yielding. "I'm so ready," she pleaded. "Let me feel you inside me."

Her delicious womanly scent made him dizzy, drunk. "My cock," he said thickly. "Be specific. Say, let me feel your cock inside me."

She squirmed sexily around his hand and whispered obediently. "Let me feel your cock inside me."

He looked into her eyes, and the battle was over before it began. She could see straight to forever, in there. Endless distances, horizons upon horizons, whenever she looked at him. He cringed from the pain he knew would follow this suicidal idiocy, but he was dead meat anyway, so why not finish the job? Grind that motherfucker into slop.

Sveti's clear hazel eyes did not waver. "Do it, Sam."

That uppity empress-of-everything tone just squeezed his nuts. He wanted to throw himself at her feet. Offer her his heart's blood. *Here, take it. It's yours, anyway.* At the same time, he wanted to drag her off that stupid pedestal. Pull her down to his earthly level, for pizza and beer. To grab and touch and hug and kiss and lick and fuck and love.

But no way. She was having none of it. She wanted a little teasing taste, that was all. Then she'd fly off again to her lonesome heights.

"I'll try to be gentle," he said. "But when I get started with you, I never know what'll happen. I forget my own goddamned name."

"I know," she soothed. "That's what makes it so good." She soothed him with a rain of gentle kisses against his jaw, and his cheek, his lips. He loved it. Though it made the pain infinitely worse.

"You can't fight me," he warned. "I won't do it if you fight me."

"I'll be good. Move off me, so I can grab a condom, okay?"

He rolled off reluctantly, as if she would vanish into smoke. She stretched to grab a condom from his stash.

He'd let her deal with the condom, but almost ended up blowing his wad right then, from her tender squeezing and stroking. She tried several times to get the thing rolled on. It kept snapping off, and after minutes of that, he was shaking with silent laughter.

She shot him an irritated glance. "You could help, you know."

He grabbed his engorged member and held it steady for her, hissing with pleasure as she smoothed the latex down.

"You said you had a contraceptive implant," he said.

"Yes." She followed up with a slow twist that made him gasp.

"But you're a virgin," he said. "Why the implant? What for?"

She shrugged. "I wasn't happy being a virgin. I figured, my life might include sex at some point, but not babies."

"No babies? Really? Ever? I thought you liked babies."

"Sure, I like them. I just don't want to have them."

That surprised him. "But you always seemed so into the little kids," he said. "Consumed, even. They hung off you. Like ripe fruit."

"As coping mechanisms go, little kids are better than most," she said. "You can't feel sorry for yourself when you're with them. You're too busy, and they don't care about your problems, no matter how bad they are. I like who I am with kids better than I like myself with adults."

"I like who you are with me," he said rashly.

"Sam," she said. "I offer you my naked body, and you stall me with questions about how many babies I want. What's wrong with you?"

"The only time you'll really talk to me is when you're offering me your naked body." He cut off her reply with his mouth and bore her down onto the bed. Her body shuddered, resisting. He lifted his head.

"You promised," he said. "Don't fight me, Sveti. Relax."

Her chest jerked as she tried to sigh out tension. "What if I can't?"

"Then we wait until you do."

"But . . . but what if I never . . ." Her throat bobbed.

"Then you'll miss your plane." He settled on top of her and resumed kissing. He would have this surrender, if he got nothing else.

It took a long time for him to get her there, but he'd have been happy to wind himself around her body forever. She kept dragging in all the air her lungs could take, releasing it in a shuddering sigh.

He timed his breaths to hers. Rolled onto his side to give her more air, and slid his hand between her thighs. Breathing with her. Hearts in unison. Slow, lazy, plundering kisses, as he played that pearly pink clit delicately with his thumb. Willing to wait, and wait. As long as it took.

He lifted his head later. The candle's flame had burned to a dim glow deep in a waxen cavity. Her hair was spread out on the pillow, her lips parted from his kisses, eyes dazzled and heavy. Soft, relaxed. Ready.

He settled between her legs. Her face looked so different when she relaxed. She glowed, from the inside, with a soft-focus shimmer.

Just a short slide down to those perfect tits, and he made her nipples gleam, teasing them to sharp, shivering points. Her heart thudded against his cheek. Her fingers twisted into his scalp. He loved the delicate bite of her little nails.

The world as he knew it was buckling, shifting into something new. He was going to pay for this, but right now, he didn't give a shit.

He settled on his knees, his cock bobbing against her decorative frill of pussy curls. He wrapped her hands around his cock. "Take me inside," he said. "Show me how much. I don't want to hurt you again."

She nodded. He propped her up, shoving pillows behind her back. She shut her eyes, flung her head back, lower lip caught between her teeth. His cockhead slipped between her satiny folds. She rocked forward, forcing him deeper. So tight. Ah, God. It had to sting, but she didn't let on, tough babe that she was.

She raised herself onto her elbows and stared into his eyes. He was balanced on a razor's edge in a motionless, agonized state of *oh-fuck-I'm-going-to-come-right-now*. She surged forward, taking in a little more. Back, a slow, clutching glide. Her body said yes, again and again with each stroke. She reached out to drag him deeper . . . *Yes*. All in.

His heartbeat thudded in his groin, wedged in the tight, fluttering embrace of her body. He braced his hands on either side of her and breathed, struggling desperately not to come. He couldn't lose control, not with a first timer, half his size. He hung on. Teetering.

"Does it hurt?" He got the words out, somehow.

"I'm fine," she said.

"That's not what I asked," he said.

"It's all you're getting," she retorted. "Shut up and move."

She sprawled back onto the pillows and gripped his chest, bucking her hips beneath him. Heaving, to get him moving.

His body had to obey. Her gaze sliced in so deep, to places uncharted. She could see all his pointless yearning in his eyes. He should flip her over, take her from behind, but that would take a coolness that he did not possess. The next best option was the dark. He reached to snuff the candle's flame, burning his fingers. Barely felt it.

Sveti made a protesting sound as the darkness fell. "Sam?"

"Shhh." He stifled her objections by kissing her.

The darkness made it harder not to lose himself to the blind, mindless greed. Her pussy squeezed around his pumping cock.

He tried to slow it down, but she was so juicy and hot, and they moved together so perfectly. The frantic momentum built, and when he became conscious of how hard they were fucking, his body would not let him stop. They were locked in that pounding rhythm. Sveti's hips braced to meet his every stroke. Energy gathered in her body, like an animal with its muscles poised to spring.

She went off like a bomb. He held her close, to savor every jolt, every sweet shudder of helpless pleasure, the scalding rush of fresh girl juice on his cock to ease the way for his own wild finale.

Now. His climax smashed down on him like a landslide.

He drifted back, damp and destroyed, to the sensation of prodding in his shoulder. "Sam," she whispered. "Let me breathe. You're heavy."

He rolled off. Sweat had chilled on his back. Dread gripped him, cold and nauseating. "You okay?" He braced himself.

"Fine," she said softly. "Wonderful. It was so wonderful."

Well. That was good. As far as it went. He got to his feet, stumbling drunkenly over her shoes on his way to the bathroom.

The condom had traces of blood. Not much, but it still made him feel like a jerk. He got rid of it and hid in the shower. This was the end. He didn't trust himself yet to face it with dignity. Ice water roared down, needle-sharp. Punishment. The time of reckoning was at hand.

Bright white light spilled out over Sveti, curled on the bed when he opened the bathroom door. She flinched from it, covering her eyes. He grabbed jeans from his dresser. Strapped on his inside waist holster.

"There's some blood again," he said. "Not too much. Sorry."

"I'm okay," she said. "It was worth it. It was amazing."

He grunted. Too late for compliments. He was not a goddamned trained seal, performing to have some dead fish flung to him.

He grabbed a sweatshirt. Sveti waited for him to say something, but he was all out of words. He flicked on the harsh overhead light.

Sveti flinched again. "Sam?" Her voice was small. "What's wrong?"

He stared at the pink smears on the sheet, the streak of grease from the candle. "Get dressed. I'll drive you home," he said. "I'm done."

Her eyes widened. "I thought you said til dawn. It's barely . . ."

He pulled his Glock 19 out of the bedstand as her voice petered out, and tucked it into the waist holster. "Close enough."

Sveti struggled into her dress with difficulty, being so sticky and damp. It didn't fit anymore. Her body had changed dimensions. Her breasts felt bigger, her skin so sensitized. She was weak in the knees and angry and hurt, but for God's sake, she was the hard-ass of this situation, not him. She had no business sniveling.

He couldn't even bear to look at her, and she'd caused this disaster all by herself. By being slutty and grabby. Trying to have her cake and eat it, too. Her fingers felt thick and clumsy. She teetered on rubbery legs as she crouched, struggling with the buckles of her shoes.

Sam stared fixedly at a point on the wall. "I'll wait downstairs, if you need more time."

"No, I'm ready now," she said, stumbling toward the door.

She followed him down the stairs, clutching the banister with a death grip. He shrugged on a leather jacket, scooped up his phone, and stuck it in his pocket. Handed her the little red evening bag, all without looking at her. Swift, economical gestures. She followed him out into the damp dawn chill, wishing she'd made more of an effort to find her stockings. She hated the thought of him finding them. Throwing them away.

"Watch the sidewalk," he said brusquely without looking back. "Tree roots have buckled it. It'll trip you."

"I see them." She picked her way over the jagged planes of broken concrete and hesitated at the car. "I can call a car, you know."

"No, you can't. Get in." He looked at her, and his eyes widened as he took in her bare shoulders. "Jesus! Where the hell's your jacket?"

"I think I left it at the reception," she said, shivering. "I'm okay."

He slipped his jacket off and held it out. "Put this on."

She shrank away. "Oh, no. I don't need—"

"Put. It. *On*." His voice slashed, making her jump. She shrank back from the flash of furious emotion in his face. It was not worth crossing him, not in his current mood. She took the jacket.

It was huge. The cuffs dangled inches below the ends of her fingers. It draped on her like a heavy cape. Warm, from his body. She huddled in it when she got into the car, so distracted that she was halfway home before she noticed that he hadn't asked for directions.

"How do you know where I live?" she asked.

He didn't answer for a moment. "It's not hard to find an address."

"So you've been stalking me?"

"Yeah." The admission was utterly unapologetic.

They sat on that for a few minutes as the dark night swept by.

Sveti took a deep breath. "I stalked you, too," she told him.

His mouth twitched briefly. "I stalked you better."

"I don't doubt that, being a cop and all. What did you find out?"

He glanced at her. "Everything."

"Wow, that's impressive," she commented. "But be more specific."

He pondered that. "Well, your landlord bugs the shit out of me."

"Walter?" she said, taken aback. "Why? He's a perfectly nice guy."

Sam grunted. "Don't like the tattoos. What's up with that hair?"

"They're dreads, Sam. You're judging him for his fashion choices?"

"Blond dreadlocks bite my ass," he grumbled. "Fucking affected."

"It's an image thing," she explained. "He leads extreme sports expeditions. He has to look hip. You won't see him today, though."

"I should hope not, at six in the morning."

"No, I mean, he's gone. He and his girlfriend, Pam, just got married. They had a big barbecue for the neighbors and took off for Queensland yesterday to surf the Great Barrier Reef for their honeymoon. They got special, patterned shark-proof wetsuits for it."

Sam grunted. "So tell me about the six three, two-hundred-and-fifty-pound goateed black guy in the upstairs apartment."

"Oh, that's Paul. Wonderful guy. Off to Chicago for the week to visit his boyfriend, William. They're struggling with the distance thing, because they both like their jobs. William's okay, but I have my doubts. He's a lightweight, and he drinks too much. Paul deserves better."

"I see," Sam said slowly.

"They're all great neighbors," she babbled on. "I'm going to miss them. Paul's all set to move down to my apartment next week. He's in love with my bay window and my clawfoot tub."

She immediately regretted mentioning her impending departure.

"So, you're all alone in that big house right now? Not a soul?"

She snorted at his sour tone. "You don't like them when they're at home. You don't like them when they're gone. There's no pleasing you."

He shook his head. "You know exactly what pleases me."

That shut her right up. She stared out the window, face smarting. She'd been so stupid. So superficial, to act as if sex with Sam

was some country she could visit like a tourist and come back un-
changed. She was inside out, exploding with feelings she didn't
know how to manage, and his seething anger buzzed against her
every naked nerve.

Grim silence reigned for the rest of the drive.

There was no parking in front of her apartment. "You can just
let me off," Sveti told him as he circled the block.

"Not a fucking chance," he growled. "I'll park."

He found a place near the end of the block, maneuvered his car
into it, and killed the engine. They sat in the chill dimness, both
mute.

She ached to say something that would be meaningful, something that would make sense of the flat finality of it. But no such
thing existed. Thanking him was wrong. She was sure he would
reject that violently. She wanted to give him some indication of
how important this night had been to her, but that would only
make things worse.

What he wanted, she did not have to give. Tension tightened,
like a knot of wet rope in her throat. This was so awful. No way to
fix it.

"So did it work?" There was a note of belligerence in his voice.

An obvious trap, but she had to walk into it. "Did what work?"

"Banging me. Is it out of your system? Do you feel better now?"

Hurt twisted in her belly, like a claw. "Fuck you, Sam."

"Ah! That's my girl! Don't let anyone inside the superhero
armor, Sveti. Don't get distracted from saving the world. Keep
yourself pure."

"Please, Sam. Stop," she said. "This is a bad way to end it."

"There were a lot of alternative endings," he said. "You didn't
choose any of them. This is all that's left on the table."

That was all she could stand. She opened the door. "Good-bye."

She didn't dare run, not in the dark, and in those heels. Thank
God there was no one in the house to see her come slinking home
in an evening gown. Not that they would judge. On the contrary,
they would probably congratulate her and tell her it was about
fucking time.

Even so, she preferred to huddle alone and lick her wounds.

She walked on the balls of her feet onto the porch, clutching the banister. Her thighs were sticky, her hip joints ached. Her private parts felt liquid and hot and sore. At least she was well and truly deflowered. She could cross that off her list of things to feel inadequate about—and replace it with a new list of stressors. Big ones.

She was going to pay for this self-indulgence. She would be viciously sleep deprived for God only knew how long, and that was the best-case scenario, if the nightmares were all she had to deal with.

The worst-case scenario saw her heavily medicated, unable to function out in the world. The conference, London, her new job, her amazing opportunity. She might have compromised that.

And to top it all off, there was the stone-cold certainty that nothing in her future sex life, whomever it might be with, could ever measure up to last night's intensity. She was dead sure of that.

She fought to get the key into the lock. The automatic porch light had not flicked on. Maybe the bulb was burned out. In any case, it was light enough to see, more or less. She finally got inside, closed the door, and reached for the hall light.

Air moved. She whirled, saw a blur—

Wet cloth clamped over her face as she was inhaling to scream.

She was jerked into a bone-crushing, smothering grip. She kicked, connected, heard a muffled grunt. Her wrist was twisted, brutally hard. She fought not to inhale again, but her arms were trapped, her eyes blurred from drug fumes. Her lungs began to heave. Her belly rolled and flopped as her blood pressure plummeted.

"Sweet dreams," crooned a rasping voice, as she fell into darkness.

CHAPTER 7

Sam's wrist would not turn to twist the key in the ignition. His fingers would not tighten around the gearshift to take the car out of park. He was paralyzed, watching through the rearview window as Sveti picked her halting way up the porch, fumbling with her key.

His jacket hung down on her to midthigh. He saw that detail by the orange glow of the streetlight that filtered in through the trees.

Why was there no porch light? He wanted to have a sharp talk about security with dreadlocked extreme sports dude. Being a giddy newlywed was no excuse for a landlord to get sloppy when he had tenants to protect.

The door opened to darkness, which he also disliked. Light should spill out when a door was opened for her. The door shut. Gone. Home safe. His cue to go. But he waited for the light go on in her apartment. He knew which would flick on first, which second. He knew her path through her apartment, how her slim shadow wavered against the curtains. Sick, pining, pathetic bastard that he was.

Her light did not turn on. He drummed his fingers against the steering column. Maybe she just felt like sulking in the dark. He did it himself often enough. Hell, he was doing it right now.

But Sveti disliked darkness. Her lights were always on. Someone had told him that was because of the organ trafficking ordeal, which had involved a lot of darkness. He should have walked her to her door, but he probably would have ended up tossing her skirt up and fucking her again, on whatever flat surface presented itself first.

The night's events had not taken the edge off of his sexual obsession. It had inflamed the problem into monstrous proportions.

Enough. She was home, choices made, ultimatums laid down. Time to go home, burn those sheets, and get on with whatever his life was going to be now. But his evil twin jerked the steering wheel around at the corner and sent him circling around the block. They said addictive substances eroded the brain's capacity for impulse control. Sveti being his drug of choice, it followed that a night of boning her would have rendered his brain into slop. No longer capable of executive decisions. He was devolving. Snarling, rattling the bars of his cage.

He cut the lights and jerked to a stop before turning the last corner, as soon as he had a sight line to the house. He turned off the engine and stared at that unlit bay window like a lovesick teenager, scrabbling for his final crumb. *Come on, Sveti. Turn that sucker on.*

He wasn't going to be able to leave until he saw that light.

A flicker of movement drew his eye. Two men came out the front door, carrying a cardboard box. Something large, like a dishwasher. Weird time, for a pick-up. They hoisted the thing up into the back of a white van. It was early. Too early. Maybe the landlord was—

No. He wasn't. The landlord and the new wife were dodging sharks on the Great Barrier Reef. The third-floor neighbor was working on his long-distance relationship in Chicago. There was nobody in that big Victorian except for Sveti. Or at least, there should not be.

The van's taillights flicked on. It jerked away from the curb. He caught the first three letters of the plate before it left his line of vision. His car roared to life and turned the corner just in time to see which way the van went at the end of the block, and juddered to a halt in the spot the van had just vacated. Instinct screamed follow, *now*, but his instinct was fucked when it came to Sveti. There could be a legitimate explanation. Sveti could be stepping into her shower, humming, while he went racing off after a couple random guys whose only crime was to be transporting stuff outside of normal business hours. Thereby cementing his status as a psycho head case, a danger to himself and others.

He groped for his phone as he sprinted toward the porch. It was not there. He'd left it in the pocket of the jacket Sveti wore. Too busy wallowing in his own goddamn hurt feelings to remember it. *Fuck.*

He wrenched the screen door open. The front door was unlocked, and a glance at the faceplate of the lock showed a coating of oily graphite dust. He flung the door open.

A crimson shoe lay on the floor, the straps torn loose. A red evening bag. Some change had spilled from it.

He dove for his car, his body jangling. *Asshole.* Second-guessing himself. Tires squealed on the curve. Not much traffic yet. They could be on the freeway, or they could have turned anywhere. His detour had cost about forty seconds, maybe forty-five. Oh, God, oh, God.

His heart thudded painfully when he saw a white van, stopped at the last light before the freeway on-ramp. He got closer, fingers white-knuckled on the wheel until he was close enough to read the plates.

The light went green as he pegged the first three letters. Same. *Yes.*

He got in line, two cars behind onto the on-ramp, breathing down panic. Jesus. No backup, no police, no phone, and he didn't dare lose eye contact for a split second. Just him and his Glock 19. Fifteen in the magazine, one in the chamber. Not even a spare mag in his pocket.

That was the cavalry.

Whack. Yuri was kicking her on the ground, calling her names: whore, dirty cunt. His breath stank like dead things. Whack. Whack.

Splash. Sveti coughed and sputtered, choking. The room spun, dim and foggy. She blinked, frantically. She was in a warehouse. Maybe a barn. A damp, ancient one that stank of mold and mouse shit. Crates and boxes were piled high, but the boxes were deformed, giving in to gravity, contents decaying. Light filtered through high, dirty windows.

Yuri stood in front of her. No, not Yuri. Yuri was in a maximum-security prison in Siberia. This man was taller, broader. His features were thick and blunt, his eyes were hot little pale points burning inside shadowy pits. His graying hair was buzzed short. His mouth was moving, but she heard nothing.

There was another man in the shadows, smaller, wearing a black ski mask. His dark eyes glittered through the slits in the mask.

Splash. The pale man heaved a plastic pitcher full of ice water in her face again. His voice boomed suddenly in her ear, volume spiking.

". . . vetlana," he yelled. "Pay attention! Wake up!"

"Wha . . . who?" She coughed out water, shuddering as rivulets soaked her chest, her back. She could not move her arms, to wipe water from her eyes, or push back the hair clinging to her face. She was bound. She could not see it, beneath her skirt, but it felt like duct tape. There was a big plastic basin full of water and floating ice.

The man held up a dripping plastic pitcher. "We need to talk."

She tried to speak and ended up coughing again. "Who are you?"

His yellowed teeth flashed. "That's not relevant."

It finally sank in. That wasn't English. The man was speaking Ukrainian. Terror stabbed, like lightning. "What do you want?"

The man set a rickety chair down in front of her and straddled it.

"Everything," he said. "Everything you have."

"My friends are expecting me," she said. "I'm supposed to be at work at eight o'clock. If I'm not there—"

"You have given notice at your jobs and volunteer activities. You sold your car, too, no? You are leaving the country."

"How do you know all this? Have you been following me?"

"Not exactly, not until just recently," the man said. "But keeping an eye on you, most definitely. For years."

"What do you want?" she repeated.

"We'll get to that. First, tell me about the man you spent the night with after leaving the wedding party last night."

She was stupefied for a moment. "What man? I went out, after the wedding. I met some friends, went to a couple of clubs. One of my friends gave me a ride home. There was no man."

"Don't lie. We followed you home from the wedding, and then to his house. You were there for hours. Did you enjoy your night of passion? Were you satisfied by Lt. Petrie, of the Portland Police Bureau? Were you left with longings unfulfilled? Tell us. Maybe we could help. My colleagues and I stand ready to serve."

Her stomach churned. "My friends will find you, and they will crush you," she said.

"They might, but it will be too late for you." He pulled out a wicked, narrow-bladed knife and hooked up the sodden hem of her skirt with it. Cold air rushed in, chilling her naked flesh still further.

The other guy moved closer to look under her skirt. To think she had fancied herself to be unafraid, of pain, of death. Hah. She had no excuse for being so arrogant. She'd gotten soft. Forgotten how it felt.

"Nice," the other man said in English.

"Yes," the pale-eyed man agreed. "Very."

She spat at them. The smaller, masked man stepped forward and jerked his hand up to hit her.

"No," the other one said sharply. "Not yet."

The man stepped back, with bad grace. The pale man leaned forward, his weight making the chair creak. He let the knife dangle between his thick fingers, like a flashing pendulum, back and forth.

She lifted her chin, waiting.

He laughed. "So haughty. Just like your whore mother."

That sent a jolt of electricity through her spine. "What about my mother?" she demanded. "What do you know about her?"

The man tut-tutted. "One thing at a time. I am going to ask you a series of questions. Answer them honestly, and we will let you go."

That was bullshit, but there was nothing to be gained by calling the man out on it. "What questions?"

"It's amazing, the resemblance." The man's low, insidious tone filled her with dread. "And Sonia wore a red slut dress, just like yours, the night she died. Poor Svetlana. All alone in the world."

"I am not alone," Sveti said, teeth chattering.

"No? I don't see anyone. Except for myself and my colleague."

Sveti closed her eyes, thinking of them. Nick and Becca and Sofia, Tam and Val, Rachel and Irina. The McClouds and their wives and kids, and all the rest. A wonderful family. She was lucky. No matter what.

But she would not debate such matters with a torturer.

Her captor scooted his chair closer and slid his fingers into Sveti's hair. He jerked her hair until her chair rocked on two legs. His bloodshot eyes were inches from hers. "Tell me about the photographs."

She shook violently in his cruel grip. "What photographs?"

"One, in particular. It appears in your TED talk. Great presentation, by the way. I was so moved, I almost donated money to help give a new start to those poor pet slaves of yours. How sweet."

"Which . . . which photo are you—"

"A photo of your mother," he said. "You displayed a slide, in your TED talk. Where did you get that photograph?"

She was utterly confused. "Ah . . . she sent it to me, years ago."

"Something is written on it, Svetlana. And there are numbers. Do you remember what is written?"

She shook her head. "Ah . . . The Sword of Cain," she faltered.

"Tell me about this Sword of Cain. Tell me everything."

She tried to shake her head, but could not move, with his fingers gripping her hair. "Tell you what? I have no idea what it meant."

"Did she send other photos from that same series? Or others taken at the same place?"

She shook her head.

"What did the letter that came with the photograph say about it?"

"There was no letter." She struggled to keep her voice steady, without success. "She sent it through the mail, like a postcard."

He let go and backhanded her across the face, so hard everything went black for a moment. "You expect me to believe that you never asked her what it meant?" he bellowed.

"It was delivered after she died!" she yelled.

He dipped the plastic pitcher into the ice water and slung it into her face. *Splash.* "You are lying," he spat out.

She gasped, sputtered. "N-n-not lying," she choked out.

"Would you like to see what the day has in store for you? I am a professional interrogator. There is nothing you can hide from me."

"I have nothing to hide! I swear it!"

"Look here." The man set down his knife and picked up a dark briefcase from a rickety card table that had been set up nearby. A small portable video camera lay upon it, too. He spread the briefcase open, tilting it up so that she could see its contents, nested in crimson velvet.

Sveti recoiled. Blades gleamed. Scissors and shears, scalpels and pincers. Things whose uses she did not dare imagine.

"The tools of my trade. One more detail . . . let me just get the angle right." He bent down over the video camera, pointing it toward her, then peering at the digital window. "Perfect," he said. "That should catch everything. And now." He pulled a ski mask over his own face, with a flourish, and his teeth flashed through the slit as he pushed the "record" button. A light flashed red. "For posterity," he said. "Once again, Svetlana. The Sword of Cain. What do you know about it?"

She bit her lip, shook her head. "Nothing," she whispered.

The man let out a theatrical sigh. "Poor Svetlana. It is going to be a long and painful day for you."

"I don't know anything!" she cried out. "It was just a picture of my mother that I kept by my bed!"

The man crouched and sliced through the duct tape that fastened her ankles. He hoisted her up by the armpits and dumped her to her knees with a jarring thud against the wet floor next to the big tub. He grabbed her sodden hair again, jerking her head so that she was bent over the icy tub, her nose mere inches from the ice water.

"We will start soft. We have plenty of time," he said. "I'm an artist, you see. I like a long, slow buildup. Tell us about The Sword of Cain."

She dragged in a huge breath and screamed, with everything she had. All her horror and fear and anger, from the depths of her being. She screamed, in his face. His mouth was open, he was yelling back, but she just kept on screaming. She might never stop.

He shoved her underwater.

The world went blue, shot through with red, her lungs already empty from screaming. Her lungs jerked in agony. Her torso was overbalanced, shoved down headfirst. She flopped and writhed, but that cruel hand held her down. Airless, frantic. Drowning.

Sam peered through the swaying tree boughs that draped the rotten, fragile roof upon which he was stretched full length. Trying not to slide down, not to make a sound, to catch a clear glimpse of the sentry by the open door. Breathing down his panic. He'd never panicked before. He turned ice cold when things got dangerous. He had a reputation for it. He didn't sweat, his heart rate didn't go up. His colleagues envied him that quality. It had never failed him.

Until now. His heart was crawling up into his mouth, and his bowels churned. How anybody could think clearly or handle lethal weapons responsibly in this condition, he did not fucking know.

Didn't matter. Scared shitless or not, he was all Sveti had.

He dragged himself up off his belly, easing into a crouch behind the cover of pine branches that draped the roof. The van was parked right below him. The building he was on looked like a derelict barn from the first half of the last century, paint peeling, wood faded to gray. In front of the barn, on the other side of the van, was a small cinder-block building, of newer make, but just as derelict.

He had not seen them unload her. They must have done that while he was making his approach on foot. Lucky their team was small, and that they weren't expecting company. The front entrance that looked down the road was the only approach they bothered to guard.

He tried not to think about what was happening inside.

The sentry was smoking a cigarette, a walkie-talkie on his belt, a ski mask, an H&K PSP in his hand. Sam had a clear shot. He could cap the guy, and was tempted to do so, but with no suppressor, he'd lose the advantage of surprise. This had to be quiet, or he'd get Sveti killed.

It had taken fifty minutes to get here. The roads were deserted; he'd been forced to hang back and risk losing them so as not to be noticed. If he shot the sentry, he could use the guy's cell to call the cops, assuming there was coverage, but it might take the local guys a half hour just to find this place, let alone get on top of things.

No. It happened now, and fast, or not at all.

At least he wasn't dealing with high security. The place had the feel of an impulse decision. The owner would be absentee Joe Schmoe from Phoenix, or somebody dead with no heirs, property in limbo.

His face itched under the mud he'd smeared on it as he reviewed his strategy. All he had to work with was what he'd gleaned from his car, the detritus of an out-of-work loser. Bottles he hadn't bothered taking to the recycling center, the gas in his tank. He'd half-filled an empty whiskey bottle with premium unleaded, ripped off the lower half of his shirt, wound it around the bottom, knotting it and soaking the dangling end of the rag in the bottle for a fuse. He corked it, leaving the bottle top free for flinging. His hands stank of gasoline. He'd be lucky not to self-immolate. A hostage situation, and he was reduced to a fucking Molotov cocktail. Problem was, it would make noise, too.

His leather jacket would have given him more camouflage than his light gray sweatshirt, and the smartphone in the pocket would have given him fifteen experienced cops to back him up.

This was what he got for being a goddamn gentleman.

If he could get that guy into a better position, he'd have a chance of jumping him. Sam lobbed the chunk of rotten wood he'd found on the roof, aiming for the cinder-block wall. It thudded dully against the wall. The sentry's head jerked around at the sound. He held still, listening. Slowly, he sidled closer to investigate. Sam willed the guy to follow the right trajectory. So much hung on pure, random chance. He fucking hated it.

Closer . . . closer. A gut-wrenching female scream ripped out from within the building. Sam lit the fuse, with trembling fingers, and let the bottle fly. The scream continued as the bottle sailed through air.

Crash, breaking glass against the cinder-block wall, then the *whump* of ignition. The sentry stumbled back with a startled shout, and Sam leaped as he reached for his walkie-talkie. He landed on the guy, smacking him to the ground. The walkie-talkie dropped. The H&K flew out of the sentry's grip, bounced, spun.

They rolled on the ground. Sam came out on top, but the guy was wiry and quick to recover. He smacked the heel of his hand up under Sam's chin. Sam jerked back in time to avoid the elbow rake across the throat. The sentry twisted free. They bounded to their feet, and Sam blocked a roundhouse to the thigh and spun, deflecting a punch to the face. A grab, a rush, and the guy went down again, Sam on top.

The man's legs wound around him, struggling to flip him. Sam grabbed the guy's biceps to pin him, wrenched loose, and slammed his fist down into the guy's groin. He howled. Sam shoved the man's legs aside and half-mounted the fuckhead's chest. An elbow strike into his face, a knee strike to the temple. He pulled away, panting. That guy was done.

He spun around, looking for that H&K. Sweet Christ. The one thing that could have upped Sveti's odds lay in a pool of flames. They licked hungrily at the weathered chunks of lumber and junk.

Suck it up. He ran inside the warehouse. Faint light leached through filthy, cobwebby windows. Nothing but piles of moldering stuff. Ancient furniture, dusty machines and appliances, piles of newspapers, boxes shredded by rodents. There was a single aisle through the heaps of junk. A door at the end of the room.

He approached it on soft cat feet and burst inside.

A big man in a ski mask was hauling Sveti's head and shoulders out of a plastic tub of water. Her eyes were closed. She sputtered, choked, wheezed. The man's gaze whipped up.

Bam, bam. Sam squeezed off two shots. The fuckhead jerked back with a shout, hand to his ear. *Bam,* he took one to the upper arm and jolted sideways, letting go of Sveti. She fell forward into the tub, struggling, but her weight was canted too far forward, and her arms were bound. She was drowning.

He lunged toward her, which was what saved his life. Bullets ripped out. A whip-slash of fire across the side of his lower back and he hit the ground, rolling up to take aim at the new shooter. *Bam, bam, bam.* Ski-mask Number Three staggered, blood pouring from his neck.

Sam sprinted for the tub, saw the torturer struggling up on one arm, and took the moment to aim a flying kick to the guy's face before he scooped his arm under Sveti's chest. He hauled her out of the water and laid her on the ground. Her chest did not move.

He smacked her cheek, pumping on her chest. "Goddamnit, Sveti! Are you going to let those assholes win? Fucking *breathe!*"

She convulsed, vomiting water and coughing.

Tears fogged Sam's eyes, but another perception clamored for attention. A smell, acrid and scary, tickling his reptile brain. *Danger.*

Smoke. Oh, fuck. Sveti was still coughing and choking, slumped on the floor in the sodden heap of crimson fabric like a wilted poppy.

Sam dragged her to her feet. "Babe. We have to run for our lives now. Up. *Move!*" He hated using that hard-ass tone when she was so fucked up, but smoke billowed in, there was an ominous orange glow out in the main room. This place was a death trap. Of his own making.

She wobbled on her small, bare feet, but nodded, still coughing, and stumbled gamely when he dragged her forward.

Flames leaped at the far end of the room, where mildewed heaps of newspaper had caught fire. The smoke was choking. Searing heat battered their faces. The door was obscured by glowing orange smoke.

He bent low, forced Sveti to do the same. They scurried, coughing and hacking down the narrow, stinking corridor, into thicker smoke, hotter air. It hurt to breathe. Sveti was slow, scrambling awkwardly, hobbled by her sodden skirt. Eyes squeezed shut, hand clamped over her nose. A little farther—he pulled on her . . .

And they were out, in the sweet cool morning. Gasping for air.

The fire roared out of the roof, only on one side, but spreading fast. Sparks swirled and flew up. Heat battered them. Sveti thudded onto her belly. Blood was mixed with the dirt stuck to her bare feet.

Sam's eyes fell on the first ski-masked guy, lying where he'd fallen, right next to the blazing building. "One second." He ran back, close enough to the blaze to scorch his face. Seized the dead guy under the arms and dragged him free of the fire.

He dropped the stiff fifteen meters away, in the middle of the clearing, and met Sveti's questioning glance. "I don't want that body incinerated," he said. "I want him ID'd as soon as possible."

"You think like a cop," she coughed out.

"Damn right." He picked her up. Her soaked dress was in tatters, her face smudged with soot. She stared into his face. Teeth chattering.

He picked up speed, going at a steady lope. She needed a hospital. Tetanus, shock, hypothermia, water in her lungs, who knew. His car came into view. He got her into it, cranked the heat up. They bounced with teeth-rattling jolts over the bumpy gravel road. He wished he had a coat to wrap around her. A blanket. Anything.

Her blue, shaking lips formed a word with no breath behind it. "Sam."

"Yeah." He pulled onto an asphalt road. The engine roared for joy.

"You came for me," she whispered. "You . . . were watching?"

"It's the upside to having a stalker," he said.

CHAPTER 8

Josef pulled out the sewing kit from his suitcase. Dental floss, from the toiletries case. He pulled out a few lengths, dropped it in the hotel room's coffee cup. Stuck it into the microwave to sterilize it.

The keyboard of his laptop was sticky with drying blood, but he ignored that, logging in to the e-mail account Sasha had used to contact the Ardova girl while the microwave hummed, doing its work. Finally. There was a new message in the drafts folder, that being the method the two of them had used to communicate without ever actually sending out e-mails. A fine plan, if no one else ever hacked into one's account. Stupid little prick. Thought he was so clever.

He clicked it open. In Ukrainian Cyrillic, capitals, bolded across the page.

DO NOT COME TO ITALY YOU ARE IN DANGER THEY ARE HUNTING YOU HIDE PLEASE JUST HIDE
I WILL TELL YOU MORE WHEN IT IS SAFE

That lying, sneaking, ungrateful sack of *shit*. Defying Josef, and his own father. The message had been sent a scant twenty-five minutes before. There was no response, as of yet, and chances were Ardova was too busy licking her wounds to be checking her e-mail.

He poised his fingers over the keyboard. Selected Sasha's text, deleted it, and typed in an alternate message.

Please come as soon as you can. You are the only one I can trust. When is your plane arriving? Send flight information.

Josef's phone buzzed angrily, vibrating on the desk. Two rings. Three. He coughed. It felt like chunks of burnt lung were coming up.

The smoke had almost overcome him. He'd crawled on boxes, smashed through a window. A long fall, but his cuts and bruises were the least of his problems. As was the bullet that had gone through his bicep.

These things were as nothing, compared to that ringing phone.

He picked it up, hit 'talk.' "Vor," he rasped.

The vor waited. There was little point pleading for mercy. It only made things worse. "She got away," he said thickly. "There was a man she was fucking. He followed us. The snakeheads are both dead."

"Ah," Cherchenko said. "So you did not question her after all."

"I had just begun," he admitted. "But I am sure she knows everything. She's coming to Italy. She left Sasha a message last night that she's flying into Rome. I just checked the account, and Sasha warned her not to come. I deleted his message and wrote another, begging her to come as soon as possible. I will take her in Italy."

"You will do as I tell you, idiot. Who knows if she will come, after your hack job? Get on a plane. I will decide an appropriate punishment as you travel. Aleksei and the others have not found Sasha, who is out there writing messages to God knows who. He is our top concern now."

"Yes, Vor," he said dully. The connection broke.

Josef stared into the mirror at his broken nose, his bloodied chin. His blood-crusted, half-detached earlobe. He pulled out his knife. Splashed it with rubbing alcohol. He stretched the torn earlobe out and cut.

The chunk of flesh thudded onto his boot and rolled to the floor.

The phone burped. He glanced at it. An airplane ticket. The flight left in only a few hours. It would be a challenge, making himself presentable enough to be allowed on an airplane. A medical facility was out of the question. There were people he could call, but no one he trusted enough to let himself be seen in such a weakened state.

No one had gotten the better of him like this since he was a boy.

The microwave dinged. He pulled out the cup of boiling water. Fished out the dental floss with the point of his knife. Threaded the needle. He palpated the wet hole in his bicep, wiping it clean with gauze. His eyes stung with smoke-tainted sweat. Fresh rivulets of blood ran down his arm as he began to stitch up the torn flesh. The needle pierced his own raw meat. Again. Two stitches. Three.

Enough. He doubled over, and vomit splattered the mirror.

He was disgusted with himself. This was nothing. He'd had his legs shattered with a hammer. His pimp had branded his ass with a hot iron when he was a boy. Now *that* was pain.

A hot iron. Yes, that would be entertaining, to use upon Svetlana and her lover. White hot, shoved deep into their tenderest places. Like the needle that he'd stabbed into his own raw, ruined flesh.

The sounds they would make would be soothing to his soul.

Sam stared at the cadaver on the morgue table, confused.

The stiff was Chinese. The corpse looked greenish in the blazing light. Sam shoved a hand through sweat- and blood-stiffened hair. "It doesn't make sense," he repeated. "The guy who questioned Sveti spoke Ukrainian. He asked about a picture her mother took six years ago, in Italy. Why would snakeheads give a shit about that? It's old, it's half a world away, and it's not their stuff."

His friend Trish's face was calm, but he knew her well enough to read her body language. Her arms folded across her chest, mouth tight.

"He's been positively ID'd," she said. "Jason Kang. Born in Hong

Kong. His wife was in earlier. She said he was a vicious, evil-hearted son of a bitch, and she's glad he's dead. He got out of the pen three months ago. He worked with Helen Wong before his stint in prison."

"Yeah, I know. Sveti sneaked into one of their sweatshops with a live camera last year," Sam said. "They sent her death threats."

Trish's shrug told him to do the math. "The wife said he didn't speak great English. Enough for his dirty deeds, but no more."

The implication pissed him off, but Trish was doing him a favor, letting him see the body. She'd been his friend for years. They'd been rookies together, he a patrol officer, she a criminologist. She was great; down to earth, funny, smart. She did not deserve to be snarled at.

"They all finished with you, down in headquarters?" Trish asked.

He kept staring at Kang's greenish face. "They Mirandized me, I gave my statement. We went through it, blow by blow. Many times."

"Who took your statement?"

"Tenly and Horvath," he said.

"Ah, okay." She nodded. "They're good. What did they think about you burning down the crime scene with two of the perps inside?"

He made an irritated sound. "I was focused on saving Sveti's life."

"Of course you were," Trish murmured. "At least you saved one of them for us. Good of you, to throw us a chunk of meat."

Sam's stomach twitched nastily, and his eyes flicked away from the dead man. "They talked to the DA," he said. "Everybody's okay with self-defense. It was self-evident, when they saw the shape Sveti was in."

"Bet the DA wasn't thrilled. Being tight with Big Daddy and all."

"Drop it." He was tense enough without thinking of his father.

"So, back to this girl," Trish said. "I've read her anti-trafficking blog. Amazing. That's one razor-focused woman. Nerves of steel."

"Tell me about it," he said bleakly. "Why the fuck would these guys be interested in Sveti's mother?"

"Maybe they weren't." Trish examined her fingernails. "Does she have emotional trauma associated with her mother?"

Sam paused. "Well, ah . . . it's hard to find any significant aspect of her life that isn't associated with emotional trauma."

"Is that so? Huh. What's with the mom?"

"Suicide. Jumped off a cliff into the Mediterranean six years ago."

Trish nodded. "Okay, moving on. Other family?"

"Her dad was murdered by the Ukrainian mob," Sam admitted. "Concurrent with Sveti being kidnapped by organ traffickers, held for the better part of a year. Rescued just in time. They'd sold her heart. She was on the slab when the cavalry stormed in."

Trish's mouth dangled for a moment. "Oh, my God, Sam."

"But these people are all dead," he repeated. "The dad, the mom, the mafiya vor. The traffickers themselves are in a maximum-security prison, monitored by her adoptive family. This stuff is dead and buried."

"Except for inside of her," Trish said.

"No," Sam repeated. "She has no history of delusional thinking."

"She was kidnapped, Sam! And tortured! You said they were drowning her in ice water! She could be excused for being delusional!"

Sam shook his head, his jaw set. Everything Trish was saying was true, reasonable, not even remotely offensive, and yet he wanted to swat it away from himself, as if she'd accusing Sveti of malicious lying.

"Sam, you need to face the facts," Trish said.

"Just drop it," he said, more sharply.

Trish's eyebrows shot up. She twitched the cover over the body and zipped it up. "Whatever," she said. "If we're done, I need to scram."

"Trish," he said, his voice weary. "I'm sorry."

She sighed and relented. "Come on, Sam," she urged. "Let's go. You need to get something to eat, get some rest. Relax. You're wrecked."

He followed her out. Eating or relaxing were not options. He was fried. Every time the day played in his head, ass-whomping chemicals dumped into his bloodstream, as fresh as they'd been this morning.

She looked back over her shoulder. "One detail eludes me. Why were you driving this girl home at dawn? Has your dry spell ended?"

He grunted sharply in answer. "Let's leave it."

Her keen blue eyes narrowed. "Ah. So it's like that, is it?"

"I wish," he said dully. "Not on her part."

"I see. Sorry." She stopped next to the exit. "What's Tenly and Horvath's take on the thug who questioned her in Ukrainian?"

"They think what you think," he admitted. "Stress flashbacks."

"It's not like anyone blames her," Trish said. "There's no shame in it. I'd be in a padded cell if a tenth of her shit was mine."

He was suddenly desperate to get out of the range of Trish's measured, pitying gaze. "I'm out of here. Going to the hospital."

"You might want to shower and change first," Trish suggested. "You walk into a hospital looking like that, they might just admit you."

Sam looked down. He'd scrubbed off the worst of the mud and soot, but the sweatshirt Tenly had loaned him was stained by his leaking bandage. The shallow trough of the bullet graze over the back of his hip burned, but he knew exactly how much worse a bullet wound could be. He wasn't complaining.

"Sam?" she called after him.

Her urgent tone swung him around again. "What?"

"This thing, this girl . . ." Her voice trailed off. "It just sounds like a world of hurt."

Sam was silent for a beat. "That's a good definition of her world."

"And you really want to go there? To live there?"

"It doesn't have to be that way!" he said, defiant. "Her world can change! Anyone's world can change, goddamnit!"

"And you want to be the one to change it?"

He waved that away. "Let it go, Trish."

"Just remember. Everybody deals with their own shit. And if she heard our stiff speak Ukrainian, then face it. Her wires are crossed."

"Our stiff wasn't the guy who questioned her," he shot back. "Our stiff was guarding the door. We don't have the questioner. He's still inside the smoking wreckage, remember?"

"And did you hear this masked questioner speak in Ukrainian? A multilingual guy like you could tell the difference between Ukrainian and Cantonese, even if you don't speak either one yourself, right?"

"I didn't hear him talk," he admitted. "It wasn't a chatty moment."

"So our Ukrainian interrogator is an equal-opportunity asshole. Maybe he has a race quota to fill, you know, for personnel."

His jaw spasmed. Sarcasm was Trish's coping mechanism. They all had their favorites. It was stupid and childish to be bugged by it.

Trish shook her head. "Just be careful, okay?"

"I will," he said. "Thanks, Trish. I owe you one."

"You owe me more than that, buddy," she called out after him.

At the car, he dug in the backseat until he found the clothes he'd been meaning to take to the dry cleaner since before his last bullet wound. The shirt was creased, and had stiff, discolored pits, but it was better than Tenly's workout rag. He pulled it on. He'd still look like hell for the hospital visit, but a slightly more elevated level of hell.

He made a straight shot for her hospital room, but an elderly woman was asleep in the bed Sveti had used.

Irrational terror zinged through him. He'd left for headquarters after Becca and Nick arrived, with the understanding that she not be left alone. He'd trusted Nick to be appropriately paranoid. He'd left the explaining to Sveti, having a long day of explaining to get through himself, downtown. So where the fuck was she now?

He waylaid the first person in scrubs that he saw, a middle-aged Latina nurse with a long black braid. "Excuse me, ma'am, but where's the girl who was in this room? Did they take her somewhere else?"

The nurse looked at the door he indicated. "Oh, yes. Her family came for her. She was discharged a few hours ago."

"Family? Which family?"

The woman's dark eyes widened at his barking tone. She took a step backward. "I don't know her family," she said coolly. "She was not my patient. She was discharged, and that's all I know."

"Thanks," he called as he loped away.

He pulled out the burner phone he'd picked up this morning before going to headquarters. He'd wanted to be able to place calls, but not receive them. No scolding rants from his father, no hysterical shit fits from his sister, no stern lectures from his grandmother. He plucked Kev's phone number out of his unassisted brain, after a few false tries.

Kev picked up. "Whom am I speaking with?"

"It's Sam," he said.

"Jesus! It's about time! Where the hell have you been? Why aren't you answering your phone? We've been calling all day!"

"My phone's AWOL. I left it with Sveti by accident this morning. I've spent the day in an interrogation room, sorting it all out."

"So I heard," Kev said.

"Where did they take Sveti?" Sam demanded.

Kev paused, too damn long for Sam's nerves. "Um, listen, Sam—"

"Nick and Becca's? Miles and Lara's? Cray's Cove? Where?"

"I think Tam and Val were the ones who ended up—"

"Later, Kev."

"Stop! Wait! Don't go racing up there right now. Tempers are high, people are being irrational, so just chill and wait a couple of—"

"They're pissed at *me?* I put my ass on the line today!" he yelled. "I killed three men for her, and they're giving me attitude?"

Kev coughed delicately. "Your ass on the line might have counted for more if she hadn't spent the previous night in your bed."

Sam stopped in the corridor. People veered sideways to give him a wide berth. "You are fucking kidding me! The only reason I saw them take her was because she'd spent the night with me! She'd have been tortured to death if she'd been home alone!"

"Don't freak. I'm not judging you. Sveti's a big girl. She can do what she wants with any man she wants as far as I'm concerned. I just don't want your ass kicked when you're all wound up. Avoid the scene for a day or so. They're protective of Sveti, and Tam's freaking—"

"I'm not the one who was hurting her!" he shouted.

"I know that, and you know that, so chill," Kev soothed. "There's no place in the world that's safer for her than Cray's Cove, Sam, so relax. I'm heading up there with Edie tomorrow, and so are a lot of the others, so stay clear of the meeting of the clans if you—"

Sam hung up. Kev called back immediately, but he let the phone buzz unanswered. Enough of this shit. Granted, Sveti, Tam, and Val didn't have the number of his burner phone, but none of them was stupid. They could have called Horvath or Tenly, or even the main switchboard.

He probably wasn't fit to drive, he reflected, as he got on the road. His hands vibrated on the wheel. But he wasn't going to fall asleep. He might never sleep again. His body tissues were marinated in adrenaline.

It was a long drive. He peeled off the interstate onto a series of smaller highways to get to Cray's Cove. He'd been there only once, not long after the bullet wound to the lung, the one he'd gotten following Bruno Ranieri around. Tam had hosted Bruno and Lily's engagement party, and since he'd taken a bullet in their service, he'd scored a pity invite. Tam had a visceral dislike of anyone who represented the law, but he'd been too curious not to check the place out. And anxious to get another glimpse of the remote Svetlana in her lofty tower. Way up there where the air was so thin. Just stars and clouds. The occasional bird.

She'd refused to speak to him that day, of course, being mortally pissed at the way he'd conducted his investigation. Hadn't stopped him from looking. Staring, even, until she blushed and fled the room.

His obsession with detail, underscored by lust, had burned the directions into his brain. He reached the driveway at midnight. There it was. Tamara Steele and Valery Janos, stenciled boldly on the mailbox.

He drove up the long, winding access road, which wended along the crest of a coastal hill. The house was an architectural marvel, parts carved right into the mountainside, parts jutting out over the cliff that overlooked a private beach in an inaccessible cove.

He bypassed the small parking lot below the house and parked next to Val and Tam's cars up in front of the garage.

The door opened as he approached. Tam's slim form was backlit in the entrance. She held a shotgun, though she knew damn well who it was, with all those cameras on her access road.

"Where's Sveti?" he asked.

"What are you doing here now? It's the middle of the night!"

"I'm not in the mood for bullshit," he said. "Take me to Sveti."

"That girl is like my daughter, and she's sleeping. It's an indecent hour. Get back in your car. Go to the motel on the highway. Come back in the morning. Maybe I'll find it in myself to be civil to you then."

"I was there for her when she needed me, Tam, so put down your goddamn shotgun and get out of my way."

She racked it back. The sound was loud in the gloom.

"Stop," she warned. "I decide who walks into my house, and when. And I am absolutely capable of filling your ass with buckshot."

"My ass isn't pointed in your direction," Sam said. "If you want to shoot me in the face, do it. But I don't think Sveti will thank you for it."

"He has a point, love." Val appeared behind Tam.

Sam was close enough now to see Tam's face. Her mouth was tight, her eyes and nose red and swollen.

"Val, would you just back me up for once?" she snapped.

"Of course," Val said. "Always. Just not when you are wrong."

Rachel appeared in the hallway, a toddler in her arms. "Mama?"

Tam's eyes did not waver. "I told you to take Irina upstairs."

"Mama, don't be mad at Sam!" Rachel said earnestly. "He saved her! Sveti said so! She'd be dead if he hadn't gone after her!"

"Go upstairs, Rachel," Val urged.

Sam pushed past Tam and her gun, and stood there, stymied. It was a large house, and the search would be long and slow and stupid.

He turned to Val. "Where is she?"

Val's eyes flicked to his wife and back, resigned. "East tower."

"Goddamnit, Val," Tam hissed.

"Face it," Val said with a shrug. "If you are not prepared to hurt him, you cannot stop him. He saved her life. You are being foolish."

"Fine, then," she snarled. "I'll just hurt you instead."

"I was afraid of that," Val said wryly. "I think that tonight will be a very long night."

"This way," Rachel said excitedly. "I'll show you."

The girl scampered on ahead down the corridor. Sam followed, his heart thudding. Tam and Val were on his heels as Rachel led him into a door that revealed an open, metal spiral staircase. Rachel's bare feet flashed at eye level as she spiraled up, light-footed even with Irina in her arms. The toddler twisted to look down over her sister's shoulder at Sam, making inquisitive gabbling sounds.

"Don't wake Sveti, Rachel," Val called. "She's exhausted."

Rachel pushed open the door at the top with exaggerated care, and put her finger to her lips. Irina pointed helpfully into the dark room. "Setty," she announced, her voice shrill. "Setty sweeping."

He was lucky there were children here. Even the thorny Tam didn't have the stomach to blow him into bloody chunks in front of her daughters. Though she clearly considered Sveti one of those daughters.

But the thought evaporated when he entered that room. Rachel snapped on a desk lamp. Tam hissed a sharp reproof from the door.

The slender figure curled beneath the blanket on the bed stirred at the snap of the light, and turned. Her eyes looked huge and bruised in her face. She jerked up onto her elbow. The blanket fell down. She wore a thin, tight tank top, loose flannel pajama trousers. "Sam?"

His tongue felt thick, taking up too much space in his mouth. "Yeah," he said hoarsely.

Her face crumpled. "Oh, God. Oh, Sam."

"Setty cry?" Irina sounded worried.

"Okay. You've seen her," Tam announced briskly. "Satisfied? We'll take it from here, Sam. She needs rest. Come on. Out."

Sam ignored her and walked toward the bed. His throat felt hot and tight, like a screw was turning in it. Every step tightened it up, to that last quarter turn that threatened to shatter the whole mechanism.

Her arms lifted up, welcoming him.

He thudded to his knees by the bed, and fell into them. He forgot Tam, the kids, Val, the rest of the world. There was only Sveti, taut and trembling. Her arms, wound around his neck, pulling him hungrily.

He pressed his wet face against her hair. For the first time all day, he could breathe.

"Out, Rachel, Irina. Go. Now." There was steel in Val's voice. Even Rachel responded to it. Sam barely heard the padding of little bare feet.

"Tamar," Val urged gently. "My love. Leave them. Come on."

Tam muttered something bitter and incomprehensible.

"She is grown," Val soothed. "She can choose. She has chosen. Obviously. Let it go. Come with me."

"Now? Seriously? Now is an intelligent time for her to make a choice like that?"

"Now is the only time," Val said.

The door shut, but he heard Tam's acerbic voice receding down the stairs. "Don't you get all zen on me when I'm this pissed."

"And when are you not pissed?" Val's plaintive voice faded away.

The last strength that had kept him upright drained away. He was boneless, spent. Clinging to her, as much to get comfort as to give it.

With their audience gone, the tears leaked faster, but he didn't want to lay that on her, so he kept his face buried in her silken swirls of hair, inhaling the scent. His ears roared and his body shook, and he was squeezing too hard, but he could not relax. His muscles were locked in that hungry vise grip of *mine, mine, mine*.

At some point, he must have kicked off his shoes. He found himself on top of her, entwined. Madly kissing her. He hadn't meant to. It was the wrong time, after what had happened, and he was a prick and a lout to come on to a girl who'd been through an ordeal like hers.

But they were dragged down, as if by the kraken from the deep, into one of those end-of-the-world kisses. Her shirt got shoved over her breasts, her legs twined, pulsing her crotch against the bulge of his cock. She kissed him back like her life depended on it, honey sweet, all open to him, offering herself. So blitzed, she'd forgotten to hold herself back.

Instinctively, he took full advantage of that. How could he not?

She made a protesting sound as he dragged himself from her embrace and got to his feet. He gestured at the door.

"Privacy," he said.

"They won't burst in on me," she assured him.

He flicked the knob lock shut as he tossed his shirt away. "You might be willing to bet your life on that, but I won't."

Sveti smiled. "Tam overreacts," she said. "But you were the hero today. She knows that."

"Whatever." He kicked off jeans and underwear; then he was on that bed, caging her in, with his heat, his bulk. *Mine.*

She had goose bumps. She needed to be sucked, licked, squeezed. He jerked her flannel pants down, along with the scrap of underwear.

Oh, God, every damn time, it wiped him out, how beautiful she was. All those dips and curves, strong muscles and delicate bones. Scrapes and bruises, too, marring the porcelain glow of her pale skin.

He started with the hurt places, kissing scraped and scabbed hands and feet, skinned knees, the bruises on her thighs. Then he got waylaid by the warm nest between her legs, those secret pink folds.

But Sveti had ideas of her own, and she grabbed his hair and yanked him up, positioning him right where she wanted him.

Right down to business, no frills, no fuss. Fine with him.

He sank into her, with a choked groan. It was inevitable and amazing and perfect, his cockhead pushing into that tight, moist nest. Loved and squeezed as it forged slowly deeper. The in stroke was a wet, slow, dragging kiss all the way down to his base, and on the outstroke, her pussy squeezed and suckled him. A few of those slow, agonizing thrusts and he was wedged to the max in her plush depths. She squirmed and whimpered, lifting herself for more, more, more.

Easy does it. He rocked inside her, eyes squeezed shut, feeling for the sweet spots, the strokes, the pace that would take her to shivering pieces. They heaved, surged, rocked. He felt the glow inside her on some inexplicable level of his being, shining like a star about to supernova.

Juicy, scalding. No latex. But the thought had no teeth, not while frantically fucking. Their hands twined, clutching as his hips thudded against hers. Their eyes locked. The contact was charged with power.

Heart-stopping. So beautiful, so painful. So fucking real.

She was right on the edge, so he slowed it down and toyed with her clit, sliding his cockhead relentlessly against that magic place that made her sob and writhe and flop, eyes wild, gasping for air—

Ahhhh, *yes*. Off she went. Long, hard, clutching throbs. She grabbed him, crying out. Nails biting deep.

She lay, splayed and limp after, dragging in shuddering gulps of air. He just rocked, waiting for her eyes to open. Waiting to pounce.

They fluttered open, all unsuspecting. He lit into her without mercy. "You left the hospital without telling me."

She blinked, nonplussed. "I didn't . . . Tam just organized—"

"You could have called."

"You didn't have a phone," she protested. "You were—"

"Bullshit. You had Horvath's number. He gave you a card after he took your statement. He could have passed on a message that you were going to Cray's Cove. I had to go to the hospital and get an adrenaline spike when I found someone else in your bed. I did not deserve that."

She hid behind her eyelashes. "It was a very intense morning," she said. "I don't know the etiquette of—"

"My ass. I killed for you today. I spent the whole day sorting that shit out. You owed me a phone call."

She twined her legs around his, swiveling with subtle, pulsing movements around his cock. "I'm sorry," she said simply.

"Good." He swiveled his cock inside her, with a slow, seductive deliberation that made her squirm and gasp. "That's a start."

"Don't be angry," she said. "They gave me some sedative, and I didn't even know what I was—"

"Stop it right there." He forged inside, savoring her delicate clutch and drag. "Don't even try to act delicate and confused and wounded on me. I see right through that crap. You are as tough as a steel cable."

She let out a jerky sigh. "You say that like it's a bad thing."

He shook his head. "Not good, not bad. Just true. You blew me off because you didn't know how to deal with me."

"And you? Do you know how to deal with me?" she asked, canting her hips eagerly to receive the slow, sensual slide.

"I'm learning," he said. "I think I'm starting to get the hang of it."

She reached up, cupping his face. "Strong is good," she said with sudden vehemence. "The strong ones stay alive."

"I like your strength," he conceded. "It makes me hard."

"I'm glad it has this effect. You're the first it ever did."

"Good," he said, staring down at the tender, shining pink petals of her cunt clinging to him on the outstroke. He gleamed, steaming hot from plunging into her sweet depths. "Stay strong, babe."

"I try," she whispered. "You're my weak spot."

He froze, breathing down the rising energy of his own orgasm. He was not done with her yet, not by a mile. There was something very wrong with her reasoning, but all his red blood cells were getting busy down in his groin, and he couldn't be bothered to thrash it out.

"Which weak spot was that?" He held his hand over her heart. "This one? Or are we talking about this one, down here?" He diddled her clit delicately with his thumb.

"Oh, Sam." Her breath hitched, hiccuping. "Oh . . . oh."

"That's not weak," he said. "That's soft and juicy and hot and alive. There's a difference, and you need to learn it." He worked the sensitive pink pearl of her clit, lifting her mound up, so he could look at it in all its shiny, flowerlike, pink glory, his cock gliding in and out.

The wave was breaking over her again. She pulled him along with her this time. He lost control, clutching her as he exploded.

He rolled to the side, after his moment of oblivion. Cold air intruded against his sweat-dampened skin. He let his cock slide out, reluctantly. They were drenched. "I didn't use a condom," he said.

She opened her eyes. "You have no diseases. I have the implant. As long as you're not sleeping with anyone else, what's the problem?"

His cock twitched with enthusiasm at this sentiment, but the words burst out of him just the same. "No," he said harshly. "You ditch the latex when you're committed. Not for a throwaway fuck buddy you're blowing off some steam with before you climb on your plane."

She sat up. "Blowing off steam? Are you *scolding* me? You should have given me this lecture before you came inside me, not after!"

"Yeah, I should have," he agreed.

"I never saw you as a throwaway! Or a . . . a fuck buddy!"

"Guess what, Sveti?" he said through set teeth. "That's what you call the ones that aren't keepers."

She made a pained sound, folded up, and pressed her face to her knees. Oh, Christ, why? He was being a raving asshole to her. Again.

"Sorry," he said gruffly. "I didn't mean to give you a hard time, particularly not tonight. It just popped out. Really, Sveti. I'm sorry."

She shook her head, still hiding her face.

He tried again. "Listen. I appreciate that you trust me, about unprotected sex. But trust is a dangerous thing. If you're not sure—"

"You think I don't know?" She looked up, eyes blazing. "Jesus! Do you think I was still a virgin at my age because I am so *trusting?*"

Sam blew out a savage sigh. "No, but you don't owe me sex, because of what happened today. Shit, I don't know what I'm saying. Just don't do anything that'll hurt you. Protect yourself. From everyone. Including me, because I can't seem to stop ranting at you."

Her lashes swept down. "That's sweet of you."

"No, actually," he said through his teeth. "On the contrary."

"But if you were wondering, I did not drag you into my bed to thank you for saving me, Sam. That was a completely selfish gesture on my part. That was all for me, me, me. Rest assured."

He was obscurely comforted by that. "Ah. Okay."

"Everybody has their vice. Some like tequila, some smoke crack, some skydive, some crave chocolate chip brownies. All I want is your . . . cock. Deep inside me." She flung her leg over him, a just-try-to-stop-me look on her face, and danced over him, her hair tickling his chest as she wedged him slowly inside her snug little hole. They gasped, rocked.

Sam held his breath, teetering on the brink. "I am willing to bet money that the word *cock* has never spontaneously come out of your mouth in your whole life before you met me," he said.

Her lips twitched. "Could be," she said primly. "It's a word I don't have cause to use much in my daily conversations."

"Another first, huh?"

Her smile widened to a beautiful grin, all perfect teeth and dimples. "You get off on that, don't you? That really yanks your chain."

He rolled her over. "Oh, yeah."

They went at it again, nothing held back. She kept stripping layers off him. A person could get so spoiled, being known like that. Having his soul laid bare, offered up to her. *Here. All yours. Take it.*

His last thought, as he sank into the pit of adrenal exhaustion, was that it was going to suck serious ass when she shut him out again.

CHAPTER 9

Sveti watched the masked figure lift Mama's writhing body high and hurl her over the stonework railing. A shriek of denial was torn from her throat. She struggled, taped to a chair, arms wrenched back. She heard a flapping sound. Silk, whipping. Her mother's red evening gown, spread out like a parachute as she plummeted toward the churning sea.

The masked figure was moving toward her. Pale eyes glittered in the slits of the mask. His breath smelled dead. He pulled off the mask.

Yuri. He licked his fleshy, purple lips as he lifted the knife—

Sveti jerked upright with a sharp gasp. Sam shifted in his sleep without waking. She was glad. She didn't want to be seen like this.

Stay strong, he said. It was good advice. She would try.

She drew her knees up tight around the sour ache. She'd expected this, even before she got nabbed. Dreams of Mama's suicide were routine. Yuri was a classic, too. But her subconscious had never tossed the two anxieties together. They were bad enough singularly.

She stared up at the intricate moon shadows on the ceiling. Her mother had never worn a red dress in her dream before. In fact, she'd never noticed Mama's clothes at all. And she'd never known nor wanted to know what her mother wore the night she jumped. The day's fog of terror was starting to lift, just enough for her to realize the implications of what her tormenter had said. *It's amazing, the resemblance to Sonia. . . . And she wore a slut red dress, just like yours, the night she died.*

This man had known Mama. What she looked like, what she'd worn. As if he were suggesting that he was the one who had killed her.

All these years, Sveti had wondered why Mama had not asked for help. Why she had not talked to someone, checked into a hospital. Or at least called her daughter to say good-bye. All Sveti had gotten was that photo in the mail, covered with cryptic scrawls. Cold comfort.

It would seem those scrawls weren't so meaningless after all.

Her mother had urged her to take the opportunity to study in America. She'd been a focused, dedicated professional, teaching French and English poetry at the university before the bad stuff happened. Absorbed by her passion for photography. Madly in love with Sveti's father. Devastated by his death. She hadn't been particularly maternal, but Sveti had loved her all the same, and had felt loved in return.

Then, suddenly, she was gone, leaving Sveti tormented by the stupid, awful fucking empty waste of it all. The terrible quiet.

But if Mama had been murdered . . .

She shied from the thought. It was a trap. She longed to blame someone besides Mama, Papa, Zhoglo. That crowd gave her no satisfaction. Just the vast silence of the dead from their direction.

But if it wasn't Mama's choice, if there was someone else to punish . . . oh, God, yes. Her hunger for that scenario could corrupt her good judgment all to hell. She had to watch herself, and keep it real.

She stared out the big window of the bed nook at the ocean. The big cloud had blown past, and the moon left a bright trail of light.

Until this morning, she'd had no reason to think anyone might have wanted to hurt Mama. Now that the possibility was unleashed, it was blundering around in her head, knocking everything into disarray. All her deepest assumptions about the world, her mother, herself.

It hurt to think about it, but she was accustomed to the trail of pain and tension certain thoughts made as they burned through her body. And at least this was a different kind of pain. It was preferable to be angry at a murderer than at Mama. At least, the sad, pitiful version of suicidal Mama that she'd been forced to swallow in place of her brighter memories. A brave, intrepid Mama, tragic victim of a terrible injustice . . . a Mama who could be avenged . . . that suited Sveti's fantasies so much better, she dared not trust it.

Dawn was glowing faintly in the sky, and she was as far from sleep as she'd ever been. Sam slept heavily on. She was tempted to wake him and tell him her realization, but that would be selfish and unfair, exhausted as he was. Besides, he would be restless and mercurial, full of strong opinions about everything she thought and said. She would end up struggling against him. Striking sparks.

The thought exhausted her.

Better to lie there, savoring the contact with his hot, naked skin, staring at his beautiful face. He looked so different sleeping. She barely recognized his bold eyebrows when they were not frowning or furrowed, expressing some strong emotion, usually about her. He seemed younger. His mouth so soft. Kissable. The tenderness that stirred inside her as she watched him sleep was strangely unsettling.

His hair was wild and snarled. She ran her fingertips just barely along the tangled locks. No hair goop, just the salt of his dried sweat.

That timid, careful caress woke him instantly. His eyes snapped open. The sudden shift in his energy made her body tingle and tighten.

"What?" he said. "What is it?"

It burst out, uncensored. "The guy who questioned me," she said. "He was the one who killed my mother."

Sam gazed at her, unblinking, for a long moment. His eyes narrowed. "I thought your mother committed suicide."

"So did I," she said. "Until now."

"What made you change your mind?"

She closed her eyes, to keep her mind from being scrambled by his direct, blazing gaze. "The guy said it was amazing, how I resembled her. How she wore a red dress like mine the night she died."

He processed that. "And why would this mean he killed her? Did he say that he killed her, in so many words?"

"No," she admitted. "But taunting me about how much I looked like her, taunting me about the dress—how would he know what she wore that night if he wasn't there? If it wasn't him?"

His gaze slid away from hers. Her frayed patience snapped. "So?" she demanded. "What are you thinking? Say it."

"Okay." His voice was carefully even. "I think that guy would have said anything to hurt or scare you. And you've got a truckload of problems already. You don't need to go digging for problems from the past. Their outcomes are fixed, and can't be changed. They can wait."

She shot upright. "I'm not digging! These problems came after me, Sam! Do you think I went out looking for those guys who snatched me?"

"Of course not," he said. "Don't get twitchy. I'll keep an open mind, but I will not open it so far that my brains fall out. I would not be doing you any favors if I did."

"I'm not asking you to! But that guy asked me about Mama's photo, Sam. And The Sword of Cain. Whatever that is, it's not in the past! He would have cut me to pieces for it. If it hadn't been for you."

Sam's face was unreadable. "I will concede. Him asking you about your mom's photo is very strange."

"I had this dream, and now I . . . oh, never mind." She swallowed the words back. He was going to think she was a fatuous fool. Dreams.

"Yeah?" he said gently. "Tell me."

She bit her lip. "I'm watching her fall. But this time . . ." She swallowed, to steady her voice. "This time she's wearing my dress."

He nodded calmly. "So your mom's got a red dress on in your dream. The guy suggested that image to you, Sveti. Very forcefully."

She covered her face. It had felt so clear when the wordless images were fresh in her head. Now it felt garbled and faraway.

"I just think it's all connected," she said. "You don't see it?"

Sam smoothed her hair off her forehead. "I don't know what to think," he said.

"It's connected," she said stubbornly. "It wasn't a suicide. She was murdered. I just . . . feel it."

He pulled her closer. "Keep on feeling," he said gently. "We'll figure it all out, in time. Try not to worry."

"Try not to *what?*" She stared at him for a moment, baffled, and then voiced her growing, horrified realization. "Oh, my God, Sam. You don't believe me, do you? You think I'm nuts!"

"Not at all," he said forcefully. "Nobody's saying you're nuts. Nobody's saying anything. Don't get uptight. Just breathe. Just rest."

His gentleness made her furious. "Do not condescend to me!"

He rocked back warily. "Hey. Simmer down."

"No!" She clambered up on top of him.

He was bewildered for a second. She kissed him, fiercely.

She was having none of this shit. She wasn't some delicate deluded girl, to be treated like fine china. She was a force to be reckoned with, and he needed to know her for what she was. Deal with her, full on.

They devoured each other with a furious tenderness. She positioned herself on the hot, rigid club of flesh that lay flat against his belly, shifting until her wet folds slid against the whole length of his shaft, painting him in long, lazy strokes with her lube.

He arched, gasped beneath her. "Oh, God. Sveti."

"Now." She reared up onto her knees and seized him by the base of his phallus. Danced over him, anointing his cockhead with teasing little swirls of contact, like kisses. When he arched, shuddering beneath her, fists clenched in the sheet, she finally maneuvered him inside herself, and sank relentlessly down. A slow, luscious caress.

They froze, trembling at the intense sensation. Neither dared to move. Wow. A marvel, every time. She could barely move, she felt so filled, but she tried, lifting herself up, sliding down. Working herself on that thick, stiff shaft. So hard. So hot. So good.

She wanted everything he had. Wanted to devour him. His energy, his strength, his heat—things she could not formulate as thoughts, but only understand with her skin, her heart, her guts, her blood. Her clutching hands, her throbbing sex. The movement of their bodies became phrases of a language she almost understood, but with some exiled, struggling part of herself that she could not quite reach.

His face was strained and taut, jaw clenched. He clutched her upper arms in a grip just short of bruising. His hips slid up, jolting into her from below, each slick stroke caressing her inside.

It stung, a little, but she was already swept into the huge surge of a shining crescendo that could not be delayed or denied.

It tore through her. Took her apart.

When her eyes fluttered open, she was sprawled limply on top of him. The look on his face squeezed her heart.

She slid off him. He shifted onto his elbow and looked beneath himself. "I think my bandage got detached. Aw, shit. The sheets."

She leaped up. "Oh, my God, Sam!"

The sheet was spotted with blood. The gauze that had been taped over his hip had ripped loose, revealing the bloody bullet graze.

She gasped. "I'm so sorry! I forgot all about your wound!"

"It was worth it," he assured her. "I didn't even feel it, swear to God. Those sex endorphins are some serious shit."

"Come on. Tam puts first-aid stuff in the bathroom cabinets."

She herded him into the bathroom. He perched on the tub while she made a fuss over his wound, dabbing with antibiotic ointment and cotton until it was decently taped up again. Torn loose by wild sex under the greedy, selfish harpy girl. She horrified herself.

"Does it still hurt?" she asked anxiously. "Are you okay?"

"What guy wouldn't be okay with your tits bouncing six inches from his nose?" he asked. "Come here, let me just . . ."

"No!" She batted his hand down and put the first-aid stuff away, then hurried to strip the sheets and the mattress cover, also stained.

She dragged them into the bathroom and set herself to scrubbing the marks under cold water with a handful of liquid soap.

Sam watched quietly. "We're hard on bed linens," he commented. "We've ruined two sets less than twenty-four hours into our affair."

She laughed silently, dumped the sodden, foamy sheet on the floor, and got to work on the mattress cover.

"I'll replace them," he told her gently. "Don't sweat it."

"That's wasteful," she said. "And it's not the issue."

"I know the issue," Sam said glumly. "It's that Tam Steele hates my guts, and my bodily fluids along with them. This will gross her out."

"She can't say a thing!" Sveti snapped. "You were a goddamn hero! You got that wound in my service! From a fucking bullet!"

"And leaked blood all over her sheets while being lustfully ridden by a beautiful nymph with bouncing tits," he said dreamily. "That salacious detail might cost me my manhood. Being in your service is dangerous, but it has some kickass perks."

She snorted in derision, but Sam's face had gone suddenly somber. "In your service," he repeated. "I like how that sounds, Sveti."

Her body tensed. The words sounded formal, antique, and archaic. Something from an epic poem, or a fairy tale. "I'm sorry," she said. "About, uh, saying . . . my service. I didn't mean—"

"I did," he said. "It's okay. I like it."

"But I . . . but you . . ." Her voice trailed off.

Sam seized her wet hand, gazing intently into her eyes. "Your service," he repeated softly. "That's exactly where I want to be."

She started shaking. The moment felt fraught with mysterious significance. Something solemn and irreversible was happening. Wonderful and terrifying. And dangerous. "Sam," she said. "Don't."

"Don't what?" Sam kissed her knuckles, stroked them against his cheek. He sank down to his knees, looked up at her. "Accept it."

She was caught in the hypnotic thrall of his gaze, a heartbeat away from saying yes, of course, anything he wanted, anything in the world. But the familiar drum roll of impending doom froze her in place.

"Accept, ah . . . what?" she faltered.

He kissed her hand again. "My service," he said. "I get that you don't want my love. How about my service? Does that go down easier?"

"I . . . I don't even know what you mean by that."

"Sure you do." His voice was implacable. "It's never been so clear. I'll serve you. Protect you, make love to you. Kill for you. Because I can. Because I choose to. Let that be the vibe. Would it work for you?"

The shaking inside her got worse. She was so afraid of hurting him, failing him. He was skating so close to that gaping abyss, and she had to herd him away from it, quick. Before he fell in and was lost.

"This is too much. It's making me nervous." Her voice was tight with panic. "I can't do this, Sam. I can't play this game with you."

"You think it's a game?" He let go of her hand and stood. A graceful, pantherish movement. "Too much responsibility?"

"I don't know what you mean."

"Sure you do. Sveti the tough babe, who takes on the world all by herself. This is just about sex. Except when it's about staying alive, but no worries, when the danger's past, bada bing bada boom, it's about sex again. Put me in my place. Don't let me forget it."

"Oh, God." She covered her face. "Sam. Don't."

"Shit," he muttered. "Forget I said it. Shutting up now. Crisis averted. Give me the bathroom for a few. I need to wash."

She stared out at the surf, unsoothed. He emerged a few minutes later, clad in a towel and a cloud of steam. "Your turn," he said.

When she finished her shower, he was still there, fully dressed and seated on the bare mattress. "Sorry I'm still in your face," he said. "I know you could use some time alone, but you have to go down first. So they all know I haven't done anything unspeakable to you."

She snorted as she pulled items out of the drawer and threw them on. Underwear, jeans, a fresh tee, a sweater. She ran her fingers through her damp hair, checked her pale face in the mirror. "I'm ready."

"No bra?" He sounded scandalized. "You can't go down like that!"

"Get out," she scoffed. "I'm small, and I have a big, baggy sweater. No one could ever tell that I'm not wearing a—"

He dragged her toward him and wrapped his arms around her.

"I can tell," he announced. "I feel every detail of those tight, suckable, rose-tinted tits. My own nipples are hard now. They're saying hi to yours. Mmmm. Hello."

She dissolved in nervous giggles, wiggling in his grip as he rubbed his chest against hers. "You're being silly!"

Sam just hung on, staring into her eyes. She realized, abruptly, that a fight as frivolous as this one was a waste of her precious energy.

She sighed out the tension. "All right. I'll put on a bra, if it makes you happy." She waited. "If you let go of me long enough to do it."

His arms dropped. He stepped back.

She grabbed the first thing she found in the drawer, and was chagrined to find that it was a sexy, peach-toned lace balcony confection. Tam had given it to her for Christmas some time ago, as a joke, and a nudge. She fastened the clasp and propped her boobs to the appropriate height. Which was to say, jacked up and in your face.

She adjusted her clothes and turned to him. "Better?"

The hot sparkle in his eye made her hairs rise in a shivery ripple, up her back, to the nape of her neck. He turned her to face the mirror and cupped her breasts, circling his fingertips.

She caught her breath as her nipples went stiff.

"A little bit better," he conceded. "The lace doesn't provide much coverage, though. I feel every last detail of your nipple hard-on."

"My nipple hard-on is entirely your fault to begin with," she said primly. "And you're being primeval."

"It's your fault," he told her. "I was cool, before, and then you come along in that red dress and I turned into a Stone Age maniac."

"I didn't wear a bra with that red dress," she pointed out. "At all."

"I was intensely aware of that fact," Sam replied. "And I'm sure I wasn't the only one."

"There was nothing inappropriate about that dress! Did you see what the Venus Ensemble wore? Mine was nothing in comparison!"

"Who knows? I wasn't staring at their tits. Just at yours." He rubbed his cheek against her hair. "Tell me something, Sveti. In what universe could you be with me? What impossible things would have to be true before you could say yes to anything other than my dick?"

She tried to pull away. "Oh, Sam, please don't. Do we have to?"

"Yes, we do." His eyes demanded the truth.

The halting words hurt her throat as they came out. "The past would have to be different," she said. "I would have to be different. I couldn't be me. Who I am, with my history. My bad, weird shit. It won't let me rest. But it's not your fault, Sam. It's not about you, not at all."

"That's not much of a comfort," he said.

"I know," she said fervently. "I'm sorry."

He nuzzled her ear. "I wouldn't want you any different than you are," he said. "Nothing. Not by a hair."

She jerked away from him. "We, ah, should go downstairs now."

He stepped back, his hands flexing and clenching. "Yeah, right."

She grabbed the tablet that lay on the dresser and marched out the door ahead of him. Roiling inside, with conflicting feelings.

So he didn't want her any different? Hah. He didn't know what the fuck he was talking about. She wanted to laugh, snarl, slap him for his presumption. Like he had any right to say that, when she wanted so badly to be the heroine of a different story, with another ending.

Anything other than what she was.

CHAPTER 10

A long, punishing internal monologue ran through his mind as he followed her through the house. Keep a few respectful steps behind your lady fair. Don't presume. Eyes down.

God, what an asshole. He never learned. Offering his sword like a samurai warrior, when all she wanted from him was what dangled between his legs.

Sveti walked like she did everything. Graceful, no wasted movement, down to business. She wanted her sex like that, too. Just jump astride her chosen mount, ride til she was done, then waft away.

It didn't matter. She could want what she wanted, and so could he, but the sex had its own agenda. It was not fun, or playful. It was like being sacrificed to the god of fire, stabbed by holy lightning, flung into the heart of the sun and being reduced to smoke and ash. It was a massive, painful shift in consciousness, every damn time. And after only two nights of it, he was totally strung out on that wild intensity.

The light shone through the loose weave of her entirely inadequate sweater, showing every perfect detail. Every slender curve. Her hair shifted and swung, light catching every wave. Hypnotizing him.

She shot a nervous glance over her shoulder, giving him a fresh jolt of astonishment at how fucking pretty she was. Even without makeup, her eyes were set off by long, sooty lashes and sharp, winged brows. Her lips were red. Slightly puffy. From lots of hard use last night.

Oh, shit. Cool it. He could not walk in there with a hard-on.

Sveti pushed open the door that led into Tam and Val's kitchen, packed with people whose collective gaze swerved right to them.

Sveti's family. The toughest sons of bitches he'd ever met on the right side of the law. Tam held court, seated on a high stool by the bar. Her topaz eyes flicked over Sveti, doing a diagnostic X-ray once-over. She gave Sam an arctic glare. "So nice of you to finally join us."

Lara, Miles' wife, ran for Sveti and hugged her. Lara, more than any of them, could relate to Sveti's ordeal, having spent months herself in captivity until Miles rescued her. She looked good, nearly two years later. Her pregnancy didn't show yet, but she had a happy glow. The last time he'd seen her, she'd been as fragile and waiflike as one would expect after her harrowing adventures. She'd been beautiful even then, but she was a knockout now, with some more meat on her bones.

He kept his eyes locked on Sveti and Lara's embrace. It was a much safer resting place than any other point in the room.

"Your timing rots, Petrie," a voice behind him growled.

Sam turned to Nick Ward and his wife, Becca, who was waiting her turn for a hug with Sveti. Liv, Sean's wife, was in line behind her.

"What timing?" Sam asked. "Being there when they nabbed her? Following her, rescuing her? Is that the timing you're refer-ring to?"

"You know exactly what I'm referring to," Nick said.

Sam shrugged. "It is what it is."

"You think the day she almost gets herself killed is the day to make your big move?"

"You're wrong, Nick." Sveti's voice rang out. "It was my move! I went to his house uninvited. I seduced him. And a lucky thing, too, or he wouldn't have seen them take me, and you guys would be getting a very bad telephone call right about now. So back off."

Nick thudded back down into his chair. He looked like he was chewing steel wool.

Sveti swept the room with her gaze. "Sam saved my life. I love you all, and you have been very good to me, but get it through your heads. I'm not a child. In fact, I've never been a child, not since you've known me. So not another word about me and Sam hooking up. That's between him and me."

Silence followed that blunt announcement, broken by Sean's soft laughter. "Seduced, hmm? Sveti, you vixen, you."

"Shut up, Sean," Nick said sourly. "I am not entertained."

"My, aren't you masterful today," Tam said to Sveti. "Getting laid appears to stiffen up your spine. Bow down, bitches."

Sveti's eyes dropped. "I'm sorry—I didn't mean to—"

"Oh, for God's sake, don't ruin it!" Tam snapped. "I like to hear some proper sass out of you! But we have more important things to talk about right now than your sex life."

"Yeah, like breakfast," Becca chimed in, from the stove. "Rachel, honey, get the toast out of the toaster and butter it, okay? I have a bacon and Swiss omelet coming out of the pan with your name all over it."

For a few wonderful minutes, eating occupied them completely. With the McCloud Crowd, the food was always good. Sam inhaled the fluffy omelet with a mountain of toast and washed it down with coffee. Sveti didn't have much appetite, but she was nagged and poked until she got around a couple of eggs and a slice of toast.

Then Rachel leaned over the table, her dark eyes magnified by the thick lenses of her glasses. "So? How did you seduce him, anyway?"

Sveti choked and sputtered on her orange juice.

Tam made a shushing noise. Nick and Becca's little daughter Sofia piped up in the silence. "What's seduced?"

"Out!" Val roared. "Rachel, take the children up to the play-room!"

Val seldom raised his voice, but it had a jolting effect. Rachel scooped up Jon, Kev and Edie's son, and scurried out, herding Sofia and Eamon, Sean and Liv's son, before her. Eamon had a keen ear for anything that disturbed adult sensibilities, and was crowing "Seduced! Seduced!" at the top of his lungs as they retreated down the corridor.

The quiet felt ominous. Tam sank onto her stool. Sam swept his eye over the assembled multitudes. There were Kev and Edie, Nick and Becca, Sean and Liv, Miles and Lara, Tam and Val. About half of the entire complement of this crowd and their progeny, and thank God for it, or the place would have been a fucking zoo. Even so, it was way too many eyes. And all of them so damn focused.

Sveti dabbed nervously at her mouth with a napkin.

"So," Nick said. "We've been working on a plan. The way things stand, we've decided it's best to keep you here on lockdown."

Tam looked at Sam. "And you're not invited," she said. "Last night was an exception."

Sveti shook her head, but Nick plodded on. "This house has the best security, and it's the easiest to defend. Plus, there's room for backup people to stay. Tam and Val's arsenal is—"

"No!" Sveti said sharply. "Are you guys even listening to yourselves? 'We've decided?' 'Keep me here?' What am I, a doll?"

"Of course not, honey," Becca said. "But it's the only option. You were snatched from your own home, and we don't know their agenda."

"I told you their agenda!" Sveti protested. "I know what they want! He wanted to know about what was written on Mama's photo!"

In the silence that followed, everyone abruptly had something to look at that was not Sveti. Her eyes widened, and a bright red slash began to glow on each cheekbone. "Oh, my God," she said. "You guys don't believe me either." She looked at Sam. "What did you tell them?"

He lifted his hands. "Just what the investigation turned up. The body I pulled out of that fire is Jason Kang. From Hong Kong. He's a snakehead goon from Helen Wong's gang." He paused. "Not Ukrainian."

She looked betrayed. "But . . . but the guy who questioned me was not Chinese! I know what language I'm hearing when I hear it! And his eyes were gray! He was white, with gray hair, buzz cut! He put on the mask right before Sam came in!"

"Calm down," Lara soothed. "You've been through a terrible experience, and no one better than we can understand—"

"You don't understand! Not if you all think that I'm delusional!"

Becca's face contracted. "Honey. We just need to keep you safe."

"The nationality of the asshole gunning for you doesn't matter, Sveti," Nick said. "Our response remains the same."

Sveti looked at Tam. "You too? You think I'm crazy?"

"I've had stress flashbacks." Tam's voice was colorless. "They suck. I would not spit in the face of a friend who offered to help."

"I'm not spitting in anyone's face," Sveti said fervently. "I've had stress flashbacks, too. But I was not having one yesterday. In any case, I'm leaving the country, so it's irrelevant. Thanks for the thought, but I'll handle this myself from now on."

Sam inhaled and braced himself. This was gonna be ugly.

Tam was the first to find her voice. "Excuse me? Going where?"

"Italy, and then England. It's been coming together the past few weeks. I was waiting to tell you until I'd nailed the details down. There's a conference on human trafficking in San Anselmo. I'm speaking on several panels and getting an award for my contribution to the fight against modern slavery. And I got a consulting job, in London. Illuxit Transnational. It's a big contract research organization. I'll be advising corporations on how to implement policies to prevent trafficking."

Nick folded his arms. "When were you going to tell us?"

"At the wedding," Sveti said. "But I, ah, got distracted. Oleg Arbatov showed up, and I had my freak-out, and then, ah . . ." Her eyes flicked to Sam and her whole face went pink.

"It's great about the award, Sveti," Kev said gently. "You deserve it. But you can't go receive it now. It's too dangerous."

"It's been dangerous from the start," Sveti said. "It'll always be dangerous. Whatever. I'll defend myself. You all taught me how."

"Like you defended yourself yesterday?" Sean said.

"Amen," Sam muttered.

"You shut up," Sveti said furiously, whirling on Sam.

Sam raised both hands meekly in the air.

"We are not going to let you get killed," Tam said stonily. "You're one of us now, and we just can't do it."

"It's not up to you." Sveti looked from one to the other of her friends. "I'll always be grateful to you. But I will make the decisions."

"I promised your father I'd look out for you!" Nick bellowed.

"That's nice, but my father should have looked out for me himself," Sveti said. "He did as he pleased. He made his choices."

"And got his guts ripped out," Tam pointed out.

"His choice," Sveti repeated. "His risk." She looked at Sam, at Nick, then Val. "I've seen your bullet scars," she said. She looked at Kev, Tam, Miles. "You all have scars. None of you ever backed away from a dangerous job. And you criticize me? You want to wrap me in tissue and lock me in a cupboard? I'm calling you on your bullshit right now!"

"This is different," Tam said. "The scum of the earth can wait for you to flatten them into paste while we get a hold on this situation. You have your whole life to fight the powers of darkness."

"And if we never get a hold on it? I stay on lockdown indefinitely? Poor Sveti with her pathetic delusions, locked up so she doesn't hurt herself. Uh-uh. I don't think so. Some opportunities won't wait."

"Your destiny will not be derailed by a single missed opportunity," Val said.

Sveti shook her head. "I won't run and hide. I want my fucking award, and I want that fucking job. I won't back down because of this!"

Val rubbed his chin. "If it was Helen Wong's gang, Europe might not be such a bad idea," he said thoughtfully. "Their ties are to Asia."

"So you're convinced?" Sveti asked. "You're so sure that what I remember is just a hallucination?"

Val looked pained. "Sveti, we must examine every possible—"

"Then examine the possibility that what I told you is what actually happened." Her voice rang out, challenging them. "I invite you to examine that, all of you. Please. Do me that courtesy."

Val nodded. "Very well, let us examine it," he said. "Go through it again now, from the very top. Every last tiny detail."

So Sveti went through the whole thing, just as she'd told it to Sam, just as she'd told it to Tenly and Horvath. Not missing a beat or a detail.

After she concluded, they all stared at one another, at a loss.

"So the Ukrainian hired at least one snakehead for this job," Sveti concluded. "I don't know why, but that's what happened."

"Tell me again about the photo," Tam said.

"I displayed it in my TED talk," Sveti said. "A picture of my father, too. Remember the photo that arrived in the mail after she died, with the poem snippets on the back? The one she sent like a postcard?"

"Let's see them," Nick said.

Sveti reached for her tablet and pulled up the first one, tapping to enlarge it. "She sent me the JPEG by e-mail, too. In the very last batch of pictures she ever sent me."

She pushed the tablet to the middle of the table. Everyone leaned to study it. Sam waited a decent interval, then spun the tablet a quarter turn. Sveti's mother had been a stunner. No surprise there. Blonde, but the full, sexy mouth, the stubborn set of the jaw, the elegant nose, the winged brows, the big, haunting eyes, all were echoed in Sveti's face.

But other than being a compelling portrait of a beautiful woman on a rocky, unidentifiable hillside, he saw nothing about the photo that could be significant to anyone but Sveti.

Sveti tapped on the tablet once again. "This was the other one that I had up on the same screen. This is my father."

Sam took a quick look before pushing it back toward the others. Sergei had passed on Sveti's amazing cheekbones. Handsome guy, dark and slit-eyed, crow's-feet wrinkled up in a feral grin. He looked tough. There were two other men, lifting their glasses in a toast. The shot had been snapped from inside a house, looking out through a window.

Becca pointed, her mouth tight. "That's Zhoglo."

Nick squeezed her shoulders. "Dead and gone."

"He haunts me, though," she said. "The bastard."

Sam leaned to examine the mafiya vor's swollen, grinning face, then the younger guy. "How about that guy?" Sam asked. "Who's he?"

"I don't know," Sveti said. "And there's no one left to ask."

Yeah, that was the thing exactly. No one wanted to say it, but there it sat, begging to be said. There was no one left to ask, and nothing left to ask about, because everyone associated with this old story was dead and gone. The phantom torturer had been asking questions about Sveti's unresolved psychological issues. Nothing that was relevant or current. He didn't know a gentle way to say it, so he kept his mouth shut. Let some other poor fool point it out.

"Your mother took this?" he asked, indicating the photo.

Sveti nodded. "She was a gifted photographer."

"Here are the pictures by Sveti's bed!" Rachel popped up suddenly. "The ones in the gold frame! I ran and got them." She held up the hinged frame triumphantly. Her eyes sparkled with excitement.

"We've talked about eavesdropping, baby," Tam said sharply.

Rachel shrugged. "If it's about Sveti, I need to know about it."

"We looked at these pictures already, sweetheart, on Sveti's tablet, but thank you anyway," Becca told her gently.

Sam took the photo frame from Rachel's hand and examined it. They were, in fact, the same ones Sveti had just shown them, but these had been trimmed to fit the frames. The shot of Sveti's mother was cut to half its original size, and something was scrawled in Cyrillic script over the top, with a couple of numbers below. The one of Sergei was trimmed, too, the third man cut away, but Zhoglo still smirked in it, his bulbous goblin face positioned right over Sergei Ardov's shoulder.

"You keep a picture of Vadim Zhoglo by your bed?" Sam said.

Sveti frowned. "No, I keep a picture of my father by my bed," she said stiffly. "It's the only one I have where he's smiling."

"His murderer is smiling, too. Doesn't that bug you?"

Sveti shrugged. "You have to take the bad with the good, if you want to salvage anything."

"You lie in your bed at night and let that monster leer at you?" he asked, incredulous. "And that doesn't hurt you?"

"Back off!" she snapped. "Maybe it does, I don't know, but I'm used to things hurting. I don't even notice."

It made him furious that Sveti should be so used to things being painful that something so fucking crazy horrible as having Zhoglo's ugly mug enshrined on her bedside table should just slip right past her. Unnoticed, among all the other crazy horrible things.

"That needs to change," he announced. He unhooked the lever in the back that held the picture in place, and the chunk of cardboard picture backing fell out, along with the picture.

Everyone watched as he twisted and snagged the kitchen shears out of the knife block on the kitchen bar behind him.

"Sam!" Sveti leaped up and started around the table. "Stop! That's *mine!* What the hell do you think you're doing?"

"Changing history." He cut into the photo, angling the shears carefully around Sergei's head to cut out Zhoglo's face.

Sveti skidded to a stop next to him, poppy red. "That was not yours to alter," she said, her voice tight. "You had no right to do that!"

He'd be damned if he'd apologize. He shook the shears. The scrap of photo fell from the blades and fluttered onto the table.

"You can't change the past." Sveti's voice quivered, dangerously.

"No?" Sam stabbed the point of the scissors in the middle of Zhoglo's face. "You can change how you think about it."

"And you think it's so simple? How the fuck would you know?"

Sean fidgeted uneasily. "Um, guys? This sounds like the kind of argument you two should have in private."

Sam lifted up the shears, with the offending scrap stuck upon the point. "Burn this ugly motherfucker," he said. "Burn him to ash."

Nick looked around. "I'm with that program," he said. "Anybody here have a lighter? Nobody smokes in this crowd anymore."

A box of kitchen matches sailed into the air from the other side of the bar, lobbed by Rachel. The box bounced on the table, sliding open. Wooden matches spilled out.

Sveti stood like a statue, fists clenched. Sam held the shears out to her. An offering.

"I know what you're trying to do," she said. "And it won't work."

"I'm with Sam," Becca said, her voice hard. "Burn it, Sveti."

Tam banged her forehead against the table. "For the love of God, finish it," she snarled. "I can't stand it anymore."

It was Becca, finally, who grabbed a match and scraped it against the box. The puff of sulfur burned Sam's nose as the flame took hold. Becca held it up to the photographic paper.

They all watched it burn in silence. Flames blackened the edges, curling green and blue, shrinking from the outside in. Ghostly shards of ash drifted onto the table, disintegrating into a puff of gray dust.

"Enough." Tam sounded unusually subdued. "Let's move on."

Sam picked up the picture frame, but Sveti snatched it out of his hands. "Do not touch my stuff again," she muttered, as she teased the backing out of the frame. The picture of Sonia fell out, along with a square of thin, almost transparent paper.

Sam held up the photograph. "What does that writing say?"

"The Sword of Cain," Sveti said. "The guy kept asking what it meant to me. I would have told him if it meant anything. It doesn't."

"Did the part you trimmed off have anything written on it?" he asked.

"Nothing about a sword," she said. "On the picture side, there were a few numbers. I figured they were phone numbers, or maybe filing numbers. Sometimes she printed several different versions of a photograph before she was happy with it, and numbered them. The other side had snippets of poetry, the address, and stamp."

"Did she send any others?"

"Not through the mail," Sveti said. "She sent me lots of JPEGs, on my e-mail. But they're just art photography. Pretty pictures of Italy."

Sam turned it over. On the back was more scribbling. Some in Cyrillic and some that appeared to be in English, but such tiny cursive, he could barely read it. "What's this stuff written on the back?"

Sveti shook her head. "Mama was cryptic," she said. "They're lines from various obscure poems. Some French, some Russian, some English, but she'd translated them all into English here. She taught poetry at the university, before Papa was killed. That first line in Ukrainian Cyrillic says, 'When you don't know which way to turn, look to the source.' Then come the quotes."

He squinted at the first quote. The writing was so miniscule. "*'Darkness from that ragged hole/pulls like a prisoner's shackling chain/drawing me into Hell's blind'* . . . what's that?"

"Realm," Sveti said. "Hell's blind realm. Peter Rodionov. It's very sad. Don't read any of them aloud, please. I'll break out into a cold sweat if I have to listen to them again."

"Is there a unifying theme?" he persisted.

She shook her head. "Only that they're all depressing. Lukyenov, Rafael, Lebedev. Poems about death. Whatever point she meant to make with them, I missed it."

Sam peered at another one. "*'Bear witness to this bowl of bones/this yellowed snarl of sticks and twigs.'* Wow. Cheerful."

"Esther Rafael," Sveti said, her face stoic. "She survived Auschwitz. She wrote about the Holocaust. Oh, and another thing. The man who questioned me yesterday? He's the one who killed my mother."

Tam's eyes dropped. Val's gaze slid away. Nick and Becca exchanged worried glances. A nervous silence stretched out.

"Sveti," Sean said carefully. "Wasn't your mom's death a suicide?"

"That's what we thought," Sveti said. "But that man talked about Mama as if he'd known her. He talked about the red dress she wore that night. How would he know if he wasn't there? Besides, Mama was not a person who would kill herself. She must have been taking pictures that made someone nervous, so they killed her. And The Sword of Cain is the key, if I could figure out what the hell it is."

Sam took advantage of her distraction to pick up the square of paper. Sveti twitched it away and smoothed it back into its folds.

"What is that?" he asked.

"Mama's last letter to me," she said.

Sam waited, but when the obvious next thing was not forthcoming, he fished for it. "And you're going to read it to us, right?"

"I'd rather not," she said. "It has nothing to do with anything, and it just makes me sad, and I really don't . . ." Her voice petered off.

Sam gazed at her, relentless. "You said everything, Sveti."

She unfolded it, with agonizing slowness, and began to translate.

> *My dear Svetlana,*
> *I write to you from Renato's atrium in the Villa Rosalba. An orange tree is heavy with fruit over my right shoulder, a lemon tree to my left. Before me is Renato's sculpture garden, full of figures from myth and legend. Atlas is my favorite. Approach him from the bench where I sit, following the tree of life, until you can see his eyes.*
> *Look beneath. Look within, to find your way through the labyrinth. You already know more about that labyrinth than any young woman should. For that I will always be sorry. Forgive me for not protecting you better. I should have taken you back to France before disaster struck. Love makes one stupid.*

Sam winced inwardly. The very last thought he wanted Sveti to reflect upon right now, and he had bullied her into voicing it.

He broke in as Sveti faltered. "France?"

"She was part French," Sveti said. "Raised in Paris. She met my father while visiting her mother's family in the Ukraine."

"And Renato? Who's he?"

"Renato Torregrossa. Her Italian boyfriend," Sveti said. "A rich Italian count. He was a bigwig in some multinational pharmaceutical company. Had a fancy villa by the sea. I never met him. Or wanted to."

"And the labyrinth, the tree of life? What's that about?"

"I don't know," Sveti said. "She just talked that way. She was a lit professor. She liked poetic metaphors." She read on.

I had hoped to spend Christmas holidays with you here, but it will not be possible until spring. I am in the middle of an assignment that takes all my attention. Come for spring vacation instead, and we will swim together in the Mediterranean in April. Don't be angry at me, love. Be strong. You'll find your strongest weapon buried in all this garbage.
   All my love, always. Until spring,
   Mama

"She died ten days after that letter is dated," she said softly.

"Where is this Renato?" Sam asked.

Sveti turned the letter over, indicated the return address, penned on the letter. "I have the address of the Villa Rosalba."

"I'll find him," Val said.

"No, don't," Sveti said. "I'll find him. I will talk to him personally."

Val frowned. "Sveti. We have experience that you do not."

"I don't want him on his guard. It makes sense for me to want to talk to someone who knew Mama and spent time with her. It's entirely different if a group of foreigners start making threatening noises!"

Tam's mouth curved. "Thank you for that vote of confidence."

"Don't touch it," Sveti said. "Promise me."

Sean drummed his fingers against the table. "Moving on," he said. "If you're going to Europe no matter what we say, who goes with you?"

"I will cover her while she is in Italy," Val said. "But we must think in longer terms for London."

"I'll check SafeGuard's roster of bodyguards," Sean said.

"I'll go." The offer flew out before Sam could gauge its insanity level. Which he instantly realized was very high.

Sveti gaped at him, blank. "Go . . . what? Go where?"

"With you," he repeated. "To Italy. And England. You know. To protect and serve."

Nick's eyes were cold. "You opportunistic son of a bitch."

Tam exchanged speculative glances with Val. "The idea has

merit. He'd be earning his oxygen. And we wouldn't have to trip over him around here. There's definitely something to be said for that."

Sveti sputtered, wordlessly. She finally found her voice. "No way!" she burst out. "I cannot afford to hire a goddamn body-guard!"

"I work cheap," Sam said.

Several men in the room exploded with quickly stifled laughter. The women in the room shot them quelling glances.

"Looking to score some points, huh?" Nick demanded.

"What if I am? She'll have her back covered all the same."

"And plenty else besides, I bet," Tam said dryly.

"You won't do her much good in Italy if you don't speak the language," Val said.

"I speak Italian," Sam said.

Val's face froze, mouth slightly open. *"Non mi hai mai detto che parli italiano,"* he said. You never told me you speak Italian.

"Non mi hai mai chiesto," Sam replied. You never asked. He continued, in Italian. "I spent time there as a child, and studied there, in college. I speak French, Spanish, and Italian. My sister speaks Japanese and Mandarin, too. I'm the underachiever of the family."

Tam snorted. "Listen to him. A Florentine accent, of all things."

"Wow," Sean said with a low whistle. "Didn't see that coming."

"I'm not surprised at all," Tam said. "You forget that Sam here isn't like the rest of us hardscrabble proles. He's the Petrie princeling, mas-saged and molded to take up the reins of global leadership."

"Shut up, Tam," Sam muttered.

"But you're a rebel, Sam," Tam went on. "You turned away from the big money to wallow in the worst cruelty that humanity can inflict upon itself. Vice and homicide, on the big city streets. Why, I wonder?"

He shook his head. It was none of her goddamn business, for one thing, and for another, he truly didn't know. He chose not to examine his own motives that closely. It never led anywhere good.

"I can't take my firearms to Europe," he said to Val. "I'll need to score some weapons once I get there. You have contacts?"

"I'll set you up," Val said. "You understand what is expected of you, no? You must be with her every second of every day."

"No, he will not!" Sveti yelled. "I will not be—"

"I'll follow her into the ladies' room when she pees," Sam broke in. "I'll follow her into the changing rooms where she shops."

"I'm not going there to shop!" Sveti's face was bright red again.

Sam pressed on. "I'll sleep across the threshold of her door."

"That I doubt," Tam said. "You'll find a warmer, softer nest."

"I can't ask Hazlett to buy another ticket!" Sveti protested.

"I'll cover my own ticket," he said.

"Money's not an issue, with Samuel Petrie," Tam said. "Did you not see the suit he wore to the wedding? His portfolio almost equals my own. And loaded as he is personally, his family is still more loaded. We're talking the top one percent of the top one percent."

"You hacked into my bank accounts?" Sam demanded. "Why?"

"I had to know everything there was to know about a man who looked at my girl the way you looked at her," Tam said coolly. "Did you think we wouldn't notice?"

"What does my portfolio have to do with me perving on Sveti?"

"Not much, but I found it entertaining just the same," Tam said. She turned back to Sveti. "He has a huge trust fund, too, but he's never touched it. It sits there, desolate, accruing interest like barnacles. This pathological lack of interest in such a large sum of money strikes me as suspicious. It hints at deep-seated control issues in his family. Though he does well on his investments with his own money. Are you bored to the point of suicide yet, Sam? Bummer about your detective job. You hero types, so desperate for validation. You have to put your ass on the line to earn the very air you breathe, hmm?"

"Leave him alone, Tam," Sveti whispered. "He doesn't deserve it."

"Aw, look at that," Tam crooned. "Defending him, how sweet. I've often wondered why a guy would choose to live in a forties-era two-bedroom bungalow in grotty North Portland and pull a government salary when he has that fat, soft cushion of money. He could just lie back on it and drift away on a slow-flowing river of bourbon, hmm?"

"Fuck off, Tam," Sam said. "You know nothing about me."

Tam's smile was catlike. "I know when I've hit a nerve."

"Stop it," Sveti said. "I don't want to watch you hit nerves."

Tam opened her mouth, paused, and closed it with a snap. "Have it your way. The point is, Sam can afford to go to Italy a thousand times over. And nothing makes a man as focused as a sexual obsession."

"It's my decision!" Sveti was on her feet. "I don't want someone breathing down my neck, following me into the bathroom! And it's not economically feasible or sustainable in any way! Who pays for it?"

"You can't stop me from coming," Sam said.

"Sure I can!" she shot back. "I'll tell the cops you're stalking me!"

"Yeah, you do that. It adds lots of credibility to your testimony. They'll figure it's not just PTSD, but a personality disorder, too."

Sveti's face contracted. "Oh, shut up."

"Just saying," he murmured.

There was an awkward pause, and Becca piped up. "Well, then. If she doesn't want Sam to go, let's look again at SafeGuard."

"I'm going, no matter who you send," he said.

Sveti slapped her hands on the table in a rare show of temper. "I can't pay for SafeGuard!"

"So opt for the bargain-basement option," Tam reminded her. "Behold, Sam Petrie, with his lustful gaze and his volunteer services, if you're uncomfortable letting us hire someone." Her eyes raked him. "But I'm sure he'll get his just recompense out of you."

Liv winced. "Ouch." She leaned over and laid a hand on Sveti's arm. "Honey. When you're in Europe, will you do something for me?"

Sveti looked wary. "What?"

Liv tugged at her hand, taking off a ring, a thick, complex snarl of yellow and white gold. "Wear this." She held it out.

Sean whistled. "Wow, babe. Really? That's the first time I've seen you take that thing off since Osterman bit the dust."

"I want Sveti to wear it," Liv said quietly. "It's lucky."

"Oh, no! I can't take it!" Sveti held up her hands. "You should keep it, Liv. It's your talisman. It saved your life!"

"And besides, I could give Sveti the prototype," Tam offered.

"No," Liv said stubbornly. "This one's better. It's been through the fire. It's all charged up and ready to rock." Her eyes flicked to him. "Kind of like Sam." When Sveti still hesitated, she grabbed the younger woman's hand and slid the ring on. "I'll feel safer if you're wearing it. God, your fingers are tiny. Wear it on your index finger. Yes, that fits."

Sveti held out her hand. The ring gleamed, lavish and voluptuous, and subtly dangerous, as if it could come to life and start writhing.

Sam eyed it suspiciously. "Is that one of Tam's designs?"

"Of course," Tam purred. "I hope it makes you nervous, Sam. That is its prime function, after all."

"Nonsense," Liv said, squeezing Sveti's hand. "It's just for luck. "

"Thank you," Sveti whispered, staring down at the ring.

"We just want you to be safe," Liv said earnestly. "And happy."

"Happy?" Sveti's mouth shook, as if she were going to burst into tears. Then Sam realized that the silent shaking was laughter.

"Yes, happy!" Liv sounded defensive. "I don't think that's too much to hope, for a person as wonderful and as deserving as you!"

"I am happy," Sveti said. "I have all my organs. I'm not chained to a sewing machine in a basement in the Philippines, or handcuffed to a bed in a Cambodian brothel. No one's chopped off my hands or put out my eyes and sent me to beg on a street corner in Bombay."

"Sveti, baby. Calm down, please," Liv pleaded.

"I'm perfectly calm!" Sveti jumped to her feet. "What do I have to be upset about? I'm fucking ecstatic, but I won't let myself be jerked around, not even by people I love, and owe." She marched out and pulled the doors shut, *slam*. Glass shivered in the mahogany frame.

Shit. She'd bailed on him again, like she had at the wedding. Left him high and dry with these people.

Sean whistled. "Whoa. That girl needs to lighten up."

"A tricky proposition," Lara observed. "Considering."

"You. Petrie." Tam's voice rang out like the crack of a whip. "So? Hop to it. What are you waiting for? Get to work."

"Work?" Sam looked around wildly. "How? What work? Here?"

Tam rolled her eyes. "On *her*." She spoke with exaggerated slowness. "Lighten her up. Show her a good time. Earn your oxygen, if you breathe it in this house. Go . . . go stir her with your magic stick."

Nick flinched. "Tam. Spare me."

"I spare no one, as Sam will soon have reason to know. Petrie!"

Her voice snapped him around as if drawn up by a tether. "Yeah?"

"Protect her, in Italy and London." Her voice was menacing. "Make her happy. Or else I will fuck. You. Up. Understood?"

He took off like a shot, to earn his oxygen.

CHAPTER 11

Sveti pressed her hot forehead against the window glass, shaking.

The door opened, making her jump. Sam, of course. He shut the door, locked it. As if he had every right to. And God knows, he did.

"You can't come to Italy," she blurted. "That wasn't the plan."

"Plans change." His voice was so calm. It maddened her.

"Not like this. Not . . ." She waved her hands. "You don't understand. This whole thing. You and me. Coming to your house the other night. It was all predicated on the fact that I was leaving. I would never have done it otherwise. I would never have led you on like that."

He shook his head. "You really know how to stroke a guy's ego. Why be so uptight? Don't worry. Take it one day at a time. Don't stress."

"It doesn't make any sense," she protested. "Following me to Europe, gratis? When your life is here, your work, your family—"

"What life?" he said. "What work? And my family bites my ass. I'm willing to put distance between me and my family. You catch me at a unique time in my life, Sveti. I have no compelling reason right now not to follow you across the world."

She squeezed her eyes shut. How bad could it get, if her pattern held? The nightmares, the flashbacks. And how did she explain that nasty, toxic shit to a gorgeous, brave, sexy, wonderful guy who just wanted to be her boyfriend? "But I can't offer you anything that would make it worth your while," she insisted. "I just can't."

"Let me decide what's worth my while," he said. "There's nothing on earth I'd rather do with my time than prevent scumbags from killing you." His dimples flashed. "And spending all my downtime draped over your naked body, of course. But hey. No pressure."

She brushed aside his invitation to keep it light and playful. "I can handle myself, Sam. Val can get me a weapon once I'm there. I have combat training. I'm not helpless. I learned to shoot from Tam and Nick; I studied martial arts with Davy and Sean and all the rest. And I know more about drugs and poisons from Tam than you ever want to hear."

"Right," he said. "You can repeat that for days on end, and I'll still keep seeing you with your head and shoulders in a tub of ice water."

She waved that away. "I was off my guard yesterday. I won't be ever again. Plus, I'll be less of a spectacle by myself. I just need to fall off the face of the earth for a while, let everyone forget that I—"

"Do not insult my intelligence," Sam said. "A girl who looks like you will always attract attention. When you start doing your thing, you'll attract even more. You'll be splashed all over every media that exists. Schoolgirls will write essays about how you inspire them. You're doing the opposite of going into hiding. Don't bullshit me, Sveti. Ever."

"But I can't make it worth your while, Sam," she said, desperately. "I swear. I just can't."

He gazed at her. A level, appraising glance that made her knees go wobbly and her face get hot. "No," she said quickly. "If that's what you have in mind, forget it. I would never trade sex for—"

"Shhh. Not at all. I never said that. You came up with it yourself, because you're all wound up. I would never think that of you."

"Sam, I . . . I'm just afraid that it will go bad. Really bad."

"Don't sweat it. Just do your thing," he urged. "Save the world, and I'll watch your back. Don't worry about my poor tender feelings or my unrealistic expectations. Those are my problems. I'll deal with them."

She took a nervous step backward as he advanced on her. "And why this great act of self-sacrifice?"

"Who said anything about sacrifice?" Another step flattened her against the window. The glass was cold through the loose weave of her sweater. "Of course, I'll come on to you. I'll be all over you, every chance I get. But it won't be payment for services rendered. Don't slap a crass label on it, Sveti. Just let it be whatever it is. Let it breathe. Let it exist."

She laughed, shakily. "Oh, you smooth, sneaky bastard."

"That's me." He put his hands on either side of her head, against the glass. "Granted, I stand ready. Give me the nod, and I'll be all over you. My tongue in your mouth, or sucking on your tits, or trailing down your spine, or between your pussy lips, lapping up your lube. I'll fuck you into sweaty exhaustion every night and every morning. But when we go to breakfast, I'll morph from abject sex slave into the perfect bodyguard. Not a hair out of place. Completely focused. We'll all get what we need. It could work, Sveti. Really."

Sveti's mouth shook, from proximity to his sensual lips, but he didn't kiss her. He just danced around it, teasing her. Leaning to inhale the scent of her hair, to nuzzle the nape of her neck.

"After a long day of saving the world, I'll bathe you, shampoo you, rub you down with scented body oil," he rasped into her ear. "Mmm."

"Don't make fun of me," she whispered.

"I'm dead serious. I'll blow-dry your hair and steam your suits. I'll pick out your lingerie. I'll carry your bags, and keep your cell phone charged, and screen your calls, and solve your computer problems. And go down on you. For hours. You'll lie there legs spread, writhing with pleasure while I lick your pussy. My payoff is your sweet elixir. Yum."

She shook her head. "A guy like you will get bored out of his mind really fast, playing lady's maid and charging up my cell phone."

"You know what, Sveti? I am totally willing to cross that bridge when I come to it. When I'm with you, the very last thing I have to fear is boredom." He suckled her earlobe. "I'm not asking for love or gratitude or promises. All I want is to keep you safe. And make you come. Let me give you a sample taste right now. See how you like it."

"You don't have to, ah . . . I already know—"

"Sample it again. You might have forgotten. It's been well over an hour." He kissed her hungrily. His lips were so hot. Soft and hungry, demanding and insisting. He slid his hand down to the small of her back, pressing her mound against the hard bulge in his crotch.

Her jeans were low rise, and loose enough for him to just slide his hand inside, over her ass. His fingers stroked tenderly into her sensitive cleft. Barely touching her labia with his fingertips from behind.

Her thighs contracted at the delicate touch.

He jerked her belt buckle loose and tugged her jeans halfway down her thighs. He sank to his knees. "Hold up your sweater and watch while I lick your clit," he said. "Watch every detail."

Sveti clutched the wadded sweater against her breasts. Her thighs quivered, trapped by the jeans that were snarled around her knees, but Sam didn't pull them down. He seized her ass cheeks in his big, warm hands, clutching tenderly as he pressed his mouth to her mound.

The sound that came out of her was unrecognizable as his tongue probed boldly between her folds, swirling up around her clit. Kissing it, suckling it, trilling. Thrusting his tongue hungrily up inside her pussy.

It felt so good. She felt so naked, exposed, with all the glass, all the light, all that enormous space behind her, as if she could fall back into bright emptiness. The cold glass against her bare ass felt good now, against her hot skin. It was pleasure, joining all the other rivulets of pleasure. They all joined into a rushing torrent that crashed and roared, carving brand-new channels of sensation inside her body. Remolding her. Then they rippled out, into a sweet, shimmering endless vastness.

Sam held her steady, his hand splayed against her belly to keep her upright. The other hand was between her legs, fingers deep inside her pussy. Just holding her. Claiming her.

She licked her dry lips. Groped for words, found none.

Sam found them for her. "You want me to fuck you."

It was not a question. She managed only a tight, nervous nod.

Sam pushed her jeans down and she stepped out of them, wobbling so hard she almost fell. Her face burned. She was abashed at how easy it was for him to manipulate her with sex.

She felt helpless and desperately eager. Vulnerable. Weak.

Sam jerked her sweater and T-shirt over her head. A flick of the clasp and the bra followed. She was naked, while he was fully clothed.

Sam's eyes swept the room. "We need fresh sheets before we use the bed again. Put your hands on the back of the couch and bend over."

She hesitated, so he guided her into the position he wanted. Arms braced, back arched, ass stuck out. Legs spread. The submissive pose triggered a rush of complicated, conflicting emotions, but nothing trumped that clawing, restless heat. She offered herself to him, shaking.

He let out a harsh, jerky sigh. "You are so beautiful from this angle. That sweet pussy. All shiny and pink. Mine."

She moaned as he stroked her from behind, up and down her labia. "Wet and soft," he whispered. He thrust two fingers inside her, forcing them deeper. His breath was hot against her shoulder. "Arch your back," he directed. "Dance for me, around my hand. Show me how you'll move around my cock when I'm inside you."

She tried, awkwardly at first, but they soon found the perfect rhythm. Every probing stroke made pleasure jolt and swell, wafting her higher, higher . . . until it tipped, and became a crashing inevitability.

She came apart, like a dandelion in the sun. Disintegrated into a frothy cloud by a puff of air, and borne tenderly away on the breeze.

When her eyes opened, Sam withdrew his hand and leaned to tug the bathroom door open, so that the floor-length mirror reflected them.

It made her gasp. Her wanton, blushing face, her dazed eyes, her tousled hair. She jerked up, but Sam's hands tightened on her body.

"Don't move." He wrenched his belt buckle loose, opened his jeans. He freed his cock, staying fully clothed as he prodded himself against her slick folds and forced himself inside her. Sveti pushed back, yielding into the heavy, slick caress of his thick phallus.

He wedged himself deep, then withdrew with agonizing slowness. In again, out again. Each slow stroke a hot, luscious lick of pleasure.

Amazingly, that breathless, terrifying tension was building again. She closed her eyes against it, pressing her face to the couch.

Sam seized a handful of hair at the nape of her neck and tugged her head up. "No, Sveti. Look at me. Look into my eyes."

She met his gaze in the mirror, and her eyes skittered away from the intensity, as if it were an electric shock. "I can't," she gasped out.

"Do it." His eyes demanded, implacable. "It's important."

She met his eyes in the mirror, saw the tension in his clenched jaw, the naked emotion in his eyes. His powerful body thudded against hers, stroking and stroking, demanding, insisting . . .

She came apart again, explosively.

This time, when she floated back, she was on the floor, with no memory of getting down there. No bumps or bruises, though. She'd floated down on a magic cloud. There was a heavy thrum of water from the bathroom. Steam floated from the open door.

Sam came out. He scooped her into his arms. "I ran you a bath."

She was too limp to protest. He set her on her feet in the hot water, which foamed and roared from the pounding jet. She sank into it with a grateful sigh. He'd found something lavender scented to throw in. Ahh.

He hit the tap to stop the water, and crouched next to the tub.

For the first time, she felt relaxed enough to just look at him, full on. Not just the usual quick, nervous stolen glance, but an all-out, blatant, ogling stare. Enjoying every beautiful detail. It felt wonderful.

Sam grabbed the soap and pulled one of her feet out of the water. She twitched, trying to jerk it away. "What do you think you're doing?"

He grinned. "Call it the audition. You know, for my body servant duties. I've never done a pedicure, but I'm a fast learner. I can't wait to paint those pearly little toenails." He leaned to kiss her toes.

Her foot jerked, involuntarily. "That's silly."

"Is it?" He yanked her foot back and planted it against his chest, heedless of the wet footprint she left on his shirt. He sudsed up his hands and dug his fingers deeply into her quad muscles, massaging her leg. Oh, God. She gasped, as tension released in a shuddering rush. After sex like that, she wouldn't have thought there was any tension left, but Sam kept squeezing, kneading, releasing layer after layer of tightness and always finding another hiding beneath it. Some of those knots inside her were so old, she didn't recognize them as pain anymore.

The sudden relief from the tightness was weird, unsettling. She didn't know herself without it. She didn't recognize the sensations in this unknown girl's body at all. She felt lost. Floating in no-man's land.

Sam was halfway down her second leg before she could gather her wits to speak. "You're getting totally soaked," she told him.

"A small price to pay. I give myself up to your service. Mistress."

She snorted. "Mistress, my ass. You're a dominating alpha male to the very core of your being, Sam Petrie. Pretend all you want, but you can't fool me. Not now that we've . . . made love."

His brow tilted up. "Say 'had sex.' You'll feel more in control. 'Fucked' would be even better, if you could cough it out."

She tugged her foot away, stung. "Ouch," she murmured.

Sam stuck his hand into the water and seized her foot again. "At least the sex works. You did fine, in spite of my dominating alpha vibe. I've never seen a girl come so hard." Sam soaked his sleeve up to the shoulder as he slid his hand up her inner thigh and cupped her muff. Her legs floated apart to give him better access. He slid his finger inside.

She sucked in air. "What are you doing?" she asked inanely.

"Washing your pussy." His voice was silky. "You're full of my come. It's the least I can do. Mistress."

She laughed, and he scooped his arm behind her shoulder and

jerked her into a fierce kiss, accompanied by a huge slosh of soapy water. His tongue plunged, his hand thrust deeply, hitting spots inside her that made a little sun come out in her body. Shining so bright.

"Would the sex-slave scenario work better if I cleaned you with my tongue?" he asked. "Because I'm all over that idea."

The words alone detonated her.

The marvelous ripples pulsed and throbbed through her inner universe, dissolving her into liquid light. She clung to the ineffable sweetness, but she felt it start to fade before she opened her eyes. A sad, empty pull, deep inside. As if something was draining away.

Sam looked at her keenly and frowned. "Did that feel good?"

"You know it did," she said.

"Then why the look?"

He had no right to read her mind so easily. "What look?"

"The look that says something sucks."

She shook her head. No point in lying. He'd see right through it.

"I don't feel strong, when we make lo—have sex," she amended. "It makes me feel . . . soft. Melted out of shape. Scared. And . . . sad."

He looked perplexed. "So? Scared and sad, those we'll work on. But melted, soft? Since when are those bad things to feel?"

"It's dangerous," she said. "It makes me feel weak. Powerless."

He was silent for a moment. He drew his hand slowly out of her body and stood up, dripping hot, sudsy water down his jeans.

"I didn't mean to insult you," she said miserably. God, this was a minefield, and she couldn't even lie her way out of it. Not with him.

"I'm not insulted. I'm confused," he said. "Sex games are for making you hot, making you wet. What the fuck's wrong with that?"

"Nothing, I guess," she whispered.

Except that her subconscious mind would punish her for giving in to it by lobbing grenades at her. How to explain something so weird?

"I think you're incredible," he said. "I still can't believe you let me get this close to you. All I want is to please you. Where in all this did I make you feel powerless? Because I am seriously missing something."

It sucked, hurting him because of that sick feeling in her belly that she could neither control nor hide. "I'm sorry," she whispered.

"Feeling soft or melted is not bad," Sam said. "That's how it feels when the sex is good. You know how good it is by the extent to which it destroys you. Look at me, Sveti. Behold, a broken man."

"I never said that the feelings were bad," she hedged. "Just that they were . . . dangerous. For me, at least."

"They wouldn't be if you trusted me," he said. "I'll give you some space. Sounds like you need it." He walked out and shut the door.

Sveti lay in the tub and listened to the hollow plop of water dripping from the faucet.

The sound was lonesome and desolate to her ears.

Sam stretched out on the couch, watching the sunset. It was the only spot in the room out of sight of the bed nook. Sveti needed to be alone, but he was not willing to go downstairs to be verbally tased by Tam Steele. Nor was he leaving this house without Sveti. The minute he turned his back, she'd bolt. He was sure of it.

He amused himself by poring over the poetry written on her mother's photo. They'd had a bad moment when he'd insisted on taking the picture out of its frame again. She had a right to be twitchy, after seeing him take kitchen shears to the picture of her dad.

He'd won that fight, at some cost, and Sveti was pissed with him now. She'd made up the bed and dozed off in it, with her back to him.

He combed through the fragments, using Sveti's tablet to research each one. First Peter Rodionov, "*Darkness from that ragged hole/pulls like a prisoner's shackling chain/drawing me into Hell's blind realm.*" Then Ruslan Lebedev, "*Oh Orpheus, do not turn your head/Love follows only the flame of utter faith.*" Then Jean-Michel Laurent, "*I am swathed in the breathless hush of night/caressed by fluttering wings of ragged and disreputable bats.*" Then Esther Rafael, "*Bear witness to this bowl of bones, this yellowed snarl of sticks and twigs.*" And finally, Vladimir Lukyenov, "*Come, shuffling souls, in rank and file/through the tall, implacable door/to the echoing vault where Death awaits.*"

Spooky, doleful, miserable shit, and it meant absolutely nothing, in regard to Sveti. Neither did the whole poems, when he read them through. It pissed him off that Sveti had been jerked around like that, and by her own mother, too. Crazy. But not surprising, considering that the woman subsequently threw herself off a bridge.

Or not. He would revise all his judgments about Sonia Ardova if she'd been forcibly thrown off that bridge. But that was another whole writhing snake pit of speculation. One thing at a time, for God's sake.

A knock sounded on the door. Sam opened it and found Rachel, with a dinner tray. The girl carried it in, along with the stern message that the food was for Sveti, and Sveti only.

"It seemed kind of mean," Rachel said apologetically. "I wanted to bring you some, too, but Mama said you could come and get something out of the fridge yourself, if you're hungry. Sorry about that."

Sam laid the tray on a table. "It's fine. I'll get something later."

After midnight, maybe. Like a slinking thief, rummaging shifty-eyed through the congealed leftovers in the fridge. God, what he was reduced to. Like Sveti's mom had said: Love made you stupid.

Rachel drifted over toward Sveti's bed. "She'll probably have nightmares tonight," she said knowledgeably. "So watch out. She gets the really bad ones when she's worried about stuff."

"Nightmares?" he asked. "What kind of nightmares?"

"You know. About when we were locked up. She gets 'em bad."

Sam looked at Rachel's remote, abstracted expression. "You remember that? Weren't you just a baby?"

"I remember it just fine," Rachel said. "They don't know how old I was when they got me, I was so shriveled. Failure to thrive, they called it. Plus, my eyes got screwed up, because I never got a chance to focus on anything farther than a few feet away from me while my eyes were developing. And the food was pus. The doctors told Mama I'd be retarded, from malnutrition. But I'm not."

"You most certainly are not," Sam agreed readily.

Rachel folded her skinny little arms over her narrow torso. "Sveti saved me," she said. "She gave us all her fresh food. The milk, the bread, the fruit. She just starved. She was so skinny when they saved her. I'd be dead if it weren't for her."

They looked quietly at Sveti's slender form for a moment.

"Sveti thinks everyone's special enough to save," Rachel said softly. "Even the broken, messed-up ones that get put in the garbage."

He nodded. His throat was too tight to speak.

"It's stupid, for her to go to London now." Rachel's voice was rebellious. "She should stay here, where my mom and dad and the rest of them can protect her! She's crazy to leave now!"

"Couldn't agree with you more," Sam said promptly.

"She doesn't listen to you?" Rachel's tone was disapproving.

Sam shook his head.

The little girl harrumphed. "So what good are you?"

Sam choked on his laughter. "Whoa. Harsh."

Rachel sniffed. "You think that's harsh?"

Sam gazed at the young girl, who tapped her foot, looking over the tops of her thick glasses. Tam's daughter for sure, with that attitude.

Rachel blew the mop that fringed her forehead upward with a puff of breath. "So you're going to Italy with her? And then to London?"

He nodded. "That's the plan."

"You're going to be with her all the time? Every minute?"

"Like glue," he promised.

She crossed her arms, chin out. "Do you have a gun?"

"I can't take one to Europe, because of their laws, but I'll figure something out when I'm there," he said. "On my honor."

Her head tilted to the side. "You love her, right?"

The matter-of-fact question took him by surprise. When he could inhale again, the answer flew right out, as if released from a cage. "Yes," he said.

"Good," she said coolly. "That way you'll be more motivated."

Calculating, for one so young. "I wish she thought so," he said.

"Just know this." Rachel's girlish voice was hard. "You keep her safe, or it won't be just Mama and Daddy coming after you. I will, too. And I'll make them look like a couple of kittens rolling on the rug."

Sam clamped down on the urge to laugh. Rachel reminded him of exactly that. A fierce little kitten, hissing. But kittens grew. Rachel was a panther in the making. "I don't respond well to threats," he told her.

Rachel sniffed. "It's not a threat," she said. "I'm just saying."

"Thank you." He kept his mouth from twitching. "I'd put my life on the line for her. I already did, yesterday. So you know I mean it."

Rachel looked back at Sveti. "Careful if you wake her up from a nightmare," she advised. "She hits. She gave Mama a black eye once."

"Yikes," he said.

"Oh, Mama didn't care," Rachel said. "Mama's tough. That was the last time Sveti had a bad one. At least while she was here."

"Was it after her mom died?"

"When her mom was killed, you mean," Rachel corrected. "But, no, I was talking about last year, when you were in the hospital."

Sam's jaw sagged. "Huh?"

"She practically lived at Legacy Emanuel when you were in the ICU," Rachel informed him. "Mama drove down to Portland to get her when you got put into a normal room. They wouldn't let me sleep in here with her, like usual. Mama did, because of her nightmares."

His mouth was dry. "Nobody told me Sveti came to the hospital."

Rachel shrugged. "Your family didn't see her. They wouldn't have recognized her if they had. Sveti's friends with a nurse who works in the ICU. She let Sveti sit with you whenever your family wasn't there."

Sam's mouth opened and closed. Nothing came out.

"You get shot a lot, don't you?" Rachel's voice was disapproving. "Mama says it's a bad habit. The worst habit a boyfriend can have. Worse than smoking."

Hysterical laughter burst out his nose. "You could say that."

"You're no good to Sveti if you get shot. Learn to duck, okay?"

"That's the plan," he assured her.

"Okay, then. My work here is done." Rachel flounced toward the door, then turned. "Don't touch her dinner, or I'll tell Mama."

Air whooshed out of him when the door shut. He thudded down onto the couch. She'd sneaked in and sat with him in the ICU when he was unconscious? God, what a waste. If only he'd woken up in time and busted her. What he could have accomplished, with months to ruthlessly play the convalescing invalid pity card. He would've had her nailed to the wall by now. He'd have closed the deal long before this seductive Illuxit bullshit ever came onto the horizon.

But what-ifs were a waste of time.

He stripped off his shirt and climbed into the bed wearing just his jeans, curling his body around hers. Her heartbeat felt rapid and hectic, as if she were dreaming. God knows about what. Something scary.

He wished he could crawl into her dreams and do battle with the monsters there. She deserved a champion, even inside her mind. Hell, especially inside her mind. She'd stood guard while he was in extremity. He could do the same. He lay wide-eyed in the darkness. Battle ready.

It happened a couple hours into his watch. Sveti exploded into movement, wailing something in Ukrainian. Good thing Rachel had given him a heads-up, because it would have scared the living shit out of him otherwise. He parried her blows and carefully rolled on top of her, containing her body without crushing it. She thrashed and yelled.

"Sveti, Sveti, Sveti," he crooned, batting her clawed fingers away from his eyes. "Sveti, it's me. It's Sam."

Slowly, her flailing ceased, easing down to a violent tremor. "Sam?"

"Yeah, it's me." He dared, finally, to lift himself, reach to flip on a lamp. "You're safe, baby."

"Sam? Oh, God, I'm so sorry. Did I hit you?"

"Nah," he lied. "Not very much. Little kitten paws." Actually, his face smarted from the blows that had landed, but even a whack on the face from Sveti was sexually stimulating. He was really that fucked up.

He pulled her close, but she wrenched away and huddled herself into a knot. Hugging her knees, hiding her face. He'd gotten familiar with that pose by now. "Nightmare?" he asked gently. "Tell me about it."

"You don't want to know."

"Yes, actually, I do," he said. "Come on. Tell me."

He waited, stroking her back. Minutes went by. Her heart rate had eased off. He lifted her hair, exposing her face. "Tell me," he urged.

She sighed, surrendering. "From when I was taken, years ago. One of our guards, Yuri. He was foul. He stank, and he was cruel, and violent, and he . . . well. Anyway . . ." Her voice trailed off.

Sam finally prompted her. "He sexually abused you?"

She shook her head. "He wanted to. He was working up to it. But the woman who watched us, Marina . . . she held him back. There had been this other girl, back in Kiev. She'd been raped by the men who had kidnapped her. She got some disease, maybe hepatitis. She had night sweats, fevers. Anyhow, when people came to test us, they found that Aleksandra's organs were no longer viable. Big shake-up. Heads rolled."

"Jesus," he muttered. "What happened to her?"

"I don't know," she said. "I woke up, and she was gone."

"I'm so sorry, baby," he said. "That's awful."

She nodded. "That's the only reason he didn't have sex with me," she said. "Marina didn't trust him not to be HIV positive, or whatever else. But he compensated by beating me. That excited him, too."

He wound his arms around her again and squeezed her against himself. There wasn't anything to say that wasn't stupid or vapid.

"Aleksandra was the one who first explained sex to me." Her voice was bleak. "That was my introduction to it. Straight from the mouth of a twelve-year-old girl who'd been kidnapped and gangraped."

Sam hid his face against her hair.

"See what my problem is? I'm as fucked up as you might expect, considering what happened to me. You don't want to get near it, Sam."

"I'll decide that for myself, thanks."

She muttered something under her breath in Ukrainian.

"What?" he said. "What was that? Translation, please."

"You're going to destroy me," she said, turning to climb up onto his body. "You might as well at least make it worth my while."

He grabbed her hands as she reached to unfasten his fly. "No."

She froze, astonished. "What? Why not?"

It was almost impossible to articulate the weird impulse, which flew in the face of everything his body screamed for. But this imperative came from someplace even deeper. "You're just distracting yourself from the way you feel," he blurted. "Don't do that. It's a dead end."

"Dead end?" She gaped at him. "Sex with you is an end in itself!"

"Not this time," he said.

"What's wrong with just changing the subject? I thought that was good! Change the bad channel! That's what they all tell me to do!"

He wrapped his hands around the deep curve of her waist. Stroking, soothing. "Running away isn't good," he said. "You have to stay with it. Not skitter away like a marble in a pinball machine."

She tried to dismount, but he tightened his fingers on her waist. "Uh-uh," he murmured. "You're not going anywhere. Stay with it."

"So you're a therapist now?" she snapped. "You weren't there with me, Sam! You would not want to stay with what's in my head!"

"I'm sure that I wouldn't, but relax. I'm trying to be real with you, and I'm putting myself way out there, so don't punish me for it."

She shook her head, baffled. "What do you want, then? For me to dwell on it? And work myself into a state? That's stupid!"

"Tell me about the dream," he said stubbornly. "Tell me all of it."

Her face contracted. She pressed her fists against her eyes. "Oh, God, whatever," she said. "If you must know. I dream that I'm making love to you. And you turn into Yuri. Suddenly, it's Yuri on top of me."

He recoiled, instinctively. "Oh, shit. That's bad."

"Yeah, it is. It's awful. Every goddamn time."

"You've had this dream before?" He was appalled.

"Oh, yes," she said. "Ever since I started having sexual fantasies about you, Sam. Which is to say, the very first day I met you."

He jerked up onto his elbows. "Me? Why? What did I do? What, you think that I'm a—"

"Not at all." Her swift smile flashed. "Relax. You're not like Yuri at all. But I became a sexually aware person in that filthy hole, and there was Yuri, the whole time, leering at me while it happened. It marked me. I can't forget feeling helpless and vulnerable. A thing to be used. I felt so naked. I had nothing but a dirty oversized T-shirt to wear."

"But what do I have to do with that?" he demanded.

She hugged her knees, propped her chin on her arms, and pondered the question. "You make me feel vulnerable," she said.

"But I would never hurt you!"

"I know that." She put a soothing hand on his chest. "You are nothing at all like him. You're wonderful. But when I feel naked and vulnerable, Yuri comes to me. And nothing makes me feel more naked and vulnerable than you. It's very strange. Very fucked up. I'm sorry. And I have no idea if it will ever get any better. The closer I am to you, the worse it gets. Nightmares. Stress flashbacks, too. After what happened in Bruno's office two years ago, I saw Yuri everywhere. On the metro, on the bus, in the supermarket, in the library. He haunted me."

"Oh, Christ." He felt helpless. "Is that why you blew me off?"

She bit her lip and nodded.

"I wish I'd known," he said.

Sveti shrugged. "I didn't want to advertise my mental health issues to the world. Particularly not to the guy I had a huge crush on."

He stared at her slender hand, which was making delicate, stimulating circles on his chest. "Do you want me to go away?"

She jerked, as if he had stuck her with a pin. "God, no! I want you here! I want you all over me!"

"Ah. Okay." He flopped back onto his back and gazed up at the ceiling, bemused. "Wow. How did we get here, to this weird place?"

"It's all your fault, Sam," she snapped. "I was just trying to seduce you. But you refuse me. You insist on an uncomfortable conversation about my feelings and how I shouldn't avoid them. You manipulate me into telling you things that hurt your feelings and freak you out."

He rolled his eyes. "Does my ass look fat in these jeans?"

Her lips twitched, and she ran a teasing finger over the bulge in the front of his jeans. "Will you sulk if I tell you the truth? Because those jeans don't fit so well right now."

That cracked them both up. They snorted helplessly through their noses. Sveti doubled over, face in her hands.

When his own fit eased off, he pulled her hands from her face, and kissed her knuckles. He tasted tears, and licked them away. Every precious, salty, magic drop. By the time he was finished, her eyes were soft and dazzled looking, her lips soft and blurred with shaking.

"Make love to me," she whispered.

Oh, God. Please. He was the flicker of an eyelash away from just jerking his jeans down and falling on her. Taking what was his to take.

He wrestled that urge right back down into the dark, primordial ooze whence it had come. This was too goddamned important.

"No," he said gently. "You should sleep. I'll watch over you."

"I don't want to sleep, Sam," she said in a small voice. "He'll come back. I hate it. I just . . . hate this."

"He's not here," he said. "He's just a thought pattern in your mind. Those can change."

She snorted. "You make it sound so easy."

He just shook his head and twitched the cover over them. "Let's try a new technique. Go to sleep being worshipped for the spectacular goddess that you are. See if that vibe helps with your nightmares."

She giggled. "And just how do you intend to worship me?"

He smiled at her and started kissing her hands.

It was a strange revelation, like the one he'd had about her feet. He'd never noticed hands before, but now, hers had suddenly become a shining, beautiful metaphor for her body, her soul. Elegant and well-formed, slender and strong. Her hands broke his heart and blew his mind and made his cock ache. They made tears well into his eyes, too.

Fortunately, by that point, she was asleep.

He didn't stop kissing her hands even then. Let her sleep rocked in a cradle of passionate appreciation. A shield against nightmares. That strange ring Liv had given her looked good on her hand.

He just wished it was his own ring gleaming there.

CHAPTER 1 2

Sunlight strobed hypnotically through the conifers lining the highway. Sveti stared out of Sam's car. She was exhausted, in spite of the fact that she'd slept through the night with no Yuri dreams. A fact so startling, she dared not even look at it too closely. She might jinx it.

Miles and Kev were in the car behind them. Lara, Edie, and little Jon had remained behind up at Cray's Cove. This was the compromise: an armed escort, a night in Sam's family home protected by Petrie Investment Industries corporate security staff, and Miles and Kev escorting them to the airport security gates the next day. Sam had proposed the plan this morning at breakfast, and put a blessed end to the awful, grinding fight with Tam, Val, and Nick. Thank God.

"Your family is not going to be thrilled," she said. "Bringing me to their home to stay the night without permission?"

"They'll hear about it after the fact. My father and sister are in Hong Kong, my grandmother is at the ranch in Wyoming with my sister's kids. Nobody's home but the staff. And it's only one night."

Sveti's smartphone buzzed. It was Bruno, Kev's adopted brother. She punched the button. "Hey, Bruno."

"Yo, Sveti. I'm in your apartment. Lily coached me through clothes and toiletries, but where are your travel documents?"

She talked him through the gathering of her passport, credit cards, and driver's license. The deal she'd made involved not going near either her or Sam's residences, which necessitated that Bruno pack her lingerie, clothes, and makeup for her. Not ideal, but whatever.

She thanked him and ended the call. "He's got my suitcase packed," she said to Sam. "He's heading to your house."

Sam grunted. "I'd rather have him rummaging through my underwear drawer than yours."

"You don't even have an underwear drawer," she said. "Just boxes. Why is that? Do you not feel at home in that house yet?"

"I don't know. Just lazy, I guess."

"Like hell you are. Anything you think is worth doing, you do, without hesitation. Even if a bullet through your flesh comes with it."

He glanced at her, looking vaguely alarmed. "What's your point?"

"No point. Just don't try to make me underestimate you."

"Ah. Well, speaking of bullets through my flesh," he said. "Rachel told me you came to the ICU to see me, when I got shot last year."

Her stomach clenched, as if she'd been caught doing something shameful. "Of course I came to see you. I was worried. Everyone was."

"Everybody didn't come sit with me for nights on end while I was unconscious," he said. "That was just you, Sveti."

She looked at the dense wall of trees. "So? What's your point?"

"No point," he said softly. "Just saying."

He tried again after a few minutes. "Is that ring weaponized?"

"There's a tiny blade that snaps out of it," Sveti said. "It doesn't have poison or explosives or corrosive spray. But it still saved Liv's life, and Sean and Cindy's, too. It's a big deal that Liv gave it to me."

"You're not going to try taking that thing on the plane, are you?"

"Tam designed it with airline security in mind. Don't worry."

The thick, ornate ring made her hand look so delicate. "Just don't cut yourself with it," he muttered.

They arrived at the Petrie estate as dusk fell. Sveti stared around once they'd been buzzed through the gate, startled speechless. The grounds were amazing, starting from the drive through the forest, then the rolling green hills with white-fenced horse pastures and stables, leading to an enormous home on the hill built to resemble an Irish country manor in a beautifully landscaped garden.

Sam parked and handed his keys to a middle-aged man in a suit who had come out the door. "Good to see you, Mr. Petrie. Are your friends staying?"

"No, we're just the escort," Kev said, as his window buzzed down. "I'll be heading right on home, Sam, if you're good here."

"We're fine now," Sam said. "Thanks. See you tomorrow."

The interior of the house was as impressive as the exterior, but Sam didn't offer to give her a tour. He had a brief conversation with the staff about dinner, took her hand, and led her up a grand staircase. Another flight, a long corridor, and he opened the door to a large attic room paneled in natural wood. A bank of windows the entire length of the room looked out on the fading cobalt sky and tossing treetops.

Sveti dropped her bag on a chair as Sam shrugged out of his jacket. She felt weirdly shy in this alien environment. "Val's clothes look good on you," she ventured. Tam had thrown a fit this morning about Sam's foul clothes, which resulted in Val's wardrobe being raided.

"Goddamn skintight Italian designer crap," Sam growled, plucking at the shirt that strained over his shoulders. "Didn't the guy used to be a gigolo or something? He dresses like a Eurotrash fop."

"Do not say a word against Val or Tam," she blurted.

Sam looked taken aback. "I'm just talking trash about his wardrobe. I'm not judging him personally."

"The hell you're not." Out of nowhere, her chin was shaking. "Those people are everything to me. They're all I have in the world."

"Jesus, Sveti. I was just bitching about his shirt."

"Well, don't! He did you a favor. It's unbecoming to complain."

She ran for the bathroom and leaned over the sink, splashing her face. Ashamed of herself for being childish and snotty.

It had just hit her, full force. She'd been too distracted to let herself feel it, overloaded by the attack, the affair with Sam. But she was leaving her beloved family behind. She'd counted on their love and support and fierce protection for so long. What an ungrateful bitch she'd been. And after all her posturing and carrying on, all her whining tantrums about being smothered, the world suddenly seemed so big and fanged and hungry. She hadn't dared let herself feel scared or vulnerable, as if admitting that she felt it would make it more real.

It felt real now. She was pathetically glad Sam was going with her. That feeling was so dangerous. That feeling was the drum roll of doom.

She didn't dare allow herself to need him like that.

Sam dredged up some old clothes from the closets while he waited for Sveti to work through her snit. It had been years since he'd spent the night here. There was a limit to how long he could be in his father's residence without morphing into a snarling animal. Usually, he managed the problem by cutting visits off well before he approached the danger zone.

Tonight no one was here to torment him, but he still didn't like the person he became in this house. Barricaded against certain attack. Wary of hidden agendas, subtle traps and decoys. So fucking tense.

He listened for signs from the bathroom. Still nothing. He should cut her some slack. After all she'd been through, she still had to deal with his smart remarks and his perpetual boner. Being put in his place just made it stiffer, which was borderline kinky, but hey. Just the fact that the elusive, mysterious Sveti was letting him into her glorious orbit was miracle enough. Let her scold and rant and bitch.

He'd stay put, panting and hopeful. Tongue at the ready.

He stretched out driving-stiffened muscles, and the sting in his hip reminded him of the bandage. He shrugged off the shirt and dug out the bag of stuff from the pharmacy.

He positioned himself in front of the mirror on the bathroom door. Tricky spot to reach. Twisting made the scab stretch and pull. Ouch.

The door opened. Sveti stepped out. "I'll do that," she said.

"Don't worry about it," he said. "I'll get Dolores to help."

"Hell with that," Sveti said softly. "This one's mine."

He liked the sound of that. He felt claimed. At least his wound.

She'd taken off her sweater and wore a close-fitting button-down brown blouse in some clingy knit. Her low-rise jeans showed a teasing strip of taut belly. As she bent over him, the shirt dangled, opening a window to the shadowy wonders within: a flash of cleavage, a cream-colored lace bra strap, a whiff of mouth-watering scent. The mirror also offered the back view, which was dazzling in its own right.

It had been too long since they'd had sex. Twenty-four hours, and a lot of those hours had been spent holding her body in his arms with his neglected stiffie throbbing away, unappeased.

Her hair brushed over his shoulder like a flow of warm water.

Then she kissed him. A brief, butterfly touch of her lips on his cheek that left him openmouthed and stammering. "Wha... huh?"

"Sorry about my tantrum," she said. "You didn't deserve it."

He stared, jaw slack. He'd been braced for a scold, and was totally unbraced for a kiss. Her hair did another soft, liquid swish. Then she started peeling off the bandage, and he started hissing obscenities.

"It's messy, but it doesn't look infected," she commented.

He twisted to take a look at the oozing slash. "There's cotton and gauze and antibiotic ointment in the bag."

She cleaned it, patted it dry, dabbed antibiotics down its length. This activity gave him an excellent view into the secret wonderland inside her shirt. He wanted to crawl in there and just stay.

He hooked his finger into her belt. Pulled her upright.

"Sam," she murmured. "Let me finish. I have to tape you up."

"Go ahead." He pressed his nose against the vee of petal-smooth skin above her shirt, savored the springy heft of her luscious breasts with his lips. Her nipples tightened to sharp points. Oh, yeah.

He cupped her ass, dragged her closer with a hungry growl.

Sveti reached down and stubbornly continued taping down the gauze, but he could feel that high-frequency thrum of bright energy building in her body, sparkling against his face, buzzing beneath his greedy, stroking hands.

She fumbled to finish, her fingers caressing the tape flat. Every stroke a tingling promise. Mmm. He liked the ministering angel routine.

The tube of antibiotic gel thudded onto the bed. Her hands rested on his bare shoulders. Her nails bit in. Fingers shaking.

He dragged in her scent the way a guy about to go underwater would drag in air. "I like that bra," he said. "Open your shirt. Show me."

A swift jerk would have done it, but he wanted those doors to open from within, flung wide and willing. Sweet surrender. That hot blush, that dazzled look. He wanted her soft and sopping wet. So he petted, stroked, nuzzled. And waited. Time measured by heartbeats.

She put her hands to the buttons. Fumbling, clumsy and shy.

The bravery and trust of that gesture humbled him, knowing what he knew about her. The hell she'd been through. She still trusted him.

It made him feel thick and stupid. Tearful, even. Ready to fling himself at her feet, make some grand, stupid-ass gesture to move her, charm her, win her. Of course, nothing so clever came to him. All he could do was press his face against her chest. Fighting for control.

When the hot fog had receded, he tugged the stretchy lace down, tucking it under the curve of her tits until they jutted proudly from a lacy harness. So sweet and full, those tips pert and inviting, the pearly undercurve flushed pink. He slid his hand up between her legs, petting her hot core through her jeans. She moaned as he tongued her nipple, sucking it slowly into his mouth. He lashed it, delicately. His tongue was a fine-tipped paintbrush, and he was painting a holy masterpiece that would endure for all time on the canvas of her sweet, perfect body.

She shivered, clutching his shoulders, then his hip. Her hand skittered nervously away from the bandage, with an incoherent apology.

"It's okay," he muttered. "Oh, God, Sveti. Lose the jeans. Please."

Her hands went to her belt—and a knock sounded. *Rat-tat-tat.*

They leaped apart. Sveti frantically rearranged her bra, buttoned her shirt. *Tat-tat-tat* again. Hard, rapid, imperious. The staff would not knock like that. In fact, the staff would not knock at all. He grabbed his gun, though anyone he would need to use it against would probably not be the knocking type. "Who's there?"

"Your father," said a chill, disapproving voice.

Sam froze. His gun hand dropped. No way. He'd called Martin, the head of security, last night. His father was in Hong Kong for the rest of the week.

Well, fuck it. He got up and opened the door.

Richard Petrie stood there, arms folded. Tall, silver-haired, distinguished. His sealed mouth and pinched nostrils said what he was too restrained to voice about his rebellious son, but he'd verbalize it soon enough. It always sneaked out somehow.

"Hey, Dad," Sam said, resigned. "I thought you were in Hong Kong."

"Counting on it, I expect?"

Sam stoically ignored that. "They said you'd be back next week."

His father's eyes flicked over Sam's chest. "Why are you half naked?" His gaze fell on the Glock, and his lip curled. "Sam. Must you?"

"This?" Sam held up the gun. "Yeah, as a matter of fact, I must."

His father leaned forward and caught sight of Sveti. He scowled. "Was I interrupting something?"

"Nothing we can't get back to later. Why are you back early?"

"Put that thing down. It's not necessary to play cops and robbers here." His father's gaze fastened on Sveti. She was as composed as ever, though he could sense the subtle get-me-the-fuck-out-of-here vibes coming off her, thick and fast. His father's gaze flicked away from her.

"What's wrong with your hip?" he asked abruptly.

Sam braced himself. "You know me. Accident prone."

His father made a disgusted sound. "Put on a shirt, for the love of God. You look like a car wreck. A fresh wound, to add to your collection. My compliments, Sam. Well done."

"He got that wound saving my life," Sveti said.

His father looked at her, startled. Sveti gazed right back, her big golden brown eyes bright and very direct. "And you are?" he asked.

"Dad, this is Svetlana Ardova, a friend of mine," Sam said. "Sveti, this is my father, Richard Petrie."

Sveti did not mouth pleasantries. His dad met her glare for glare.

"I was not speaking to you," he informed her, icily.

Her chin went up. "I speak when it pleases me."

This was going south at warp speed. He hastened to intervene. "So, uh, Dad. What brought you back so early?"

Sveti crossed her arms over her tits, zapping Richard Petrie with a death-ray look, as if she wasn't facing down a billionaire financier whose ass was kissed by everyone. Except for his wayward son.

"You're the reason I'm back early," his father said. "I learned you'd been in another deadly shootout involving the Chinese mob and a half-drowned prostitute."

Sveti's eyes narrowed. "What half-drowned prostitute is that?"

"The one from the escort service you called. My investigator took pictures." He clicked on his phone and handed it to Sam.

It was a shot of Sveti in the evening gown, tottering up his steps. Lit up in the porch-light's glare, she looked so exotic and out of context, he could see why she'd be mistaken for a call girl. Sveti glanced at the picture and maintained a sphinxlike silence. Taking the high road.

"You've got it wrong," Sam said. "An investigator? Seriously?"

His father grunted. "We booked a flight immediately when we heard. Your grandmother as well. Dinner will be served in half an hour. Your companion can stay up here. Your sister and your aging grandmother do not need to meet her. Dolores can bring up a tray."

"Sveti's been a friend of mine for years, Dad," he said. "Her life is in danger. I brought her here for the night because I trust your team. I thought we'd be no trouble, because you were out of town."

"Protection from whom? Her pimp?"

"She's not a call girl, Dad," Sam said through his teeth. "Don't say that again. I'll come down to dinner, but Sveti comes with me."

His father looked like something had curdled in his mouth. "Bring her, if you must. Explain her to your grandmother, who turned eighty-seven last week, by the way. She could have used a phone call. You've been sulking for months, and she misses you. Don't be late, please."

His father marched out, closing the door smartly.

Sam listened to footsteps recede, trying to breathe. Everything just got way more complicated than he'd bargained for. "Sorry," he said.

"It's not your fault," she said. "But is it true, about not having seen your eighty-seven-year-old grandmother in months?"

He gave her a narrow look. "Don't you dare judge me right now."

"I'm not judging," she said. "But I have a lot of bitter experience with this. Death comes without warning. And it's very final."

"I lost my mother when I was fifteen," he said. "I know about the finality of death."

She was quiet for a few moments, eyes downcast. "I'm so sorry," she murmured. "You go on down to dinner. I'll stay here. I'm not hungry anyway. Being taken for a sex worker killed my appetite."

"No way. You're coming with me. He has to get used to this."

"Used to what?"

"Us," he said bluntly.

Sveti had that terrified look in her eyes again, the one that always came over her when he dared to invoke a possible future with her.

Too fucking bad. He was sick of backing down, pussyfooting around it. There was no way this woman was getting away from him. The sooner she understood that, the better for everyone concerned.

"Sam . . . I don't think you should . . . now is not the time to—"

"Now is the only time," he said, grim and relentless. "Start learning to tolerate my family. You're going to need the practice."

CHAPTER 13

"Hollandaise sauce, Svetlana?"

Sam's older sister Connie's voice was artificially bright and sweet as she held up the sauce boat. She was a pretty woman, tall and statuesque, with long, gleaming chestnut hair.

Svetlana murmured her thanks and held up her plate to have buttery sauce drizzled over her blanched asparagus. Sam and his father glared stonily at each other, over an abyss of silence. All attempts to break the silence sounded weak. Baby birds, cheeping in the void.

Connie gamely tried again. "So, Svetlana. Do you, ah, have a green card?"

Sveti smiled behind her napkin as she dabbed at her lips. "No," she said. "I have a passport. I've been an American citizen for years. I went to high school in Washington, on the coast, where my adoptive family lives. After that, I went to the University of Washington."

"An American success story!" Sam's grandmother, Moira, seized eagerly upon the new topic. "Like us! Augustus Petrie crossed the Atlantic in seventeen-ninety in search of opportunity. And he found it."

"Have you found yours, Svetlana?" Sam's father asked. "Or are you still looking?"

The question felt like a trap, so she chose her words carefully. "Yes, certainly. I've been very fortunate in the friends I've made here."

"It must have broken your parents' hearts to have you go so far away, though," Moira said. "What does your father do, dear?"

"He was a police investigator," she said. "He's been gone for many years now. He died in the line of duty."

"Oh, I'm sorry," Moira said, blinking rapidly. "And your mother?"

"I lost her, too, six years ago," Sveti said.

"Tragedy at every turn." Richard forked up a bite of salmon.

"Watch it, Dad," Sam said.

"A tale of woe calculated to bring out your pathological hero complex," his father said. "Orphaned by a bullet, eh? Classic."

"He was disemboweled, actually," Sveti said.

Connie's fork clattered on her plate. They stared at the fish, which had been opened, filleted, and sprinkled with herbs and almonds.

Constance's chair screeched as she shoved it back. She scurried out of the room with her hand on her mouth.

Sam's father swallowed his mouthful with an audible gulp, and coughed. "I beg your pardon?"

"He was undercover, investigating a mafiya boss," Sveti explained. "He was betrayed. It ended badly."

Sam's father wiped his mouth. "Dramatic."

"Yes, it was." Sveti was unfazed by his tone. He thought she was making this up. If only. What she wouldn't give to have it be untrue.

"I'm surprised after such trauma that you would want anything to do with someone in police work," Richard Petrie said.

She glanced at Sam. "I'm surprised, too," she admitted.

"Not that I'm in police work," Sam said. "You've killed that."

The senior Petrie did not deny it. "No one could blame a father from trying to keep his son from destroying himself!"

"I'm blaming you anyway," Sam said.

"Calm down," Moira soothed. "Sam, have some more potatoes."

"Do you care to explain what you were doing on the six o'clock news? Putting fresh cadavers in the morgue?" Richard demanded.

"They were torturing her." He indicated Sveti. "I objected. That was how they came to be cadavers."

Connie came back and sat down carefully at the table, still very pale, and with a shiny forehead.

Richard turned to Sveti. "Why did these people attack you, if I may ask?"

Sveti took a sip of wine. "I'm not exactly sure."

Petrie, Sr. looked down his nose at her. "Oh, really."

It took talent, to load just three syllables with such a quantity of contempt and disbelief. Sveti reminded herself that this man's opinion meant nothing, changed nothing. "Really," she affirmed. "My prime theory is that they want information my mother was gathering when she was murdered. I don't have it, but they think I do."

"Dear God." Moira put down her fork and pressed her napkin to her mouth. "Your mother, too? Spare us the details this time, dear."

"They could also be a local gang who traffic people from China for slave labor," Sveti said. "I inconvenienced some of them last year. They weren't pleased." She shrugged. "Who knows."

"Ah." Richard turned to Sam. "I see that your choice in lady friends is as colorful and haphazard as your other life choices."

"I try, Dad," Sam said. "Always."

"So, Sam, dear," Moira interjected, with false cheerfulness. "Let's look to the future, shall we? Do you have any plans?"

"Yes, I'm going to the airport tomorrow," he replied. "I'm starting my new career. In Italy. With Sveti."

His father blinked. "Excuse me? Italy? What new career?"

"I'm going as her bodyguard." Sam stuck a forkful of salmon in his mouth as that grenade bounced and rolled into the enemy camp.

"But . . . but that's insane!" his father said. "Bodyguarding?"

"Her life is in danger," Sam said. "She needs protection. And my career prospects are ever narrowing, thanks to you. Bodyguarding is more interesting than private investigating. Following cheating spouses and wayward sons around. Big yawn. I'd be good at forensic accounting, but it would bore me into an early grave. I could join the military, I guess, if they'd have me. As beat-up and long in the tooth as I am."

His father's mouth was white. There were dents beside his nostrils. "You'd truly go to such lengths just to spite me?"

Sam shook his head. "No, I'm going to Italy because I want to. But I would prefer it if you kept your tentacles out of my professional life."

"What will you be doing in Italy, Svetlana?" Connie broke in.

Sveti briefly explained about the conference in San Anselmo, the award ceremony, and the London job.

"Martin," the senior Petrie called. "Bring me my tablet, please."

The uniformed server passed it to him. The older man poised the little pen over the keyboard. "The name of the organization? I'd love to see the announcement for this award. Congratulations, by the way."

Sveti gazed at him. "Are you trying to catch me in a lie?"

Petrie blinked innocently behind his glasses. "If the shoe fits."

"It doesn't," she said. "Look up the Tran-Global Business Organization against Human Trafficking, and this year's Solkin Prize."

"Better yet." Sam plucked the tablet and pen out of his father's hands, tapped the flat-screen keyboard. "Watch the reason she's getting this prize. It's because she has a set of solid brass balls. She busted a sweatshop slavery ring single-handedly, right here in Portland."

"Good Lord." The elder Petrie scowled at the tablet with distaste.

"Oh, Sam," Sveti murmured, alarmed. "Really? Now? At dinner?"

"He should know who he's dealing with," Sam said stubbornly.

Connie and Moira leaned forward to watch the video clip, curious, but Sam's father pushed the tablet away, his lips very thin. "Later for this, if you don't mind. I would like to finish my dinner in peace."

Sam shoved his chair back. "True to form," he said, as he got up. "You always cut people off before they have a chance to get to the point. That way you never risk having to change your mind."

He stalked out of the room, to Sveti's dismay. She got up to follow.

"No! Leave him," Richard snapped. "There's no point, until he's had his sulk, and who knows how long that will take. Years, maybe."

"Dad!" Constance shot Sveti an embarrassed glance. "Sorry," she added. "My father and Sam tend to bring out the worst in each other."

"It's so frustrating for Richard, you see," Moira confided. "Sam is so gifted. And I don't just say that because I am his grandmother. His grasp of finance was . . . well, almost magical, his professors and mentors said. He shocked people with what he could do."

"He was already at it back in high school." Connie had a harder edge to her voice. "Sam the wunderkind. He interned with a hedge fund when he was sixteen one summer, and earned them twenty-two million dollars in a single weekend, just messing around. Taking risks he was not authorized to take. But he got lucky." Her tone indicated that she considered this ability to be entirely wasted upon her brother.

"He sees patterns, you see," Moira explained. "Other people just see a mass of data, but Sam sees connections, shapes, trends."

"He could have gone anywhere," Richard said bitterly. "Any bank or brokerage firm in the world would have paid him top dollar. He could have started his own company. Or had mine. The whole world flung itself at his feet, and what did he do?" His voice shook with old anger.

The woman Sam had called Dolores came in, bearing what appeared to be chocolate mousse cake, drizzled with raspberry sauce.

"I don't know, actually," Sveti admitted, as the woman served her.

"He threw it away!" Richard thundered. "He switched his major from economics to criminal psychology, his last year in college! After graduation, he applied for a job at the Police Bureau! As a patrol officer!"

Dolores froze, tray in one hand, plate in the other. Eyes wide.

"And he made detective after only a few years, right?" Sveti pointed out. "I'm sure this ability to see patterns is what makes him such a gifted investigator. It's not like he joined a motorcycle gang."

"You saw his scars!" Richard bellowed. "Do you know how close he's come to being killed? And all this just to spite me! To punish me!"

"Dad," Connie said. "Don't yell, please. You're embarrassing us."

"And now, he wants to chase some seductive little chippie across the world!" He raked her with a scathing gaze. "Bodyguarding? Unpaid, I expect? I hope for his sake that you intend to make it worth his while."

"Mr. Petrie," she said, her voice quiet. "That is enough."

Richard Petrie got up and walked stiffly out of the room.

Dolores hastily finished putting down the plates of cake. "I'll get the espresso," she mumbled, scurrying out.

In the silence, Connie and Moira's attention was drawn once more to the sound of the video clip Sam had set to play on the tablet. Sveti leaned over to see what was happening in it. Oh, dear. One of the young women was about to show the camera the festering welts on her back, from having been savagely beaten with electrical wire. Sveti pressed 'pause' and met the two women's questioning gaze with a smile.

"Not before dessert," she said gently.

Sam opened the bedroom door and stepped inside. Sveti sat cross-legged on the bed, tablet glowing in front of her. She wore gray jersey pajamas and a tank top. Bland, cheap stuff that turned Grecian goddess graceful when draped over that regally upright body.

He closed the door. "I'm sorry," he said. "That was bad."

"It's okay," she said. "I'm tough."

He looked down at the tablet. "What are you doing with that?"

"I just told Hazlett and his assistant about my arrival tomorrow."

His heart rate kicked up violently. "Are you fucking kidding me?"

She looked up, big-eyed and startled. "What? Sam, the guy is my future employer! I don't consider him a security risk!"

"Maybe not him, but your own e-mail account might be!"

"But I have to communicate with them!" she protested. "I'll miss most of the conference! I was supposed to be on two panels tomorrow!"

"You're missing the panels because you almost got killed," he said through his teeth. "Please. Keep your priorities in order."

She tapped at the keyboard, hair swinging forward to hide her face. "I'm sorry. I wasn't thinking. I should have said something to you."

"Damn right, you should have." He was perversely irritated at her for having apologized too quickly, since he wasn't done being scared and pissed yet. "I hope you're not tweeting about your trip. It's a good bet your would-be killers are following your Twitter feed."

"I'm not an idiot, Sam. I just sent the message to Nadine, and checked the account where Sasha and I message each other. That's all."

"Sasha?" He was bewildered. "You mean Alex Aaro? He messages you?"

Sveti snorted at the mention of one of the McCloud Crowd's most prickly and reclusive companions in adventure. "God, no. I would never presume to call Aaro by a nickname. Only Nina can do that. And Tam, when she's being provocative."

"Which is always," he commented.

Sveti's lips twitched. "I'm talking about my friend Sasha. The one who was imprisoned with me and Rachel by the organ traffickers."

Sam's lungs froze. "Oh, fuck me. Aleksandr Cherchenko? The son of Pavel Cherchenko, the head of the Ukrainian crime syndicate?"

She frowned. "Yes, the very one."

"You're chatting, online, with the son of a mafiya vor?" His voice had risen to a hoarse bellow. "Do you have a death wish?"

"Calm down!" she snapped back. "Sasha is my closest friend! We went through hell together! We trust each other absolutely!"

"Is he smart enough to cover his tracks? Doesn't he shoot up heroin? Val said he's a junkie! You think he's completely on top of it?"

Sveti's lips tightened. "Val should not talk about that. Sasha's had problems with drugs, yes. Who could blame him, after what happened?"

"Let's not even start," Sam said grimly. "That's a classic dead-end conversation if I ever heard of one."

"Fine," she said crisply. "Sasha and I have an e-mail account. We leave messages for each other in the drafts folder. No one else knows."

"How do you know? Someone could be logging his keystrokes! What exactly have you told him?"

"Sam, please. Calm down. I didn't tell him—"

"Do you have any idea how easily what you do online can be monitored? Every last tiny fucking thing!"

"Don't yell at me! I haven't written anything tonight except a message to Hazlett's assistant, Nadine! I was only checking Sasha's account because I was expecting a message from him!"

"Yeah?" He tried to slow down his breathing. "Why is that?"

"Because I sent him my TED talk ten days ago! We had a big fight about it, months ago, when I was preparing the lecture."

"Why?" he demanded.

"He said I was crazy to drag that old stuff up and trot it around. He got kind of hysterical about it, actually. It was weird."

"Huh. So he has some sense. More than you do, that's for sure."

Sveti's mouth was tight. "I told him that burying the past doesn't help you rise above it. I promised I'd come see him, when I got to Rome, first thing. Before going to San Anselmo."

"You did *what?*" he bellowed. "Holy fucking *shit!*"

Her hands whipped up to cover her ears. "God, Sam, don't do that! It's not his fault, what happened to him, or whose son he is! No one gets to pick! I trust Sasha with my life! And I love him!"

"Love him?" He was breathing heavily, as if he were running a race. "Define 'love,' Sveti."

Her gaze flickered away. "Not that way. Like a brother, I mean."

He could breathe again. "So did he answer you? Where's the rendezvous point with this soul brother of yours? Did he answer you?"

She hesitated, not meeting his eyes. Staring down at the tablet. "Yes," she said. "He said, please come as soon as possible. That he needs me. And he asked about my flight info. That's all he said."

He braced himself. "And you gave it to him?"

She shook her head. "I haven't responded yet. It seemed . . . odd. He didn't mention the lecture, or scold me for going through with it."

"Does he scold you a lot?"

"Not as much as you do," she said tartly. "But it doesn't matter. I'll just go to the house in Rome and talk to him directly."

"Ah. Okay. How about we just write our obituaries right now, and save our families the trouble?"

"I've been there before, Sam," she said wearily. "Three years ago, with Tam and Val. I left in one piece. Pavel Cherchenko has no issues with me. All I ever did was be his son's friend. Sasha even visited me for a couple of months in the States, before Mama died. I was hoping he'd stay, but his father made him go back when they went to Italy."

"Sveti, why don't you just call the guy?" he demanded. "Ask him how the fuck he is and be done with it!"

"Sasha can't talk into the phone," she explained. "He stopped speaking while we were locked up, and it never really came back. Even now, it's very difficult for him. He can only talk easily to me in person, or to his brother, Misha. He loves that kid. Says he's a genius with computers."

Oh, that was just fucking great. So the guy was a mute, too. Sam fought to keep his voice even. "How the hell did you communicate with him back then, if he couldn't talk?"

She shrugged. "I don't know, but we did. Sign language, eye contact, mind reading. When I saw him in Rome . . ." She shook her head. "He was like a ghost. Like when we were locked up. It's so hard, Sam, to come back to the real world. He never really made it back."

"You came back," Sam pointed out. "I've never heard you blaming anybody, or taking drugs because of the pain."

"I made it most of the way," she said quietly. "I was luckier. I had my friends to show me how to be strong. Sasha was all on his own."

Sam reached down and spun the tablet around to look at the message, still open in the e-mail account. Just two lines of Cyrillic.

"Don't go to Italy," he said, though he knew it wasn't any use.

"I won't think any less of you for it. And your family would weep for joy."

She looked up at him. "And do what, Sam?"

"Hide," he said promptly. "I'll help you. I'll hide with you. I'll stick to you like airplane glue. Don't go."

Sveti closed the tab on the browser. "I'm not being stubborn for the sake of being stubborn," she said. "I see your point, and I know it's valid. But I know something else, too. If I let them put me on the run, I'll run until they kill me. It's like running from an angry dog. The dog has no choice but to pursue. It's his nature to chase and maul you."

"Not if the dog doesn't find you," he said.

"And live my life hiding from angry dogs? Letting them define my existence, my actions, my choices?" She let her twisted hands fall open. "That's prison, Sam. I've been in prison. I won't go back. I'd rather die."

That jolted him, nastily. "Don't say that."

"I'm going to find Sasha," she went on. "I'm going to find Renato, to ask about Mama. I'm going to speak at the banquet and receive my award. I'm going to run at this thing head-on, screaming and waving my arms. I'm following my instincts. They've kept me alive so far."

"Actually, no," he said. "The other day, it was not your instincts that kept you alive, Sveti. It was me."

"Yes," Sveti said. "It was you. And thank you."

"I wasn't fishing for thanks," he said. "I was making a point."

"Point taken. But I still have to go. Sasha's my responsibility. Don't feel compelled to go with me, if you can't support my—"

"Stop," he said. "Hold it right there. Don't even say it. There are no circumstances under which I would let you go to Italy alone, and you know that perfectly well. You know how I feel about you, and you are exploiting it. You are jerking me around, Sveti. Without mercy."

"Oh, God, Sam." Her shoulders slumped in a rare moment of weariness. "That's not true. But I'm so sorry you see it that way."

"It's weird," he went on. "You're so brave about everything else. You'll run straight at this, waving your arms, here I come, you pussy motherfuckers. But you won't take that kind of crazy chance on us."

Her eyes were wide, and trapped looking. "Sam, I—"

"I want you to run at me like that. No retreat, no excuses, no prisoners. Bowl me over, mow me down, blow my mind. Why do only bad guys get that turbo-charged mojo from you? Where's my share?"

"I don't understand how to be what you want!" she wailed.

"You've got a mistaken idea of how it's supposed to feel," he said. "What, you think you're not supposed to feel scared? It's the human condition! It's not specific to you! We all feel it, unless we medicate it. You're afraid of pain and loss and death? Get over it! Join the club! If you wait until you don't feel scared, you'll wait into your grave!"

She looked up, eyes hot. "Do not tell me how to feel, Sam."

"I'm not telling you. I'll show you. Take off your clothes."

She rolled her eyes. "Oh, please. Give me a break."

"Really. Your body knows what you want. Let it show you."

"No," she said sharply. "You are so arrogant."

"Not arrogant," he corrected. "Purposeful. Focused. You know damn well I'll make it good for you."

They stared at each other. "Come on, Sveti," he coaxed. "Put my arrogant ass right back in its place. If you have the nerve."

She gave him a long, appraising look and shook her head. "You're too angry right now. At me, your father. Everyone."

The red fog intensified. His hands fisted. "You're afraid of me?"

"Not at all," she said. "But the answer is still no."

Fuck it. He would never understand how that chick's mind worked. He yanked his clothes off. Slid into the bed, turning his back.

Sveti puttered around for a few minutes, then flipped off the light and slipped into the bed beside him. She cuddled against his back. The contact refreshed his long-suffering boner right back up to full salute.

"What happened to your mother, Sam?" she asked softly.

"Lymphoma," he said. "I was fifteen."

She was quiet for a moment. "I'm so sorry."

He nodded. "It was bad. My dad's been under constant attack ever since her funeral, being one of the richest eligible widowers on the planet. But he stays true to her memory. He was so angry when she got sick. Her cancer didn't care how much money he had, or who he knew. It made him frantic. It was the first time in his life that he ran into something that he couldn't control."

"Not the last time, though," Sveti said. "He can't control you."

"Yeah, right," he snorted. "Me and cancer. We're par."

"You and your father are very similar," she said. "So intense."

He laughed, harsh and mirthless. "Not. I could have been the high king of world finance, they like to say. Like him, only more so. Bet they told you that when I stepped out of the dining room, right?"

"Yes, actually," she admitted. "They said something like that."

"They've got this family myth about my tragic lost potential. Carrying on about my wasted prospects makes them feel better. But it's all crap. I'm not like him. Not at all."

"No? Then why did you change your major? Why not become the high king of finance? Did you hate it?"

Sam closed his eyes, groping for buried memories. It felt as if he were talking about another person, not himself. "No," he said. "I didn't hate it. It was kind of great, actually. So was the attention I got for it. Pull a bunch of money out of your ass, and the whole world wants to suck your dick. It was hard to resist, particularly after Mom died. It was a hell of a distraction. And we were all so fucking miserable at home."

"But you did resist, in the end," she said. "Why?"

He lay there, pondering the question. He'd never actually analyzed the motives for his choices before. He preferred action to reflection, at least when it came to his own life. But he didn't want to bat Sveti away.

She deserved better than that, whether he had it to give or not.

"It was the summer before senior year," he said. "I went to a party off-campus. There was a girl, Elaine. A friend of mine. Funny, smart. She got drunk, or someone slipped something into her beer, which is more likely, because she claimed she only drank one beer.

Some guys carried her upstairs and raped her while she was unconscious."

Sveti made a pained, wordless sound.

"They wrote demeaning comments on her body with felt-tip pens. Insert breast implants here, do liposuction there. That kind of thing."

"Oh, God," Sveti whispered. "How awful."

"Yeah, she had to leave school. Spent some time in the psych ward. Tried to kill herself. It was bad. The police did what they could, but she'd been out cold, so no witnesses." He paused as he pulled it from his memory. "I was so angry. I couldn't go to class, or work on my thesis. I just obsessed about who could have done it. I went around talking to everyone who'd been at that party, their roommates and friends. I recorded what they said, what they didn't say. Spent my nights staring at the ceiling, hashing it over, until it started organizing itself. I targeted the likeliest assholes. Got them to my apartment. We weren't friends, but I spoke their language. I got them drunk and stoned. Led them on. One of them started boasting. I caught it all on my recorder. He named the other two."

"Wow," she said softly. "Your very first criminal investigation."

"Didn't help Elaine much. She appreciated the effort, but she still lives at home with her folks. No love life, no job. But it sure helped me."

She dug her fingers into his shoulders and tugged until he finally turned around to face her. The look in her eyes made his face go warm.

"That was a great thing to have done," she said.

He was abashed. "It felt real. More real than money games, or economic theory. For the first time in my life, I really gave a shit. It was a whole new level of being connected. I saw my future self, stuck inside my own swelled head, in a penthouse apartment. Fancy cars, expensive girlfriends, getting my ass kissed. I compared that to how I felt when I watched the police cuff those dickheads in front of their own frat house. There was just no comparison. At all."

"Did you ever tell your father this?" she asked.

"I think I tried, but he never made it to the punch line. He just saw it as rebellion. But it was more like . . . redemption."

The space Sveti opened up with her smiling, radiant silence felt safe, protected, giving rise to thoughts he usually would not let himself think, and then to even deeper ones, spiraling up and surprising him.

"I heard this old song once," he said. "How you've got to serve somebody. Good or evil, you have to choose. Whatever you do is always in the service of something. I didn't know whose service I was in when I played with money, but I knew who I served when I nailed the assholes who hurt Elaine. It felt more right than anything ever had. Until now."

Her eyes went wide and wary. "What's now?"

"You," he said.

She jerked up onto her elbow, looking vaguely alarmed. "What does that mean? That's what this is all about for you? Serving a cause?"

"Nope," he said. "No cause, Sveti. Just you."

"I don't get it," she said hastily. "I don't know what you mean."

"Maybe not," he mused. "You never had to awaken to it, because you've never been asleep. It comes to you so naturally, you can't even see it. Ask the fish what the ocean is. Ask Sveti what service is. You can't answer. It's just who you are."

She shook her head. "You've idealized me, Sam. I'm not so altruistic as that. I can be as vain and silly and superficial as anyone."

"Sure you can, babe," he said quietly. "Sure."

"So . . . so you just want me because I'm this freakish martyr?"

He smiled. "Don't even try to twist this around on me. You're the most beautiful thing I've ever seen on this earth. I can't stop trying to get close to you. I won't be chased away. You make me feel like I did when I woke up from my money dream. The world was so loud. Everything looked so bright. Things meant more. I love that feeling."

"I don't want to be a symbol for somebody," she said nervously.

"Fuck symbols," he said. "Be my lover. Be my lady."

She hugged her knees to her chest for a long moment, and then suddenly sat up and peeled her tank top off. His heart raced as she pulled off the pants, her underwear. "You said, when you were in your money dream, everyone wanted to suck your dick," she said.

"Uh, yeah. I did." His dick, happy at being nominated, twitched and jumped. Sveti pulled the coverlet back from his naked body and seized his throbbing cock in her hand. Stroking, twirling. Oh, man.

"What does it for me is hearing how you woke up," she said.

"Oh, Sveti," he said shakily, as she slid down his body.

He flung his head back and gasped sharply as she sucked his cock into her mouth. Oh. So. *Good.* Hot, wet, and eager, that sweet pull and clutch and glide, the teasing swirl of her clever tongue. Licking, hand-twisting. She sucked him in deeper, harder, with long, beautiful mouth-fucking strokes. Deep-throating him. Her luscious mouth clasping him was so pretty. Eyes closed, cheeks pink. Wild, sensual abandon.

"I'm on to you," he said hoarsely. "You're trying to distract me, just like always. I throw my heart at your feet, and you distract me with a blow job. Not fucking fair, Sveti."

She lifted her head. "Do you want me to stop?"

He shook his head, helplessly. She bent down to the task again.

She brought him close to coming, but he just made an incoherent pleading sound in his throat, held her still, and breathed as the throbbing pulses of a dry orgasm shuddered through him.

She lifted her head. "Don't you want to come?"

"I am coming. Just without ejaculating. It's great. You tired?"

"God, no," she said with a soft laugh. "I love it."

"It's awesome," he told her. "But I want to come in your pussy."

She clambered up over his body. He positioned his cock beneath her, nudging and prodding it into place. They sighed and moaned together as she took him inside. That swelling surge of mutual pleasure.

She settled onto him, seeking the angle, the rhythm. Finding it quickly. He pumped up into her body, twining her fingers with his. "Be my lady," he said again. Because he just could not fucking stop himself.

The feelings flashed over her face. Longing, fear. Grief. He could see that she wanted it. She just didn't believe she could actually have it.

She cupped his face. "I'll give you everything I have to give."

He stopped moving. "Another brush-off? We can't get past this?"

"Does this feel like a brush-off to you?"

"Yeah, it does. I know your tricks." He lifted her, sliding out.

Sveti gripped his upper arms, in a panic. "Don't," she pleaded. "Don't leave me like this. I need to feel you come inside me. Please."

He squeezed his eyes shut, against the fog of hurt, and anger, and lust. Bombs, set to detonate on every level of his being.

"From behind," he said. "Turn around. If you want it."

"But I . . . but . . ."

"Or not," he said. "I cannot stare into your eyes while I come and then have you shove me away again. Your choice."

It took her a few seconds, but she was as jacked up as he was. She scrambled off, turned. Got on her hands and knees.

Sam gripped her waist, nudging her thighs wider, and slid his cock slowly, deeply inside her sweet, tight wet heat, and oh, God, he'd been fooling himself if he thought that switching positions was going to make it any easier to balance on this fucking tightrope.

"Sam, I'm not shoving you away," she said "I'm just—"

"Enough talk," he said hoarsely. "Let's finish this."

It didn't matter that she couldn't see his face. She could feel everything he was in the tight, shaking grip of his hands. Every stroke jolted him deeper into that lost, unmoored place in his mind. No lies or secrets, just burning ardor, driving them up to the edge—

And beyond.

CHAPTER 14

The only good thing about this ungodly hour of the morning was that Sam didn't risk running into his family. He prodded Sveti out of bed in time for a shower and coffee. Miles and Kev arrived right on time.

At the airport, Sam grabbed Sveti's arm when she made a move toward the check-in kiosks to print out their boarding passes.

"Not here," he said. "We're getting new tickets."

"What? I just bought these yesterday! They're not refundable!"

"You've been on that manifest for a full day, and you babbled about the flight times online," he said. "We're taking a different flight, routed through a different airport. There's one that leaves a half hour later, routed through London. We'll take that one."

"I did not babble! I sent one e-mail! This is so *wasteful!*"

He pulled her up to the ticket counter, flanked by Kev and Miles.

Sveti overheard his conversation with the ticket agent, of course.

"First class?" she exploded. "Last minute? You're joking, right?"

Sam turned to her. "I am in a serious fucking mood, Sveti," he said through his teeth. "Do not fight me right now. You will lose."

Sveti's face was hot pink. "At least let me pay for my own!"

Sam pushed her card back. "It wasn't your decision. I pay."

"It's safer," Kev offered cautiously. "It's exactly what I would do."

"Me too," Miles said, still sweeping the crowd with his eyes.

Sveti fumed all the way down to the security gate, but once there, she mellowed out enough to hug Miles and Kev.

"Thanks, you guys," she said, voice quivering. "For everything."

"For what? I didn't get to shoot anyone. Or even thrash anyone." Kev sounded disgruntled. "It would have been a privilege to pound on any piece of shit who messed with you, sweetheart. You take care now."

Sam herded Sveti through the airport security routine. Tablets, phones, laptops. Liv's ring clattered into a plastic basin and went through the X-ray machine without a hiccup. Hell and damn.

He started to breathe a little easier when every passenger had filed past, observed and X-rayed by his eyes as they passed. Sveti was tucked into her window seat, and the plane doors were shut. Ahhh.

She was still sulking about his alpha dog posturing. They'd been tense with each other ever since the soul-baring sex last night. His umpteenth declaration of undying passion. He had to scale those back.

At this point, she could barely look him in the eye.

She put her earbuds on as soon as they got under way. He was dismissed. Just as well, as he could use a little downtime. Before they had left Tam and Val's house, he'd scanned the photos of Sveti's parents and a translation of Sonia's letter. He took the documents out to study. Sweet relief, to throw himself into data crunch mode.

He'd compiled a list of lenses through which he'd looked at them. Poets' dates of birth, dates the poems were published, stanzas in which the lines appeared, etc. He'd read all the historical context. Nada.

But he could feel the puzzle's desire to be solved. It was a subtle quality of energy, pulsing, trapped, and wanting to flow free. He was attracted to it. That was why he was a detective. Hell, that was probably one of the reasons he was nuts for Sveti. That woman was a knot needing to be untied if ever there was one.

Sveti had caught the thought wave. She glanced over at him as if he'd spoken her name. She pulled out the earbuds. "What?"

"Didn't say anything," he said.

"What are you looking at?" Sveti leaned over to peek, and let out a pained sound. "Oh, God, at those? Why?"

"What else have I got to look at? You got a better idea?"

"I flogged those to death years ago! Let them rest in peace!"

"Fresh eyes," he said. "You never know."

She was shaking her head. "It's a dead end, Sam."

"You just can't stand the way it makes you feel," he said. "But I don't have any of that baggage. I might as well take a look."

"I did not run away from it!" she said, stung. "I could write a master's thesis on any one of those poems and their social, linguistic, and historical context! I gave those damn quotes everything I had!"

"Don't get uptight. I won't hurt anything by looking at them."

She tossed her hair and settled back into her seat, tucking her earbuds into her ears. Dismissed again. He gazed at her. Admiring the way her jeans fit, the way her hair swung. Liv's ring looked heavy on her hand, resting on the table. He admired her slim fingers against the open flight magazine. Saw the title of an article. Something about TSA.

Acronyms. Yeah. He looked at the poems again. Typed in a new category. Tried the first letters in every quote, the first letters in every word, the second letters, the third. All gibberish. He was getting out into total derivative obscurity, but hey, whatever. It was a long flight.

He typed in the poets' names, in the order Sonia had listed them. Made an acronym of their first names. PRJEV. Last names. RLLRL.

There it was. That tickle. An itch wanting to be scratched. Tangled up energy wanting to be soothed, smoothed.

When you don't know which way to turn, look to the source.

What was the source but the poets themselves, in this context?

He reached out and tapped Sveti's arm. "Hey."

She jumped. "Hmm?" She tugged her earbuds out. "What?"

"Your mother, in her letter. She talked about a labyrinth."

"Yes, she did." Sveti waited for more.

"When you don't know which way to turn, look to the source."

Sveti looked blank. "I know. So?"

"Did she ever mention an actual, physical labyrinth? Any kind of place that a person might need directions through?"

Sveti shook her head slowly. "Not that I can remember. Why?"

"Look at the names of the poets. The last names."

"I have, Sam," she said wearily. "A million times."

"Look again. The first initials of their surnames. RLLRL. Right, left, left, right, left. When you don't know which way to turn, she said. Maybe she was giving you directions through something."

Sveti's lips went white. She opened her mouth, closed it again.

"Not that it changes much, if you don't know where the labyrinth is," he added. "It's like having the pin code, but no bank card."

Her hand came up and covered her mouth.

"Oh, baby," he said, alarmed. "What? You okay?"

She shook her head, fumbling for the airsickness bag. She shoved the tray table up. "Bathroom," she croaked, and fled.

Nice work. Make the lady toss her diet Coke, why don't you.

He got up to follow her, and slouched against the wall outside the bathroom for what seemed like forever. He was just raising his fist to knock when the door opened. Sveti emerged, pale, but composed.

"Sorry," she said. "It just got too real for me."

"I hear you." He held out his arms. She came into them, as if their bodies were magnetized. His body vibrated in tune with hers. It felt so good, but he didn't dare get used to it.

Sveti couldn't even pretend to watch her movie anymore. She'd hit the wall and sat there shivering, lips bluish. Sam called for cookies, sweetened tea, then bullied until she put the seat back and footrest up.

"I have to look at everything I ever thought I knew about my mother all over again, in relation to this," she said shakily.

"Not right now you don't," he said. "You need to chill. Just shut down for a while. Close your eyes. I'll sit right here and watch over you."

She gave him a nervous, haunted look. "I can't sleep here," she said in a hushed voice. "What if I . . . what if—"

"If you have a nightmare, you have one. No big deal," he said. "I'll wake you up. I'll keep it all together. Don't sweat it. I've got you, Sveti."

She gave him that swift, gorgeous smile. "Wow," she whispered. "Thanks."

He tucked her blanket and his own over her. Held her hand until she dozed off. Kept sitting there, like a fatuous fool, still holding it. He loved how it felt, when she trusted him.

He loved it way too much.

She ran through a dank, dripping cave with a sense of growing dread. She had to do something, save someone, but time was running out. Then the cave was a cinderblock tunnel, insulated pipes snaking along the ceilings. There was a hole in the roof. Light spilled in, the golden light of the sun. A hand reached down to help. It was Sam, and she leaped to grasp it, but it was too high. The light blinded her. She fell short.

Then she was in her bed, the bare, dirty mattress she'd slept on during her imprisonment. Magically, Sam was with her, and his presence turned it into a bower, a haven. He kissed her hands, twining his body with hers. She melted for him, opening—and everything went cold.

Sam's face receded. Yuri's rotting leer hung over her, reddened eyes triumphant, foul breath hot in her face . . .

"Sveti? Sveti! Wake up!"

She startled awake with a cry. Sam was bent over her, his hand cupping her cheek. She jerked away from his touch, panting. "Sam?"

"It's me," Sam said. "He's gone. It's just me now."

"How did you know that I was . . . that he . . ." She stopped, licking her trembling lips. "How did you know?"

Sam shook his head. "I don't know. I just knew that I needed to wake you up." He leaned down, covering her cheek, her jaw, with a rain of hot, soft kisses. "I needed to remind you of who you are."

She gulped, throat shaking. His hand stroked up, beneath the blankets, between her thighs.

"You're so hot, here," he whispered. "Were you dreaming of me, before that butthead came in and messed it up for you?"

She nodded.

"I want to go back into that dream with you. Tell me where I was. I'll re-create it for you, right now. And I won't let anyone elbow in."

She laughed at him. "What, Sam, do you think you can chase my Yuri dreams away by fucking them out of me?"

"Worth a try, don't you think?" He stroked the hot spot between her legs as he flattened her into the seat and whispered into her ear. "So hot. So sweet. I want to lick you right now. Do you want my cock?"

She laughed. As if it had to be said. "But I can't . . . we can't—"

"Say it anyway. You know I love to hear it." His voice was a caressing buzz against her senses. His hand teased, pulsed, stroked her through her jeans at just the spot where she needed him most.

"Yes," she whispered. "I want your cock."

Another slow stroke, and . . . oh, God, she was almost there . . . and his hand slowed, just as she was about to pitch forward into a glorious free fall. He grinned and took his hand away.

She stared at him, quivering. Poised to explode. "Sam!"

He didn't pretend to misunderstand. "Just a couple more hours," he said, his voice silky. "Don't worry. I'll take care of you. In good time."

"You sadistic bastard!"

"Not sadistic, just practical. A guy uses what tools he has."

"You'd use sex as a tool, on me?"

"Shhh," he murmured. "Not against you, baby. For you. I want you to ache for me. I want you in physical discomfort from how bad you want me to fuck you. That's how I want you. All day. Every day."

"That's kinky and controlling," she snapped.

"Too bad," he said. "You drove me to this. If I can't make you love me, then I'll make you crave me. Because I can, Sveti. You know it."

"You're pissing me off," she told him. "On purpose."

He grinned. "Be pissed. It won't change the ache. Every time I make you come, you'll want more. I'm going to pound that nail, babe. I'll pound it, and pound it. Until you're so stuck on me, you can't move."

She tore her eyes from his smoldering gaze. "Enjoy your sexual power fantasies. I won't have time to cater to them when we arrive."

"Oh, cruel Sveti," he murmured, laughter in his voice, just as the intercom announced that the flight would be landing in forty minutes.

She spent the rest of the flight trying to ignore him.

The next argument began in the passport control line, when she told him their first stop. Which was Sasha.

"It'll be too late to speak on the panels anyway, even if we drove straight there," she explained. "I'll only make it for the gala this evening, so I might as well find Sasha now. He's the real reason I came to Italy. The conference is just a pretext. I can't think straight until I know he's okay."

"I can't believe that after what happened, you're voluntarily seeking out a mafiya vor's son," Sam said. "Your synapses aren't firing."

"Sasha had nothing to do with what happened, Sam."

"He's living high on the hog on his daddy's dirty money, Sveti."

Sveti shook her head. "That's not Sasha. You'll understand when you meet him. And you're being unfair. So his father is a mob boss. Mine was a cop. Yours is a tycoon. Nobody chooses. And I trust him."

"Don't toss the word *trust* around when you're talking about a junkie," he said. "It's like punching your own self in the face."

She looked pained. "Sam, we went through hell together! We could barely breathe in there. There was hardly any light, hardly any edible food. We almost lost our minds. It hurt him. I know, because it hurt me, too. He was all I had to keep me sane. Rachel was just a baby who clung to me to survive, but Sasha was there for me!"

Sam just looked at her. His expression gave her a strange, nervous feeling in the pit of her stomach. "What? What's the look?"

"Just jealous," he said. "All that passion from you. All that loyalty. Lucky Sasha."

"Sam, that's stupid!"

"I was there for you," he said. "Sasha gets a break, even if he's a junkie. But there's no break for me, is there?"

Her first response was anger, but it faded as the scene played, in brutal detail. Him, bursting through the door, against all hope.

Yes, Sam had been there for her. But she couldn't say it. The channels were stopped up. She felt like a volcano straining to explode beneath mountains of solid rock.

She shifted gears, instinctively. "So giving myself over to your voracious sexual appetites does not count as giving you a break?"

The guy behind them in line choked and sputtered.

Sam's mouth twitched. "Talk a little louder, Sveti. I don't think they heard you in the baggage claim."

She nudged him toward the window of the customs agent, her face hot. "Go on," she hissed. "We're holding up the line."

At the arrivals hall, she was startled to spot a man holding a placard with her name on it. She was about to say something when Sam jerked her around and dragged her in the opposite direction.

"Don't look at him," he said harshly. "Just haul ass."

"Sam, relax," she soothed. "Probably Hazlett is just—"

"No, there's no reason anyone should be waiting for you. You didn't communicate your new flight number. The flight that went through New York landed two hours ago. If it's Hazlett's guy, he's overly focused on you, waiting too eagerly. And if it's not Hazlett's guy . . ." He steered her toward a tall man, holding a sign that read WESTWICK INC.

"You had a driver meet us?" she said.

"Not a driver. I don't like to be driven, but neither do I like to stand in lines at rental agencies. I called ahead, had a car delivered."

A scrawled signature later, she was being handed into the plush leather interior of a sleek silver Audi, waiting right outside. "What rental agency has cars like this?" she demanded, when he got inside.

"Do not give me any shit about that, or anything else for a while," he said. "Driving in Rome takes up a lot of disc space. I don't have any left to navigate your convoluted thinking process.

Today is a good day to die, Sveti. Tell me where the merciless mafiya vor lives."

Sveti pulled the address from her phone and passed it to him.

"He doesn't live here," she said. "He bought this house for his wife, Marya, but he never lived here. He's always off on business."

Sam snorted. "Business? Nice euphemism."

"Sam, I have to make sure Sasha is okay. I don't have a choice."

Sam guided the car through dense traffic. "Being compelled to do something crazy and self-destructive, against your better judgment?" he said, finally. "Yeah, I can relate to that. But I don't have to like it."

Her chin went up. "Feel free to leave," she said. "I'll get a cab."

"You're missing the point," he said grimly. "It was never a choice."

Sam was quiet for the hour and a half or so that it took to get out of the airport and through the morning rush hour in Rome. Sveti was nervous, too, but she could not afford to admit it to him. Her last visit here had been disquieting. Pavel Cherchenko had been absent, to Tam and Val's relief, but she'd met Sasha's mother, Marya. A thin, grayish woman who reeked of alcohol and never looked anyone in the eye. She'd died of liver disease not long after. Sveti had been unsurprised.

They parked two blocks from the lavish eighteenth-century palazzo. Sam followed her to the door. She buzzed the bell, which bore no name.

"*Chi e'?*" someone barked.

"I am Svetlana Ardova," she said. "I'm looking for Sasha."

The pause was so long, she'd reached to buzz again. The door lock suddenly released. Sunlight spilled through arched windows into a large entrance hall, making the pink veined marble walls glow.

An elevator began to hum. Someone was coming down.

Sam jerked her closer to his body as the silver doors slid open.

A thick, slab-faced guy glared out at them. He wore an expensive suit. A weapon bulged beneath it. Sam's head was aching from clenching his teeth so hard. He hated being unarmed. Not that he could have carried a gun into Pavel Cherchenko's lair in any case, but still. The man barked out something inquisitive in Ukrainian.

Sveti replied in the same language, asking again about Sasha.

Another query, and the guy jerked his lantern-jaw toward Sam.

"I'm Sam Petrie," he said. "Her boyfriend."

"I have to search you," the man said in thickly accented English.

Sam submitted to the pat down, but stiffened when the guy approached Sveti. "Watch where you put your hands," he growled.

The menace in Sam's voice froze the guy. He searched Sveti, with careful, gingerly gestures, and then gestured toward the elevator.

Sveti asked about Sasha again, but Slab Face ignored her.

The elevator opened directly onto a lavish *salone*. Spindly baroque furniture, Persian rugs on a vast expanse of gray-veined, gleaming marble. A pallid, sullen boy with longish dark hair waited for them.

Sveti gasped. "Sasha?"

Sam was taken aback. That couldn't be right. This kid was Rachel's age, and Rachel had been a toddler in the Zhoglo days.

"That is not my name," the boy said in British-flavored English.

"Oh, of course. You're Misha," she said, also in English. "I'm sorry. You looked so much like Sasha when I first knew him."

"I am nothing like my brother," Misha said.

"Of course you're not," she said warmly. "You're your own person. Sasha told me about you. He's so proud of how talented you are with computers. He told me you're a genius."

"He lied," Misha said icily. "Drug addicts always lie."

"He wasn't lying about you," Sveti said.

"Shut up about Sasha. Andrei didn't want to let you in. I made him, because I wanted to warn you to stay away from Sasha."

Sveti's smile faded. "I was hoping you could help me find him."

"Why?" Misha demanded.

"I love him," Sveti said quietly. "He's my friend."

"Stop loving him. Find a better class of friends. He's junkie scum, and a traitor, too. He'll be dead soon. Don't waste love on a corpse."

Wow. Brotherly love at its most warming. Sveti pressed a hand against her belly. "Why do you say that? What has he done?"

"None of your business. I'm doing you a favor, and I don't owe you any favors. Stay away from my brother. Forget he exists."

Sveti stared into the boy's face with that look, as if she could see a million miles inside him. "A heart can't forget," she said.

"Such a stupid heart might get a bullet right through it."

"Time to go, babe." Sam took Sveti's arm. When the threats of deadly violence started to fly, that was their cue to fuck off, pronto.

But Sveti resisted, digging into her purse for . . . what? A business card. Oh, of course. It made perfect sense to give her contact info to this mouthy, pimple-spotted little dickhead who dared to bully and threaten her, just to make it convenient for him to continue his abuse at some later time. "Sveti," he muttered. "Goddamnit. Don't."

Sveti held out a card. "Here's my number, and e-mail. If you want to talk to me about Sasha, or anything else, please, call me."

Misha flinched away. "Take it back! I don't want it!"

Sveti kept her hand outstretched. "Please, Misha."

"I don't want to talk to you! And I don't want your card!" The kid's voice was wobbly, as if he were about to cry.

Sveti's arm lowered as she gazed intently into his eyes. She placed her card on the edge of the marble mantelpiece. "I'll just leave it here."

"No!" Misha yelled. "Take your fucking card!"

"Tell Sasha I looked for him, if you hear from him," she said, as gently and calmly as if the kid weren't screaming obscenities at her.

Andrei was as taciturn escorting them out as he had been on the way up. Sveti did not attempt to speak with him again. He saw them to the door and shut it smartly in their faces.

Sam hustled her along so fast, she stumbled over her own feet.

"What do you make of all that?" she asked him.

"Let's get away from this place before we discuss it," Sam barked. "That kid was scared shitless. And now, so am I."

"Hey!" A shrill voice sounded. Sam shoved her behind him and looked up. Misha Cherchenko hung over one of the ornate, carved stone balconies on the first floor. He waved Sveti's business card in his hand.

"I told you to take your fucking card back!" he shrieked. "Stick it up your ass! You make me sick!" He flung the card, which fluttered and swayed on air currents before landing on the sidewalk ten yards away.

Sveti started toward it. Sam grabbed her arm. "No, Sveti!" he said sharply. "Enough! This is the part where we fuck off!"

"Let me go, Sam." She wrenched herself out of his grip and ran lightly to the card, and picked it up. She looked up. "Misha?"

"Take it! Get out! Go!" The kid's voice cracked from screaming.

Sam scooped his arm around her shoulders and half-shoved, half-carried her down the sidewalk. "You've pushed me too far. There could have been ten guys in there, with bad intentions. Never again, get me?"

"Sam!" She barely registered his tantrum, she was so busy scrambling not to trip, and staring at the card in her hand. "Look!"

"At what? My life, flashing before my eyes?"

"No, at the card! Look at the card!"

He finally heard the excitement in her voice. He stopped, looked.

A phone number was scribbled hastily upon it. A time, too. 15:00–16:00. They used a twenty-four-hour clock here: 3:00 P.M. to 4:00 P.M.

His stomach sank at the look on her face. "Don't give me that big-eyed hopeful look. It's probably a trap. That kid is not normal."

"Of course he's not normal," Sveti said. "You said yourself that he was scared shitless. And all that swearing and screaming was forced."

"Sveti," he said. "I'm begging you. Do not add Misha Cherchenko to the list of people who are your personal responsibility to save."

"Sam." She planted her feet, forcing him to grind to a stop, and slid her hands up on either side of his face. She gave him that wide-eyed, radiant, soft-focus angel look. "Sam, breathe."

His groin tingled. He was such a chump for this woman, it embarrassed him. He popped the trunk of the car and pulled out a briefcase. Once the Glock 19 inside was tucked into his waistband his heart rate came down, but he had a way to go before he hit normal.

Sveti was startled. "That is one full-service car rental you've got!"

"Val and I worked it out days ago. His contact will bring me more hardware tomorrow, in San Anselmo. This will tide me over for now."

Sveti dialed the number. A phone rang on the other end. A voice responded, tinny, distorted. *"Un momento,"* Sveti murmured, and held out the phone to him. "Italian," she said. "Would you . . . ?"

He took the phone. *"Con chi parlo?"* With whom am I speaking?

"Noi siamo La Gelateria del Corso," said an irritated, older male voice with a Roman accent.

"Dove siete locati?" Where are you located?

"Al centro!" the guy responded truculently. Downtown.

Sam pushed his luck a little further. "Downtown of what town?"

"Sul serio? Castellana Padulli! Don't waste my time!" He hung up.

Sam pulled over in the next free spot. Typed the *gelateria* and the town into his phone. Waited while it sifted data, churned out mileage.

"So?" Sveti demanded impatiently.

"It's an ice-cream shop," he said. "In a small town south of here."

They stared at each other. Horns blared. Traffic swirled outside.

"Sasha must be there," she said.

"Not necessarily," he said. "That kid is fucking with you, Sveti."

"I want to go to this ice-cream shop. Could we get there by four?"

He thought about it. "Maybe, but it's two hours from there to San Anselmo. We can't drive there, do whatever we end up doing, and make it back in time to check in, find you formal wear, and get cleaned up for the gala. So, ice cream in Castellana Padulli or the Solkin Prize?"

Sveti's gaze slid away. "Shit," she whispered. "But what if this window of time is only a one-day thing?"

"Then he should have communicated better. Sasha's waited this long. He can wait a little longer. If this is Sasha, of course."

"Okay. The gala. But I'm going to Castellana Padulli tomorrow."

They were quiet as Sam wended his way through the thick traffic. Then Sveti spoke up again. "Misha must feel guilty," she said.

"Why?"

"Sasha said that Zhoglo made his dad choose which son to sacrifice to the organ traffickers. He put it like a favor. Your choice, go ahead, discuss it with your wife. The two-year-old or the ten-year-old, either one is fine with me. Sasha told me he was glad he was picked. It would've been worse, having his little baby brother condemned."

"Oh, God, Sveti. That is so fucking horrible," Sam said sharply. "Did you have to tell me that?"

She was silent for a moment. "I guess I didn't," she said, her voice small. "I just . . . Sasha is special. I wanted you to understand that."

Goddamn. He didn't have time to indulge in compassion for the problematic mafiya spawn. His systems would go into conflict.

He had to stay streamlined and simple. Thing one, keep Sveti alive. Thing two, seduce her at every opportunity. Thing three, don't think about the future. These iron-clad imperatives would keep him sane, and on top of this crazy mess. Nothing else could intrude.

"Jesus," he muttered. "And I thought my family was fucked up."

She choked on a giggle. Out of nowhere, they were both snorting nervously under their breath. It felt perverse, to laugh under these circumstances. As if by doing so, they were letting down their guard.

"Stop it, Sam," she choked. "Not funny. At all."

"You started it."

But the furtive chortling lightened the atmosphere, just a little.

It occurred to him as he pulled onto the Autostrada that he was living out one of his fondest Sveti fantasies. In a hot sports car speeding through the Italian countryside. The plan: Buy her a sexy evening gown, take her to a party. Sunset over the Mediterranean.

Good food, good wine. Blow-your-mind sex. What wasn't to like about that scenario?

Just his girlfriend's complicated death wish. But if he wanted her attention, he had to dance to her tune.

And oh, what a weird melody it was.

CHAPTER 15

The hotel Sam took her to in San Anselmo was very luxurious. She followed Sam into the baroque palazzo, where a graceful atrium opened right out of the lobby, and palm fronds waved over people seated at wrought-iron tables, sipping drinks in the late-afternoon sun. It was not, of course, the hotel where she had a room paid for by Illuxit, but she was too exhausted and preoccupied to make a fuss.

Sam dealt with check-in, and Sveti listened with half an ear to his sexy, perfect Italian while staring into a display case that showcased a local jewelry artisan. The pieces reminded her of museum displays of Byzantine jewelry that Erin, Connor's wife, had curated. Spirals of beaten gold, round cut stones. It reminded her of Deadly Beauty, though Tam's style was more edgy and modern. The similarity lay in the pieces' savage sensuality. They were beautiful, fierce, menacing. An emerald ring and matching pendant earrings were particularly gorgeous.

Sam slid a possessive hand around her waist from behind. She wanted to melt into him. And she fought the impulse, on pure principle.

"You like those earrings?" he murmured into her ear.

"They're beautiful," she said. "The ring, too. Stunning. The jeweler is very talented."

"Do you want them?" he asked, his voice elaborately casual.

She jerked, as if shocked with electricity. "Get out! They're emeralds, Sam! They cost eighteen thousand euros! I can think of a hundred things I'd rather do with eighteen thousand euros!"

He snorted. "Of course you can."

His attitude bothered her. "You think I'm being sanctimonious and humorless because I don't value fine jewelry?"

"Fine jewelry has its place in the grand scheme of life."

"Not in my scheme," she said vehemently.

Their room was a fresh shock to her sensibilities. It wasn't a room at all. It was a freaking ducal apartment. A huge baroque sitting room with complicated molding, stunning mosaic tilework, and French doors that opened onto a private terrace overlooking the sapphire sea. The bedroom had a massive carved teak four-poster swathed in dreamy folds of mosquito netting. The bathroom had a sunken marble tub, a two-person shower. Antique frescoes of shepherds and chubby angels.

"What the hell?" She turned on him. "I can't afford this place!"

"I never asked you to," he said.

"Yes, and that's why it pisses me off! Where are we?"

"The Hotel Aurelio. I thought of it right away when you said this thing was in San Anselmo. I stayed here with my sister and mom when I was a kid. In this very suite." He looked around, his eyes faraway. "I have good memories of this hotel. I wanted to be here with you."

Oh, great. Cut her off at the knees, why didn't he. "It's lovely, but there are plenty of perfectly nice *pensioni* that cost a fraction—"

"I like this place," he said. "It's my choice, so obviously, it's my expense. You asked a whole hell of a lot from me, back in Rome. Now you can return the favor and start acting like a fucking grown-up."

She stared at him for a moment, stung. Fine. So she would. She sat down in one of the wingback chairs and pulled out her phone.

"Who are you calling?" he asked.

"Hazlett, of course," she said. "To tell him I'm here. It's rude, that he sent someone to pick me up and I never showed. Or even called."

"Don't tell him where we are," Sam said.

"Don't be absurd," she snapped. "What am I supposed to say?

I'm sorry, but I can't tell you my hotel. You might be an assassin, so I'll just meet you at the party, 'kay? See you there!"

"You just love to make it hard for me, don't you, Sveti?"

His unconscious play on words roped her into it. Her gaze flicked to his crotch and just as quickly away. His erection strained against the denim. His eyebrow tilted up, asking what she wanted to make of it.

She turned away. "No distractions, please."

"Fine," Sam said. "Tell everyone. Post our location on the Internet. Don't forget our room number. The Ukrainian mob can triangulate your phone signal now, so fuck it, what's the worst that can happen?"

"Shhh." She focused all her attention on the ringing phone.

"Illuxit Transnational," a low female voice answered.

"Can I speak to Michael Hazlett? This is Svetlana Ardova."

"Oh, good! I'm so glad you've finally gotten in touch. Mr. Hazlett was beside himself when you didn't arrive this morning! This is Nadine."

"Hi, Nadine. I'm so sorry about that. I ended up coming on a later flight, and, of course, my phone was turned off. Can I speak to him?"

"Of course. We're glad you decided to come at all, after having such a horrific experience. One moment, while I track him down."

She kept her eyes averted from Sam's still figure as she waited.

"Svetlana!" Hazlett's deep, booming voice jolted her nerves. "Just in time for the gala! We missed you on the panels."

"I'm so sorry I missed everything," she said.

"I'm relieved you're here for the awards ceremony. It would have been embarrassing to make excuses to the donors. I expect to get sizable contributions to Illuxit's anti-trafficking foundation from my friends, after they see you speak! And not to be crass, but the attack you suffered certainly does ratchet up the drama factor, hmm?"

"Ah . . . I . . ."

"Drama sells! But I don't have to teach you any tricks, not after the way you played up the shock value on your video log to crowd-source funding for the victims! Brilliant job, brilliant. Silver linings, right?"

"Ah, yes," she said weakly. "Of course."

"I'll send Nadine over as soon as she's free, and a man from my security team as well. Where are you located?"

"Oh. Ah, I . . ." Her eyes slid to Sam, who watched intently. "That won't be necessary. I've brought a friend with me, and he's—"

"Is he a professional bodyguard?"

"Well, actually, he's—"

"Whatever he is, he could use backup. I had rooms reserved for you at La Perla Del Doge, my dear. You could still move into them."

"Thank you, but I'm fine where I am," she said. "I thought you would change your mind about having me associated with Illuxit now."

"On the contrary. I anticipated this. Anyone who actually changes the status quo will make enemies. That's the cost of contracting experts who genuinely walk the walk. I'll send my people right over." He paused. "Assuming that you tell me where you're located."

Sam's gaze burned the side of her face. She knew exactly how he was going to react to Hazlett's security descending upon them, and cringed at the thought. "We're at the Hotel Aurelio," she said. "But don't send a security agent. I'm quite safe with my friend—"

"Nonsense. I invited you, so your safety is my responsibility. Corporate security is a pain in the ass, but I've gotten used to it, and so will you. Excellent, then. Nadine will be there soon to help you with anything that you might need. Until tonight, then!"

"Yes, thank you, but about security, please don't—"

"Wonderful talking to you. I must run. The conference is in full swing. *A presto*, Svetlana. Can't wait." The connection broke.

Sveti let the phone drop, feeling Sam seethe. With all she had to stress about, she had to feel intimidated because the man with her might throw a sexually charged temper tantrum? To hell with that.

"So," she said. "We're on, then. For tonight."

"Yeah, I heard. With the big man's security team all over us."

"I tried to tell him no," she said.

"I guess he doesn't listen too well. It's something he and I have in common. Was the mutual ass-kissing session pleasurable?"

The hairs on her neck all stood on end. "Don't be ugly, Sam."

"You think that's ugly?" he asked. "Babe, you have no clue."

"I don't want to," she said. "You crossed the line a long time ago."

"Are you going to put me in my place now? The Sveti smackdown. My dick is tingling at the thought. I love it when you're stern, baby."

"You're being an asshole," Sveti said. "One more comment like that, and we part company. I'll take my chances with the Illuxit team."

His eyes burned. "And you think I can be dismissed like that?"

She couldn't withstand the seething heat in his glance sitting down. She got up and threw her shoulders back. "I have enough problems, Sam," she said. "Do not become another problem for me."

"But you're attracted to problems. You exist to solve problems. The bigger the better. And I'm plenty big enough for you, Sveti."

She stared at him. "The only reason we're still in the same room is because that thing with Misha stressed you out," she said quietly. "I was grateful for your company. I wouldn't have had the nerve to do that alone. For that reason only, I'll cut you some slack. But no more."

"Thanks for the pity points," he said. "That's real sweet."

The intense glow in his eyes was palpable, on her skin, in her mind. That electric tingle, that liquid melting.

The absolute inevitability of sex, about to happen.

Her knees wobbled, and her thighs clenched, and she was getting wet. She was furious with her body's helpless animal response, preparing for sex just because a man looked at her that way. It gave him too much power. She kept her back to him as she rummaged for her toiletries. "I'm taking a shower." She fled into the bathroom.

The hot water pounded down as his words on the plane echoed in her mind. *I'm going to pound that nail, babe. I'll pound it, and pound it. Until you're so stuck on me, you can't move.*

It wasn't just sexy blather to make her pant and squirm. It was literally true. She had to take back control. Before this destroyed her.

She took her time, blowing her hair dry. Some lip gloss and mascara, some scented cream. She wished she'd brought some pretty lingerie into the bathroom with her, but she would have to put her faith in the shock value of stark nudity, used as a blunt force instrument.

One last panicked look in the mirror, a few deep breaths to drag in some oxygen to compensate for when he took her breath away.

She flung her hair back and slapped the door open.

Sam turned when he heard the bathroom door open. The shirt in his hand fell to the floor, forgotten.

He couldn't get used to how beautiful she was. His mind went into apeshit overload—bells ringing, lights flashing, steam shooting out his ears. All the blood in his body racing down to the party spot. She lifted her arms and spun, with the sinuous grace of a prima ballerina, back arched, tits out. That fierce, I-own-you-sucker glow in her eyes. Wow.

He cleared his dry throat. "Is there a point to this floor show?"

Her brows lifted. "If you have to ask, maybe it's wasted on you."

His hands clenched. "No," he said. "That will never be wasted on me. Count on it."

"That's comforting. Certain assertions were made, on the plane, Sam. I'm holding you to them. Take off your jeans."

He hastened to obey. Jerking the jeans down, kicking them to join the shirt. He walked over to her, higher mental functions hijacked by the power radiating from her. "So. How do you want this to go?"

She considered the question. "Make me wet."

Whoa. Time out, while his head exploded. "Happy to comply, but I've never seen the bitch goddess persona. Where did she come from?"

"You talk too much. I suggest you put your mouth to better use."

He was obscurely delighted by this, but kept his cool as he swept the mosquito netting aside. "Lie back," he said. "I live to serve."

"No, you come to me," she commanded. "And get on your knees."

He let out a low whistle. "Wow. You sure you want to play with this vibe right now? You can't take it back, Sveti."

"If you're not up to it, I have a lot to do," she said crisply. "I need to shop for a dress anyway, so I'll just be on my—"

"No, no, no." He was over there on his knees before he was even conscious of moving. "I'm up to anything. Always. Know it."

Who cared. On his knees, on his back. Anything that got that sweet little pussy warmed up and ready for action was fine with him. He gripped her ass, stroking the warm, silken skin of her thighs with his cheek, tongue straining eagerly to probe up that tender, juicy cleft.

He pressed up her mound, to open the shiny pink secrets and leave them naked to the artistry of his lashing tongue. He wallowed, nose rubbing her clit as his tongue delved, licking and stroking and probing the magic spots that made her moan, and melt, and yield.

So good, to score that sweet, shivering surrender.

She swayed, whimpered. Her hands twisted in his hair. His senses dilated into something new, to suck up more details, more data, subtle nuances. With that inner eye wide open, he could sense the energy rising in her body, and pilot it. He could take her right where she needed to go. She was afraid, but there was no stopping it now. They tumbled through inner space . . . and oh, sweet *God.*

What a beautiful sight. Sveti coming, against his face, around his hand. Clenching his fingers. He was dazzled, drunk. Wet with her lube.

And so, so ready to fuck.

He rose to his feet, tossed mosquito netting out of his way to make space, but she put out an arm as he was about to push her down.

"Wait," she said.

Impressive, that she could maintain that imperious voice, after that orgasm. A rosy mist of sweat made her dewy and soft, and her face pink. The copious lube made the ringlets on her mound gleam black and wet. Juicy sweet. "Wait for what?"

"Lie down on the bed," she said. "On your back."

His jaw dropped. "Still? You're still in that place?"

"Just do it, Sam."

Fuck it. As long as she was naked and touching him, it was all good. He wrenched the coverlet off and reclined. She gazed at his stiff, empurpled cock against his belly, taking her own sweet time.

He massaged his cock as he stared up at her. "So? What now?"

She clambered onto him, her perfect tits bouncing and swaying as she straddled his thighs, and ran a slow, appraising finger up the shiny, reddened length of his cock, stopping for a moment to swirl her palm over his cockhead. She gave him a few tight, bold squeezes, root to tip.

He arched beneath her, groaning. "Oh, God. Sveti. Please."

"Hold it up for me." Her voice was utterly cool, remote.

He gripped his cock in his fist and presented it to her with silent pleading, but she wasn't done with the torment. She poised herself over him, one hand braced on his chest, the other opening herself. Brushing her hot pussy lips over his aching cockhead. Wet, teasing little kisses. Languorous, undulating. Taking him in, making him wet, shiny.

Making him wait. This was payback. There would be no mercy.

She rolled his cockhead sensually around her clit, eyes closed, head flung back. Intent on her own pleasure. Then she opened her eyes and gave him a challenging stare. Goading him.

Something nameless and dangerous stirred inside him. They could crash and burn if they went too far down this road, but she just kept pushing, and he was too jacked out of his mind to stop her.

"It's dangerous to tease," he said, thickly.

"You should have thought of that on the plane," she replied.

"That was different."

"Of course, since you were the one doing it. Poor Sam. Feeling put-upon?" She pulsed her hips, sliding his shaft between her slick folds. It emerged happy and gleaming from that hot, voluptuous kiss. She swayed, head tossed back, dancing over him. Pleasing herself.

As if he weren't about to flip her over and fuck her hard.

He fought it. Wary of scaring her. He wasn't going to last much longer. Her scent fogged his senses. The little wet sounds, that scalding, voluptuous lick of contact, it was driving him to the screaming edge of reason. But she'd said at the start that she chose him for a lover because he wasn't afraid of her.

She cried out as he rolled her over, and struggled furiously beneath his weight. "Sam! I didn't say you could do that!"

"Nope, you pushed me here on purpose. Because you like me this way." He cut off her response with a kiss, ravaging the moist sweetness of her mouth. She slapped his chest. He barely felt it, he was so intent upon sinking his stiff cock into her quivering sheath.

She was primed. One deep, deliberate thrust into her slick depths and she went off. Her cunt clenched and fluttered, the muscular pulses clenching like a fist. She almost dragged him over the edge with her. He held back, by some supreme effort of inner balance.

He waited, rocking tenderly in her tight little nest to silently remind her that this was not over. When her eyes fluttered open, they were smeared with mascara. He loved that look. Disheveled, undone, sprawled wide and yielding. That naked look in her eyes. No games, no walls. Just the feelings she had for him that she could not hide. Not when he had mastery over her body. He loved those moments.

Fleeting though they always were.

Her pink tongue darted out to wet her soft, full lips, and his cock twitched eagerly in response, begging for action. He thrust, swiveling.

"I'm not done," he said.

Her gaze fluttered up, met his eyes. "I know," she whispered.

He cupped her face in his hand, gently forcing her to meet his eyes. "I want to fuck you from behind again."

Her pussy tightened around him, a little fluttering clench. He loved being able to read her. Knowing what she secretly liked.

"Still playing power games?" she asked.

"You started it," he said. "It worked for you. Spectacularly."

"No, it was you who started it," she pointed out. "On the plane."

"Who cares?" he said. "If it's a game, it's a good game. Between equals who like to play, and know what they want. Understand?"

The crease between her brows indicated that she did not.

"Equals," he repeated. "Meaning, sometimes, I kneel before Her Magnificence and subserviently pleasure her with my tongue, and sometimes, my love-slave concubine presents her hothouse flower of a pussy to me to be fucked from behind. In any case, I can be counted on to make you come screaming. No need to get uptight. If you trust me."

She gave him a short, nervous nod. Old ghosts, old shames. The two of them had to push through the fear.

Pulling out almost killed him. His cock shone, radiated scorching heat. "So?" he prompted her. "Show me that you trust me."

He moved aside. She rolled over and got onto all fours, her body shaking. Her hair swung forward, hiding her face. Her arms shook. He positioned himself behind her, marveling at the perfect shape of her ass, the shadowy marvels between as he gently urged her legs wider.

"Do you want me?" he rasped.

"Yes," she whispered.

"Invite me. With your body. Show me."

It was beautiful to behold, the graceful arch of her back, the swirl of hair dangling down, the shy, sensual glance back.

She cried out at the first thrust, but she soon braced herself, rocking back to meet him. The bed rocked in time with the heavy slapping rhythm. He could have exploded then and there, but he had a point to make. He tuned in to those secret senses that bloomed open whenever he fucked her, swiveling, stroking. Driving her to that place in her head where everything sharpened to a fine point—

And detonated, together. The force of it blotted out the world. There was just wave after throbbing wave of blinding pleasure.

They collapsed on the bed. The last thread of consciousness he had was dedicated to not crushing her. He lifted himself away, sometime later, and sprawled alongside her. Boneless.

"You could trust me more," he said.

"I try," she whispered. "But it's a mistake, to play games. Dominance, submission. It makes me feel . . . ashamed."

Fuck. "Ashamed?" He jerked up onto his elbow. "It's not about dominance and submission! It's about pleasure! Have you been listening to me at all?"

"I don't know," she said. "I just know that I'm lost, in all this. I can't find my way." Her voice shook.

He held out his hand. "Let me lead you. Trust me. I'll take you through the dark. All the way to the other side."

Sveti's eyes flicked from his hand to his eyes. She did not take his proffered hand. Wary of a trap.

"It's not a power game," he urged. "It's give-and-take. Look at the sorry state I'm in. I'd do anything. I'll follow you around like a lap dog, when I'm not beating assassins off you. Is that not submissive enough? What the fuck else do you want from me? Leather and chains?"

"Sam . . ." She rubbed her face and shook her head wearily. "You're a man. It costs you nothing to play at being submissive."

"Play?" He stared at her. "You think I strut around like the king of everything just because I have a dick? I know how it feels to be at someone's mercy. You've had me on my knees for years, so don't give me shit about my dominating attitude. I know how to sit and beg and roll over. You've seen me do it. Hell, babe, you taught me how."

A knock on the door jarred them. He was on his feet, yanking on his jeans. Sveti leaped off the bed and scrambled toward the bathroom.

"Who is it?" he called.

A female voice answered. "I'm looking for Svetlana Ardova."

He edged into the sitting room, gun in hand. "Who wants her?"

"I'm Nadine Muller," the voice said. "Is she there?"

Sveti opened her mouth. Sam put his finger to his lips and waved her into the bathroom. "Who gave you this room number?"

"I know the concierge," she said. "Federico's a friend of mine."

"I'm going to have a talk with friendly Federico about security."

"Actually, Federico is discussing security right now with Silvano, one of Mr. Hazlett's team." A business card slid under the door, followed by a UK driver's license. He examined them. The license looked real. Her name was right. "That's me," she said. "Mr. Hazlett sent me. Satisfied?"

Not really, but when would he ever be? He cracked the door.

A slender blonde stood there, in an elegant black and white dress. Flaxen hair, a kittenish face that matched the one on the license. He peered into the corridor. Handed the woman her card and her license.

She took the license, leaving the card. Her eyes flicked over his bare torso, his half-buttoned jeans. Drying sweat. The reek of sexual discharge. Tough shit. That's what she got for sneaking up on people.

She cleared her throat. "I've come at an awkward time, Mr . . . ?"

"Petrie," he said.

She waited for more. "Is Svetlana here?"

"Yes, I am." Sveti emerged from the bathroom, fully dressed in a graceful, dark blue wrap dress and blue pumps. Remarkably put together for a woman who had been in a state of sexual collapse moments before. "I'm sorry to greet you this way. Come in. Sam, why don't you take your turn in the bathroom while I talk with Nadine?"

The two women's eyes fixed upon him, expectantly.

Right. As if he was going to go wait meekly in the bathroom and leave her alone in a room with a strange woman. Not in this universe.

"Nah, I don't think so," he said blandly. "I'll just stay here."

Sveti's mouth tightened. "I'd like to talk with Nadine. In private."

"I won't interrupt you," he said. "I'll just sit here. Talk away."

He dropped in a chair, the gun dangling from his fingers.

"Ignore him," Sveti said, her voice chilly. "He's behaving badly."

"Who is he?" Nadine asked. "If you don't mind me asking."

"Sam Petrie, a friend of mine," Sveti said.

"Bodyguard," Sam corrected. "I'll accompany her everywhere."

"Ah." Nadine's smooth brow creased. "That might be a bit awkward, because the gala tonight is by invitation only. But don't worry, Mr. Hazlett's security team can take over for—"

"It won't be a problem," Sam said. "I'm on the guest list."

Sveti's head whipped around. "You're *what?*"

Nadine looked blank. "But this function is—"

"I'm a donor," Sam said. "Look me up. Samuel Petrie."

Nadine gaped. "Samuel . . . oh my! You're *that* Samuel Petrie?"

"Yeah," he said. "That's me. No worries. I'm on the list."

"I should think so!" Nadine's entire demeanor had changed. Her eyes sparkled. "We'll roll out the red carpet!" Her gaze flicked back to Sam's torso with renewed interest. "Well. You two are busy. I'll leave this envelope with the info for tonight. A car will come at eight—"

"We'll go on our own. The address of the venue's in the envelope?"

"Of course, with directions. If you'd prefer, we can—"

"How much did he donate?" Sveti's voice was crystal sharp.

"One point two million USD!" Nadine bubbled. "One of our biggest private donations so far, aside from Mr. Hazlett's! Now we know who brought it in! You have more resources than we realized!" She nudged Sveti's arm. "We didn't know you had donors to bring to the table!"

Sveti's face had gone white.

"Actually, there's something you can help us with," Sam said.

Nadine snapped to attention. "Anything! Say the word!"

"Sveti doesn't have a dress for tonight," he said. "And for obvious reasons, I don't want her wandering the streets to shop for one."

"Sam!" Sveti hissed. "I can handle this myself!" She looked at Nadine. "I have a dress in my suitcase that would be perfectly—"

"Price is no object." He ran a practiced eye over the dress Nadine wore. "That looks like Dior. Did you get it here?"

She preened. "Quite an eye, Mr. Petrie! I bought this in Florence, but I do shop here. I know which shops would have what you need."

"Could you contact them? Have them send us some possibilities in a size four. We'll probably need alterations, too. Since she's short."

"Sam! You are embarrassing me!"

"Shhhh, I got this," he soothed. "Sveti, what's your shoe size?"

Sveti crossed her arms over her chest, mouth flat. He reached for the flats next to her suitcase and examined them. "Five and a half, narrow." He glanced at Nadine's elegantly shod feet. "I think we can trust you to find the right thing. For the dress, tell them romantic, clingy. Think old Hollywood. Earthy colors would work, rust or moss greens. Not black, or white, or anything too loud or bright."

"I'll get right on it!" Nadine bustled out, all smiles.

Sam closed the door behind her and braced himself to face Sveti's fury.

CHAPTER 16

Sveti stared at Sam's broad, muscular back, obdurately turned to her. She could not breathe. *Price is no object.* Her ass.

"One point two million dollars," she said. "Holy. Fucking. *Shit.*"

"I do a lot of charitable giving." Sam's voice was gruffly defensive. "I checked into Illuxit's anti-trafficking foundation. They met all my criteria, and I still hadn't met my philanthropic quota for the year, so what the hell? I thought you'd approve."

"I would, under any other circumstances!"

"What's wrong with these circumstances?" He spun around, scowling. "I don't get it! What is your fucking problem?"

"Just how rich are you?" she demanded. "Spell it out for me."

"I don't know," he said. "Depends on the day, what's happening with the market. You know, wars, coups, earthquakes, plane crashes, terrorist attacks. Pretty rich by almost anybody's standards, I guess."

"What does 'pretty rich' mean to you?"

"What do you care?" he demanded.

"Normally, I wouldn't," she said. "I would never have asked such a vulgar, invasive question if you hadn't started swinging your money around and knocking things over. But since you did, I feel entirely justified. Is this money that you inherited?"

"No," he said. "I just work with money I've made myself."

"Made from what? Not from a homicide detective's salary."

He huffed out a sharp sigh. "I'm good with money, Sveti. After college, I invested in some tech start-ups that did well. I reinvested my profits with other ventures, and did well with those, too. Playing with money is something I do to unwind. Sort of like masturbating."

"Except that you ejaculate into your bank account," she said.

He snorted. "Great. So now I'm scum because I trade for fun?"

"For fun?" she repeated. "With that pocket change, you can afford to give Illuxit's anti-trafficking foundation one point two million?"

"Among other gifts." He sounded annoyed. "I've given away about six million this year, so far. It's just something that I do. And? This is relevant exactly why?"

"Tam said you had money," Sveti said. "But I never thought it was on that scale."

"Why think about it at all?" he asked. "I don't, because I don't find it particularly interesting. That's why I didn't pursue it as a career."

She waved that away. "Don't you see the position you've put me in? Here comes the new girl, the one who fucked that rich donor! Nice dress, wink wink, nudge nudge."

"Sorry," he said stiffly. "I didn't mean to put you in a bad place. It just never occurred to me that throwing a big chunk of money at a worthy cause could possibly have a downside. For anyone."

"Of course you didn't," she said. "You wanted to control me, and control the situation, with your money. Because you can."

"Bullshit," he snapped. "I give money away all the time. What the fuck else do I have to spend it on? I don't do drugs, I don't drive fancy sports cars, I don't have a high-maintenance girlfriend to impress. Or maybe I do, now. One point two million is pretty high maintenance."

"Not funny, Sam. I can hear the gossip. Fund-raising with your ankles in the air, har de har har!"

"I have a solution," he said. "It's elegantly simple."

"Enlighten me."

She could feel his body heat, smell his salty sweat as he rested his hands on her shoulders. "Let's make it clear to everyone that you won't be fucking any other donors," he said. "You'll just be fucking me."

She edged backward. "How do you propose we advertise that?"

"Marry me," he said.

She stiffened, staring at him. Unable to breathe. "Sam," she said. "Don't. Be. Difficult." She bit the words out slowly, one by one.

"There we go again. You hate my money, just like you hate my abdominal muscle tone. But the cat's out of the bag, right? Why not indulge myself, and throw a tantrum as only a rich playboy can? Why not just swing my moneybags around, breaking all the china?"

"Why didn't you tell me? I had to hear this from Nadine!"

"I guess I knew instinctively that my investment portfolio would be a huge turn-off for you," he said. "On the level of, say, genital warts."

"So you lied to me deliberately?"

"Hell, no!" He sounded aggrieved. "You wouldn't even give me the time of day, Sveti, for years! Then, when you finally did, I got distracted by sex and violence. Money was never relevant. But don't worry, it's not contagious. Not unless you marry me."

"Don't try and make a joke out of this," she snarled.

"Then don't make such a big fucking deal out of it! Let me spend some cash on something I genuinely care about, for once!"

She waved her arms in frustration. "But not like this! Designer dresses and shoes, brought up to my hotel suite, like I'm a rock star, or royalty? I can't swallow it! It's not my scene!"

"Look at it like a role-playing game," he suggested. "I play the part of the spoiled playboy indulging his whim. You play the whim."

"I'm not a whim, Sam! I won't pretend to be one!"

He rolled his eyes. "The operative word here is *play*, Sveti."

"I suppose you're used to role-playing games, with your modest two-bed in borderline North Portland with the broken sidewalk, right?"

"What, you think I should act like a rich man?"

"I would never presume to tell another person how to act. But I do know it's not healthy to pretend to be something you're not."

Her gaze locked on his smoldering eyes.

"You want me to drop the masks, Sveti?" he asked softly.

"I'm not afraid of reality," she said. "And I'm not afraid of you."

She was on the bed, pinned beneath him so swiftly, there was no time to gasp or flail. He shifted his hot bulk a little so she could breathe. His naked torso felt so hot, so hard. Her fingers clenched convulsively against the thick muscles in his chest. Nails digging in.

"This is the deal." His rough voice tickled her ear. "I like you feisty and difficult and uppity. I do not want you cold and dead. I will do whatever, and spend whatever to that end, whether you like it or not. And call me spoiled and frivolous if you want, but I want you to have a hot dress and sexy shoes for your big party. I'm just selfish that way."

"Sam, get off."

"Spit all the nails you want, but I'll win." His voice drifted lower, a smoky, sensual rumble. "I'll never get tired. I'll never give up. I will wear you down, because you know in your heart that I'm right, to insist on your safety at all costs. And you know what else your heart knows?"

"Don't tell me about my heart. My heart is my own business."

Sam slid his hand up between her thighs. She shuddered with startled pleasure, arching so hard she lifted him up.

"I know more than you do about what's going on in there," he whispered. "I know what your body says. Your body doesn't lie."

"You're fantasizing," she scoffed, squirming under his weight.

"Sure, babe." He slid his fingertip over the gusset of her panties. "You want the naked truth, no masks? You like me this way. You like me strong. You like to push, and you want something hard to push against. And I've got something really hard for you right here, Sveti."

She opened her mouth, but nothing but a breathless moan came out as his finger teased her panties aside and slid delicately inside her.

Sam's face contracted. He thrust deeper. After having washed up, she was slick and soft and ready for sex all over again, and he'd gotten her that way with words alone. With his power games and his posturing and his sexy talk. Her face was hot with shame, but it didn't keep her hips from jerking up to meet his hand, or the muscles inside her from clenching convulsively around his fingers.

Sam reared onto his knees, tossing her skirt up. His stance was arrogantly wide, displaying the thick bulge in his jeans. He inhaled the scent on his hand. Licked his fingers. Waiting. So damn sure of himself.

Oh, to hell with it. She reached for his belt, almost angrily, and yanked it loose, tugging on the heavy buttons of his jeans. His cock sprang free, bobbing against her hand. He shucked his jeans, then resumed his blatant, show-off pose, with his big phallus jutting toward her, the blunt tip swollen and red with eagerness.

A quick tug, and the gusset of her panties gave way. He shoved the ruined garment up to her waist and shoved her thighs wide.

"Damn it, Sam!" she snapped. "What did you do that for?"

"Saving time. And making a point," he said, with a swift grin.

"It's a stupid point!"

"Yeah, terribly wasteful," he agreed. "Shhhh." He nudged the blunt tip of his cock barely inside her. Pulsing, hinting, promising.

"Sam," she whispered. "Please."

"Of course," he said. "But first, tell me something. No masks."

She clutched his shoulders. "What?"

"You like me," he said. "I'm not talking about just liking the way I fuck you, or how my dirty power games get you all hot and bothered, or any of that. I'm talking me. Just me. At least a little bit. Don't you?"

It hurt, in her throat, like some wild thing trying desperately to get out, but a mountain of rock crushed it. Wouldn't let her speak.

He waited, looming over her. Eyes relentless. He cupped her face, and kissed her, with a sweetness that broke her heart.

It lightened the load, just long enough for her to whisper it. "Yes."

He entered her, slowly. So good, so sweet, both gasping with pleasure. Each long, gliding stroke caressed a million shivering points of delight. Momentum gathered, and soon they were locked in a straining knot, panting and heaving. Struggling toward that shining prize.

Waves thundered through her, tearing her wide open, inside her chest, her head, exploding out into infinity.

It mellowed, slowly, to the tender glow of starlight on the water.

She opened her eyes when he pulled out of her. Cool air, against her wet skin. He still knelt between her spread legs, sliding his fingers boldly inside her, clasping her mound. Blatantly possessive.

"I love to see my come dripping out of you," he said.

Her throat was too parched from yelling to reply.

The phone rang. She jerked up, but Sam gestured her down and reached for it. "Yes?" He listened. "Give us ten, then send them up."

Sveti slid off the bed as he hung up. "Samuel Petrie," she said. "I didn't go through hell and back again to be a rich man's bed toy."

His face hardened. "We don't have time for me to get my feelings hurt about that," he said. "Your ten minutes are ticking away. Get to it."

It took a judicious combination of charm and ruthlessness to get rid of Nadine and the saleswoman from the boutique, both of whom had accompanied the wheeled rack of plastic swathed garments up to Sam and Sveti's suite. But no one needed to witness the knock-down, drag-out fight about to take place between him and his stubborn girlfriend.

A very generous tip satisfied the boutique lady, giving him further reason to be glad that Sveti was in the shower. He had to pick his battles carefully. Good thing the prices weren't marked on the garments themselves. He'd arranged for them to be charged to his bill.

He sat down on the bed outside the bathroom door after he got rid of the would-be spectators, and tried to occupy himself with his laptop, check his messages, think strategically. No luck.

The sound of running water eventually gave way to the sound of a blow dryer, which he construed as progress. He glanced through the dresses, discarding several immediately. He leafed through the contents of the envelope Nadine had given Sveti, taking note of the venue, the Villa Fenice, a half hour down the coast.

He plugged the address into his phone, studied the route. Straight-forward enough. He loafed.

Finally, the door clicked, and Sveti emerged, swathed in a thick white terrycloth robe. She'd blown out her hair into swirling waves.

Hot. Shiny. Gleaming. His fingers wanted to wind into it, and pull.

He muscled it down. This was sexual excess, even by his own pig-dog standards. "The clothes are here," he said. "I'm ready for the show."

Her face took on a look he'd come to know well. He braced himself. "Sam," she said quietly. "I don't want to be dressed like a doll."

He let out a careful sigh, his mind racing for strategies to manage her. "It isn't a power game," he said. "I'm not trying to buy you. I know you can't be bought. Can we reframe this whole thing?"

Her brows twitched together, suspiciously. "How?"

"Look on it as an art installation," he suggested. "You've gra-ciously consented to participate, as a favor. Because you like me."

Her lips twitched. "Art installation?"

"Yeah, let's see what happens if we put a stunningly beautiful young woman into a hot dress designed by a renowned artist of high fashion. Doesn't that sound like a fun art project? Will you in-dulge me, just this once? From here on out, it's sackcloth and ashes, I swear."

She laughed, and let the robe fall. "You're so full of shit."

Whoa. Got him, every time. She wore nothing but a nude thong. It made his palms sweat. He dried them against his jeans and grabbed the first dress, cream-colored taffeta shot through with rainbow iridescence.

Sveti dropped it over her head and shook it into place. She gath-ered her fall of heavy, swirling chestnut hair into her hand and turned her back. "You said you'd be my lady's maid."

Oh, yeah. He took his time doing it up, skimming his knuckles along the warm perfection of her skin. Memorizing the curve of her spine, the dip of her waist, the flare of her hip. A hot haze of lust made his toes curl in his shoes and his dick pulse against his jeans.

He lingered over the top hook, reluctant to lift his hands away.

She dropped her hair and turned. "So? What do you think?"

His mouth went dry. He studied her from the front, then walked around her, looking from every angle. "Too virginal," he said finally.

Her eyes widened. "Really? I thought you'd approve of that effect! I figured you would want a dress that said, 'Hands off.'"

"This dress doesn't say that," he said. "It says, 'I'm a defenseless, clueless innocent, so sneak me out of the debutante ball to the gazebo, and ravish me in the moonlight.' It says, 'Fair game.' You are not walking out the door in that thing."

She glanced down at the dress. "Good Lord. I had no idea a dress could say all that."

"That dress is now reserved exclusively for our fantasy sex play. The game I call 'The Deflowering.'"

She let out a crack of laughter. "Why would you need to play that game? You lived it firsthand!"

"It doesn't count, since I didn't know til it was too late."

"Oh, shut up." She swatted at his chest. He seized her hand and kissed it. And kissed it again, trailing kisses up her wrist, her arm, until her hand shook and her eyes were dilated.

"Sam," she whispered. "It's late. Let's, ah . . . try the next one."

"Yeah," he said hoarsely. "Right."

The next dress was a dreamy, rose-spattered chiffon thing, with a lot of asymmetrical fluttering ruffles. It hugged her torso and fell around her, graceful and romantic. She turned, making the ragged, layered skirt flutter out in a floating swirl. Pretty. But he shook his head.

"It says, 'Please don't hate me because I am beautiful," he said. "Fuck that shit. You don't owe anyone any apologies. Take it off."

She turned to the mirror, bemused. "Wow. You have incredibly focused opinions about women's fashion, for a straight man."

"If you're the girl inside the dress, then yeah, I do," he said.

The next offering was cobalt blue chiffon, with soft, swirling knots of fabric sculpted over her torso, molded to show every contour. It hugged her hips and flared into a mermaid frill around her feet.

Sam circled her, eyes narrowed. "This one says, 'How dare you look at me, peon. Begone, lest I strike you down with my magical triton for your insolence, and turn you to a cowering sea slug.'"

She laughed at his nonsense. "Not the vibe I'm shooting for."

Somehow, out of nowhere, this had become fun. What a high, what a buzz, to make Sveti smile. It made him giddy.

Even knowing that her mood could change in a fucking heartbeat.

He pushed that thought away as he fastened the hooks on the last dress, but the thought disintegrated when she turned to show him.

It was soft like velvet, but flowing. Brown-tinted, golden green. Forest moss, hit by a beam of sunlight. Fabric twisted gracefully over her perfect breasts, and fell from a high empire waist to skim her curves. It brought out her hazel eyes, the raw cedar tints of her hair.

He found himself thinking of stories his mother had read to them. Schlocky girl stuff about fairies and dryads whenever it was Connie's turn to pick. Sveti had just stepped out of one of those stories. That bold, yet cautious look in her eyes. As if he were a dangerous magical beast, but she knew she had the power to bend him to her will.

He cleared his throat. "That one," he said. "That one's a winner."

She twirled, smiling at the mirror in a rare show of vanity. "I agree, for once," she said. "It's very nice. How much does it cost?"

"Don't even start," he said. "I'm hard already, just looking at you in that thing, so don't provoke me. I might end up getting all masterful and overbearing. Just to prove a point."

"Really?" She twirled, making the skirt flare. "What kind of point?"

He tilted her face up and kissed her hungrily, until she was dazed and breathless. "The kind of point that might mess up the dress."

*   *   *

"Break his other knee," Pavel Cherchenko said.

"No!" Misha shrieked, as Ivan lifted the baton over the wretched, bloodied Andrei, who lay broken and unrecognizable on the floor. "It's the truth! It wasn't Andrei's fault! He didn't know! I'm sorry we didn't tell you as soon as she arrived, but I didn't know that you wanted to—"

"Liar. Of course you knew. You spy on everything I do, my son. Andrei is an idiot, yes, but you are not. I had people waiting for her at both airports in Rome and Milan, and you knew it. But what bothers me most is what a bad liar you are." He swatted the back of Misha's head, smashing his face onto the gleaming surface of Pavel's desk.

When Misha dragged himself back up, blood streamed from his broken nose, along with the snot brought on by his womanish tears.

And this piece of shit was all he had to call his heir.

"I'm sorry." Misha's voice gurgled. "It was me, only me. Not Andrei. I told him to bring her up, and I—"

"He should have called for instructions." Pavel punctuated this with a savage kick to the kidney. Andrei shrieked. "He shouldn't have listened to a snot-nosed, lying little boy." A crunch of broken ribs. "He should have realized what you were doing." A boot heel, ground onto the man's genitals. Andrei jackknifed, in spite of his shattered vertebrae.

"Please, stop, stop, stop," the boy moaned. "Please." He sobbed silently, eyes closed, blood streaming down his neck into his shirt.

Pavel gazed at his son with a bitter taste in his mouth. He'd entertained hopes for Misha, even after the blow that Sasha had dealt him. Bright Misha, with his talent with tech, his facility with numbers. A freak, yes, but in this day and age, one needed an edge. Misha was unscarred by Zhoglo's punishment. Marya and Sasha had been gutted, but there was still hope for Misha. Or had been. Now he was not sure.

He was still angry at Sasha, for not being strong enough. For not appreciating what his father had done for him, by murdering that scum Zhoglo. He had to remind his own self every morning that he had actually done it, as he woke from the nightmares in which Zhoglo was grinding his boot into Pavel's face. He was not that wretched slave any longer. He had freed himself. Killing Zhoglo had ignited him.

He had avenged Sasha, but had his son shown gratitude for his father's efforts? Had he valued the possibilities his father had given him? No. The worthless turd had curled up into a ball. A mute wraith of a boy who would not speak, who lost himself in drugs. First vodka, brandy. Then as soon as he was old enough to go and seek it out, heroin. His boy, floating away, on a fucking lake of opiates. He could forgive a great deal, after what Sasha had suffered, but not betrayal.

Sasha had to die. It would be a relief to everyone. Most of all to Sasha himself, he suspected. But Pavel was appalled to find that the taint had corrupted Misha, too. Something had to be done. Something severe.

His offspring hunched, shaking and leaking before him. He slapped the boy, *whack*. "Stop crying! I watched the footage. You knew about the hidden cameras. I saw you playing to them. That screaming and carrying on, so overdone. Not like you, sullen, constipated clam that you are." *Whack.* "You turned your back to the camera in the library to write on her card. And throwing the card onto the street? How did you plan to justify that to me? Svetlana Ardova's cell phone number might have saved me time. I don't suppose you memorized her number?"

"No," Misha whispered. "I didn't even look at it."

Pavel took the baton from Ivan's hand. *Crack*, he brought it down on Andrei's scapula. Misha's moan was drowned out by Andrei's shriek.

Pavel panted as he stared at the man twitching on the floor, ruining the fine Persian rug. Rugs were replaceable. Sons were harder to come by. But when a thing was ruined, it was ruined.

He would give Misha one last chance, for Marya's sake. Not that he owed the bitch anything. She'd been weak. Giving in to despair. He'd worked so hard to make it up to her, but even Sasha's return from the dead did not slow her descent. From the grave, she kept her grip on him. Guilt, shame, at being powerless to protect his family.

He hated her for it. He hated them all.

"Where are the thermal generators located?" he demanded.

"I don't know! I don't know anything about—"

Whack. The slap rocked Misha's head back. "Why are you helping Sasha?" he bellowed.

"I just . . . wanted to know he was alive." Misha sobbed, silently.

Pavel leaned into his son's cringing face. "What did you write on the card you threw down to her?"

Misha's eyes were full of mortal dread as he raised them to his father. "I . . . I didn't write anything."

Pavel picked up his letter opener, an antique stiletto, its hilt adorned with precious gems. "One more lie . . ." Pavel said, nudging the side of Andrei's bloody face with his shoe.

Misha hesitated. "If I tell you, you won't hurt him anymore?"

Arrogant little shit, daring to bargain with him. Pavel forced his voice to softness. "Of course. Tell me, and his suffering will end."

"It's a phone number," Misha admitted. "Sasha sent me a note, one day, when I was at school. It's a *gelateria*. In Castellana Padulli."

"Tell me what is special about this *gelateria*."

"He checks it. If I show up, he sends a message. Where to meet."

Pavel's hand contracted around the jeweled hilt. "So you have been in contact with Sasha. And you said nothing."

"I met him, just once," Misha whispered. "Two days ago."

"Where is he?"

"I don't know." Misha's voice was strangled. "He wouldn't tell me. He has a remote camera set up, to watch for me. He has organized it so I cannot ever know where he is. To . . . to protect us both."

"Protect you? Hah."

"I'm sorry," Misha said brokenly. "Can I go? Please?"

"To warn Sasha? No, you stay here until this is finished. You are a liar, and a traitor, and stupid. I despise stupidity."

"Father, please—*no!*"

Misha's wail of protest choked off as Pavel drove the stiletto through Andrei's eye. He hesitated. There were precious gems in the hilt, after all. He pulled it out and wiped it on Andrei's suit coat.

"Wrap him in the rug and take him away," he said to Ivan and Yevgeni, who stood watching. "Take Misha downstairs, to the room."

Misha's mouth was slack with horror. "But . . . you said . . ."

"I said, his suffering will end. And it has ended." Pavel patted Misha's clammy cheek. "But yours, my son? Yours is just beginning."

CHAPTER 17

Sveti stared out at cliffs of silvery stone that glowed pink with reflected tints of the sunset. A cool breeze scented with aromatic wild herbs blew in the window. She wore a gorgeous evening gown, she was in a sexy car with a hot guy in a tux who made her delirious with pleasure, about to receive a prestigious award for her achievements, to be fêted at a lavish party—and she was still capable of feeling miserable.

Leave it to Sveti to tie the pretty bow on top of her present into an unbreakable knot that could only be released with the slash of a knife.

She glanced at the car that was following them. Silvano, Hazlett's security agent, and his driver were in it. Sam had insisted on driving his own car. This was the compromise they had struck, with great difficulty and a lot of incomprehensible male snarling, all in Italian.

"This isn't sustainable," she said.

"What's not sustainable?"

"This security situation," she said. "How much does it cost, to pay someone to follow you around all the time?"

"Hazlett would only hire top-of-the-line people, so you can be sure that it costs a fortune. What do you care? You won't be paying."

She shook her head. "It won't work. There's a point of diminishing returns. When people decide that I'm more trouble than I'm worth."

She regretted saying that the second the words left her mouth. As if she wanted to hasten the day that he made that decision, too.

"You underestimate the cosmic mega-bullshit people are disposed to tolerate in order to be close to you, Sveti."

"Oh, stop it, Sam." She stared out the window. "Don't try to soothe me or flatter me. I'm just trying to think this through."

He made little smooching sounds. "That's the sound of me kissing your ass. Wow, all I do is think of your ass, and boom, my pants don't fit. What's a little mortal danger or a few pesky trust and intimacy issues when I can peel down your panties and—"

"Stop." She blocked her ears. "I need to concentrate on what I'm doing tonight. Don't melt my brain with your sex talk. Please."

"No, actually. I disagree. I think it would do your brain some good to be melted. You've got concentration totally nailed, Sveti. What you need is to chill the fuck out. You need to laugh."

She stared down at her lap. "I've never been great at that," she said. "Please, don't make it a requirement. I can't do it on command."

"Don't turn what I just said into a brand-new problem for you," he said. "Consider this. I've been watching you take yourself way too seriously since the day I met you. You can see with your own eyes how much my enthusiasm has wilted. Go on, look. Touch, if you want."

She snorted, her mouth twitching. "I said, stop it."

"Hah! Success!" he crowed. "I'll do anything for a laugh from you, even humiliate myself by sporting a boner in evening wear. Slap a red clown nose on me and watch me go."

"You are the furthest thing on earth from a clown," she said.

He grinned. "That's not true. You're further, so the job falls to me by default. Laughter is a great tension reliever. Almost as good as sex. I guess if I can't make you laugh, I can make you come. You're so covered."

She snorted helplessly into her hand. "Oh, God, stop it, you'll make my makeup run. It always comes back to sex, doesn't it?"

"It goes there on its own. No conscious help from me, I swear. Who can blame me, when you're wearing that dress?"

"By the way, you never told me what this dress said," she pointed out. "You just said it was a winner. Didn't it talk to you, like the others?"

She was trying to play along, to lighten up, like he wanted, but the glance he cast at her was surprisingly somber. "Sure, it talked to me. It said, 'There is a God.'"

Her face went hot. "Sam," she whispered. "You're overdoing it."

"And you need to work on accepting compliments."

"Maybe I do, but not right now," she said. "I think we've arrived."

Sam slowed at the wrought-iron gates, set in a high stonework wall. The road swirled in curving switchbacks up the hillside, through perfectly manicured grounds and terraced gardens toward the Villa Fenice, a ducal palace on the top of the hill.

The sun had set, leaving a fiery streak on the horizon that faded up to violet and then to deep cobalt blue. A single star glowed on the horizon. They drove into a rotunda that circled a fountain, a cluster of winged marble angels pouring water from urns, their dimpled limbs in a complicated tangle. A fragrant profusion of flowers bloomed everywhere. The air was heavy with their scent. The rotunda was full of high-end automobiles and uniformed staff driving them away.

Sam helped her out, gave his keys to an attendant. They strolled toward the entrance. The building was creamy white stone that had absorbed the sun's heat all day and now seemed charged with power and radiating trapped energy. Torches flickered in sconces that flanked the entrance and the mirrored double staircases. There were no artificial lights. Sam took her arm, leading her across the flagstones and up the massive marble steps.

She spotted Hazlett in the arched entrance, across the wide expanse of marble paving stones. He hurried toward them. He was even more tanned than the last time she had seen him, and seemed far younger than his forty-eight years. She felt the subtle tension from Sam ratchet up, thrumming through her arm and into her body.

"Svetlana," he said. "I am so glad. In spite of everything, here you are. Nothing can keep you down. You are an inspiration."

"Michael," she murmured, wondering frantically what to do with her hand, because Hazlett was not letting go, and his grip was tight, and hot. And now he was patting her with his other hand. Trapped.

He utterly ignored Sam's presence.

Sam stood there quietly at her elbow, sizing him up.

"Sam, this is Michael Hazlett, my new employer," she said. "Michael, this is Sam Petrie. I told you about him."

"Ah, yes." Forced to acknowledge him, Hazlett's glance flashed over Sam. "The one who rode to your rescue? The famous Mr. Samuel Petrie, the Illuxit Foundation's new mystery donor? You caused quite a stir with your gift." He did not release Sveti's hand to shake Sam's.

Sam just looked at him. "You're the founder of Illuxit?"

"Yes." Hazlett flashed his teeth. "Biopharmaceutical development and commercial outsourcing. One of the biggest worldwide."

"So, essentially, your company organizes clinical trials for new untested drugs in third world countries? Have I got that right?"

"Among other things," Hazlett said. "We've helped develop some of the most important, top-selling drugs on the market, but I've recently stepped down from direct leadership. It's time for Illuxit to give back, so I'm concentrating on the Illuxit Foundation. Most specifically on initiatives to combat trafficking, and funds to help the victims."

"Yeah, I read up on that before I donated," Sam said. "It looked well organized. Particularly now that she'll be associated with it." He jerked his chin in Sveti's direction. "She'll set you all straight."

"Oh, yes," Hazlett said with a big smile. "She's unique. So utterly focused and rigorous. That's what we need. She has an almost . . . well, a cutthroat quality, I might say, for lack of a better term."

Sveti winced. "There must be a better term."

"Consider it a compliment." Hazlett's teeth flashed. He turned back to Sam. "I watched that video of the slavery ring exposé, and I contacted her immediately. She's ferocious. As unique as she is lovely."

Sam's grin looked feral. "Don't I know it."

"I'm sure you do," Hazlett said. "I knew she was the one when I saw her video. That's my passion, you see. Finding the pressure points. It's a discipline that applies to any field of human endeavor. Finding the place to poke to make someone jump, or the exact point where medicine must be applied in order to be effective, or the precise place where the money must be spent to make a difference. In this case, Svetlana is the perfect woman. In the right place, at the right time, she could change the world. I'll be privileged to be nearby and watch it happen."

The men stared each other down. Svetlana wanted to melt into the ground. "So," she said tightly. "Shall we go on in?"

"Please, get a glass of champagne," Hazlett said. "I have a friend coming up the drive whom I must introduce you to. I'll join you soon."

Sam and Sveti strolled into the vaulted, frescoed entry hall. It was lit with dozens of candelabra. The warm glow made the arches of cobalt blue sky from the loggia that opened toward the sea intensely vivid. On the terrace outside, waiters wandered with trays of champagne flutes. Both of them refused. Sam gave her a questioning look.

"Why not?" he asked. "It's time-honored relaxation trick number three. Although numbers one and two are still my favorites."

She shook her head. "I have to be brilliant tonight, remember?"

"Ah, yes. How could I forget, with Hazlett fawning all over your hand. You're the perfect woman! Carefully chosen to touch that precise magic place that will cause him to erupt in paroxysms of bliss!"

She glared. "Don't you dare get into a pissing contest, Sam."

"I won't start one, but I won't back down from one either."

"Svetlana! Mr. Petrie!" Nadine hurried toward them, resplendent in a stunning teal taffeta gown with a vast, pouffy skirt.

"Call me Sam, please," Sam said.

She smiled, flirtatiously. "All right, if you insist. Thanks, Sam. Svetlana, excellent choice of dresses! It was one of my favorites, too! It looks stunning on you. Armani is just classic."

"Sam picked it," Sveti admitted.

"I'm not surprised." Nadine looked through her lashes at Sam. "I must run and take care of business. Enjoy yourselves!" She hurried off.

She raised an eyebrow. "You made quite the shirtless impression on Nadine, didn't you?"

He lifted her hand, kissed it, and kept kissing it. "Who?"

"There she is! Svetlana! Let me introduce you to a friend of—" *Crash.* The champagne glass of the tall, salt-and-pepper haired man next to Hazlett shattered on the floor.

The man stared at Sveti, eyes wide. *"Dio mio,"* he whispered.

Sam drew her toward himself. "What the fuck?" he muttered.

"Renato, are you all right?" Hazlett asked. "What's wrong?"

The man tried to speak, his mouth working. *"Per l'amor di Dio,"* he whispered. *"Uguale. Ugualissimo."*

"Uguale to whom?" Sam asked sharply. "Someone clue me in."

"Sam?" Sveti clutched Sam's arm. "What is it?"

"You evidently resemble someone this guy knows, babe."

Two white-clad attendants appeared, one with a broom, another with a long-handled dust pan. In tandem, they swept up the shards and as swiftly disappeared. More arrived, one with a mop, another with a dry cloth, and a third, holding out a fresh glass of bubbling wine.

The tall guy did not deign to notice. He just kept staring at Sveti. Hazlett waved the champagne bearer impatiently away.

"I'm sorry." The man's English had a heavy Italian accent. "Forgive me. I was not expecting—but you're just so much like her. Your eyes, your lips. It's extraordinary. I . . . I was not prepared."

"Who?" Sam and Sveti asked in unison.

"Sonia," the man said.

Sveti gasped. Cold sucked on her from below. Her blood pressure dropped. Sam's arm slid around her waist, strong and bracing.

She rested her hand on it and squeezed, drawing strength from him. There was so much of it to draw. "You knew my mother?"

"Yes." The older man's eyes looked shiny. His mouth was set. "We were together. For over a year, before she died."

"Oh, God." Sveti's heart gave a painful thud. "You're the *conte*. Renato Torregrossa. With the villa on the sea."

"Yes. Here, look. I have her photo on my telephone, always. I transfer it over every time that I change phones." He pulled out his smartphone, thumbed around on it, and held it up to Sveti.

Sveti leaned forward. Yes, it was her mother. Dressed in some flowing white gauze thing, laughing. She was next to Renato, their heads together. Renato had held out the phone to snap a selfie.

Her heart clenched. Grief, and a blaze of raw, childish jealousy. Who the fuck did this arrogant old Italian *conte* think he was? Having snapped pictures of her mother that Sveti had never seen, sharing days that Sveti would never remember? He had a piece of her that she would never touch. He'd been with her, spoken to her, touched her, more recently than Sveti had. By a year and a half. *Bastard.*

She clamped down on her emotions. She would not make a spectacle of herself, and be that pathetic crazy girl. *Poor thing. She's been through so much, you know. Understandable, really.*

No. Her jaw ached from clenching. "She told me about you."

"It's true." Hazlett's fascinated gaze darted from Renato's cell phone back to Sveti's face. "The eyes, the mouth."

Sveti felt Sam's arm tighten. "Yes, we were very similar. Everyone always said so." Her voice seemed to come from very far away.

Sam spoke up. "This can't be a coincidence," he said, to both Hazlett and Torregrossa. "How do you two know each other?"

"Oh, we've known each other for decades," Hazlett said. "Illuxit has partnered with TorreStark for years. We organized the clinical trials of all of their latest revolutionary cancer care drugs. Renato and I have also been close personal friends for many years. When I turned my attention toward philanthropy, he drew my attention toward you, Svetlana." He patted Renato's shoulder. "You have him to thank for all this." He gestured around at the glittering throng, the candlelit hall.

"Ah." Sveti's eyes flicked to Sam. His face was grim. "Well, then," she said awkwardly to Renato. "Thank you. I suppose."

"No need." Renato wiped his eyes and gave her a brave smile.

"It's the least I could do, for Sonia." Renato squeezed her hand. "She adored you, *cara*. She was so proud of you. How you'd come through your ordeal triumphant. How you rose above it. Just magnificent."

Her jaw throbbed. Who was this asshole, to know about her ordeals? The details of her past were private, to say nothing of her mother's opinion of them. Mama's pride and adoration might have been better directed by paying more attention to her daughter.

She could not bring herself to smile. She tried to pull her hand back. Renato clutched it tighter.

"So many times I wanted to approach you," he said earnestly. "You're the only person who could understand how unique she was. But I hesitated to contact you. I was afraid to open old wounds."

Oh, puh-leeze. Her hand shook with the urge to yank it back.

"She is buried in the Torregrossa family mausoleum, at Villa Rosalba," Renato said. "I could take you there, if you like."

That information made her vibrate like a plucked string. She had a vague sense of having known that fact, once, and then deliberately forgetting it. She nodded. "Yes," she said quietly. "I would like that."

"I'm staying at the Villa Rosalba myself, in fact," Hazlett said. "Renato is always my gracious host when I'm in Italy. Stunning place."

"Svetlana, why don't you come and stay, too?" Renato asked. "It would be lovely to have you! You could see where your mother—"

"No," Sam broke in.

Renato blinked, his face going blank. He was noticing Sam's existence for the first time. "I beg your pardon?"

"Sure, you're pardoned," Sam said. "But no. She's not staying anywhere, with anyone but me right now."

"But I . . ." Renato broke off. "I hope you aren't insinuating—"

"Nope, not insinuating anything," Sam said smoothly. "But no."

"Sam!" Sveti hissed. "Please! Hang on to yourself!"

Sam shot her a look that scared her.

Hazlett put a hand on Renato's arm. "Svetlana was violently attacked a few days ago," he explained. "Her companion is feeling understandably protective."

Renato's eyes widened. "*Santo cielo!* I can guarantee that my home would be absolutely secure, however."

"Why not come by tomorrow?" Hazlett suggested.

"We have plans," Sam said blandly.

Sveti looked at him, disoriented. "Ah, we have . . . what?"

"Remember?" he said softly. "Our big ice-cream date?"

Oh, God, yes. She pressed a hand to her forehead, feeling queasy.

"Excuse me?" Renato said, his voice chilly. "Ice cream?"

"You are invited to Villa Rosalba, too, Mr. Petrie, of course," Hazlett said, after an insultingly long pause. "If that is the issue."

"No, it's not," he said. "And I'll be sticking to her twenty-four/seven, no matter where she gets invited. It's just that Sveti and I had plans for tomorrow. A little romantic getaway."

Hazlett gestured at the panorama of sea, the fading streak of sunset, the mountains towering up. "Is this not romantic enough for you?" he said, his voice jovial. "Where are you going?"

"It's a secret," Sam said. "A memory from my childhood."

"Perhaps visiting her mother's grave might take precedence over your sentimental jaunt for gelato?" Renato's voice was acid.

Sam's eyebrows went up. "I suppose it might. Sveti? Your call."

Oh, great. Put her on the spot. She just looked at him, lost.

"Sveti and I'll talk about this in private, and get back to you," Sam said smoothly.

Renato turned to Sveti. "I loved your mother, Svetlana. I'm so grateful for the opportunity to get to know you. So, Michael? Shall we introduce her to the Hallerbachs first, or Lucia Rutigliano? I've been working on Conrad Hallerbach all week. At this point, he's expecting a celestial visitation."

They swept Sveti off between them with Sam close on their heels.

The evening passed like a feverish dream. Her eyes swam, in the shimmering blur of candlelight. She met so many people, shook so many hands, was kissed on the cheek endlessly. She noticed food and wine in front of her at one point, but could not eat any. Michael Hazlett recounted her abduction and rescue story to everyone he introduced her to. She felt paraded naked through the crowd, her horrific tale offered up like a calling card. But she kept it together, like always. She felt like a remote-controlled robot, her emotions miles away—but for one.

She was passionately glad to have Sam there. Always a step away, even if he had to elbow some diamond-studded dowager or tuxedo-clad tycoon physically away from her. He'd just give them a sweet, charming smile and stand there, monolithic. Never ceding an inch.

Every time she looked at him, his conspiratorial grin gave her strength. He was her anchor, and her shield. Her private place. One sweet, precious thing that did not belong to these people. It was hers.

No, not just hers. Theirs.

The awards ceremony was the hardest part. Being shy and introverted, she found speaking in public difficult in the best of circumstances, but she'd learned ways to cope. She'd polished a speech weeks ago, before the wedding, Sam, the attack. But the girl who had prepared that speech was a different Sveti, someone she no longer even recognized. She was something raw and torn open now. Utterly new.

She stared down at this expectant crowd and began to speak.

The whole tale. Papa's punishment, the abduction. Aleksandra, Yuri, the rescue. Her stolen family, her stolen childhood. Her stolen heart, ransomed in the nick of time. She told them what she'd done last year in Portland, and why. It was her job, to be the face of the faceless slaves and trafficked innocents. She offered her experience up like a sacrifice, with all its shock and entertainment value.

They looked up at her, judging and appraising, and she tried not to hate them for it. Stupid, to resent a person for being lucky. For having a father to protect you from monsters who would tear out your heart. For having a mother who would not jump off a bridge. Or get thrown, for that matter.

She used her favorite trick for staying centered as she stared out. She just remembered that each face she saw was once a helpless newborn baby, and that all would one day stand at the doorway of Death, the great equalizer. The gap between her and them was not so wide. And Sam was always there, waiting. Giving her his strength.

"If not for the people who rescued me, my heart would be beating inside another woman's body," she concluded. "My corneas would be on another person's eyes. My kidneys filtering someone else's blood. I have to pay it forward. The Illuxit Foundation Victim's Fund will be an even bigger, wider net, to catch the ones who fall. Let's spread that net of hope and healing together."

The applause was loud and prolonged. Everyone stood. Several hands reached up to help her down from the stage, but she stepped straight into Sam's arms. He hugged her, tightly. "Crushed it," he whispered. "Beauty, brains, and a heart of gold. What a huge turn-on."

That approval from him gave her a sweet little rush, before Hazlett scooped her up and flung her to the crowd again. She was passed from hand to hand, hugged and squeezed by tearful ladies who told her how moved they were, how brave she was. Checked out by keenly interested men, all of whom swiftly retreated from Sam's menacing stare.

All except for Hazlett. His hand came to rest against the skin of her shoulder, left bare by the plunging back of her gown. It fixed there, hot and damp, as if it were stuck to her. She wanted to shrug it off.

It took hours to work through them all, but finally she stood at the dessert buffet, sipping an espresso and wobbling on those treacherous spike heels Nadine had sent. Hazlett kissed her hand, with a courtly flourish. "Excellent," he whispered.

"Your mother would have been so proud," Renato said, beaming. "You played that crowd. Completely in control, and yet completely open at the same time. I was more moved than I can express."

She stuffed a sharp comment behind a tight nod and smile. Sam spread her wrap over her shoulders.

"The crowd is starting to thin," he said.

"Thank God," she replied. "I'm dog tired."

Sam passed her a small plate piled with lemon cream profiterole and tiny, chilled cannoli. The sugar gave her a welcome jolt.

"So, my dear," Renato said. "Not to pressure you, but have you given some thought to my invitation to Villa Rosalba?"

"I haven't had a second to think. Could I come the following day?"

Renato looked regretful. "Actually, no. I'm closing up the Villa Rosalba and going back to Milano the day after tomorrow, and Michael, too, has pressing business in London. I hope you can come tomorrow."

Shit. "I would love to see the Villa Rosalba," Sveti said. "Mama talked about it so much in her letter. Especially her last one."

Renato looked out at the sea, dabbing beneath his eyes with his finger. "Ah, did she," he said, voice muffled. "What did she say?"

"She described the sculpture garden in the atrium," Sveti said.

Renato smiled wistfully. "Yes, she loved the sculpture garden, and the views. And the maze. We spent hours strolling in it sometimes."

Her hairs prickled up, a chilly shudder. "A maze? Really?"

"Yes, planned in the eighteenth century, by my great-great-great grandfather. The maze amused her. Do you still have her last letter?"

Sveti hesitated, jealous of her treasured letter. The only thing remaining of her mother that was exclusively hers. "I have it somewhere, in my things," she hedged. "It's not the kind of thing you throw away."

"Certainly not. I know it is presumptuous, but do you suppose, if you find that letter, that you might let me read it?"

She hesitated, suddenly speechless. Mind blank. Her mouth opened and closed, no words forming. "Ah . . ."

"Don't answer." Renato waved his hand. "It's just . . . forgive me. I miss her. Even seeing a letter she wrote. It would mean so much to me."

"Do you read Ukrainian?" Sveti asked.

He blinked at her, as if the question made no sense. "Ah, no."

Sveti swallowed, to calm her throat. "I understand your desire to see it," she said. "But I don't have it with me here in Italy. I'm sorry."

Sam shifted closer, leaning on the railing. He was staring out at the moonlight on the sea, but she felt the focused quality of his attention. He knew that she had Mama's letter. That she was lying.

"Ah, there he is," Renato said sourly to Sam. "Mr. Petrie. The faithful pit bull."

Sam lifted his espresso cup in salute. "Woof, woof."

"You never left her side the entire evening," Renato commented.

"Guilty as charged," Sam said.

"I suppose the size of your gift to the foundation gives you a feeling of entitlement to the young lady's attentions?"

Sveti caught her breath at the guy's blatant, needless rudeness. She braced herself for an unpleasant scene, but Sam kept his cool.

"Not at all." The gaze he gave the *conte* was very direct. "The bullet graze I got on my back when those guys tried to kill her gives me that feeling. I bought that feeling of entitlement with blood, not money."

"Ah, *beh*," Renato muttered, rolling his eyes. "Just so."

"May I ask you something, Renato?" Sveti hastened to change the subject. "And excuse me if this causes you any pain."

"Of course," he said. "Ask away."

"The night that Mama died," Sveti said. "What was she doing?"

Renato's mouth tightened, and his gaze slid away. "There was a reception, at the Villa Rosalba. We were celebrating the launch of Milandra, our new cancer care drug line. She went out into the grounds, and never came back." He passed his hand over his eyes. "There is a footbridge that leads over a gully between one ridge and the next. She was found on the beach below it the next morning."

Sveti gulped. "What . . . what was she wearing?"

Renato frowned thoughtfully. "It was red," he said finally. "A long evening gown. Low cut, crystal beading. She looked stunning in it."

A cold thrill shook her. Sam's arm slid around her waist.

Hazlett turned from a conversation with someone else to them. "So when shall we expect you tomorrow? Breakfast, lunch? After the ice-cream jaunt that simply can't wait? Dinner's fine, too, right, Renato?"

"Of course," Renato said. "Anytime is fine."

"We'll call you tomorrow with the timing," Sam said calmly.

Hazlett bent over her hand and pressed a long and lingering kiss against it, looking soulfully up into her eyes. "You have destroyed me."

Sveti tugged vainly on her hand. "Michael. Please. Don't."

He let go. "Excuse me. I was overcome. Til tomorrow, then."

"Or not," Sam ground out.

She struggled not to stumble over her feet as he towed her away.

CHAPTER 18

The minute they were on the road, Sam let out the throttle, window open. He needed air, after hours of suppressing the urge to crush that groping motherfucker into the slime that he was.

Sveti's eyes were closed, avoiding the issue. He didn't blame her. She'd just delivered a piece of emotionally wrenching performance art, followed by hours of hardcore public relations. He'd be catatonic if he'd been called upon to do what she had just done. And brilliantly, too.

But Hazlett felt entitled to place his hand on Sveti's shoulder and leave it, as if Sam weren't watching. Under any other circumstances, Sam would have simply removed the guy's hand. As in, permanently separated it from his body at the shoulder. But fucking up this gig for Sveti would not help his cause.

So he'd swallowed it. He'd felt it burn, like a hot coal, all the way down, and it kept on burning deep inside him. Hazlett saw him staring, and left his hand right where it was, eyes glittering. Arrogant prick.

"Sam?" Sveti said, her voice small. "I'm, ah, sorry about the—"

"Don't," he said.

She glanced at him. "Don't what?"

"Don't touch it," he said. "Not tonight. I'm on a hair trigger, and you're tired, after doing your thing all evening. We'll save it."

She was silent for a while. "Okay," she whispered. "If you'd rather."

"Believe me, it'll keep. I'm not going to forget one second of it."

She stifled a giggle. "I never thought you would. But I want to know what you thought of everything. Except for, ah . . ."

"Except for your future boss fondling you right in front of me?"

She sucked in air, eyes closing. "Oh, Sam—"

"Sorry, sorry. That just slipped out. I'll start with the good news."

She glanced over, surprised. "There's good news?"

"Yeah," he said. "The good news is you. You're fucking amazing, Sveti. You could sell ashes to the demons of hell and have them put their e-mail addresses down on the mailing list for more."

"Oh." She sounded startled. "Wow."

"It's not like I'm surprised. I saw your TED talk."

"You did?" She gaped at him. "Really?"

He tried not to laugh. Only about a hundred times. "Of course. But seeing you do your thing, in real time, in that dress? I'm in awe."

"Don't overdo it," she said. "So? What's the bad news?"

"You asked me for it, okay? Let the record show."

"Recorded," she assured him. "Let 'er rip."

"Okay," he said. "This whole thing stinks."

Sveti stared out into the night for a minute. "That assessment doesn't astonish me anywhere near as much as you might expect."

"I hate it," he said. "More than before. In Portland, the idea of leaving Helen Wong's snakehead thugs thousands of miles behind us made some kind of sense. After today, it no longer does."

"So you did think I was hallucinating," she said. "About the guy asking me about Mama, in Ukrainian. About The Sword of Cain."

She didn't sound pissed, but he still felt defensive. "We all thought it," he said. "You can't blame us. Anyone who's experienced violent trauma knows how it fucks with your head for years afterward. There's no shame in it, no reflection on your worth. Is that clear?"

"Sure," she said. "But you still should have listened to me."

"I do nothing but listen to you!" he exploded. "I've been chasing you around like a fucking idiot for years, trying to listen to you! You should have started talking to me sooner!"

"That, Sam, is an argument for another day." There was a hint of laughter in her voice.

"Besides, if you'd convinced us, you would not be here now!" he went on. "We would all be sitting on you, at Cray's Cove! The selling point of this Europe trip was that you were safer thousands of miles away from the snakeheads, and that it would be healthier for you to be distracted by conferences, prizes, parties. A fancy new job."

"And you," she said.

"Sure. I'm the Great Distractor. But things look different now. The guy who, unbeknownst to you, hooked you up with your new boss and would-be sugar daddy is the very guy your mom was sleeping with and partying with the night she parted company with a bridge. That's bad."

"You're a fine one to talk about sugar daddies, Sam."

He clenched his teeth. "Can we stay on topic?"

"I'm not the one who strayed from it," she said crisply. "There's the dress, too. Renato says she really did wear a red dress that night."

"Are you going to show Renato your mom's letter?"

She hesitated. "No."

"Why not?" he demanded.

Sveti lifted her chin angrily. "It's mine," she said. "She sent it to me. He already had his piece of her, and it was more than I got. I'll keep my pathetic crumbs for myself, thanks very much."

"So you're keeping it from him out of spite?"

"I am not spiteful!"

"Don't get mad," he soothed. "I don't blame you. I wouldn't show it to him either, but that's just because I think he's a dickhead. But if you're not being spiteful, then letting him see it takes nothing from you. So what's the real reason you're not showing it?"

She could not answer. He waited for a moment.

"It's fear, right?" he prompted. "You're afraid."

"Of course I'm afraid," she snapped. "I'd be a fool not to be!"

"Then listen to your fear," he said fiercely. "I'm afraid, too, and

I'm listening to mine. This whole thing, Sasha, Misha, Hazlett, Renato? It smells like a huge, festering clusterfuck in the making. The smart thing to do now is to back away, very slowly."

Sveti let out a slow sigh and shook her head.

"I think we should just keep driving," he said. "Straight to the airport. I think you should disappear. Now. And for a long time."

"Disappear to where?"

"Hell, I don't know. A cabin on a lake somewhere in the ass end of nowhere, in British Columbia, maybe. They say Ecuador's nice."

She choked on a giggle. "Oh, please. Doing what?"

"Playing house," he proposed, rashly. "With me."

She shot him one of those scared, big-eyed glances.

"Come on," he urged. "It would be fun. Can you cook?"

She shook her head. "Cornbread, from a box. I'm terrible."

"We're set, then. I love cornbread."

She shook her head, laughing. That silly Sam and his romantic notions. But he was alarmed at how quickly the fantasy of the cabin on the lake took him over. He could practically feel the wind off the lake, ruffling the water. Mountains soaring up, aching mountain greens stark against a vivid blue sky. Cup of coffee in one hand, the other clamped around Sveti, all soft and relaxed in her bathrobe, as they sat on the steps, watching hawks wheel in the sky in the morning. Oh, hell yeah.

"I can't back away from this, Sam," she said.

The fantasy shattered. He tried to exhale his frustration, but it filled right back up again. "What a surprise," he muttered.

Sveti rubbed her temples, squeezing her eyes shut. "Try to understand," she pleaded. "I need to find Sasha. He's in trouble, and I want to talk to him, and hold his hand. Before something horrible happens to him, too." Her voice began to wobble. "Something horrible always happens." She shot him a wet-eyed, blazing glance. "Not you, Sam. Don't you dare let anything happen to you! Understand?"

"Perfectly," he said. "I'm tough. Don't worry."

"I'm not leaving until I see my friend. And my mother's grave."

Sam swallowed his reply. If she wanted to bring out the big guns, there was nothing to do but shut the fuck up and be good.

They drove back to the hotel in silence. Once in their suite, he shed the tux and pulled on sweatpants, without turning on the lights. Moonlight streamed through the windows, shining on the sea, lighting up the swirling patterns of mosaic tile. He sat on the bed and waited while she did her interminable girl stuff in the bathroom.

The door finally opened. Light spilled in. Sveti was silhouetted in the door, just long enough for him to get slammed by the heart-stopping effect of her body in the brief nightgown of cream silk. The swell of her breasts tented it out, the jut of her nipples barely denting the fine fabric. Lots of smooth, perfect leg extended below the lacy trim.

Then she turned the light off and stepped into the room. She paused until her eyes adjusted. He couldn't see her eyes, but he didn't need to. He felt her breath. Was tuned to the frequency of her every cell.

She moved across the geometrical blocks of moonlight that slanted across the floor, glowing like a ghostly angel. She wafted through shadow, then through light, then shadow, then light again. He stopped breathing when she was about ten feet away, but jarred his lungs back into movement by sheer force, so that he could smell her.

That sweet cloud of warmth and mystery, moving inexorably toward him. So momentous, so desirable. So fucking dangerous.

She stopped, close enough to him to touch. "I'm sorry, to be such a big problem for you," she said.

He grunted. "Not sorry enough," he muttered. "Don't sweat it. I'm not a victim. I volunteered for this crazy shit. I could leave at any time."

"But you don't. Because you're a good guy." She laid her hand on his chest. Right over the bullet scar.

He stifled the bark of laughter. *No, I don't go because you finally let me touch you.* Nah, that wouldn't fly. He'd score more points letting her think he was a righteous dude rather than a sex-crazed lug with hormonal brain melt. He seized the hand that lay on his chest, kissed it, and rubbed it against his cheek. He'd shaved, for the sake of the gala, but he already had a bristly rasp on his cheek mere hours later.

"I couldn't have gotten through that speech if you hadn't been there," she said. "The state I was in, after meeting the *conte*. I was a mess. You held me together."

He kissed her hand again. "I'm glad if I helped, but it was all you," he said. "You rocked it. You were amazing."

She laughed, bitterly. "Yeah, people love it when you rip out your heart and throw it to them as a blood offering."

He laid his hand over her heart, fingers splayed over the thin silk. The steady throb of her heart pulsed against his palm. "It's still going strong in there," he said. "Plenty of heart. You could fling it to the hungry masses all day long and never use it up. The more you throw, the more you'll have. It's as big as the sky. If you trust it. Just . . . trust it." He kissed her hand again. "Please, Sveti."

Moonlight glinted on a tear that flashed down her cheek and dropped on her breast, blistering the flawless satin.

Christ, he never learned. He just kept hammering at her.

"Sam," she whispered. "Just take this for what it is. Don't ask it to be something else, something more. Because I just . . . I can't."

"Why not ask for more?" he asked. "You're brave, talented, brilliant. You've done amazing things. You could learn this. To be with me, to trust me. To let me love you. A person can learn anything."

She sat down on his lap and wrapped her arms around his neck, and his glands went nuts. His dick tingled.

"Thank you," she murmured into his hair. "For standing by me."

"Don't thank me," he said. "You know damn well that I'd give up body parts for the privilege."

"You made me strong tonight," she whispered.

He grunted. That was problematic, since he didn't approve of her presence here, and didn't want to sustain it. But he didn't want to kill this moment, either. She could dismantle his defenses with a hug and a few smooth, artless moves. Sit that juicy little thing down on his hard-on, press those soft, scented tits against his face, and he'd fall right into line. She said jump, he'd say, sure, babe, over what cliff?

But the tough pep talk didn't slow him down. His body was miles ahead of it, kissing her ravenously. Her cheeks and lips were wet. His tongue slid into her mouth. She shivered in surrender, opening to him.

She pulled away and swept aside the bed canopy. She slid off his lap and clambered onto the bed on hands and knees. With a view like that to precede him, he followed as if dragged by a harness into the mysterious inner sanctum of the tented bed.

She reclined, propped up on her elbows, shivering as he stroked her from her knees up to the baby-soft warmth of her inner thighs. Warm, smooth skin, the graceful shape of her thighs, the swirling puff of ringlets between. The lickable, kissable, fuckable pouting folds of her beautiful cunt, shining and hot. He slid his fingers into her slick heat. She arched and sighed, squeezing around his fingers. He shucked the pants, let his cock spring out, heavy and stiff. Sank his fingers knuckle-deep into her wet warmth, finger-fucking as she bucked and trembled, nightgown shoved up. Spread open, offering it all to him.

Except that it wasn't all. Not even close. He'd gone forward as if frequent, prolonged bouts of wild sex would make up for what she wouldn't give him. It wasn't working out, but he still could not stop.

He inhaled her sexy scent, and lapped his tongue hungrily around her clit while his fingers plunged and delved. She arched off the bed, whimpering as she clenched around his fingers in a wrenching climax.

He wedged his cock into her tight, slick little hole while she was still quivering with the aftershocks, and pumped lazily in and out.

He arched over her, staring straight into her eyes.

"This isn't enough," he said. "I want more from you. You think you can manage me like this? Just drop your panties and give me a little treat whenever I start to bitch and whine?"

She shook her head and cupped his face with her slender hands.

"I'm giving what I have to give," she said. "It's yours, anyhow.

You know that." Moonlight shone full on her beautiful eyes, swimming with tears. "Take it if you want it."

He took it.

Sveti slept long and deeply. She was usually jolted awake by nightmares before dawn, no matter how tired she was, but today, the sun was high when her eyes opened. She felt rested, relaxed.

Then her eyes met Sam's, and last night's events thundered through her head. Her face heated. Her thighs squeezed around the tender ache. He'd peeled back so many layers of her, to some secret part deep inside that flowered madly just for him.

She blinked back hot tears, just thinking about it.

Sam lay on his back, his thickly muscled arms folded back behind his head. So handsome, even scowling. He looked as if he'd been awake for a long time, staring, cogitating, seething. Lying in wait for her. His jaw was set. His mouth looked grim and tight.

"Good morning," she said.

He stared at her for a moment. "That remains to be seen," he said. "It depends on what's required of me. Today's agenda bites my ass."

Oh, boy. He was in one of his moods. This was going to be complicated. She sat up, shoved her hair off her face, groping for something to say that wasn't going to make things worse.

Her phone rang. She jerked up to respond, but Sam was quicker, and closer. He snagged it with his long arm and held it out of her flailing reach as he examined the number. *Buzz. Buzz.*

"Is this your slobbering lech of a future boss?" he asked. "If so, don't answer. I do not want to listen to you talking to him." *Buzz. Buzz.*

"Give me that!" She wrenched the thing out of his grip and stared at it, flustered. The number was unfamiliar.

"I don't know this number," she said. "It's no one in my family."

Sam peered at it. "That's an Italian cell phone. Don't answer."

She shot him an eloquent glance and hit 'talk.' "Hello?"

She waited. Silence, but no beeping. The silence had depth. The line was open.

"Who is it?" Sam asked.

She waved for him to be quiet. "Is someone there?" She barely made out the faint sound of breathing. Her first thought was Sasha, but Sasha had long since given up trying to speak on the telephone. The words just wouldn't come out.

The next possibility bubbled up out of nowhere. "Misha? Is that you?" she asked in Ukrainian.

Sam's body went rigid next to her. "What the fuck?"

"Shhhh. Talk to me," she coaxed whoever was listening. She glanced at Sam, who looked ready to erupt. "The line's open, but no one's talking," she said to him.

"So hang the fuck up!"

She shook her head. "Misha," she said softly into the phone. "I'm your friend. Sasha loves you so much. He worries about you, and brags about you. How bright you are, how special."

"Sveti!" Sam hissed.

She turned her back on him and kept talking. "Remember that I'm here for you. Call me whenever you want. I'll always listen."

A click, and the live silence went flat. The listener was gone.

She let the phone drop, afraid to meet Sam's eyes.

"Have you lost your goddamned mind?" he bellowed.

"Evidently." She was still surprised by what she'd done.

"That could have been anyone! What the hell did you say to him?"

"Stop yelling," she said quietly. "Nothing dangerous or compromising. I said I'm his friend. That Sasha loves him, that I'd be there for him."

Sam rubbed his face violently. "Oh, fuck me."

"Stop carrying on," she said. "I have a lot to do today, so—"

"Yeah, about that." His hand clamped around her arm. "We have stuff to talk about first. Stuff we put off, from last night."

She went still. "Sam—"

"You can't expect me to deal with that guy. It's too much to ask."

"It was embarrassing," she admitted. "I'll make it plain that I'm not interested sexually. It's just a matter of being extremely clear."

"I could make it clearer," Sam offered. "With my fists."

"You just have to trust me," she said quietly.

"You are not the problem! He is! That guy wants to fuck you!"

"You think all men want to fuck me," she snapped.

"That would be an accurate assessment. But that guy thinks that he can. He's sure that he will. And touching you in front of me gets him off. That is sick, sociopathic bullshit. You shouldn't be exposed to it. The guy's a prick, Sveti. You cannot work for him."

"Sam, you're exaggerating the problem—"

"You think we've got problems now? If he puts his hand on you again, I'll tear his head right off his neck. I'm not speaking figuratively."

She was openmouthed. "Ah . . . you're scaring me, Sam."

"Good," he said roughly. "Then we're starting to communicate."

"Listen to me," she said. "No harm will come to me if I just go have breakfast at the Villa Rosalba."

"Why?" he demanded. "Why go there at all? What for? What do you think you're going to accomplish? You think you'll wander freely in the *conte's* house, poking through his stuff? You think after six years that you'll find some trace of your mom there? You're dreaming!"

"That's not the only reason," she protested. "I want to see the atrium, and Atlas, and the maze. Her bones are in the mausoleum! I want to pay my respects. Is that so hard to understand?"

"And I'm supposed to nod and smile while he gropes you?"

"No! I expect you to trust me to handle the situation in my own way!" she yelled back. "I'm not an idiot, Sam!"

He laughed bitterly. "Idiot, no. Babe in the woods, yes."

"You're wrong." She sat up very straight. "You're being irrational. I understand your feelings, but I won't be controlled by them. I'm sorry it makes you angry. Bottom line? It's not up to you. This is my decision."

"That's your final word?"

"In this case, yes." She stretched to snag the gauzy canopy so she could slip out of her side of the bed, as climbing over Sam's big body to get to the draped tent opening did not feel like a good idea right now.

His big hand pressed against the small of her back, pinning her down, and he rolled on top of her. Oh, God. He was so long. Dense, hot.

She went still. "Sam?" she said hesitantly. "Not a good time."

He slid his thigh between hers, opening her. "Last night you said this was mine. You were very specific about what's mine, and what is not and never will be mine. But I can lay claim to this, right?" His hand slid up her thigh, stroked her cleft. Wet from last night's excesses.

"I said a lot of things last night," she said. "That doesn't mean—"

"Shhhh." He pushed her hair aside and licked the birthmark on her neck, a slow rasp as his thick cock prodded her wet folds. He forged inside, in a slow, slick glide. "I want what's mine. It'll probably be the only satisfaction I get today, so I'll take it while I can."

His voice was cool, but his body was so hot, and his solid weight grinding against her, that slow, deliberate penetration, made her limbs go liquid. Her lungs jerked for air, shuddering as he slid his thick cock slowly deeper. Rocking, sliding, swiveling. So deep.

She dragged in more air. "But you're angry. And cold. I don't like that. I don't want you inside me when you're like that."

"I'm not this way by choice," he said. "You're not the only one ripping your heart out, offering it up. I've been doing that since we hooked up. Your answer's always the same. You don't like me angry and cold? Fine. If you want me to bounce for joy, you know what to do. Are you going to do it?"

"I . . . I . . . Sam, that's not—"

"Of course not. I know you're not. I'm just making do with the crumbs that I'm offered." He slid his hand lower until his finger found her clit, caressing it as he fucked her harder, and deeper.

She pressed her face to the pillow, muffling the strangled sounds, canting her hips to meet each slick, hard stroke like an eager little love slave. She loved it and she hated it. How could it feel so good when she was this angry? "You manipulative son of a bitch," she choked out.

"I might be a son of a bitch, but I'm going to make you come so hard. You love the way I touch you, even though you don't want to love it. Just like you don't want to love me."

"Goddamnit, Sam!" She writhed and struggled beneath him, but every move just seemed to stroke his big cock against every shivering sweet spot inside her, driving her wild. "Stop talking that way!"

"Not until you come." He worked her with terrifying skill and timed it just right. Letting go just as she took off, so that he was pumping his essence into her as she bucked and thrashed and wailed.

She was a shaking mess afterward. Her nightgown twisted up around her ribs. Fighting for breath beneath his weight.

He lifted himself up, out of her body. She couldn't even move. She felt flattened. In every way. On every level.

"I'm good to go, then," he said. "I got my morning treat. A quick shower, and I'll be ready to do your bidding once again."

"Fuck you," she said, shakily. "You're punishing me with sex."

"You call that punishment? The way you came? Let's keep it real simple. A time-honored arrangement any guy can understand, even a bonehead like me. I do what you tell me to do, and you let me fuck you."

"You're trying to make me feel cheap," she whispered.

Sam laughed harshly. "Who's making who feel cheap? You'd already be my bride, if I had my way. But I don't get my way, Sveti. I just get a treat tossed to me, now and then."

"So this is your strategy now? Fucking me into submission?"

"No, my strategy is to fuck you into screaming orgasms."

"I don't feel the difference!" she snapped. "This domination kick you're on makes me nervous. Scale it back. Or we'll have problems."

"But you like it that way," he observed. "From the very first, we've played with that vibe. It makes you explode. And I think it makes you feel . . ." His voice trailed off, eyes narrow, as if he were afraid to say it.

She sat up. "What? Makes me feel what? Spit it out!"

He shrugged, still hesitating. "Safe," he said finally, his voice low.

She stared, aghast. "Safe? Sam! Are you crazy?"

He shook his head. "You slept nine hours last night, Sveti. Nine, with no nightmares. Yuri didn't come to you."

She shook her head frantically. "No, Sam. You've got the wrong idea about me. You're going down a dangerous path."

"Those are the only paths you tread, baby. I'm just following after you." His gaze was steely. "You're not having breakfast with Hazlett, today or any day. Put it out of your head. Simone will be here soon with more hardware for me, so I'll take the first shower."

He strode into the bathroom. The shower began to hiss.

Sveti dragged herself up into a sitting position, limbs still weak and shaking. She stared at the bathroom door, appalled at where this was going. Where it had already gone. Over the line. Barreling onward.

She hugged herself, shivering. Wondering if she'd somehow invited him to morph like that, with her unconscious longing for someone strong to take charge, tell her what to do. Keep her safe.

It didn't matter, in the end. Maybe it happened because of the way she responded to him in bed. Maybe it would have happened no matter what she did. Either way, it was not acceptable.

She might love his fierce, conquering vibe in their sex play, but she had struggled through dark places, and come a long way up to the light. She'd attained a sense of power, autonomy, choice. It was very hard won, and no one was taking it away from her. Never again.

Sam was out of the shower before she'd finished formulating her thought. He marched around the room naked. Yanked his clothes on without looking at her, dragged his fingers through his wet, tangled mane of hair. His phone rang as he was shoving his feet into his shoes.

He grabbed it. "*Sì?*" He listened. Said something terse in Italian. "Simone is on his way up," he said to her. "Don't leave this room."

With that, he strode into the *salone* and shut the door.

So. The little woman was dismissed. Not a thought of inviting her into the meeting, or asking if she wanted a firearm, too. It just didn't occur to him, and why would it, the way she shivered and sighed, begging to be ravished. Fuck that. No more.

She hurried into the shower. Threw on a white linen dress, a pair of sandals. Her phone beeped as she was brushing her hair.

Breakfast on the terrace with Renato and me at Villa Rosalba?
Short drive—a half hour at most.
Rocco and Silvano waiting for you downstairs.
Yours hopefully. M.

She felt almost faint, at the momentous choice that text message posed. She opened the connecting door just a crack. Sam was conducting a lively conversation in Italian with Val's guy, Simone, over a table covered with guns of various shapes and calibers. They were talking shop, and would probably be at it for a while.

She didn't have the energy to face him down about this. And a massive power struggle with Sam was a poor use of her energy in any case. She texted Hazlett:

Coming.

Seconds later, her phone burped.

Excellent! A presto.

It was the architecture of the old baroque palazzo that made it possible to leave discreetly. Connecting doors were everywhere, and in the back of the bedroom was a door that communicated with what was probably a servant's stairway. Locked, of course, but from the inside. She scribbled a quick note to Sam.

Going to Villa Rosalba. Accompanied by Illuxit Security. Don't worry.

She left it on the crumpled bed and hurried down the narrow, dingy back stairway.

Outside the lobby, a limousine idled. Silvano leaned against it. He opened the car door for her.

It made her chest hurt, imagining how angry and betrayed Sam was going to feel, but he'd driven her to it. And he might be right about Michael Hazlett being a big prick, but she'd draw that conclusion for herself, thanks. Nor was she particularly interested in drawing it today.

It was the Villa Rosalba, and whatever secrets it might harbor, that beckoned her this morning. Neither Sam nor Hazlett was going to keep her from it. So everyone could just back the fuck off already.

She pulled out her phone and turned the ringtone off.

CHAPTER 19

The Villa Rosalba was perched on a ridge over the sea. It was a small, graceful Renaissance castle, made of pale gold tinted stonework. Sveti stepped out of the car and into the blazing sunshine. Her smooth-soled sandals slipped and slid over ancient cobblestones.

Renato came out to greet her, dapper in a pale linen jacket, a silk scarf knotted around his tanned throat. Oozing with money, and the native arrogance that sometimes accompanied it. How could Mama have chosen this effete nobleman, after Sergei Ardov? Her father had been the polar opposite of this guy. Fiercely handsome. Pragmatic, stern, ascetic in his habits. Focused on work to the point of obsession.

Hazlett came out to greet her, too. She suffered through the ritual, being kissed on both cheeks, her beauty exclaimed over, blah blah blah. Her smile felt stiff, aching. Stapled on.

"You look pale, Svetlana." Hazlett cut into Renato's rhapsodizing, thank God. "Have you eaten anything yet today?"

"Not yet," she said. "But I'm not all that hungry."

"Well, find an appetite. They're setting out breakfast on the terrace right now," Renato said. "Come, let me show you the house."

The palace was an exquisitely restored gem. Harmonious, vaulted rooms full of light, glowing with restored frescoes and graceful loggias overlooking the sea. At one point, she was led along a breezeway that bordered a large atrium in the center of the building. A sculpture garden was featured, arrayed around an ancient fountain.

"My mother told me about this atrium," she said.

Both men stopped and turned to look at her. "Did she?" Renato asked. "What did she say?"

"Just how beautiful it was," she said. "And that statue of Atlas."

"Oh, yes. Atlas. She loved it. I'll show it to you after breakfast."

Sveti had to force herself to eat. There was pastry, fruit, cheeses, prosciutto, and salami. She took black coffee, berries, a small pastry.

"Your mother and I always breakfasted on the terrace when the weather permitted," Renato said. His eyes darted to the pastry in her hand. "She had a fondness for those. *Ricce con crema*. Her favorite."

The food in her mouth became a tasteless lump. It dried out her mouth, to think of Mama lounging on this terrace like a pampered, fluffy poodle. Nibbling sweets with this self-important idiot.

There had to have been a good reason. Some powerful, driving motive, for doing something so out of character. The abstracted, cerebral scholar who Sveti remembered had never cared about luxury. She would not have married Sergei Ardov if she had. Her mother's early life with her rich father and ex-pat mother in France had been much more luxurious. With her beauty, she could have had her pick of men.

"I'm so sorry, Svetlana. How clumsy of me, to speak of her," Renato said gently. "I shouldn't have."

Sveti forced herself to swallow. "Not at all," she said. "This is why I came, after all. To talk about her." She put the pastry down uneaten.

"I'm surprised that your pit bull did not join us," Hazlett said. "Is he loosening his grip? Or did you slip away when he wasn't looking?"

Sveti choked on coffee, clapping the napkin to her lips just in time to save her dress. "Please don't call him that. His name is Sam Petrie."

"I didn't mean to be disrespectful," Hazlett said. "But I'm glad we have you to ourselves. Mr. Petrie was, well, overwhelming. I understand his protective attitude, of course. And I applaud it."

"I owe him my life," Sveti said.

"And I will always be grateful. However, he struck me as controlling. His attitude seemed one of ownership, you might say."

Sveti shook her head. Even if it was true, it was none of his goddamn business, and even less so was the fact that Sam felt the same way about Hazlett himself. "That is between myself and him," she said.

"I know I'm taking a risk," Hazlett said. "But you're young, and all alone in the world. Don't let your natural gratitude for his heroic rescue cloud your judgment. That's all I ask."

"My judgment is just fine, thank you," she said.

"Your mother would never have wanted you to get involved with anyone who might limit your possibilities," Renato said.

"Don't preach to me about what my mother would or would not have wanted," she retorted.

Shocked silence followed that reproof.

Sveti bit her lip. "Sorry," she said tightly. "That was uncalled for."

"Not at all," Renato said. "I'm the one who should apologize."

There was an expectant pause, as if both men were waiting. Renato examined his fingernails. Hazlett sipped coffee.

Renato cleared his throat. "I guess I should just come out with it. Are you ready to see where your mother is laid to rest?"

"Yes," she said. "Thank you. I would love to."

"I'll sit this one out," Hazlett said. "I know you'd rather be alone."

Sveti got up, her belly fluttering. Which seemed silly. What she was about to see was static and eternally unchanging. She followed Renato off the terrace, through a flowering walled garden, then alongside a high hedge. "Is this the maze you spoke of yesterday?"

"Yes, it is," Renato said. "I would be delighted to show it to you. Would you like to see it before, or after . . . ?" He paused delicately.

"After, please." The tomb scared her more. It made sense to confront the bigger emotional ordeal first.

The garden gave way to fruit trees and a vineyard and, finally, an ancient marble mausoleum.

"My family has been buried here since the sixteen hundreds." Renato unlocked the door and led her into the dim, stifling, narrow marble room. He gestured at a panel on the wall. "She's here. Next to the place destined for me. Where I would have put my wife, if I had married. A nod toward lost dreams, romantic old fool that I am."

Sveti stared at her mother's name on the gleaming metal plaque affixed to the stone. She put her hand on the marble, trying to visualize her mother's face. All she could see was the image from her dream. Her mother in the red evening gown, falling backward into the darkness.

The mute slab of stone infuriated her. She wanted to smash it.

"Do you want some privacy?" Renato asked. "I can wait outside."

She made the decision abruptly. She wanted out of this stifling trap. There was nothing here. No answers or insights, just the maddening silence of death. "I can't feel her here," she said. "Could I see the maze? And the atrium? Maybe I'll get more of a sense of her there."

Renato's smile was sad. "I know just how you feel. Come."

He led her back the way they'd come, to the tall wall of topiary they had walked past before. "This maze was planned and planted in the early eighteen hundreds," he told her. "It's multicursal, with a central island. There's a fountain with an ancient Greek statue of Athena in the center, and statuary at the various nodes. The hedges are two meters high, so I dare not leave you alone in it. You might never come out." He chuckled.

She could not bring herself to smile back.

He led her through the entrance. Instantly, the high, narrow corridors made her feel stifled. There was not enough room to walk side by side unless they were uncomfortably close, shoulders touching, but when she tried to edge ahead of him, he just lengthened his stride.

She pulled the sequence of poets out of her memory and turned right at the first node, not even glancing at the statue.

"Svetlana?" Renato hurried after her. "Will you let me guide you?"

She forced herself to smile. "Just let me wander a little," she said. "Please? I don't need to solve it. I just want to experience it."

He shrugged, looking vaguely troubled. "As you wish."

Left, at the rearing horse. Left again, at the lovers. Another right, at a snarling griffin—and then left again, at a plumed soldier.

And she was facing a blank, impenetrable wall of dense green foliage. Smooth turf beneath her feet. Nowhere to go. Nothing to see.

It was a blind alley. There could be nothing here to guide or illuminate her. Not unless it was buried in the ground.

It hit her like a fist in the gut. She should be used to slamming up against blank walls by now. Tears welled up, to her horror. She did not want to blubber like a little girl in front of this man. God, please, no.

She put her hands to her face. Started silently sobbing. *Shit.*

Renato placed his hand on her shoulder. "Oh, my dear."

She shook her head. "I'm sorry. What was I thinking? That she would stroll around a corner and meet me here? I feel so silly."

"Don't, please. If only she could." He passed her a handkerchief.

"Let's go," she said, snuffling into it. "May I see the atrium?"

"Certainly. Whenever you're ready."

Sobbing in front of him had evidently made Renato feel that he had license to touch her now. He took her arm. Good thing Sam wasn't there. And even so, she missed him so badly.

The carved bench in the atrium was made of the same marble the mausoleum was fashioned of, gray with streaks of orange. She sat down. "This is where I'd like to have a moment alone, if you don't mind."

"Of course." Renato patted her shoulder and then strode away.

Alone, at last. Sort of. Anyone could stroll by on one of the porticoed walkways that surrounded the garden. The breezeway with the loggia on the second floor also was open to the atrium, and dozens of windows looked out on it from the third floor. She could be seen by anyone looking down. But her heart fluttered, to be at the very place her mother had described. Mama had invited her to sit right here. Had asked Sveti to see something, to understand something. But what?

What, Mama? What did you want me to see? Her eyes burned with unshed tears. She ached to answer the call. Still longing for approval from someone who was dead six years. Someone who hadn't cared enough to have her daughter come visit for Christmas. And where did that thought come from? It distorted her perceptions.

Now was not the time for goddamn hurt feelings.

It was so hard to think clearly when she had such a complicated emotional agenda. She was behaving as if by solving this mystery, she could somehow regain that intimacy with Mama that had been stolen from her. She could explain, justify what had happened.

She'd so much rather see Mama as a heroic, self-sacrificing crusader against evil rather than just a pampered mistress. A suicidal failure who didn't care enough to live, even for her daughter's sake.

There might be nothing here at all but her own hopeful fantasies.

She looked around at the trees. Mama had mentioned the "tree of life," but there were only palms, orange, and lemon trees here. Atlas stared at the ground, a look of grim endurance on his face. The burden of the world that had been loaded on his back had broken away and been lost hundreds of years ago, but he got no relief. She could see it in the constant, ceaseless effort in his face, in the desperate bulge of muscles in his back. His burden had been lifted, but he hadn't even noticed. He carried on as if it were still there. It was his whole identity.

That weight would always crush him. No relief was possible.

She tore her gaze away. *Follow the tree of life.* How did one follow a tree? Trees were rooted. By definition, they did not move. She rubbed her face. Was surprised to find it wet. She wiped away mascara sludge. What had possessed her to wear a white dress? It was just asking for trouble. Makeup, coffee, who knew what else. Danger at every turn.

When she blinked the tears away, the patterned tiles beneath her feet swam into focus. The design looked like a flowchart, or a root system, stylized and intricate. Her eyes followed them up. The lines coalesced into the bole of a tree; a serpent twisted around it, forked red tongue darting.

She rose to her feet and followed it.

The tree trunk led straight up the path, then branched three ways. The left-hand branch led straight toward Atlas. The images were scenes from the book of Genesis. Some she recognized, some she did not. Adam and Eve were easy to identify, the fig leaves, the serpent, the apple, the angry angel with the flaming sword. The fountain gurgled faintly in her ear. She heard distant conversations, in other parts of the house. Birds chattered. Parakeets screeched. Bees hummed.

She stopped when she could see Atlas's eyes. *Look beneath. Look within,* the letter had said. She looked down.

It took a while for the images to come into focus. The first tile was of two men on either side of an altar, one carrying a sheaf of grain, the other carrying a lamb. The next was a man with a sheaf of grain on his back, who appeared to be yelling at a pissed-off looking angel.

The third image was half-hidden, beneath dried vines and petals of what looked like honeysuckle. She nudged them aside with her foot.

The angry man from the last image was striking another man down with a sword. Blood pooled beneath the fallen man. The sword was red. The killer's face was a mask of senseless rage.

Cain and Abel. It was The Sword of Cain. Her heart galloped.

She slid her foot from her sandal, touched the tile with her toe. It was loose. She pushed the tile as far in its groove as it would go, wedged her toe beneath, and pried it up. There was a cavity beneath it.

"Ah, there you are! Communing with your mother, Svetlana?"

She jerked her foot away, heart jumping up into her throat, and smiled as Hazlett walked toward her. He held two champagne flutes filled with pale, bubbling liquid. She nudged the tile back into place without looking at it and slipped her foot into her sandal. Her heart thundered. Oh, God, the guy's timing sucked. So very badly.

Hazlett's carefully shaped brows furrowed. "Did I startle you?"

"Oh, no. Just lost in my thoughts." She tried to shimmy her foot back into her sandal. The last thing she wanted was to fuss with her shoe and pull his gaze down, drawing his attention to that loose tile.

But why the secrecy? Why was her heart pounding? Hazlett wouldn't care if she found something connected to her mother. Renato would be over the moon with delight. She could just bend down right now and satisfy her curiosity. Why the hell not?

She just couldn't. Her muscles had frozen, and her vocal apparatus, too. There might be nothing hidden under that tile. The place was hundreds of years old, after all. Probably half the tiles were loose.

But Mama had written her a cryptic letter about it. Things she had not confided to Renato. She might have nibbled pastries with him, and shared her body with him—but she had not shared this.

Sveti edged away from the tile without looking down, and took the glass. The sling-back strap was still trapped under her heel.

"Try some Prosecco," Hazlett urged. "Are you feeling all right?"

She gulped the fizzy wine. "Sad," she offered. "I'll always regret not saying good-bye to her. It just doesn't get any easier with time."

Hazlett's eyes went soft. He seized her hand. Fingers closed tight. His grip was forceful. Not more so than Sam's, but it was an entirely different sensation, to have this man seek to impose his will on her physically. A man she did not know, or trust. She disliked it.

But her presence of mind was trashed from finding the tile. She took another swallow of Prosecco, for lack of anything intelligent to say.

Hazlett tucked her arm into the crook of his elbow. "Walk with me," he urged. "I want to show you the chapel. There are frescoes some say were painted by Giotto himself."

"I . . . I'd love to see them." Her loose sandal flapped loudly against the tiles. She contracted her toes to keep it pressed to her heel. Her stomach was roiling. "One moment. Let me just fix my shoe."

She bent down, glad for the opportunity to pull free of his arm.

She rose up and . . . oh, wow. Head rush. A wave of cold, dark. Sweeping upward, washing over her head. She stumbled. Oh, no. *No.*

Svetlana? Svetlana, are you all right? Svet . . .

Hurt. It burned, a fire on the side of her head. The light blinded her when she tried to open her eyes, so she kept them shut as she struggled to figure out what the hell was going on, listening to the voices swirling in and out of focus. Italian. She couldn't catch a word.

She fought to orient herself. "Where am I?" she croaked.

"With us, at the Villa Rosalba. You're perfectly safe, and you're going to be fine. Don't be alarmed," a male voice responded.

It all clicked into place moments after. That was Hazlett—but she had asked her question in Ukrainian. She forced her eyes open. They watered copiously. "You speak Ukrainian?" she asked in English.

He patted her hand. "One doesn't conduct international business deals for decades without picking up a few things."

She tried to sit up and fell back, wincing. "What happened?"

"You fainted." Renato's voice. "I'm not surprised. It was an intense morning for you, emotionally."

That observation bugged her, obscurely. Her intense emotions were not on display for his entertainment.

The loose tile, the tree of life, The Sword of Cain all crashed back into her mind. She still had not the slightest desire to say anything to either of these two men about it, but she was bursting to tell Sam.

She missed him so badly. She put her hand to her head and found a gauze bandage around her forehead. "What's this?"

"You hit your head on the bench when you fell," Renato explained. "Dr. Argillo examined you and bandaged you up. It's a small wound. Just a little blood to wash out of your hair."

A short, middle-aged woman in a white coat leaned over Sveti, peering into her eyes. She shone a bright penlight into both of Sveti's eyes and spoke in rapid, staccato Italian.

"She says you don't have a concussion, but that you should be carefully observed for a while," Hazlett translated. "Of course, we would be happy to observe you. What could be more pleasurable."

Like hell. She wanted Sam. She wanted to soothe his ruffled feathers, tell him what she had seen. She struggled up into a sitting position. The doctor scolded, but she ignored it. A woman hurried in and spoke to Renato. Renato held up his hand for her to wait.

"It appears your fearsome protector has arrived," he said. "From what Agata says, he seems very agitated. I'm not surprised."

"So you did slip away." Hazlett chuckled, smugly. "You sly minx."

Thank God. Her rush of relief was so intense, tears filled her eyes.

Hazlett's gaze narrowed. "I have to ask. Do you want us to let him in? Has he become problematic? We could distance you from him, if you want us to. Now would be the perfect opportunity. Just say the word."

She almost laughed. Problematic, hah. He might be a problem, but he was, by God, her problem. "You have the wrong idea," she said. "Please, let him in. I want to see him."

"If you wish." Renato looked disappointed. He spoke to the girl called Agata. She scurried off to do his bidding.

"Just remember," Hazlett said, "if you change your mind, tell me."

"I appreciate the thought, but I'm fine. Really."

The door burst open and Sam strode through, a terrified-looking Agata hurrying in behind him, babbling shrilly in Italian.

"Sveti?" He looked at her, horrified. "What the *fuck?*"

"It's not as bad as it seems," she assured him. "Don't freak."

"What happened?" He rounded on Hazlett, his gaze accusing.

"She fainted," Renato said. "She hit her head."

"She'll be fine," Hazlett added soothingly.

"Says who?" Sam spun around. "Has she been seen by a doctor?"

"Yes, I have, and you can speak to me, not over my head," she said. "This lady is a doctor. She has examined me. Calm down."

Sam started firing questions at the doctor in rapid Italian. Sveti was too exhausted to try to follow their conversation.

Sam turned to her after a moment. "You ready to go?"

"No," Hazlett said. "She needs to stay under observation."

"You are welcome to stay with her, if you must," Renato said, with ill grace. "Please, do stay for lunch."

"Thanks, but no." He looked at Sveti. "Let's get out of here. I'll observe you like you've never been observed before. Can you walk?"

God, she hated to leave without looking under that tile, but no way would she get another moment alone. And she still didn't want to share her discovery. "I'm fine," she murmured. "We can go whenever."

She got to her feet, tottering. Sam scooped her into his arms.

Hazlett grunted, his narrowed eyes sliding over Sam. "Remember what I said, Svetlana," he said. "Anytime. Just call."

She looked up at Sam, who was glaring at Hazlett. "Would you stop being ridiculous, Sam? You're embarrassing me. Put me down."

"No," he said flatly.

The doctor trotted behind Sam, rapping out instructions. He helped her into the car. She waved at Renato and Hazlett, and dug in her purse for her sunglasses. The blazing sunlight hurt her eyes.

And Sam's deafening silence hurt her ears.

CHAPTER 20

Sam focused his attention on the hairpin turns on the coastal high-way. The slightest provocation and he'd be breaking things.

After about twenty minutes, she gave it a try. "Sam, I'm sorry if—"

"Don't." The word slammed like a karate chop on whatever she meant to say. "You have a head injury. Don't start. We'll both regret it."

She subsided, intimidated. He focused on the road. He was ashamed of himself. Had been since the door to the bedroom had closed behind him. Throwing his weight around, using his strength against her. Sex, as a weapon? Those were toxic gray areas, slippery slopes, guilt trips, power trips. Deal breakers. If he were her, he'd tell him to fuck off and die. If his sister told him a guy had treated her the way he'd treated Sveti, he'd beat the shit out of that Nean-derthal fuckhead and feel justified doing so. He might have al-ready killed whatever they had.

That scared him out of his wits.

"Sam?" she tried again. "I wasn't in any danger—"

"I found you with your head bandaged!" He pulled out her note and tossed it onto her lap. "You scared the living shit out of me, Sveti!"

She looked down at the crumpled note, smoothing it. "You did the same thing to me this morning."

He gulped over the rock in his throat. "I know," he said. "I know."

A couple minutes of fires-of-hell writhing followed, until Sveti broke the silence again. "Did you get anything from Simone?"

"Yeah, I got myself another Glock 19, and a .357 Taurus snubbie for backup. And a Micro-Glock for you. Spare magazines. Ammo."

"You got a gun for me?" She sounded startled.

"Of course I did," he said. "You said you can handle one, right?"

"Ah, yes," she said.

"I got a waist holster for you, too," he said. "Smallest size they make. And a thigh strap." He glanced down at the exposed length of her shapely thigh. "For when you wear the girly stuff." He glanced at her face. "You thought I was going to treat you like a helpless fawn, right? Blinking big, innocent eyes like Bambi? I know how tough you are, Sveti. I want you armed and dangerous. It makes me feel safer."

He was heartened by the smile that flashed over her face.

"He had a good selection," Sam said. "I wanted to get everything he brought. I was in the mood to blow shit up."

She shot him a wary glance. "Sam," she said. "About that."

"Don't," he warned.

"We have to talk about it sometime!"

"I'm hanging on by my teeth, Sveti. I don't want to push you farther away from me. If you give a shit about me, if you care about whatever we have together, then please, help me do that."

She gave him the big-eyed look. "Okay. But for the record?"

He braced himself. "What?"

"I really do give a shit," she said.

That opened up a little space in his chest. Enough to actually breathe. After a few minutes, he was the one to break the silence.

"Learn anything about your mom?" he asked.

"Yes, in fact," she said. "Renato showed me her tomb."

"Any astonishing revelations?"

"Don't be sarcastic. And yes, in fact. There were."

He waited, intrigued. "So? Spill it. What?"

"Well, the maze was a dead end. I followed the directions and slammed nose-first into a hedge. But I found the tree of life."

"No shit," he said. "Found it how?"

"It was on the tiles, in the atrium. The tree, with images of the Genesis creation story. And there was a tile with a depiction of Cain murdering Abel. He's holding a bloody sword."

"The Sword of Cain," he said quietly. "Son of a bitch."

"Exactly," she said. "That tile's loose in the floor, with a cavity beneath, but Hazlett barged in as I was about to peek inside."

"And you didn't want to tell Renato?"

"I was too flustered to think clearly," she admitted. "Hazlett interrupted me as I was lifting the tile. I panicked, and shortly after, I passed out. So embarrassing. I'm not the fainting type. I need to figure out how to get back in there. I have to look under that tile."

"You're kidding, right? By stealth? Without telling Renato?"

"I'll get myself another invitation," Sveti said. "Preferably overnight. I'll look while everyone's asleep. That's the simplest plan."

"That's just fucking brilliant, sweetheart." Sam's jaw tightened. "You love to put me to the test, don't you?"

"This isn't about you, Sam." She sounded exhausted. "And it's not about Hazlett, either. He didn't come on to me at all, by the way."

"How about what he said at the end?" he demanded. "Anytime you're ready to trade up and unload the ball-and-chain boyfriend, he'll sweep you away into bliss and perfection. Wasn't that the subtext?"

She shook her head. "Sam," she said gently. "We're degenerating."

He bit the rest back and parked. Sveti looked at the turn-of-the-century hotel, perched on a cliff over the sea, as so many buildings around here were. "Where are we?"

"At our new hotel, in a new town," Sam said. "I don't like having your admirers at the Villa Rosalba knowing where you are. Or having a driver turn up to carry you away when I'm not looking. Makes me wonder what the fuck I'm doing here at all."

She got out as he heaved the suitcases out of the trunk, and he glanced at her with a frown. "Sit back down," he said sharply. "I'll ask someone else to get the bags, and I'll carry you up to the room."

"No, I can walk," she assured him. "Really. I'm back to normal."

He gave her his most baleful look. She gazed limpidly back.

Now was no time for a fresh power struggle. He left the bags where they were and offered her his arm. "Compromise?"

She rolled her eyes and took his arm. "Okay."

This hotel was smaller than San Aurelio, but just as beautiful, and check-in was swift. He hustled her up into the room. Once inside, he pushed until she sat down on the bed. They stared at each other, for an excruciating interval. He took a deep breath and went for it.

"Okay, here goes," he said. "I was a controlling dickhead this morning. In bed and out. I apologize. I will never do that to you again."

She blinked up at him. "Ah . . . thanks."

"Don't thank me yet. I'm not through," he said.

"Well, then. Finish, by all means."

"I accept that I behaved badly," he said. "But I have to be able to trust you. We've got to work as a team. You can't run out on me. It was stupid and lazy not to face me down. Not to be straight with me."

"I wasn't in any danger, Sam," she said.

He held up a warning hand and shook his head.

Sveti sighed and went to the mirror that hung on the wall. She started undoing the gauze bandage wrapped around her head.

"What the hell are you doing?" he demanded.

"Getting rid of it. It's not necessary. It makes me look like I'm at death's door, and I just bumped my head a little. It's stopped bleeding."

"How does it feel?"

"A little tender, but the headache's gone," she said. "I don't need it, Sam. And it makes you act weird with me. All careful and nervous."

He harrumphed. "Maybe you should put it back on. Maybe that's a better vibe for us right now. Safer."

Her chin went up. Her glance was like a honed blade. "Safer, my ass," she said. "I'm not afraid of you, Sam Petrie. Not one little bit. So don't be afraid of yourself. It's silly."

The look in her eyes made his body start to hum and rev. His heart jolted and started to pound. Oh, Jesus, this was a bad idea. This went beyond slippery slopes. This was a sheer cliff.

"I'm sorry for going off alone," she said. "You drove me to it, but it made me miserable. I was relieved when you showed up. Even as furious as you were."

"Are," he said. "Present tense. I'm still furious."

"Ah. I seem to bring that out in you," she murmured.

"We need a reboot," he said.

"I'm all for it," she replied.

"Any brilliant ideas on how we might accomplish that?"

She hesitated. "I have one idea," she said. "It's not too original, and I don't know how brilliant it is, but it seems to work every time."

His heart kicked up to a mad gallop as the heat in the room went up. "Sveti," he said carefully. "You have a head injury."

"I told you, I feel fine." She swept up her hair with both arms. "It was a very strange morning. Very intense. I need to feel close to you."

"Yeah?" he said stupidly. "How close?"

She kicked off her sandals and slid both her hands under her crisp, flirty little skirt, pulling off the wispy scrap of white stretch lace panties. She tossed them aside and approached him, sliding her hands over his shirt. Fingering his buttons. She smelled so good. He wasn't going to be able to say no. He wasn't going to be able to control the sex, either.

So what else was new. He was almost starting to get used to that.

She opened his shirt, brushing her fingertips over the pattern of his chest hair, the jagged scars. She leaned forward, and her little hot pink tongue flicked out to swirl around his nipple. She pressed her hand to his solar plexus, feeling the frantic thud of his heart. She jerked his belt loose and wrenched open the buttons of his jeans.

He seized her wrists as she pulled his cock out. "Oh, my God."

She sank down to her knees and took him in her mouth.

He sucked in a sharp, rasping breath and flung his head back. This was going to kill him. So raw, so good. Pure electricity. Too much, that hot, suckling vortex, the tender, luscious swirl of her tongue around his aching cockhead. The long, wet pull . . . oh, God.

He opened his eyes and caught sight of them both reflected in the mirror across the room. Himself, chest bared, face contorted in a primal grimace. Sveti on her knees in front of him, hair loose. Still in her virginal, girlish white dress. Like some kinky schoolgirl sex fantasy.

He cradled her head gently, careful not to touch the hurt part. "Stop," he said, but it was a shaking, pleading tone. No authority.

Sveti looked up, squeezing his stiff rod. "Don't you like it?"

"I love it. But we can't. Not after this morning. It's too weird."

"So let me fix it." She lashed him voluptuously with her tongue.

He keened with agonized pleasure. "Wait." His brain was too fried by sex hormones to get the thought out in one piece. "I don't want to be managed and soothed. I don't want you to fix us with sex. I don't want to be trained with it like a circus animal. I don't want that dynamic." He grabbed her under her arms and tugged until she stood up.

Sveti sighed. "Sam. Relax. You're overthinking this."

"Oh, yeah?"

"Yes," she said. "Sometimes a blow job is just a blow job."

"This isn't just a strategy to blow me into a sweeter mood?"

She smiled. "My strategy is to blow you into a screaming orgasm."

His laughter made his chest shake, as if he were sobbing. "You just love throwing my words back in my face, don't you?"

"When the words are perfect for the occasion, yes. Do you feel that I'm manipulating you right now, Sam?"

He held up his thumb and forefinger, touching. "Little bit."

"I'm not." She rucked the skirt of her dress up above her hips. He could see the puff of her pubic hair. She lifted up one foot and perched it on the bed. "Feel me. You told me yourself. My body can't lie."

He just stared at her, breathing hard. His ears roared.

She seized his hand and guided it between her legs. "Feel me. When I come all over you, then tell me how manipulated you feel."

His fingers fluttered across the damp seam of her pussy. He slid them between her folds, finding her hot, slick. Exquisitely yielding.

He yanked her into his arms and kissed her, fingers delving more boldly, thumb circling her clit. The kiss grew ravenous, furious.

"You melt me," she gasped against his mouth. "I want that, Sam."

"You got it," he said breathlessly. "Wait, just a second."

He clawed the coverlet down, leaving just the altar of naked white linen like untouched snow. He shoved his jeans off.

Sveti twisted, straining for her zipper. "Shall I take off the dress?"

"I can't wait," he said roughly, shoving her skirt up. He pushed her thighs apart and stared at her beautiful pale thighs, the nest of dark, damp curls. That gleaming, perfect pink pussy. All his.

She pulled him to herself. "I need you inside me."

He kissed her again. "It's going to be intense, once we get going, the way I am today," he said. "You need to be sopping wet."

"I am wet. You felt me." She sounded anxious. He could feel in her clutching, trembling fingers how she needed to grasp something, affirm it before it could slip away from her.

"Not yet." His voice was savage. "I will decide when you're ready. You are going to relax, and trust me to take care of you. Have you got that straight? Because I will just repeat myself until you do!"

She jerked in a sobbing breath, clutching his shoulders. Her fingers dug into the cotton fabric, trying to trap him there.

He slid his fingers into her hair, avoiding the sore spot. Protecting it. "You with me?" he asked. "Are we good? Do you trust me?"

She bit her lip. "I'm with you," she whispered. "I trust you."

That took him apart, unexpectedly. He had to sink down and hide his face against her breasts. His shoulders shook. What suckass timing. Right now, when he was trying to be all masterful and studly, to show her she was in such good hands. Right now he had to fall apart?

Sveti's arms tightened around him. Then her legs, a whole-body hug. He felt her soft lips, pressing his forehead. Sweet benedictions. She'd ended up comforting him. How fucking backward was that?

When he finally dared to lift his face, her eyes shimmered with tears. Her mascara was long gone, just a shadowy smudge accenting her eyes. No major landslides this time. He brushed her tears away. Sucked them greedily off his fingers. Hot, wet, salt. His.

"Sorry," he muttered gruffly. "Lost it."

She smiled, luminous. "Anytime. I like to be trusted, too." She lay back, squinting at the sunlight flooding in the window. "It's so bright."

"Does it hurt your head?"

"No," she said. "It just makes me feel so naked."

"Good. That's exactly how I want you." He stroked tenderly down her body, inside her thighs. Spreading her gently open.

Sam made a low, choked sound. "Look at that sweet, beautiful thing. All pink, in the sunshine," he murmured. He spread her labia, exposing her most intimate parts. "I want to suck on your clit."

The words racked her, a shudder of emotion. "Oh, God, Sam."

"It'll calm me down." He grinned mischievously. "It'll make me sweet and tractable. Can I have my dose of happy juice?"

She shook with half-hysterical laughter. "Stop it. Don't joke about that, after all the drama! It's not fair!"

"I know, but hey, you laughed, right? I'll do or say anything to make you laugh. And if you came for me, ahhh. Right against my face. Pure heaven. That would be it. I'd be your helpless slave forever."

He put his mouth to her, stroking his tongue up her folds. She gasped. Swirl, suckle. Stroke and plunge. He got his hand into the action, fingerfucking her. Engaging all the hot spots at once.

She was tense and quivering for a few minutes, but she finally gave in. Trusting him, even when he drove her to that naked leap into the void. He pressed his mouth to her clit while the waves pounded her. Fingers shoved up deep into her pussy. Squeezed with each hot pulse.

Now she was ready. A lake of slick, hot lube to ease his way.

Her eyes popped open as he settled over her. She moaned softly at the nudge of his cock, forging inside her. She clung to his shoulders.

He kissed her hungrily, his tongue dominating her mouth. It was majestically slow for many sighing, trembling minutes, but soon the hot, electric lick of pleasure got them both going. She started bucking under him, inciting him with her body to ride her harder. He obliged.

It was deep, pounding, amazing, every stroke. She whimpered and gasped as her pussy licked and clutched his cock. More. Harder. Each thrust more impossibly awesome than the one before. Winding them both up again to that terrifying swell of energy. He muttered incoherent encouragement into her ear as she bucked, wailed, throbbed.

He exploded. Energy blazed through his chest. He was unmoored, lost in the void. She was the cord thrown out to save him.

When he came back to who he was, where they were, she was petting his damp back, as if memorizing the shape of his muscles, his bones. "Sam," she said softly. "There's something I need to clarify."

His eyes popped open. His body tensed. "Yeah?"

"About what you said this morning," she said. "When you went all scary alpha on me. And you said that it makes me feel safe."

"Uh, yeah. I did," he said. "Sorry about that. What of it?"

"It's not your alpha vibe that does it for me. That's fun, in bed, and I get off on it, sure. But that's not what makes me feel safe."

"So what's your point?" he demanded. "What does?"

"You, Sam. Just you. Who you are. The way you treat me." She cupped his face. "You make me feel safe. And it's keeping Yuri away."

The realization hit him all at once. The weight of that tremendous responsibility. Someone so precious, so wary, trusting him that much.

What if he fucked it up? Failed her?

He hid his face against the satiny coils of hair on the pillow and hung on, to her, to himself. His body hummed, like a power source that had switched on. He blazed with it, like a torch.

He'd keep making her feel safe if it killed him.

CHAPTER 21

They were quiet on the drive to Castellana Padulli, careful not to disrupt the truce they'd established. Sam had grumbled, but he'd gotten ready without a fight, thank God. She couldn't face another one, though the make-up sex blew her mind. She crossed her legs, squeezing the hot glow. Her body's constant, tingling animal awareness of him.

Her phone rang, not long after the first signs announcing the highway exit that would lead to Castellana Padulli.

"Who is it?" Sam asked when she hesitated, staring at the phone.

"It's the same number from this morning," she replied.

He shot her a blazing glance. "Don't answer this time."

She hit 'talk.' "Misha? Is that you?" she asked in Ukrainian.

In the silence, Sam cursed and pounded the steering wheel.

"I wish you would talk to me," she said into the phone. "Maybe you're afraid of being overheard. I understand. I know you're in pain. I want to help. I'm here if you need me, Misha. Just call."

The line clicked. The caller was gone. She let the phone drop.

Sam exploded. "What the *fuck* makes you think that asshole is Misha? You've got ten different bad guys breathing down your throat right now! This is sloppy wishful thinking! Use your goddamn head!"

She stared at her lap, biting her lip. He was right, but the impulse had been so strong, she couldn't reason it down. She shook her head.

"Babbling sweet nothings to a manipulative pervert is dangerous!" Sam raged. "Whoever it is, you're encouraging him to jerk you around some more! If it's Misha, he can find his balls and announce himself, like a normal person!"

"Normal? Misha?" She snorted. "That's a lot to ask of him."

"Don't even start. I'm sick of your excuses for your damaged mafiya soul brothers." He flipped on the turn signal for the exit ramp.

Castellana Padulli had a walled historic center on top of a steep hill, with cobblestoned streets. The *centro storico* was a traffic-restricted zone, so Sam parked in a garage, and they strolled up the road that wound around the hill and through the arched gate into the center.

Sun-bleached vistas spread out around them, an undulating patchwork of orchards, fields. The sun beat down. She sweated in her white linen sundress and the crocheted cream mohair shrug she'd tossed over it in case it got cooler. Cats who were the same silver gray as the lichen-mottled stones darted like shadows. Fragrant wild herbs and flowers hung in ragged bunches from joints between the stonework.

Sam took her hand as they went inside the ancient arch that marked the entrance to the old town. He wouldn't meet her eyes, still pissed about the phone call, but his hand felt good. Her fears and doubts were flooding in as she remembered Misha's panicky hostility. This could be a trap, and she was dragging Sam into it.

And this might also be a blank, anticlimactic letdown.

But she couldn't share her doubts with Sam. She'd maneuvered him into this against his will. She was so grateful for his brooding presence, but she wished they could be real partners, brainstorming, bouncing ideas back and forth. Supporting each other.

But she couldn't impose her agenda on him by force. She cared so desperately about finding her answers, and he just didn't. All Sam cared about was her. Keeping her safe. Making her come.

Right. And she was complaining? God. Life was so weird.

The Gelateria Del Corso was on a piazza near the town's cathedral, in a small, lovely shopping district. There were tables, umbrellas, a handful of people having coffee or ice cream. Inside, behind the counter were two adolescent girls with hairnets and pimples, scooping gelato. Neither seemed good candidates for questioning. Where was the man who'd answered the phone? He at least was an adult.

They sat down, ordered. He had coffee-flavored gelato. She had crème caramel. She stared out at the pigeons strutting, the blueness of the sky behind the cathedral's bell tower, wishing her fiction was reality. That she really was just wandering the charming hill towns of Italy, eating fabulous gelato with her gorgeous, complicated, demanding lover between bouts of incredible sex. Instead of . . . well, hell. She wasn't even sure what she was doing, but whatever it was, Sam disapproved of it, with all the force of his outsized personality.

A dark-skinned man, Indian or Pakistani, entered the *gelateria*'s sheltered area, carrying an armful of long-stemmed roses. He proceeded to offer roses to all the women at the *gelateria*, flashing white teeth at each of them as they refused. He left a rose on each table, including theirs, and made the rounds once again to collect the unsold flowers.

Sveti picked up the rose he had left beside her and passed it to him with a smile. *"Grazie, no."* It was the full extent of her Italian.

The man's white teeth flashed, and he gave Sam an apologetic look. "No," he said. *"Lei è bellissima. Tenga pure."*

He backed away without taking the rose.

Sveti looked at Sam. "What did he say?"

"He's just giving it to you, because you're so goddamn pretty," Sam said, disgusted. "He's got quite the racket going." He dug into his wallet, pulled out a ten-euro note, and held it out.

The guy wagged his finger in denial. Sam stood, towering over the guy, and held out the money again.

"Tenga," he said in a voice that made the man's eyes go big.

He extended his hand and Sam slapped the ten-euro note into it.

"Buona sera," Sam said sharply.

"What was that about?" Sveti asked, when he was seated again.

"No guy gives you flowers when you're with me," he said. "You get flowers, I pay for them. Assuming he wants to keep those pretty teeth."

"Wow," she murmured. "That's very primordial of you."

"Babe, you have no idea." He gave her a look that zapped her to her core. "There's the guy I talked to, behind the counter."

Sveti let out a measured breath and got up, tossing her half-eaten gelato into a waste bin. Sam followed close behind as she went inside. It appeared he was not going to volunteer his linguistic skills for this encounter. On principle. Whatever. She'd be a grown-up and manage on her own. She gave the man a big, radiant smile as she approached the counter. That got his notice quickly. He smiled back.

"Excuse me, sir. Do you speak any English?" she asked.

"Little bit. Little *francese*, little *tedesco*. More, for the pretty girls."

"That's wonderful. I'm looking for someone who might have been here recently. A young man named Sasha. He's thin and pale, with dark hair and dark eyes, and he has trouble speaking. Have you seen him? Or heard of him?"

The man's smile vanished. His eyes darted out toward the street. "No." The warmth in his voice was gone. "I don't see nothing like that."

She pulled out her card. "If you do see him, could you give him—"

"No!" He waved her card away. "I don't tell no one nothing."

Sam reached for his wallet. *"Mi faccia almeno pagare il gelato."*

"No, no, no," the guy babbled. "No, *il gelato è gratis. Offre la casa. Vada ora.* Get out. Now. Please."

Sam slid his arm around her waist and pulled her against him as they walked toward the exit. "Smile," he muttered. "Kiss me."

She obeyed without a thought, but was startled by his brazen answering kiss. He let her come up for air as they walked into the piazza, and leaned in to her ear. "Someone got there before we did and scared the living shit out of him. Which suggests that we're being watched. Keep smiling, sweetheart."

She smiled as fear settled into her belly like lead.

"Congratulations, babe." He grinned at her, eyes glittering with razor-sharp concentration. "This is special. Only with you."

"Stop it, Sam. I'll apologize later, I promise. On my knees."

"Ah, now there's a happy thought." He spun around, just a care-free guy on vacation with his girlfriend. "If we live through the afternoon, you'll spend a long time on your knees to make up for this."

"Don't be crude," she snapped.

"Stop looking scared. At least pretend to look forward to your apology. Kiss me again. Grab my ass. Laugh. Act."

"Stop jerking me around," she hissed. "You're pissing me off."

"I get this way under stress," he said. "I default to sex, my favorite coping mechanism. Could be worse, right? At least sex is life affirming."

She snorted. "Right. So now what?"

"We fuck off, fast. And once we're someplace safe, and your long, yummy oral apology has calmed me down, I will kick my own ass for letting you talk me into this."

She realized that she was clutching the rose so tightly, she'd snapped off the head of the flower. The red blossom hung limp and forlorn. The sight gave her a pang of premonitory dread. She put her finger under the bloom to hold it straight, which was when she felt the shred of paper wrapped around the stem.

She glanced down. *Svetlana* was written on it in Cyrillic.

She let the hand holding the flower drop. "Sam," she said.

He hustled her swiftly along. "What is it, baby?"

"The flower the guy gave me? There's a note on it. Wrapped around the stem, right under the blossom."

He didn't react or look at her. "Could it just be a piece of tape?"

"It has my name written on it."

"Oh *fuck*," he hissed. "Don't look at it til we're in the car."

Once in the car and speeding away, she unrolled the scrap. "Via Savoni 84, Torre Sant' Orsola. It's an address." She typed it into her smartphone GPS. "A town about twenty kilometers from here."

"Tell me you don't want to go there now, Sveti," he said.

She stared at him. "Of course I want to go there now! Why did you think we came here at all, Sam? For my health?"

"Yes! You saw the guy in the ice-cream shop! This address is probably just a more discreet place to shoot you in the head and stick you in a hole than the main shopping district of a tourist town!"

"Why would Misha go to the trouble? He had me in his clutches in Rome! If he'd wanted to shoot me, he could have done it then! Easily!"

"Yeah, I know! I remember every second of it, believe me."

"He could have killed us, but he didn't. He threw me a clue." She craned her neck to look behind them. "No one appears to be following."

"The look on the ice-cream guy's face was enough reason not to go to the address on that note."

Sveti held up the paper. "And the look on Misha's face is enough reason to go. This is my only possible point of contact with Sasha."

"Well, it's burned now, babe."

"My point exactly! If not now, then never!"

"You think Sasha will never be able to find you again? That's stupid! You don't hide, Sveti! You damn well should, but you don't!"

"Sasha would only go to such insane lengths if he were scared to death. He's trying to protect me with this cloak-and-dagger spy stuff."

Sam flipped the turn signal on and jerked the car to a stop at the side of the road. He reached for Sveti's phone. "Give me that thing."

She handed it to him and waited as he stared at the digital map, eyes darting between it and the rearview mirror. Constantly monitoring.

"We should be taking this to the police," he said.

"That won't help Sasha," she said.

"You're so sure? How are you supposed to help, if they can't?"

"He'll tell me when he sees me," Sveti said quietly.

Tires squealed as the car surged into movement again. "Yeah, baby, I just bet he will."

*   *   *

It took a couple hours to get to Torre Sant' Orsola by the route Sam took. He circled, backtracked, puttered around on back roads, even parked the car in the alley of a small town and dragged Sveti into a bar for a tense twenty minutes, while he stared at the street outside and gnawed a prosciutto sandwich. She was too tense to eat anything.

By the time they finally arrived at Torre Sant' Orsola, he was as convinced as he would ever be that they had not been followed. It was insane to drive into this rendezvous with no idea what they would find. It was a peculiar sort of torture, to feel so responsible for her while at the same time having no veto power over her decisions. If he refused to play, she'd do whatever the fuck she wanted, alone. She'd demonstrated that this morning. She never backed down. He'd have to restrain her physically to keep her from her suicidal bullshit. Nor could he distract her with sex. He'd tried, but it didn't matter how many orgasms he brought forth. As soon as she caught her breath, *boing,* she bounced right back. Up and at 'em again. More pigheaded than before.

Via Savoni proved to be a sad, seedy place, once an expanse of olive orchards. In the middle of the last century a factory had been built there and then subsequently abandoned. Its roof was caved in. Huge slabs of rusty, corrugated metal hung askew. The place was surrounded by nondescript smaller buildings that had grown up around it like mushrooms and been abandoned in their turn.

Number eighty-four was a scarred, featureless door in a long, rough concrete wall, the faded, stenciled number barely legible. The roadside was overgrown with weeds and strewn with garbage.

Sveti rang the bell. They heard a metallic rattling noise from the inside, but there was no subsequent movement or sound.

She rang again. Wind sighed, in the grass, the bushes. The smell of manured fields drifted on the breeze, acrid and heavy.

"Ehi!"

Sam almost jumped out of his skin.

It was a kid who had called out to them, maybe ten years old, on a beat-up pink bike that was much too small for him. He was tanned a deep brown, dressed shabbily, with broken flip-flops. His bike rattled and thudded over the broken pavement as he approached. He stopped about ten meters away. His dark eyes were sharp and calculating.

"*Venite,*" he said. When they did not move, he frowned, and beckoned impatiently. "*Aò! Movetevi!*"

"*Tu chi sei?*" Sam demanded. Who are you?

The kid ignored his query. "Sveti?"

She nodded. The kid beckoned and turned, tottering away on his bike. Sveti followed and Sam kept pace, his hand on his gun. He hated having a young kid in this mix. The situation had lacked only that element to make his stress complete. Put a fucking cherry on top, why didn't they. Throw in a toddler, maybe a gurgling newborn.

The kid made sure they followed, but kept a careful distance from them as he led the way through the deserted buildings. Finally, he stopped by a gate, which was slightly open and askew on its hinges. He pointed to it and pedaled away like the demons of hell were chasing him. Sam was glad to see him disappear. One less target to feel responsible for.

There was an acre or so of orchard inside the gate, bounded by a stone wall with broken glass jabbed into cement adorning the top of it, jagged and hostile as shark teeth. Sveti slid sideways through the broken gate before he could stop her. He followed swiftly after.

There was a squat, miserable little building made of roughly poured concrete. The windows were shuttered, the door closed.

Sam pulled Sveti back as she reached for the door, and shoved her behind himself, putting his fingers to his lips. He pushed the door open, bursting in with his gun drawn.

It was dark inside, the air stale and close. Light from the door poured in, revealing a table with a glowing laptop and a tangle of wires and cables. There was a cheap metal bed frame, covered by a bare mattress. Upon this cot a figure lay, flattened and insubstantial, more like a shadow than a person. The figure shifted, moving slowly.

"Sveti?" His voice was gravelly. He sat up.

"Sasha? Oh, Sasha!" She ran at the guy.

Sam was intensely uncomfortable to see Sveti kneeling on a

filthy floor in her crisp white dress, her arms around another guy. The situation did not improve when his eyes adjusted and he saw more details of the nasty little room. Unsavory stains on the mattress, plates of spoiling food with flies crawling on them. On a chair next to the bed was a plastic bag of white powder, a spoon, a syringe, a lighter.

He'd seen way too much of that poisonous shit, after years spent in police work. He hated the soul-killing addictive drugs. What they did to people, kids, families. What people were disposed to do to obtain them.

Sam stared at the guy, whose chin rested on Sveti's shoulder. He'd seen people in very bad shape, but not since his mother's death had he seen anyone on this side of the dividing line between life and death look as bad as Sasha did. His dark hair was lank and unwashed, his eyes so lost in shadows, they stared out of gray pits. His lips looked blue, his cheeks caved in. His skin was yellowish gray.

His arms, wrapped around Sveti, were thin, but his hands seemed unnaturally large, hinting at the size he should have been if his weight had been normal. Sasha's eyes opened and saw Sam observing the slovenly scene, the baggie. His gaze slid away, ashamed.

Sveti asked a question. Sasha replied in the same language.

Enough bullshit. He hadn't come this far to be linguistically cut out of the conversation. "Does he speak English?" Sam asked.

Sasha's lips moved. He coughed, closed his eyes. "Yes," he said, his voice halting and scratchy. "It is n-n-not perfect, but I—"

"Use it, imperfect or not, and keep me in the loop. Tell us what's going on. Why the scavenger hunt mindfuck to get us here?"

Sasha stared at him, blinking, and turned to Sveti. "Who . . . ?"

Sveti shot him an entreating look. "He's, ah . . . he's my—"

"Her boyfriend," Sam supplied. "And bodyguard. We need to get the hell away from this place. We're too isolated. Too exposed."

"He's a friend who's helping me," Sveti corrected quietly. "His name is Sam Petrie. He's a police officer. You can trust him."

"But can we trust you, Sasha? What are you doing, other than getting high and moping in the dark? Practicing for the tomb?"

"Sam?" Sveti sounded shocked. "What the hell?"

"I'm doing him a favor," he replied, unrelenting. "He doesn't need sympathy. He needs his ass kicked."

Sasha turned to Sveti. "Why are you here?" he coughed out. "I begged you not to come. Told you they were h-h-hunting you. The m-m-message. Did you not see it? Why didn't you . . . l-l-listen?"

"That's not what you said in the message!" Sveti protested. "You told me to hurry, that you needed me! You asked for my flight info!"

Sasha shook his head. "Josef d-d-discovered our e-mail account."

"Before you go on, clarify something," Sam said. "Are you high? Because I don't have any thought cycles to waste on a drug dream."

"Sam!" Sveti gasped, horrified. "Don't talk to him that way!"

Sam gestured at the powder. "I'm justified. It's in my face."

Sasha met his eyes. "No." His voice was stronger than it had been so far. "I am clean. I've been waiting, ever since I saw you on my monitor at the *gelateria*. I had Saleh bring you the note." He choked on the long speech, coughing, and then went on, looking at Sveti. "I thought you were safe, in America. With your friends protecting you."

It pissed Sam off. This guy had the privilege of Sveti's love, and yet he had allowed her to see him in such squalor. He should be strong for her, after what they'd shared. How dare he fuck up this badly.

Sasha murmured something halting in Ukrainian. He flicked a guilty look at Sam, and repeated in English. "Sorry, to let you see this."

"We'll get you out of here somehow," Sveti said.

"No." Sasha seized her hands. "It is too late for me."

"That's defeatist thinking! Don't talk that way!"

"Shhh. I am a dead man, after what I did."

Sam crossed his arms. "What did you do, Sasha?"

Sasha's gaze darted to him. "I . . . I be-be-betrayed my father. I t-tried to ex-ex-expose him. I have tried before . . . but he did not . . . know it was me. This time, I was caught in the act. They will kill me."

Sam groaned. So they were right in the middle of a mafiya family betrayal. Sweet. That was just fucking priceless. "What do you mean, you tried before? You make a habit of it?"

"I . . . I t-t-tried, once," Sasha said. "I d-d-did not want Sveti in danger. I b-b-b-begged her not to come."

"You didn't beg loud enough or long enough," Sam said harshly. "What about the guy selling roses? The kid on the bike? What happens to them if your mafiya buddies come down on you?"

Sasha's throat bobbed as he swallowed. "I had . . . no choice."

"No? You're not locked up. I see choices all over the place." Sam looked around. "You chose to stay here. To have people bring you food, which you then chose not to eat, or dispose of. That baggie is a choice. You're making lots of choices. You're just making the wrong ones."

"Stop scolding him!" Sveti said hotly. "Don't you see it's hard for him to talk?" She turned to Sasha. "Ignore him. He's being an asshole. How did you betray your father?"

"I tried to expose . . . a deal. Years ago." It took forever for Sasha to cough the words out. "He bought . . . thermal generators from an arms dealer. In A-A-Abkhazia. Stuff the S-S-Soviets left in Georgia, after the Cold War. I intercepted the messages. The cores were strontium-90. Already p-p-pulverized. They . . . they spent almost thirty million euro."

"Who is Josef?" Sveti asked.

"One of my father's men. The worst one. He went to find you. To question you."

"Oh, him. So that's his name." Sveti shuddered. "Yes, we've met. Sam saved me from him. What are thermal generators?"

"Radioactive materials. For powering nuclear plants," Sam said. "Dirty bomb?"

Sasha nodded. "Or more than one."

"And we should believe this why?" Sam demanded.

Sveti looked astonished. "Why would he lie?"

Sam looked at the baggie. "He abuses mind-altering drugs. If he told me where to find the nearest toilet, I would question his credibility."

"He has no reason to make this up!" she said angrily.

"I don't know. I might go to some crazy lengths to justify lying around in a rathole with only a bag of smack for company," Sam said.

Sasha's eyes flashed. "I can prove. I tried to tell a journalist. I tried to show him proof. I thought, when it is on Internet, the press, there is no going back. But they killed this man, in front of me."

Sveti winced. "Oh, no. Oh, God, Sasha."

"Mauro Mongelli is the name," Sasha said, still staring at Sam. "He was murdered. Look, on your phone. You will see. Look. Go on."

Sam pulled out his phone and tapped the name into the search engine. Interesting, that Sasha spoke more clearly when he was pissed.

Mauro Mongelli, columnist. Killed in a hit-and-run in Rome, stolen car, driver still at large. Foul play suspected. He looked at Sveti. "It happened right about when they came after you," he said.

"I didn't know who to tell," Sasha said. "I had to tell someone, before I . . . before they kill me."

"They won't kill you!" Sveti's eyes glowed with fervor. "I won't let them! We'll get you back to America. My friends will help protect you!"

Sam suppressed a snort. Sveti had a rosier idea of the extent of her adoptive family's generosity than Sam did. He could imagine how Tam, Val, Nick, and the others would feel about nurturing the drug-addled offspring of a mafiya vor, with bloodthirsty goons out to whack him. With their children toddling around them? Nah. No matter how much Sveti loved the guy, that was going to be a very tough sell.

Sasha read his mind. His shadowy eyes darted to Sam and away again. "I do not think they will be so happy to see me, Sveti," he said.

"They'll help you, for my sake! You're like my brother! Mama would have wanted to help you, too. She wrote to me about how she saw you when she came to Italy. She loved you."

"She told me once that if . . . if you save others, you save yourself, too," Sasha said. "But I n-n-never save anyone, Sveti. I . . . t-try, but I only put people in danger. You, Misha, Mongelli. And your mother."

"My mother?" Sveti's voice was fearful. "What about her? Why did Josef come hunting me? Why did he ask about Mama's photos?"

Sasha struggled to speak for over a minute. His painful throat clearing and false starts were the only sound in the room. "Your mother . . . your mother . . ." He kept trying, but the sound strangled itself.

"What? What about her?" Sveti's voice was getting high and thin.

Sasha forced out a sharp breath. "She was killed because of me."

Sveti knelt on the filthy floor, paper white and immobile. Sam's skin prickled. He felt as if the building were a tomb, sealing itself around them.

"How?" Sveti asked.

"My fault." Sasha lifted his face. His eyes were wet. "She was here investigating the lab. That was why she came to Italy."

"What lab?" Sam prompted. "Spit it out, for Christ's sake!"

"The lab that my father . . ." Sasha coughed again. He looked at Sveti. "Does he know? About your father?"

"Only that he ran afoul of a guy who gutted him," Sam said.

Sasha coughed, struggled. He looked at Sveti, gesturing at Sam. "You tell him," he said. "The lab, in Nadvirna. Tell him."

"My father was undercover," Sveti said, her voice without inflection. "Investigating Zhoglo. They were doing illegal medical experiments with radiation. Killing people. My father blew up the lab, the scientists. He destroyed the research."

"They killed him," Sasha added. "And kidnapped you."

"Mama tried to investigate," Sveti went on. "She said she found a mass grave, but they never found any bodies. Paranoid delusions, they said. They locked her up. What does it have to do with Mama's death?"

"They opened a new lab," Sasha said. "Here, in Italy."

Sveti's hand drifted up to cover her mouth. "Oh, God."

"Yes, they d-d-did it all again. The research, the testing. It was my fa-fa-father's idea. He had ties with the local mafiyas, the Camorra, Cosa Nostra, the 'Ndrangheta, to provide test subjects. But these were not mental patients and orphans, like Zhoglo used. They used refugees from Africa, coming ashore in Italy. He bought boatloads directly from the traffickers. They put ashore, were met with food, blankets, and herded into trucks to be taken to a refugee camp. Or so they thought."

"And you were involved?" Sam asked.

Sasha's mouth twisted in a bitter smile. "He tried to involve me. That was why he called me back, when I was . . . v-v-visiting Sveti. He brought us down to Rome, he bought that house. He thought it would do me g-g-good, to be involved. That it would make a . . . a m-m-man of me. But I . . . I refused, to p-p-participate. He was . . . so angry at me."

"Oh, Sasha," she whispered.

Sam suppressed the urge to say something sarcastic. Sarcasm was all that could distance him from this tale of utter wretchedness.

"I still don't get it," Sveti said. "Where did Mama fit into this?"

"She contacted me while she was looking for the lab," Sasha said. "She wanted my help, to take them down. But they were watching me, after I came back from America. She found it on her own. I met with her only once, while Josef was gone on some other job. She gave me copies of the pictures. And I . . . I told her about the thermal generators."

"Why?" Sam asked. "Why did you involve her at all?"

Sasha's smile was bitter. "I did not have many . . . p-p-people to . . . confide in. I had to do something, but I . . . could not do it alone. Sonia came up with a plan. To steal the thermal generators right out from under them. She was amazing." His eyes had a wistful glow of hero worship.

"You couldn't have just called the cops?" Sam asked.

"Sonia tried that once before and ended up sedated in a mental institution for three years," Sasha said. "She insisted. First, the press. Then the police. So there could be no cover-up."

"Okay," Sam said. "So you came up with a plan. And?"

"She came up with a plan," Sasha specified. "I just did what she told me. I monitored, as they were moving the generators. We saw an opening. Ambushed the truck. We stole The Sword of Cain. Just the two of us." There was pride in his voice. The words slid out, unimpeded.

"Our mistake was not killing Josef and the driver," Sasha went on. "We used drug darts, and when they woke, they remembered a masked woman with a sexy body who spoke Ukrainian. My father knew Sonia was in Italy, that she had tried to find the mass grave in Nadvirna. He did not suspect me, but he took her. And killed her."

Sveti hugged herself, rocking. Her face hidden against her knees.

"She never told them about me." Sasha's voice broke. "She didn't tell them where we hid the g-g-generators. They did not break her."

Sam cut him off before he could start to cry. "Where did you hide the generators, Sasha?"

Sasha wiped his eyes on his sleeve. "Here."

Sam's body went rigid. "What the fuck? You mean . . ." He looked around the tiny room, nerves jangling.

"Not in this building," Sasha clarified. "Behind the old foundry. A Camorra boss owns it, but it has been abandoned for years. It was just a temporary hiding place. I never meant for it to stay there for six . . . six years. But they were watching, always, and I was paralyzed. No one else knew, after Sonia died." He paused. "Until now."

Sam wanted to clutch his brow. "Oh, lucky us."

"I am glad I had a chance to tell you," Sasha said to Sveti. "She was so brave. She saved me. I wanted you to know that, before . . ."

"Before what?" The insight was like ice water in Sam's face. "That baggie. It's your ticket out, right? You're going to load that needle with a lethal dose and drift off with the unicorns and rainbows. And leave your friend to clean up your mess? Is that your plan?"

Sasha's eyes fell.

"Sasha?" Sveti's eyes darted between them. "That's not true, is it?"

Sasha would not meet her eyes. "It's a better death than the one they would give me."

"That's how you repay her?" Sam demanded. "By offing yourself? She's been let down by a lot of people. You're not joining the club."

"I couldn't think of what else to do!" Sasha's voice got stronger.

"Then think harder!" Sam yelled. "That night, ambushing the truck, that was it for you? Your finest moment? Life is asking more of you. Pull another shining moment out of your ass, Sasha. Now."

Sasha flinched. "No," he said. "You d-d-don't understand—I—"

"You are using her, and I will not allow it. Get up off that bed. Get outside. Both of you, out of this place. I need some air."

"But I . . . but I can't stand the light—"

"Too fucking bad. You want a mausoleum, die first. We'll talk about the details while we go to the police. I'll call around, make sure that whoever we talk to isn't dirty. I'll call people at home, too. We'll spread the word. Everyone will know about it."

He was going to pay for his tough-love attitude, but the guy needed a boot sunk in his ass, and they had to blow this mess open and turn it into someone else's problem before the hammer came down.

Sveti helped Sasha to his feet. He tottered out the door like an old man, wincing away from the half-light of dusk. "I c-c-can't be out here."

"Let's go," Sveti said gently. "Come to the car. We'll fix this. We'll find a way to protect you. I'll stick with you, Sasha. It'll be okay."

Great. Sam wanted to bash his head against the concrete wall.

"I can't come," Sasha said. "Being with me is dangerous for you."

"I don't care about the danger!" Sveti said. "I want you anyway!"

"Go, tell the c-c-cops," Sasha said, stroking her hair. "I'll stay here. When they come, I'll show them. And I'll tell them about the lab, too. I do not know where it is, but at least they will know that it exists."

"I will not let you stay here to kill yourself! We'll find you a place to hide! Someplace beautiful where no one can find you. Please, Sasha!"

Sasha looked tempted. Then his gaze darted toward the building.

Sam read that look and the impulse behind it. "No," he rapped out. "Come if you want, but you can't bring your stash. If you're coming, then keep walking. Right foot, left foot."

Sasha turned to Sveti. His eyes were sad. "I can't," he whispered. He turned to Sam and opened his mouth. "I—"

Whannnggg, a bullet ricocheted off the concrete by his head. A shower of grit stung them. "Get down!" Sam bawled.

A huge, dark shape cannonballed down from the roof and took Sveti down. Sam leaped up with a shout, the Glock drawn.

Bam, bam, bam. Bullets thudded the ground at his feet, driving him back. Three more men stepped out of the trees, guns drawn.

They were pinned.

CHAPTER 22

It was the one who'd tortured her in Portland. Josef. His breath stank like rotting meat. An odd thing to fixate on, with a gun barrel shoved under her chin. Josef's grip was grinding agony. He didn't care if he broke bones, ripped cartilage, snapped tendons. He specialized in damage. Her wrists were crushed in his enormous paw. No way to grab the gun strapped to her thigh. She wiggled her fingers, to try for Liv's ring. His hand tightened until she gasped, her vision going black.

It had happened so fast. She still couldn't believe it.

Pavel stepped forward. She'd only seen him once, eleven years ago. He and Sasha's mother, Marya, had come to the place where the children had been held after their rescue. Pavel had looked bad then, and he looked worse now. His face was grayish, pitted, sagging.

He stared at his son with naked loathing.

"Traitor," he snarled to Sasha. "Get down on the ground, like the turd that you are." *Bam.* He fired a shot between his son's feet.

Sasha danced back. One of Pavel's men struck him against the back of his head, sending him stumbling forward. A kick to the small of his back planted him face-first at Pavel Cherchenko's feet.

Pavel kicked his son in the face. Sveti cried out in protest, Sam flinched. Sasha did not make a sound. He drew himself into the fetal position, huddling to protect the most vulnerable parts. A trick they had learned with Yuri, and his thick boots. Yuri had liked to kick, even the little ones. Sveti and Sasha had drawn his attention away from the smaller children whenever possible. Sometimes at great cost.

Pavel hooked his son by the collar of his shirt and yanked him up without much effort. Sasha couldn't weigh much more than Sveti did. He looked at Sam. "Put down your weapons, slowly," he said in English. "Or he blows the girl's kneecap off."

The gun jammed deeper into the soft spot under her chin so hard, it was impossible to speak. She locked eyes with Sam, wishing she could tell him mind to mind how beautiful, how valiant he was. How grateful she was. How sorry that she'd gotten him into this.

The thoughts were locked in. A swarm of terrified birds frantically beating their wings against the bars of their cage.

Sam crouched and laid the Glock 19 on the ground.

"Kick it away from yourself," Pavel said.

Sam did so.

"Search them," the boss barked in Ukrainian. "Cuff him."

One of Pavel's men ran his hands over Sam's body and made a triumphant sound when he found the ankle holster with the snubbie. He took the revolver and jerked Sam's arms back, ratcheting plastic cuffs around his wrists. Josef ran his hands over Sveti's body, pinching and groping. He growled when he found the pistol strapped to her leg, and pinched her thigh viciously as he ripped the Velcro strap loose.

Pavel walked over to Sveti. "So, my son. At last I have my hands on something you care about." He lifted up a lock of her hair, fingering it. "So this is the famous Svetlana. Scrawny, ey? Hardly bigger than when you both came out of Zhoglo's black hole. Have you fucked her?"

Sasha did not answer. Pavel kicked him again, this time in the ribs. He shuddered but did not cry out.

"No, you have not fucked her." Pavel sounded exasperated. "What's wrong with you? Don't you like girls? My men will be happy to try her. Josef can hardly wait. But he had better go last, considering what he has in mind."

Sasha rasped the words, in one explosive breath. "Don't hurt her!"

"Tell me where you hid the thermal generators, if you don't want to see this cunt cut into stew meat."

Tears rolled down Sasha's face. He nodded, jerkily.

"Where?" his father thundered.

Sasha looked up. "Here," he whispered. "I'll take you to them."

Pavel squinted. "You hid my generators on Camorra property? Shit-brained fool." A kick to Sasha's kidney. "Get up. Lead on."

The seven of them formed an odd procession following Sasha. Sveti willed the boy on the bike to stay away. Magpies darted, insects hummed. It was warm, even at dusk. The smell of festering weeds in a ditch prickled her nose. Weirdly peaceful. Just their feet, crunching on gravel, broken glass as they walked around the decaying foundry.

Huge chunks of wall were missing, windows were smashed, the roof had caved halfway in. Birds swooped high in its vaulted rafters.

"Faster," Pavel growled.

On the far side of the building was a large, asphalt parking space, cracked and sunken. Ramps and loading bays. A long, low building with many doors that could have been storage, garages.

Sasha led them to the last door, through the thick foliage that had grown up around it. Prickly pear, fig. A tangle of dusty, dry-looking vines covered everything, twining over the boughs of a wild orange tree that bristled with long, brutal thorns. They tore at her skirt and her legs as Josef dragged her along.

Sasha stopped. Josef pinned her against the concrete wall. Thorns stabbed into her back, her arm. A branch fell over her shoulder, draping like a stole. It stabbed its stiff spines into her neck.

Sasha indicated the metal door. Tried to speak. Choked on it.

"Where is the key?" Pavel demanded.

Sasha cringed. "I do not have it."

"Who does?"

Sasha's mouth worked. *Sonia*, he mouthed.

Pavel cupped Sasha's head and slammed his face into the door. Sasha fell to his knees, leaving a bloody splotch on the door.

Pavel gestured to the man who carried a shotgun. He swung the weapon up, taking aim at the lock.

"Stop!" Sam yelled. "Holy God, there's pulverized strontium-90 in there! You're going to shoot right into it? Really? Do you want to die?"

The man with the shotgun hesitated, exchanging glances with Pavel. The vor shrugged and made a swift gesture.

The guy shifted his stance and shot the door at a sharp angle.

Boom. The sound hit Sveti's body like the mallet of a gong. The heavy door swung inward, a jagged hole where the lock had been.

The dark room was empty.

They stared into the space, silent. Everything was so clear. Every leaf, every thorn sharply outlined. The bird calls were crystalline and shrill. The orange-yellow of the prickly pear fruit glowed in the half-light of dusk, hanging voluptuously out of the leathery, scarred cactus.

Sveti flexed her hands to see if she could touch Liv's ring, and Josef's grip tightened inexorably, until the bones ground.

She somehow managed not to scream. After Yuri, she knew that reacting to pain only excited such monsters. Made them want more.

Sasha's face, beneath the flow of blood from his nose, was a mask of blank bewilderment.

"You dare to make a fool of me?" Pavel asked softly. "Still?"

"No," Sasha said. His mouth shook. "It . . . it was here."

Pavel grunted. "Then the sneaky bitch moved it. She trusted you as much as I do. Good judge of character, ey? Even at betrayal, you are a failure." He looked at Sveti. "Can you tell me where my property is?"

Sveti shook her head.

Pavel gestured at Sam. He was jolted forward by the gun between his shoulder blades. "You," he said in English. "Petrie, isn't it?"

"I don't know where the generators are," Sam said flatly.

"Very well. Since no more business can be conducted, we will move on to the entertainment of the evening," he said in English. "Josef, take Svetlana into that room and teach my son the price of betrayal."

"No!" Sasha yelled hoarsely, lurching to his feet. "*Tato*, no!"

Josef made a thick, snarling sound in his throat and picked Sveti up. He hauled her toward the door.

"Wait," Sam said sharply.

All eyes swiveled to Sam. "I wouldn't do that," Sam said to Pavel. "She's the only one who could find your property for you."

"Could she?" Pavel said. "She could tell us nothing in Portland. Granted, you showed up before Josef could show his skill, but still."

"Sonia sent her a letter." Sam's gaze darted to her, full of urgency. "Full of clues. She's been working them out. It hasn't quite jelled yet. But she's the only one who could put it together."

Pavel turned to Sveti. "Do you have this letter?"

"It's at the hotel," she said. "With my things. In my suitcase."

"You are lying." Pavel gestured at Josef. "Go on. Begin."

"It's The Sword of Cain, right?" Sam said. "It's all in the letter. Numbers, directions. She just has to crack the code. Don't be so quick to kill the golden goose, like you did with Sonia. Sveti's the key."

Sveti's body clenched with dread. *Shut up, shut up, please. Do not draw that man's lethal attention upon yourself any sooner than you have to.* But it was too late. Pavel had turned his snakelike gaze on Sam.

He was considering Sam now. Evaluating how much pain he could inflict. With him, upon him. How best to inflict it.

"You are smart boy, hmm?" Pavel said. "Her father thought he was smart, too. You know what I think? I think you're a lying prick. You're trying to buy time. There's no time for sale. You are of no use to us, except as incentive. It appears she likes you. We studied you, after Portland. Spoiled rich boy, playing at being cop, no?"

"If you say so," Sam said evenly.

"What a stupid game to play." Pavel walked around him, appraising him. "I was there, the day Sergei Ardov's guts were ripped out and piled onto his chest. I'm sure she told you the story."

Sveti made a barely human sound. The realization was so sharp, like a knife stabbing. The reason she was so terrified of loving Sam. The reason she panicked and always held herself back.

It was because of this. It was her worst, depths-of-hell nightmare, and she had made it come true. With her own hands.

A muscle twitched in Sam's jaw. "I heard about that, yes."

"I will slice you open right here. Pull your bowels out while you watch," Pavel mused. "Just like her father. It seems appropriate. The cunt can watch us begin and then hurry back to her hotel with one of my men to fetch her letter. We will see how long it takes her to solve this puzzle while we unravel your guts. She'll have a time margin, you see. Sergei lasted, oh, the better part of a day, but he was a tough old bastard, with Cossack blood. You Americans are soft. I give you three hours, maybe less. You'll die of shock, and fear." He smiled. "And surprise," he taunted, "that it's actually happening."

He looked at Sveti, enjoying her panic. "We'll cut him carefully," he said. "He won't bleed out. He'll lie here with his abdominal cavity wide open, intestines spread out for the flies to sample. Are you motivated?" He chuckled. "Yevgeni, show them the knife you'll use."

"*Tato*," Sasha begged. "Don't. Please."

"And *you!*" Pavel backhanded his son, sending him reeling. "I will think of something special for you, too. You thought you were so clever, hiding here? You think you are smarter than me? We just followed her!"

"You are exactly like Zhoglo," Sasha said to him with surprising clearness. No hesitation, no stutter, no cough.

"No, I am not!" Pavel hissed, stung. "I killed Zhoglo! I defeated him for you! It was all for you, you ungrateful piece of shit!"

"You defeated nothing." Sasha's broken nose bubbled with blood with each breath, but his voice rang clear. "Zhoglo just found a new body to inhabit. Yours was perfect, because no one was home. He possessed you. He owns you. You are pathetic."

One of the men slapped Sasha on the back of the head, sending him stumbling forward again.

"Let the boy speak," Pavel said. "It's just the sound of a baby whimpering when he does not get his mama's tit."

"Don't speak of my mama. You killed her, too."

For that one moment, everyone's attention was focused on the emotionally fraught interchange between the vor and his son.

Sam twisted, sprang up. His forehead smashed into the face of the man holding him.

Josef's grip slackened for an instant. Sveti jerked her hands free, seizing the thorny branch. Josef grabbed her wrists again. She pulled back against him, with all her strength . . . and then reversed direction suddenly, driving the long, stiff thorns straight into Josef's face.

He screamed. So did she. *Bam. Bam.* His gun went off in her ear.

A shower of prickly pear fruit pulp rained down on them. Joseph clawed at his face. Blood streamed from one of his eyes. He was screaming, but the gunshots had deafened her. She barely heard them.

Sam's foot spun through the air, connecting with Josef's gun hand, but he lost his balance, stumbling to his knees. He rolled back up again. Josef's gun bounced and spun on the broken asphalt.

Pavel's mouth was wide, in the deafening silence. His gun swung in strange slow motion to aim at Sam.

Sasha leaped up and flung himself in front of Sam.

Bam, bam, bam, bam. A heavy vibration thudded, deep in her body. The bullets jerked Sasha this way and that. He crumpled on top of Sam, bearing him backward, onto the ground.

Sveti dove across the broken asphalt for Josef's gun. Pavel swung his pistol around. "Do not move a muscle, whore."

Sveti froze, then drew her hand back slowly. She could not tell if Sam was alive. Sasha made wheezy, sucking sounds. Shot in the lung. Sam had been shot in the lung once. She remembered it so clearly. It was right after she'd met him. And fallen madly in love with him.

Thoughts spun in her head, buzzing and frantic, uncoupled from the events that were unfolding. Pavel walked around Sasha's slight form, still sprawled over Sam's legs and torso.

"I wish you had never been born," he said to his son.

"Me too." Sasha's hand jerked out from under his blood-drenched shirt. *Bam.*

Pavel stared down, astonished, at the revolver in Sasha's hand. Then at the small hole, right in his heart. Blood leaped out, arching and spattering. Flooding down his shirt.

He crumpled to the ground on top of Sasha, eyes blank.

"*Tato,*" Sasha whispered.

"Vor!" the guy with the shotgun bellowed.

Bam. Bam. Bam. Sveti opened fire on the man, with Josef's gun. The guy's shotgun fell to the asphalt, bouncing out of reach as his legs buckled, folded.

He sank to his knees, sagged to the side on his ass, clutching his belly. Blood seeped through his fingers. His eyes were wide.

There was only the sound of labored breathing. From all sides.

"Sveti." It took all his energy to punch the sound out to her. He was leaking, blood pressure dropping. "Baby. Look sharp. Talk to me."

Sveti jerked her gaze from the guy she'd gut shot. Josef's Beretta PX Storm compact bobbed dangerously in her shaking grip. "What?"

"Baby, it's me. Sam." He made his voice louder. "I need you."

The stunned blankness in her eyes vanished, and she jolted into movement. "Sam. Oh, God. Sasha." She scrambled over to them, on bloodied hands and knees, laying the gun down. "You're shot?"

"Don't know, exactly. I can't use my arms. I don't want to move, and jar him. Get Pavel off, and lift Sasha so I can crawl out."

Sveti heaved Pavel off with a grunt of effort and slipped her arm beneath Sasha's blood-drenched body. He made a thin keening sound.

Sam crawled out from beneath Sasha. His shoulders felt torn from their sockets. He glanced at the gun that had fallen from Pavel's hand. A Kahr PM9 Black Rose.

"You're shot, too? Oh, God, Sam!"

"I think most of the blood is his," he said. "I caught a couple bullets that went through him." He looked down, evaluating as best he could without his hands. Chest, upper thigh. Lucky his femoral artery wasn't nicked.

Sveti's eyes widened in horror. "Sam! Your chest!"

"Must have caught on my rib," he wheezed. "Hurts like a motherfucker, but I can still breathe okay. How about him?"

She lowered Sasha to the ground and struggled out of her cro-cheted sweater. Sasha's red, sticky hand lifted, seeking blindly. Sveti clasped it while she pressed the shrug against his wounds.

Sam scooted over. His wrists were bleeding, he felt the hot slick-ness, though his fingers were numb. But Sasha was way worse off.

The guy's eyes were open, and brilliantly lucid, considering the size of that pool of blood. Chest. Gut. Groin. All bullets he'd taken for Sam. Sam's death wounds, intercepted.

He caught Sasha's eye. "Thank you," he said. "You crazy bas-tard."

Sasha coughed. Flecks of blood and lung spattered over his lips and chin. "Not for you," he croaked. "For her. Save her."

The previously hidden force of Sasha's character blazed out along with that directive. "Yes, I will." *If she'll let me. She's fucking hard to help.* He left that part out. No point tormenting a dying man.

Sasha tried to speak, but there wasn't enough air to vibrate his vocal folds. Sam leaned down to hear him whisper. "What?"

"I didn't . . . join the club," Sasha whispered.

"What club?" Sam demanded.

"Of the people who let her down."

Sam stared into Sasha's eyes and felt like ten different kinds of shit. "You sure didn't," he said, feeling helpless. "You saved her."

Sasha turned his head and whispered something to Sveti in Ukrainian. She whispered back. Then Sasha's haggard expression softened into a look of dumb relief. He was gone.

Sveti pressed her finger to his throat. Tears ran down her face, mixing with blood. Sasha had lasted longer than most would have.

But now was not the time for mourning. Enough being a pussy-whipped asshole. This girl was going back into the vault, with Tam and Val and Nick and all the rest of them to guard her until this mess was cleaned up. Completely, and for all time.

"Baby, you have to get these restraints off me," he said.

Sveti looked up. "Oh, God. I'm so sorry. I . . . I didn't think." She scrambled unsteadily to her feet and looked around. "How . . . ?"

"A knife," he reminded her gently. "They took mine, but these guys will all have them. If they were going to gut me, they have to have good blades. Go on, search the one I head-butted."

She knelt by the man's still form. "He's dead," she said, as she rummaged through his pockets.

"Yeah, I know," Sam said wearily.

She found a knife and hurried over, sawing at the plastic.

The cuffs came loose, along with the wave of pain. Oh, fuck. *Fuck.*

The first thing he did when he could use his fingers was to close Sasha's eyes, after which he just sat there, in slack-jawed overload. Sveti clutched the knife in her shaking hand, shoulders hunched.

He put his hand on her shoulder and tried to make his voice gentle, but it was too thick to sound anything but harsh and aggressive.

"He's gone, baby. We can't help him now. We have to go."

"We have to get you to a hospital," she said.

"I'll be fine," he said. "I'm not at death's door."

"You have been *shot!*" she snarled. "Don't you dare play your bullshit macho games with me!"

"I'm fine," he repeated, breathing down the nauseous giddiness. He looked around the grisly scene and his guts twitched, uneasily. The math did not add up. "Hey, Sveti. Where's the other guy? Josef?"

Sveti struggled to her feet and looked around. "I don't see him."

That zinged him right out of his trance. "That sucks ass," he said.

She helped him struggle to his feet. "I'll call an ambulance?"

"While we wait for Josef to bring back some of his friends? We'll be better off if we move ourselves. Can you imagine trying to give directions to the medics? I don't even know where the fuck we are."

"Then I'll get the car and bring it back," she said.

"I don't want you out there alone, with that scumbag around."

"I'll take a gun," she said. "I can handle a gun."

"I noticed that," he said. "What's with your hand?"

She looked down at her bloody hand and forearm. "Oh, I grabbed a thorny branch. Shoved it into Josef's face. I think I got his eye."

"Wow. My warrior princess." He took a step, but his legs were rubbery. Sveti caught him, and he almost brought her down with him.

"I'll go get the car," she said, her voice shaking. "Wait here, Sam."

"No, we stick together. Find our guns. Get that Saiga, too. See if he has another ten-round mag for it, too. Check his pockets."

She scrambled to gather it all up. His Glock, back into the waist holster. His ankle holster. The snubbie. Her Micro, in the thigh strap. He'd leave the Black Rose and the PX Storm for the cops, but he wanted that shotgun, at least til they were home free. Sveti gestured at the man she had shot, who was now only barely conscious. "What about him?"

Sam's own belly scar tingled nastily, just looking at the guy. He remembered how it felt. Innards torn up, life leaking out. Death rising like a swift dark tide. The man panted, with swift, shallow breaths. His frantic eyes met Sam's and then fell to the gun in Sam's hand.

Sam shook his head. "He would have raped you and ripped my guts out in front of you. Let him die alone, in his own good time. We'll tell the authorities about him. Let's go."

"One last thing." Sveti crouched beside Sasha, straightening his limbs. She folded his arms over his chest and bent to kiss his forehead.

Sam stared at the body of the man he'd judged and scolded. He swallowed over the tight, burning ache. "Hurry," he rasped.

The trip back to the car was a nightmare, without the guidance of the kid on the bike. They got disoriented, which doubled the agonizing trip. Sam shuffled like a zombie, leaving a trail of blood, but giving up wasn't an option. He was too heavy to drag, and he dared not leave her alone.

At one point, the boy popped up and skidded to a stop, eyes huge.

They must look like horror movie escapees. Sveti's white dress was plastered to her body. Her hair hung in blood-matted strands. Sam looked worse, draped over her shoulder. Shotgun clutched in his grip.

Sam fixed the kid with a menacing stare. *"Hai visto un altro tizio in giro?"* Have you seen another guy around here?

The kid nodded. *"Se ne andato con la macchina."* He left with the car.

"*Ti ha visto?*" He saw you?

The child shook his head violently.

"*Bene,*" Sam muttered. "*Vattene. Sparisci.*"

The boy didn't need to be told twice. He pedaled frantically away.

"What was that about?" Sveti asked.

"He says the guy drove away, and didn't see him," Sam said. "I hope to God it's true."

Their car came into sight. Then came the task of prying the key out of Sam's blood-stiffened jeans pocket, it being unpleasantly close to one of his nastiest wounds. Sveti pried them loose, to the tune of his foul, virulent cursing, and dumped all their weapons into the trunk.

She unlocked the car, now smeared with blood where Sam had sagged over it, and strapped him into the passenger's seat. She got the car onto the road and floored it. He almost instantly started to drift off.

Her voice sounded far away. "Stay with me, Sam! Don't pass out!"

"Call the cops." He put the words in a bottle and sent it bobbing gently across the ocean stretching out between them. Wider, wider.

"First, let me find you a hospital! Damn it, Sam! Look at me!"

"Castellana," he muttered. "Follow . . . signs. *Ospedale.*"

"Yes! I'm not an idiot! I know that much!" she snapped.

He gathered all his energy to launch another bottle into that swiftly widening ocean. "Sveti. Tell me . . . something."

"What?" she prompted. "Anything! Keep talking! Stay with me!"

"The last thing Sasha said. In . . . Ukrainian. What was it?"

She tried to speak, but her words choked off into a sob. "He said, be happy. Goddamn him! It's a sick joke. Your best friend is bleeding to death in your arms, and he says, be happy? Fuck that! Fuck happy!"

"No." The water was so wide now, so vast, but he had to say this to her. It was so important. "Don't. Sasha's . . . right."

"What?" He could barely hear her high, frantic voice. "Stay awake, Sam! I need you! Don't leave me alone!"

"It's not . . . too much to ask." His voice was groggy. "Happiness . . . for you. I want that, too. I'm with him. I want that."

"Fuck!" She swerved out of the path of an oncoming car. Its shrill horn dopplered out behind them. "Goddamnit, Sam! This isn't helping!"

But he couldn't understand her anymore. He was looking at Sasha's face now, on some mysterious plane of existence between life and death. The dead man's dark, direct gaze burned right into him.

He looked back, chastened. Nice move, dude. Hell of an exit.

Sasha had done it. He'd pulled off another shining moment of pure, high-octane heroism, and Sam had to love him for it, even though it was a brutal fuck-you-and-the-horse-you-rode-in-on.

As well as a mortal challenge. Sam could practically hear the guy say the words as he sank down to a deeper layer of consciousness.

Top this, dickhead. Go on. Knock yourself out. I'll be watching.

CHAPTER 23

A golden thread in the darkness led him through the maze of evil dreams. Blood, violence, gunshots, guts, screams. Dead, empty eyes.

He clung to the thread, following it blindly. Trusting it.

Shrill beeping, smothering gauze on his face. People manipulating his body. So much pain. He finally clawed his way up close enough to the light to frame the sensation. To name it.

The clasp of her hand. That was it. Sveti's hand was the golden thread, and the touch of her skin on his was the sweet, unspoken promise that there was something worth waking up for.

Even so, he regretted opening his eyes. The light hurt.

Several attempts later, he kept them open long enough to place himself. A hospital room. Scarred metal bedstead. Walls painted a pale, industrial green. A crucifix hung on the wall in his line of sight.

He swiveled his eyeballs in his head, which was harder than it should have been. They felt swollen and dry, as if they had sand embedded under them. An IV was stuck in his arm. He shifted, experimentally. He was not intubated, nor did he have a catheter up his dick. Excellent. Things had been far worse for him than this.

Sveti sat beside him. Her left hand was bandaged. She had bruises and scrapes on her face, her arms, the unbandaged hand.

"Hey." She gave him her brief, lovely smile. "You're awake."

"What day is it?" he croaked.

"It's Tuesday. You've been out for more than a day. You had a bullet against your ribs, and you have stitches everywhere. You're a hot mess."

"Police?" he croaked.

"Of course. I talked to them for hours. I told them everything I know. The guy I shot was dead when they arrived on the scene."

"Josef?"

"Disappeared," she said. "No trace of him."

Then someone needed to hover over her with a gun. "Where's Simone?" he demanded.

"He's here. I called him right away. I was sure you'd want that. He's right outside your room."

He sighed his relief. "Have you called Val and Tam and Nick?"

"Simone talked to Val. They're all coming day after tomorrow. Your father and sister should be here, too, early tomorrow morning."

He jerked like he'd been stuck with a pin. "Who? What?"

"I called him," she said. "He was beside himself. He just texted me their arrival times." She indicated her phone.

"Let me see that." He took her phone, which had a new star-burst shatter marring the screen. Sure enough, there was his father's private number. An arrival time, an airport code. His dad's usual stern synthesis. He let the phone thud onto the mattress.

"Sweet God," he muttered. "Just kill me now."

"They'll just scold you," she said gently. "They love you."

"Never mind them. How about you? Are you good?"

She dropped a sweet little kiss on his hand. "I'm fine."

He was horrified to feel the tears well into his eyes. He was still so fucking scared. All stoved in and fucked up, and if Josef or whatever other asshole wanted to hurt her walked in, he'd be helpless to stop him. "You have to go home, Sveti," he said. "Now. You can't stay here."

Sveti's gaze slid away. "Soon," she soothed. "Not quite yet. I needed to talk to you about that. I couldn't leave until I let you know—"

"Leave?" He jerked up and fell back with a hiss of pain, his ribs screaming. "Leave for where? With whom?"

"Calm down. I'm just going to the Villa Rosalba for the night. You know. To look under that tile. We talked about that."

"Fuck, no!" He tried to jerk up again.

Sveti murmured in dismay and pressed him back down onto the pillows. "Sam, be calm! I'll be fine!"

"Hold it right there," he said, voice shaking. "Let's touch back down into the realm of reality, just for one goddamn second, okay?"

Her mouth thinned. He knew he'd lost her, right then. She wouldn't hear him talk. She'd do whatever she damn well pleased, just like always. "I see reality very clearly," she said.

"Yeah? You're aware that Josef is out there, pissed as hell about the thorns in his eye and his sudden change in career prospects," he said. "And that he's now convinced that you know where tens of millions of euros' worth of dirty bomb materials are, or at least that you could figure it out, given the right incentive. You know firsthand that he is an expert at providing that kind of incentive. And you propose to wander off alone, maybe tour some Roman ruins? Go to a spa?"

"Do not trivialize what I am doing," she said.

"Then don't trivialize the danger! You need to stay with Simone! You need bodyguards on you, twenty-four/seven, until Tam and Val and Nick can take over! You cannot be alone! Ever!"

"I won't be alone," Sveti said.

"Excuse me?" He paused as realization sank in. "And just who exactly will be keeping you company, babe?"

She squeezed his hand. "Sam, it's just for one night. And I—"

"Hazlett," he cut in. "Hazlett's going with you. Moving in on you while I'm out of commission. That's great. That is just fucking *classic*."

She winced. "Oh, God, Sam. Please."

He suddenly noticed her clothes, which were incongruously elegant, with her scrapes and bruises. The coral silk blouse, the loose linen pants, perfectly pressed. "Where did those clothes come from? The last time I saw you, you were covered in blood. I don't remember that outfit. Where the fuck did you get those clothes?"

Her face stiffened. She crossed her scratched, bruised arms over her chest. "Michael brought them to the hospital for me."

"Michael, billionaire philanthropist and personal shopper?"

The chin went up. "I'm sure Nadine picked them out."

"Aw. How sweet. And you're going to spend the night with him now? Tell me you're shitting me. Please, Sveti."

"I'm not going to spend the night with him! I am going to look under that fucking tile, because I can't eat or sleep until I do!"

"So tell the cops! Let them look! I do not give a flying fuck what secrets your mother hid there! All I know is, she died for them, Sveti, and Sasha did, too! You are not getting in line to be next!"

She gave him the regal empress look. "You heard what Sasha said, about the dirty bomb? The lab where innocent people were murdered? The grave where their bodies are hidden? And you don't think it's important enough to follow up?"

"Sure, it's important, but it's not your job to do it! And that's only assuming that what Sasha said was true!"

"Pavel appeared to believe it. Why shouldn't we?"

He shook his head and hissed at the ensuing *whanga-whanga* inside his skull. "I can't even begin to count the ways that guy was messed up," he said. "Maybe he was dreaming up things he wished he'd done. He didn't have the nerve to do anything like that alone."

"He wasn't alone. And my mother had nerve for ten," she said.

"True, but really? Sasha saves the world while putting the shaft to his mean, evil dad? Talk about a wish-fulfillment fantasy. I'll believe it when I see the bomb materials with my own eyes."

"It didn't look like a fantasy to me when he was bleeding out on the ground," she said frigidly.

"I am not diminishing his sacrifice," Sam said through his teeth. "And I'm not saying bomb materials weren't stolen. I'm just questioning if he could actually have been the one who stole them. Your mom isn't around to corroborate. And they sure as hell weren't where he left them."

"He throws himself in front of a hail of bullets for you, and yet, you continue to underestimate him," she said.

Oh, *fuck*, ouch. Sveti had the art of the merciless zinger nailed.

"This is about more than me staying safe," Sveti went on. "Sasha didn't lay down his life after asking me to hide under the bed until it's safe to come out. Mama gave up everything for this!"

"And she got a jack shit return on her investment! I'm sorry to say this, but I don't give a rat's ass about bombs and labs and bodies. All I care about is getting you someplace safe. Go. The fuck. *Home.*"

Her mouth trembled. "So," she whispered. "Here we are again."

"Yeah, here we are. But my job now is not to pander to your suicidal whims. It isn't even to fuck you senseless, much as I enjoy it. My job is just to keep you in one piece. That's all. That's it."

Her face crumpled for an instant, before she got herself back under control and smoothed it out. "That's the problem," she said. "I'm not in one piece. I'm in a million pieces, Sam. I have been for years."

His stitches pulled, stabbing lines of fire jabbing in his guts, his rib, his thigh. "I'm sorry about that," he said awkwardly. "But you can put the pieces back together in the safety of Cray's Cove."

She threw up her hands. "I won't be in danger at Villa Rosalba! Michael's security team will be all over the place!"

"Great. That makes me turn cartwheels for joy."

"Sam, haven't you ever had a thing burn in your mind? A thing that just won't let you go? Remember Elaine, in college? That's what this is for me! If you care about who I am inside, you'll understand!"

He grabbed her hand and held up three fingers of his other hand.

"Three things," he said. "One. Your family trusted me to keep you safe."

"My family does not dictate—"

"Two." He held up his second finger. "This one's more important. You're my woman now, like it or not. Being in a gun battle with you clinches it. It's my evolutionary duty, mandated by the incontrovertible laws of nature, not to let you eat a bullet, if I can help it."

"Sam—"

"The third thing," he proceeded relentlessly. "Your crazy friend

Sasha laid some very heavy karma on me. If you get hurt, he will haunt my ass into the next life and beyond. And I'm in no condition to pay my debt to him right now. Can you not give me that much, while I'm lying here with a fucking IV drip in my arm? Is that so much to ask?"

She wiped at her eyes. "I will be completely safe," she insisted. "Please, be reasonable, Sam. I'll always be grateful. You saved my life."

His bark of laughter hurt his chest. "Yeah, well. You *are* my life."

She gazed at him, eyes soft, openmouthed. "Oh, Sam . . ."

"Yeah, I know," he snarled. "Don't start. I know. You don't have it in you, you're too damaged to love me, blah blah, fuck you very much, let's have more wild sex now. I'm in love with you, Sveti. I'm out of my head. That's my only excuse for some of the shit I've pulled."

"You? You've done nothing but protect me!"

He grunted in disgust. "Yeah? The ice-cream date, at Castellana Padulli? Going to the death-trap address on that note? Seriously? Coming to Italy at all was dumber than shit. I should have just trapped you in my bed in Portland, like a good sex maniac. I can't believe I shoved my head that far up my ass, and left it there for so long."

"My choice. Not your fault. I'm sorry I put you in danger."

"I can't take it anymore," he said. "I'm officially done. If you care about me, collaborate with me. Have some fucking mercy on me."

"I do care about you, but I care about this, too! Renato is leaving tomorrow morning, and Villa Rosalba will be closed up, indefinitely. They both came back when they heard what happened, and I thought even you would agree that it's safer for me there than—"

"You thought wrong," he said. "I don't agree. It's not safer."

"Just give me this," she pleaded. "One night. One last try. No one will attack me or seduce me. I don't want anyone but you. I'm trying so hard, Sam! Let me find some meaning in all this horrible shit!"

He stared up at the ceiling, the glaring overhead light. That headache slammed heavily into his skull with every heartbeat.

The price of that head-butt. The silence stretched, tense and tight. Then tighter.

He shook his head. He couldn't go with her. He couldn't physically restrain her. But he'd be damned if he'd give her his blessing.

"No," he said. "I'm done."

"Oh, shit. *Shit*," she hissed. "Please! Don't turn this into a stupid ultimatum! I'll be back tomorrow! After that, I'll be good, I promise!"

"Don't come back tomorrow," he said. "Don't come back at all."

Her eyes were full of torment. He looked away from them.

"You can't mean that," she whispered.

"I mean it," he said. "Enjoy your freedom, Sveti. Try to be careful."

"Don't throw us away over this! I have to do this, at all costs!"

"We both know what the cost is," Sam said. "Pay it and go. We're all done here." He closed his eyes. He couldn't bear to look at her.

She got up but did not leave. "Simone brought you a car," she offered. "I parked the one we used before in a garage across the street. When I told him that it was covered with blood, he said to—"

"Take it," he said. "You need a fresh, untraceable car, if you want to go out and challenge your bad guys all alone."

"I'm not challenging anyone! Keep the new one. I'll just rent—"

"Take the car and go."

"Sam—"

"For the love of Christ." He put his hand over his eyes, blocking her out. "Please. Don't make me beg."

He waited. The door clicked open, and after a long, torturous pause, it clicked shut again.

Sam opened his eyes. He was alone in the room. So. It was done. She'd left the parking ticket on the little table next to the bed.

He stared at the crucifix on the wall. It came clear to him, for the first time. The point of having a crucifix in a hospital room. It had eluded him thus far. He'd had some vague idea of comfort, tradition, prayer.

But it wasn't about comfort at all. No way. That crucifix was to put things into perspective for the poor bastard on the bed. The unspoken message being, *You think your shit is bad? You call that pain?*

Yeah, his shit was bad. He struggled to breathe.

Sveti leaned on the wall outside Sam's door to keep from falling.

After the events of the last twenty-four hours, she would have expected to be burnt-out and empty. But letting her barriers down for Sam had opened up a vast new capacity for suffering inside her. Oh, lucky girl.

"Svetlana! There you are!"

She wiped the tears off her face and did not try to smile as Hazlett strode toward her. If only she could get what she needed from the Villa Rosalba without having to do a smiling PR song and dance for it. But that was the price she had to pay. One of the many. She'd bargained away her own heart for this. "Hey, Michael," she said dully.

Michael gestured toward Sam's door. "How is your friend?"

"He feels terrible, but he should make a full recovery," she replied. "His family will be arriving soon."

"Excellent." He gave her a toothy, approving smile. "So you won't feel like you're abandoning him!"

Hah. Right. Her feelings must have shown on her face. He laid his hand on her shoulder. It felt heavy and hot through the thin silk.

"Is he upset?" he asked. "About you coming to the Villa Rosalba?"

She shrugged, that being none of his fucking business.

"Predictable. I anticipated that. But he can't expect you to sleep in a hotel room alone, or to wander the corridors of the hospital all night, eating out of vending machines and sleeping in an upright chair!"

"He just wants me safe," she said quietly.

"Well, and so you will be. Finally. Don't get me wrong. I appreciate what he did for you, though perhaps keeping you out of the situation altogether might have been more intelligent."

"Don't blame him," she said. "He tried."

"Not hard enough, in my book," Hazlett said. "Ready to go?"

She hesitated, looking at Sam's door. She could still change her mind. Run back into that room. Stay forever under Sam's sheltering arm. It was wonderful, under there. Warm, safe, exciting, sexy. Fun.

Everything she could want. And she did want it, desperately. But it meant staying forever in this tortured limbo.

Sasha and her mother had both begged her, in their own ways, to take this next step. If she turned away, she would live and die always knowing that she'd fallen short and failed them. It was time to stop being poor little Sveti, flotsam on the tide, swept here and swept there. She had to grow up and do the hard thing. She'd heard that phrase thrown around both in jest and in earnest for years. Only now did she really understand what it meant.

This was her hard thing. She'd had hard luck, and plenty of it, but the hard thing was not the same as hard luck. The hard thing was consciously chosen, its painful consequences stoically accepted.

Walking away from Sam was the hardest thing of all.

She followed Hazlett with the car Simone had provided, detouring to her hotel, so she could pick up her clothes, computer, and tablet. She had no idea how she got through the rest of that evening at Villa Rosalba. Drinks on the terrace with Michael and Renato, a late dinner she could not eat, invasive questions about her disastrous adventures. She performed like a puppet, chatted, smiled. Polite and articulate. Was this how she would feel for the rest of her life? She'd traded the vivid realness of being with Sam for this? Small talk, dull superficiality, crushing boredom? God, how depressing.

Shortly after dinner, she caved. "I'm so sorry, but I can't keep my eyes open any longer," she said. "Would you gentlemen excuse me?"

"Of course." Hazlett got to his feet. "I'll show you to your room."

He took her up a stonework staircase that led to the breezeway on the second floor. The moon was bright in the sky. Wall sconces glowed on the loggias that opened out upon the garden below. It was a Renaissance fantasy, and she was completely numb to it.

Michael unlocked a room and handed her the key. She turned to go in, and he stopped her with a hand on her shoulder.

"Svetlana," he began earnestly. "You've been through such an ordeal. If you need company, any time of the day or night, please, call on me. I'm right across the courtyard. Second room from the left."

"Thanks," she murmured. As if. In your dreams, buddy.

"You're troubled," he said softly, stroking her shoulder with his thumb. "Is it about your . . . I'm not quite sure what to call him."

"Friend," she said. "He's my dear friend." Always, and forever. Tension rose inside her. She didn't want Hazlett's oily curiosity brushing up against that awful sore spot, not even slightly.

"Just friend?" he demanded. "Nothing more?"

She pried off his hand. "Not a good time, Michael."

He was instantly contrite. "Sorry. I won't put pressure on you."

How very civil of him. Wow. She stared blankly. The situation felt grotesque, against the backdrop of blood, death, and heartbreak.

His expression was one of stoic fortitude. "I can be patient," he told her, soulfully. "When something's worth waiting for."

Wait until the sun exploded, then. "Good night, Michael." She shut the door in his face with no further salute.

Now she had to just wait, without going batshit. She'd be smart to sleep a few hours, but sleep was almost as laughable as Michael Hazlett coming on to her, with gunshots still ringing in her ears, and Sasha's body barely cold. And Sam saying, *Don't come back at all.*

She sat on the bed, doubled over. The images that flooded through her made her rock, moaning. Sasha, jerking and twisting in midair as he took those bullets. He had been taking bullets for everyone for his entire fucking life, and he'd never gotten any thanks for it. She was so angry, so confused. So grateful Sam had not died, but damn Sasha for not finding some brilliant way out of that trap other than his sacrificial goat routine. And God, what a thing to criticize someone for. Self-sacrifice, heroism. It was so fucked up. So wrong.

One thing, at least, was clear. She didn't care what bridges she burned. She wasn't going to London for the Illuxit job. It felt wrong now.

Of course, everything felt wrong right now. They said not to make life-changing decisions when depressed, but if she followed that rule, she'd never make any decisions at all. Life was too short to tolerate Hazlett's smug smile, his groping, squeezing fingers. She had plenty of other things to grit her teeth about. She didn't need to go looking for more.

But the thought didn't take up much space in her head. Nor did she appreciate the beautiful room, the priceless antiques, the moon on the veranda. The serenity of the place mocked her. An industrial wasteland, with caustic fumes, smokestacks, bursts of angry flame stabbing up into a dingy sky. That would be more appropriate.

Hours crawled by. She paced. Powered up her laptop, poked through the JPEGs. She set up a slideshow of photos her mother had sent her from Italy. Many were of Villa Rosalba. It occurred to her that Mama had not sent a single picture of Renato.

At three, she unlocked her door and stepped into the breezeway. There was a rhythmic night chorus of insects in the garden. The sound was shrill and ominous. Beckoning her to her doom. No big deal. Doom was her natural habitat. She knew her way around it like a pro.

She walked down the corridor. No one stirred. Down the stairway. Into the sculpture garden. She made her way to her mother's bench, with the view of Atlas. Grateful for the sconces and their dim, wavering light. She was an antenna, tuned for the faintest sound of movement. What an idiot, not to get her hands on a flashlight.

The light that filtered through the thick foliage was barely enough to follow the pattern of the tree trunk tiles. It got more difficult farther out, where the shadows were deeper, but once her eyes adjusted, she began to see the dim outlines of the images on the tiles.

She found the tile with The Sword of Cain. Abel's blood seemed black, but she'd seen so much blood recently, her brain filled in the color.

She dug her fingernails into the space around the tile and pulled. It was heavy, awkward. The cavity beneath was a well of utter darkness.

She laid the tile down, wincing at the rasping clank it made, and reached down blindly into the darkness.

Deeper . . . deeper. She leaned forward, braced herself on the other side, reaching . . . and oh, God, *no*. Water.

Her touch released a whiff of festering plant matter. She groped around, in slime and muck, and found what felt like a plastic sleeve, the kind one put in a spiral binder. It was brittle, stiff.

She felt delicately around for the edges and grasped it between her thumb and forefinger. She lifted it out.

It was stiff, misshapen, stinking. It dripped.

She laid it gently on the ground and leaned forward again, teeth and belly both clenched, careful not to inhale. She quartered the watery space and felt again. Every last centimeter of that slimy cavity. Small things wriggled and squirmed away at her touch. She kept at it, hoping for a sealed item, something plastic, vacuum-wrapped. Something that might be somehow protected from six years of mold and seep.

There was nothing. When she drew her hands out, they were fouled with muck. She set the tile in place, smearing it as she did so.

But there was nothing to hide, or to gain from all this stealth. Her hope had flatlined to steely calm. Whatever was in that plastic sleeve was too light to be anything but paper, and nothing paper could survive proximity to water for any period of time. Let alone six years.

She got up, holding the plastic between thumb and forefinger. Renato or Hazlett could pop out like a horror movie cliché, with lurching zombie hordes along with them, and she would not blink. She had no secrets to defend. They had died and decomposed along with Mama.

Fuck. Them. All.

She went upstairs, not bothering to tiptoe. She did not allow herself to look at the envelope as she marched down the breezeway.

She laid the thing on the desk and trained the lamp on it.

It was stiff, deformed. The plastic was too clouded to see the contents. She tried to tease the contents from inside the sleeve, but it was adhered to the plastic. She took scissors and cut it open. The paper had slid down to the bottom of the envelope in a shapeless wad.

Just in case, she examined it thoroughly, fiber by fiber. Nothing.

She'd gone to these crazy lengths and paid this unspeakable price for a lump of discolored, shredded wood pulp.

She stared at it, hot-eyed. What brainless cow stuck a piece of paper into a hole in the ground under the open sky and then died before she could tell anyone where to find it? Her mother had been an intelligent woman. Where in the *fuck* had she put her brains?

To be fair. Mama had never meant for it to be a long-term hiding place. Nor had she ever intended to get murdered.

She'd been so desperate for some storybook closure, but such a thing didn't exist. It was a cheap trick her mind had played on her, to escape from the cruel stupidity of reality. And now, the cruelest one.

She had traded her future with Sam . . . for this.

She went into the bathroom. Yesterday's scrapes and bruises stood out in stark relief on her pale face. Scratches, from the thorns. The lump on her head was still sore. She wondered if it was getting infected but couldn't summon up the energy to care. All she could focus on right now was how stupid she was.

Stupid, and very alone.

Moping. Becca lectured her about that, but it wasn't like she didn't fight the despair. She tried hard to channel her energy in a positive direction, to turn her back on the pit of despair. But the pit of fucking despair had her name all over it. There was a magnet at the bottom, pulling on her.

She'd thought she was fighting back. The grand, definitive fight, but it had all come to nothing. How would she fight now?

She didn't even know where to begin. What muscles to flex.

After the tenth time she'd washed her hands and could still smell the festering slime, she concluded that the clinging stench was all in her head, like a whole lot of other highly undesirable things. She dried them on the fluffy white hand towel and walked back into the room.

In the dimness, her mother smiled from the screen, a ghostly apparition. Sveti gasped, jumping, and then laughed without mirth. Jumping at nothing. She'd put that slideshow up with her own hands.

Mama's smile mocked her. How could she smile, after cheating her daughter out of her best chance at happiness? It was the JPEG of the photo in her bedside frame. On the printed copy, she'd trimmed off the side with the tumbled rock and hillside and most of the numbers, too, in order to center Mama's face and fit the frame. It seemed odd, to see the image without "The Sword of Cain" and the numbers over Mama's head.

The image faded, transformed. Now it was a gnarled olive tree against a sunset-tinted sky. Then the ruins of a Roman bath carved directly out of the rocky seaside, lapped by the waves. That faded and was replaced by a crumbling tower on a peninsula, the lurid colors of the graffiti on its walls bright against the vivid blue-green of the sea.

Sveti walked closer, hypnotized by the stream of images. She hadn't been able to bear looking at them since Mama's death. Now, each photograph felt like a message she almost understood. It stirred in her brain. Teasing, beckoning. She had to pin down that ticklish flash, translate it into something concrete. Something she could use.

She stopped the slideshow and got into the folder of JPEGs, clicking around until she found Mama's portrait. It filled the screen.

This was the first time she'd looked at anything in that picture other than Mama. Her head was framed in one half. The half Sveti had trimmed off showed a rocky hill with a dark cleft in the rocks, a heap of tumbled boulders in front. At the far right was the edge of a concrete building. A chain-link, razor-wire fence encircled it.

She closed her eyes, picturing the numbers Mama had written. Only the first two digits of each number had remained on the piece in the frame. A 40 on the top, a 14 beneath. The rest of the digits had gone out with the trash, years ago. She remembered thinking, seven digits? Phone numbers, maybe. She didn't give a shit whose, under the circumstances. No one she wanted to call. That was for damn sure.

One never knew what to value while one had it. Only when it was snatched, smashed, or thrown away did one begin to understand. It had been that way with her parents, her childhood. Her innocence.

Just not with Sam. She'd known he was a treasure from the start.

She pushed that thought down before it could derail her, and found a program that accessed the metadata. Her mother had used a digital camera. It might have geotagged her photos.

In fact, it had. And the first two numbers of the longitude and latitude matched the written numbers on her photo. Forty. Fourteen.

She stared at them, terrified to get her hopes up again. She'd gotten slapped down so many times. It could just be random. But it was all she had left. That was reason enough to take it and run with it.

She found a program that would pinpoint the exact location of those coordinates. It was the middle of nowhere, about fifteen kilometers outside a town called Pozzo di San Ignazio. A satellite photo showed a couple of buildings, jagged rock formations. There was a road, but not a very distinct one. The land right behind the spot was rugged. Rocks, cliffs, gullies. Driving time, over two hours, according to the computer.

What was this but one last muscle she could flex? She'd take anything, no matter how thin or improbable, just to keep moving.

She dug into her suitcase for more appropriate clothes. Jeans, a button-down shirt, a light jacket. Her waist holster, her Micro-Glock. The most practical shoes she had, the sporty green kicks she'd worn on the plane.

She dropped the filthy plastic sleeve and its miserable contents into the plastic bag she'd wrapped around her kicks, and shoved it into the bathroom trash. Her mother's letter went into her purse, with her tablet, the maps, and satellite photos. Her phone would function as a GPS device, too, so she dug for it in her pockets. Then her jacket.

Where on earth . . . ?

Oh, God, no. When she'd shown Sam the text from his father, she'd never taken her phone back. She'd left it lying on his bed.

Shit. Phoneless. Not good, but the alternative was to wake someone and beg the loan of a cell phone, which opened up a mess of other potential problems and delays. Her hosts might even insist on accompanying her. God forbid. She'd end up murdering them both.

This bad business was between her and Mama's ghost, which took all her attention, and left none for lecherous philanthropists or fawning socialites. Besides, it didn't feel right to use Hazlett's security personnel, now that she fully intended to blow him off. Likewise, all reasons for being civil to Renato Torregrossa had rotted into slime beneath the tiles of his atrium. He was now free to go fuck himself.

She could buy another phone. The problem was the effort it would take to find a place to buy one here, communicate with personnel well enough to buy the right product, and then figure out how to activate it.

Her problem-solving capabilities had been maxed out long ago.

She could get in touch with Val's contact, Simone, but that would put the world in touch with her, and she was too raw. She wanted to float in a bubble of silence. No scolding, no admonishments.

She was going out to flex her very last muscle. It wasn't a whim. It was a bid to save her soul.

CHAPTER 24

Dawn threatened on the horizon. No time to lose. She went to the security room, trying to cobble together enough Italian to tell whoever manned the room at night that she needed to open the gate, but she need not have bothered. The room was deserted.

Strange. After all Hazlett's self-congratulatory carrying on about his security, no one was at the vidcams? But she was in no mood to quibble with her luck. She took a flashlight from one of the shelves and sat in front of the monitor. Its screens showed different infrared images of the property. She clicked around until she found the app on the toolbar that opened the gate. She clicked "open." Watched it grind wide.

The enormous entrance door was four meters tall. Gently as she tried to close it, the door made a muffled *boom*.

She took the hairpin curves of the access road fast and sped out the open gate unchallenged. It felt strange and lonely, with only herself to rely upon again. In just a few days, she'd gotten spoiled. Started to count on Sam's forceful personality, his fearsome competence at just about everything. She'd gotten used to having a high-powered, super-deluxe resource constantly at her fingertips. His energy kept things moving fast, facing forward. No time for dark thoughts, creeping doubts.

And the way he made her feel about herself. A siren, a seductive goddess. The outrageously generous way that he gave of himself. He'd flung everything he was before her as an offering. *You are my life.*

And then made it impossible for her to accept it.

She lost it. Had to pull over, on some beautiful highway overlook to cry it out. It didn't feel like a crying fit. It felt like a seizure.

When she could breathe again, she got back onto the road and followed signs to the Autostrada. She stopped at a rest area coffee bar, grimly determined to act like a grown-up and take care of her wretched self. No one was around to nag at her to eat breakfast, thanks to her own brilliant maneuvering, and today was not a day to fast. Who knew how much walking and climbing she might have to do? Some coffee, a yogurt, and a pastry later, she bought some gas and pressed on.

Like her departure from Villa Rosalba, driving to the coordinates on Mama's photo was easy at first, just a matter of following signs. But once beyond the unbeautiful, shabby little town of Pozzo di San Ignazio, road signs no longer coincided with the maps. She got turned around several times until she realized she was better off ignoring signs and just following the satellite picture. Then the road butted up to a concrete barrier. She parked the car and continued on foot.

After a forty-minute walk up the deserted, winding dirt road, she came upon a tall chain-link fence that was chained shut. Large signs warned her that it was *proprietà privata*, and *attenti ai cani*. Dogs, no less. Whoop-de-do. Dogs, wild boars, fire-breathing dragons, bring them on. She draped her purse crosswise over her shoulder and climbed the chain-link fence. The kicks were the right shoes for the task, having enough flex in the toes to hook into the links, but they weren't great for the climb that followed—miles of steep switchbacks, as the sun got higher and hotter. She stuck to the rough, rutted road, which had been abandoned to the weather and was washed out in some places into a slippery cascade of dirt and shale. There were huge tumbled boulders, steep drop-offs. Scrambling over it was slippery and exhausting.

The road descended into a canyon, its walls rearing up on both sides to block the sun. The heat beat down anyway. A fox disappeared into the bushes. Lizards darted, the occasional snake wiggled across the road.

The buildings came into view a few minutes after she began looking for them. She wasn't sure she was in the right place, it looked so different. The chain-link fence in the photo was now rusted out and knocked down. The building, some featureless prefab construction, had been new in Mama's photo, but now it was battered, discolored. The shutters had been ripped off, the windows broken. Graffiti was scrawled on the façade, satanic symbols predominating. Some rooms had fire damage, with blackened streaks around the window frames.

Her footsteps slowed as she approached the door. It was repellent, but the force that had pushed her thus far was like a gun to her back. She'd paid for this with her own heart. She would take what she had paid for.

She was grateful for the flashlight, once inside. The light that filtered through the filthy windows was barely enough to see.

The place stank. When her eyes adjusted, she saw why. It was unspeakably foul. Someone had built a fire in the middle of the room, and the bones of various small, half-burned animals were inside it. Human waste dotted the floor, as well as corpses of other animals, drug paraphernalia, used condoms. It looked like a meth den. Not surprising, if this was in fact the abandoned lab. Even afterward, an evil place attracted more negativity, more despair. She steeled herself to look through it. The front area, then a series of what must have been laboratories, looted and fouled. Broken glass crunched under her feet.

In the back were large rooms made of cinder blocks and concrete. They were windowless, with drains built into the floors for easy hosing down, and industrial bathrooms attached, with metal toilets and sinks all streaked with dried, ancient filth. The remnants of big, heavy locks were evident on even heavier door frames. What appeared to be a vidcam mount could be seen high in the corners of each room.

A holding pen, for the test subjects. That was what this room was. She knew this room. She'd lived in several like it herself, for months.

She longed for Sam's bracing presence. His caustic observations would put all this into perspective. He would keep this sick, creeping dread and sadness from making her feel hollowed out.

But she did not have Sam. This was her cross to bear, not his. It was smart of him, not to get sucked into her vortex. Look at the shape he was in after just a few days with her. Almost dead.

She forced herself to go on, but the rest of the place was innocuous. Storage spaces, a filthy, looted kitchen. She walked out a doorway that was wide open to the elements, the door having been taken off its hinges and carried away. There wasn't much outside, just more dirty, weather-beaten ugliness. Rock, scattered garbage. The ground sloped down, first gradually, then sharply, into a gully. It had been used as a garbage dump. There was a snarl of rotten plastic bags, plastic bottles, cardboard boxes. Narrow mattresses, rusty bed frames. Too many bed frames. They'd gotten sloppy. So sure that their tracks were covered, or that no one cared enough to notice their evil deeds.

She crawled down to look more closely. Garbage was garbage, and this pile was more depressing than most, but she picked her way down and clambered out onto the pile. It was steep. She risked tumbling and sliding all the way down the hill, in a cascade of weatherbeaten trash.

That phrase in Mama's last letter echoed in her mind. *You'll find your strongest weapon buried in all this garbage.* She'd been so annoyed with that. Mama should have known better than to have inflicted an empty, facile New Age truism on her, after what she'd been through.

Then again, she'd taken an anthropology class, years ago in college, and heard a lecture about how much could be learned about a culture from studying its garbage. Garbage talked, the professor said. Nothing else in this goddamned mess was talking.

So whatever. It felt stupid, forced, but she climbed out onto that garbage to listen to anything it might have to say to her.

It was so quiet here. The wind had picked up, ruffling her hair and drying the dusty sweat on her face. There were even more bed frames than she'd thought, piled up on top of each other, higgledy-piggledy. There were various patterns of mesh. Interlocking circles, swirling mazelike coils. And . . . what was that? A flash of pale blue.

Her stomach clenched, but she got down and forced her hand through the torturous patterns of wire. Straining for the little thing.

It was a little stuffed bear. She got hold of its ear, but almost ripped it off. The fabric was rotten from exposure to the weather.

Suddenly, she wanted that fucking teddy bear with all the single-minded resolve of a three-year-old. She flung bed frames aside, heedless of spiders and scorpions that scattered at the sudden movement. She got close enough to pull the bear free, slicing her thumb on a broken IV bottle in the process. It was covered with the fibrous egg-laying fluff left by insects and arachnids. Still in one piece. Barely.

It had been made of pale blue chenille. One of its button eyes was gone. Stuffing poked out of the hole, so that it gave her a rakish wink. Its seams were rotten, and probably an entire ecosystem was nesting inside it, but she cradled it as if it were a newborn, careful not to let the blood from her cut thumb stain it further. Her hands shook.

Here it was. The reason she was here. The bear was her catalyst. Her link, to the little child who had treasured it.

The link broke through the ego barrier. It let her feel it. It reminded her what she was willing to bleed for.

There was no other building to explore. She'd seen every room, every closet. The sensible thing to do now was to go to the police, to Tenente Morelli, the woman who had interviewed her yesterday, who spoke excellent English. She could tell the Tenente her suspicions, let the cops open an investigation and make whatever they could of it.

But she had no sense yet of having done her duty. She wasn't finished here yet. But with what? *With what, Mama?*

She hiked up the gully once again and around the building. Maybe the spot where Mama had snapped her fateful photo would have a message for her, the way the atrium had. Or should have had.

The spot was hard to find. Everything had changed. The chain-link fence was a tangle on the ground, the building had decayed, the rocks had shifted. But she finally found it. As close as she could figure.

Mama had been so careful to frame that cleft in the rocks in the exact middle of the other half of the picture, and the way she composed her pictures left nothing to chance. The cleft looked like a cave opening.

Well, and so? Sveti tucked the teddy bear into her bag, walked over to that pile of boulders, and began to climb.

There was a narrow opening at the top. Just wide enough for a small, narrow woman to wiggle through on her belly.

Once inside, the roof rose up into the shadows, and the floor sloped swiftly downward. She was in a large cave, the back of which was lost in darkness. The only light came from the slot she had just slithered through. It had the air of a cathedral, with light streaming down from the rose window high above, and the rest of the room a vast, mysterious darkness. Bats fluttered, startled by a visitor.

She hated darkness. They'd been punished with it often. It was so easy for the lazy Yuri and Marina to slam the door and cut the lights.

Fuck you, you whining little shits. Take that.

She'd refused to get phobic about it. She couldn't afford another crippling hang-up. But she still hated it.

She dug out the flashlight and shone it into the chamber. The cave sloped down, and farther back, the roof was not high enough to stand. The mineral formations were pale, weird shapes in the darkness, the light flickering eerily over their pallid surfaces.

She stuck her finger into the bag, brushing her fingers over the teddy bear. Could there be more clues in this cave? Was that the message of Mama's picture? She closed her eyes and asked, like a prayer. A plea, aimed down, up, out. Anywhere it might get a benevolent listening voice. This place must be thick with ghosts.

She cradled the bear and thought of the child who had carried that toy. *Help me. You deserve to have your story told.*

She rooted herself, eyes squeezed shut. The air was heavy and humid, smelling of bat droppings. A hollow drip sounded. Her sliced thumb throbbed. Burned into her closed eyes was the pattern of interlocking metal rods and rings. A three-dimensional labyrinth of . . .

Labyrinth. She had fixated on Renato's garden maze as the labyrinth. But could it be this? Her directions were . . . for this cave?

Oh, God, no. If she got lost in here, it would be like going back into the black hole where the traffickers had held her, but worse, and forever. She'd die alone in the dark. Everyone had their limits, and this was hers. She would do what Sam had begged her to do. Pass it to the police. Have them assemble a team of spelunking professionals, with maps, equipment, lights, ready to face this godforsaken cave and reveal all its secrets more effectively than she could ever hope to do.

She opened her eyes and a little girl stood right in front of her.

It was a hallucination, of course. She knew that so completely, she wasn't even particularly startled. Brought on by stress, suggestion, exhaustion. The little girl was maybe three, dark skinned and barefoot. She wore a stained white cotton blouse and loose cotton pants, with flowers embroidered on the hem. She sucked her thumb, staring up at Sveti with huge, liquid brown eyes. Her hair was a tangle of black curls.

She reminded Sveti of Rachel, all those years ago. Those big, dark gleaming baby eyes, full of terrible knowledge no child should have.

As Sveti watched, she turned and scampered, swiftly and silently, into the dark . . . to the right. Like the first poet. R for Rodionov.

Just like that, she couldn't leave. She couldn't make a decision based on fear when a little child reached out to her. Real or illusion, it made no difference. The imperative was exactly the same.

Wow. Following visions, now. She probably needed antipsychotic drugs. But they were in short supply here, so she'd just go with it.

She turned on the flashlight and followed her little friend. It was nice, in this bleak, awful place, to imagine that she had company. It was a childish mind game, of course, but if it helped, who gave a shit?

Help or no help, she was so fucking afraid. She heard Tam's voice echo in her head. Endless, gruelling combat training sessions. *Don't allow fear to control you. Fear is just a fantasy. Pop the bubble.*

Intellectually, she understood that, but no amount of pep talking could keep her from feeling it. Fear of pain, darkness, but most of all, fear that it was all for nothing. Cruelty, for its own mean, stupid sake.

She would find some meaning in this, goddamnit. She would slap some down on top of it by brute force and bolt that fucker down.

It was slow going, through the big, confusing chambers, and the choices of left or right were by no means obvious. She had to explore each new cavern before she even understood which direction a person could choose to go at all. Some were full of deep, black pools of water, the minerals around them slippery with condensation, like wet ice.

And so it went. Vast mineral monuments, like the trunks of huge trees. Cascading waterfalls of frozen stone. Huge phallic pillars and massive, tumorous lumps. She wished the little girl would simply appear and lead her on, but she did not see the little girl again. It had just been that one brief flicker, because she wanted it too badly. The little girl had slipped through the chinks in her mind's armor only because she had not expected her. Ghost, hallucination, or vision, none of those entities could be forced. They did what they damn well pleased.

She memorized every landmark, marking the image in her mind for her reverse journey. That cathedral ceiling, that batwing arch, those kissing columns, that fat, warty monolith. She was so focused on this, she did not allow herself to feel the breathless panic. Then she saw light, far ahead. She was so relieved, she started to cry.

The chamber she emerged into was as large as the entrance chamber, at least twelve meters tall, with a big opening at the top a couple of meters across. A covering had been laid over the hole, she could see the straight line of corrugated metal silhouetted against a white sky. It looked as if the earth had given way, enlarging the hole.

Plant roots hung down. Tufts of grass and foliage furred the opening. A beam of light blazed in, like a bolt of heaven reaching down to her. She almost heard celestial music.

The realization unfurled slowly, because her eyes were still blurred and blinded by tears and the sudden influx of sunlight. But as she blinked and rubbed the wavering haze away, it opened up inside her, like a sinkhole somewhere around her liver.

First she saw the one right at her feet. Not believing it. Then she saw another. Then still another. And once she saw those, she saw them everywhere. They filled the entire chamber.

A sea of human bones.

CHAPTER 25

It was a charnel house. Bones filled the room, but the highest heap of them was right under the opening itself.

They had been dumped from the hole from above, allowed to fall any which way. It appeared that the earlier ones had been put into body bags, but the more recent ones not.

They had gotten sloppy at the end.

The exposed bodies were all desiccated skeletons. Many had been disassembled, perhaps by small animals. A faint smell of corruption hung about them, but they were shriveled and yellowed and dry.

Many of them were very small.

Sveti thudded painfully to her knees on the jagged rocks, next to one of the smaller ones. Its flattened skeleton was so tiny. It must have been so little, maybe two or three. The size Rachel had been when they were rescued. Scraps of fabric clung to the tiny leg bones. There was embroidery on the rotted cloth. Flowers, bleached and colorless.

She hugged herself. The sound coming out of her throat felt too high for human ears to hear. The pressure would implode her throat.

She vibrated with shaking sobs for these lost voyagers. This innocent baby. All the little girls and boys who would never be saved.

And for her own wretched self.

When the shaking had spent itself, she felt empty and exhausted. The angle of the sun blazing down into the hole had shifted. Its beam shone down, right onto the little skeleton. The grasses and flowers above had let some of their seeds drift down and take root, even in that deathly place. Grass sprouted, and twisting plants twined around the small rib cage. A few small white flowers bloomed here and there.

That sent another wave of pain lancing straight through the hot, unstable jelly that used to be her heart.

She pulled the toy bear out of her purse and tucked it tenderly between the rib cage and the arm bone of the tiny skeleton.

"Thank you for helping me," she whispered. "I'll stop the people who hurt you. And I'll pray for you. I'm not good at it, but I'll try."

Her knees wobbled as she stood. The shifting light had now illuminated a plastic cord that dangled down from the hole, knotted at various intervals. She had not seen it, so shocked had she been at the bodies. She wondered if her mother had left it there. She could not imagine anyone else having a reason to climb down, or up. For the murderers, this hole had been a one-way street.

Who knew if it was securely fastened at the top. Or if she could even make it up, exhausted as she was. But the alternative was crawling through that twisting cave again. She could not face the darkness a second time. Not after what she had just seen.

The rope hung about five feet short of the cave's floor. She picked her way, as carefully and respectfully as she could around the scattered arm and leg bones, rib cages, skulls, and reached to grab it. She leaped.

The rope creaked as she swung, back and forth, over that surreal backdrop of bones. The rope did not break, but it took all the strength she had to climb it. She was lucky for Tam's and Val's insistence on upper-body strength. *Fight biology*, Tam said. *Be stronger than ninety-five percent of the men you meet. If you can't crack the top five percent, cleavage and eyelash flutter and surprise will take care of the rest.*

All those pull-ups and push-ups and back strengtheners were what saved her now. She worked her way up, huffing and groaning. The afternoon sun burned. She sweated, in her light jacket. The rope sawed against the dirt and rocks of the opening, sending earth and dangerously large rocks pattering onto her head and shoulders.

Her hands burned, scraped raw against the harsh synthetic fibers of the rope, but she moved steadily upward. When she finally laid her elbow on the overhanging lip of turf, it collapsed beneath her weight, sending boulders and clods tumbling down onto the bones below.

And again. And again. The hole was almost twice as big as it had been before she finally found ground solid and stony enough to bear her weight. She scrambled up on it and crouched there, shivering.

The rope had been knotted around a downed metal pole for a huge chain-link fence, sunk into a now-exposed well of cement that lay on its side, dangerously close to the opening. The rope was frayed, brittle from sun and wind and rain, heat and cold, fewer than half of the fibers intact. It could have snapped under her weight. Or the massive lump of cement that had held the pole could have rolled down inside the hole and crushed her. But it hadn't.

The opening had once been covered by a large square chunk of metal and camouflaged by a pile of rocks, but time and weather had carved away at it and opened it to the sky again. A path alongside the inside of the chain-link fence led right to the hole.

She staggered to her feet and stared down into the hole. It was a twelve-meter drop, minimum. Maybe more like fifteen. She could barely see the bones now. They were lost in shadow. The spotlight of the sun had vanished. Too low to clear the lip of the ledge.

She felt the impulse to extend a formal gesture to these people whose deaths had been stripped of all ceremony. She bowed to the dark hole. "I'll do my best for you," she whispered. "I promise."

Her voice was thick and froggy, from the dirt and the damp, and weeping. She emerged from the rocky outcropping, looked around to orient herself. She was in a narrow canyon, barely 200 yards from the bottom of the garbage dump, downhill from the abandoned lab, a corner of which was visible up on the ridge. After that endless spirit journey through the underworld, she'd expected to be miles away, but she was only a few hundred yards from where she'd started.

The gully full of garbage spilled down into the narrow canyon where she found herself, but the canyon itself and the rough road that snaked through it were blocked by heavy-duty industrial fencing still in intimidating good repair and covered on the top with loops of cruel-looking razor wire. There would be no climbing that. She'd slice herself to ribbons. The sides of the canyon were sheer, with jagged overhangs.

She could hike down the canyon in the opposite direction, and try to clamber out and circle around somehow, but who knew how long such a detour would take? Alternatively, she could climb up that long, steep, slippery cascade of garbage in the gully.

She opted for the garbage. After all, Mama had told her not to be afraid of garbage. It was a metaphor for her life. And after a cave full of decayed human bodies, what terrors could a garbage dump hold?

But as with most things, it proved to be harder than she'd anticipated. She slipped and slid on rotten plastic bags, which broke open under her feet. Broken glass, test tubes, vials, and syringes burst out. She was climbing a mountain of biohazardous waste.

About twenty feet up, she lost her footing by stepping on a plastic box lid that acted like a sled, and set her tumbling and rolling down the pile, sliding between yellowed and rotting mattresses. She bounced her hip agonizingly hard against something very solid and stationary, and came to rest in a tangle of rusted bed frames. Dazed and panting.

When she looked up, she saw the bumper of a car, poking out of the wreckage. Dirty, but whole. Not rusted, or dinted or scarred.

She pried some garbage away and saw a headlight. Not a broken one. She moved a sheet of corrugated plastic, a couple more bed frames, and peered into the cab of the vehicle. It was a smallish white panel van. The windshield was streaked with mud, but it was whole. It was dirty, but not ruined enough to warrant being buried under a pile of garbage.

She yanked a box away and uncovered a tire. The treads looked deep and sharp and new. In southern Italy, a car would only end up in a heap like this after it had been scavenged down to the bare frame.

The words from Mama's letter rang in her head. *You'll find your strongest weapon buried in all this garbage.* It had never occurred to her that Mama might have meant it literally.

On top were mattresses. Heavier things were piled to the sides. Sveti dragged away enough to expose the passenger's side door, which was unlocked. Inside, the car smelled stale, but not rotten. It was a Mercedes panel van. The seal had kept humidity out. On the seat was a plastic sleeve with a sheaf of paper, a thumb drive. A handwritten note, in her mother's graceful script. First in Italian, then English.

> *Per favore, consegna questi documenti alla polizia.*
> *Questo veicolo contiene pericolose sostanze radioattive.*
> *Please deliver these documents to the police. This vehicle contains dangerous radioactive substances.*

Well, then. There was the punch line, but she was in no mood to appreciate the joke. Her nerves could not be jolted more than they had been already. What she'd found in the cave had broken her heart wide open. This part was nothing. Just some delicate, careful mopping up.

She had to see if the stuff was still inside. She realized, as she kicked and flung garbage clear of the sliding door, that she had tears running down her face, into her nose. She had to wipe her face on her sleeve before she could see clearly enough to slide the door open.

Inside was a large, opaque yellow plastic container, with the symbol for radioactivity stenciled on the top and sides. She stared at it, wondering with a small part of her mind just how shielded that container actually was. She should get away from it until she knew.

She slid the door shut and started piling the shell of garbage back on top. Evil intentions, heaped on top of evil deeds. But it all stopped today. Those bastard fuckheads were going down.

She pulled the sheaf of paper out of the cab. There were photos: of the lab, of the contents of the van, what was in the pit. There was a map, clearly marked. The pin drive must contain still more information.

The van had no keys, or she might have driven it straight to a police station. She knew how to hotwire a car in theory, but she had no tools, and it was difficult, with a car full of modern electronics. Plus, there was the locked razor-wire fence. And to top it off, it might be radioactive. Miserable as she was, she had no desire to cosy up to strontium-90, and she probably wouldn't be able to maneuver the van over those heaps of garbage anyway. It was not an off-road rig.

She shoved the photos back into the plastic sleeve and the thumb drive into her pocket, and grimly set herself to burying the van in garbage once again, as completely as it had been hidden before. It would be a crass twist of fate to have the vehicle discovered, looted, or stolen by the subhuman creatures that had looted the abandoned lab. And an even more horrible joke if innocent local kids happened across it.

That done, it was a long, hard, sliding scramble up the steep mountain of trash to the top of the gully. Then she faced the long hike back to the car. The sun was low, and she did not want to be on this road when night fell. She felt unpleasantly visible up here. She could be seen from far away, and there was no place to hide. No trees to speak of. No place to run on the tumbled rocks.

Hours later, she got to the first chain-link fence. It was harder to climb it this time. Her legs felt hollow, floppy and rubbery. Her scraped, bloody hands burned against the sharp wires. Every downhill step toward the car seemed to rattle her loosened bones.

Bones. So many. Burned into her mind's eye. When she closed her eyes, she saw them, heaped and scattered, gray and tan and yellow.

She was relieved to find the car where she'd left it, at the concrete barrier. She'd traveled so far today, it had been like going through a magic portal. A hundred years could have passed in the world outside. Her car might be a rusted fossil. The world changed beyond recognition.

But it was just where she'd parked it, shiny and new. She tucked the papers under the seat and got under way.

This was the part where Mama had come to grief, after all her effort and sacrifice, and the same fate could easily befall Sveti. She had to be sharp and canny and quick. Right now, she felt anything but.

Of course, if she hadn't misplaced her fucking phone, she could have called Tenente Morelli right now and told her everything. Morelli would not need the backstory explained. Sveti cringed at the thought of going into a small-town police station, trying to make something so horrific comprehensible to whoever spoke the best English. They might think she was crazy, or on drugs. She'd be exposed and alone for a long time before she could prove her claim was true.

She wanted Sam so badly. Beneath the day's turmoil ran the constant, sour current of missing Sam. Even a screaming fight with him would be welcome. The thought of fighting with Sam was oddly bracing. It focused her enough to make a plan of action.

San Anselmo was a couple hours away, but it was bigger than the towns around here. She would go to that police station and search out a cop who spoke English. Beg for the use of a phone. Arrange for some heavily armed person to come to keep her company, as Sam and Tam and Val and Nick had insisted. She should have done that yesterday, but she'd been too busy sulking because that person could not be Sam. But she didn't even have the energy to properly scold herself right now.

First, she'd copy the papers, photos, and documents. When she got to the cops, she'd speak to Morelli, just to spread the joy. She'd call home, tell Nick, tell Tam and Val. She'd widen the net of people who knew until it was too big for anyone to contain. She'd have accomplished at least that much. Whether they killed her or not.

Step Two, if she survived Step One, was to drive straight back to Sam's hospital room and tell him the story. He would not be able to shut her up or throw her out, as injured as he was. She'd tell him she loved him and missed him so badly, she wanted to die. That she'd been a brainless asshole to flounce out the door by herself, that she wanted to burden him with the monumental pain in the ass that was Svetlana Ardova for the rest of his natural life. She'd collaborate. She'd be safe, sensible, as good as gold. Forever. Cross her heart.

It would be too late, of course. He being the kind of man he was. When Sam's mind was made up, he didn't un-make it. He would tell her to fuck off. Then, of course, the world would end.

Let it. The world had ended so many times today. What was one more time? She had nothing to lose. Not hope. Not pride.

She circled around a long time in San Anselmo before finding an electronics shop. The gangly man with the large Adam's apple behind the counter spoke a little English, but he stared with big, scared eyes for a while, his throat bobbing, before he dared to speak to her. He took pity on her when she begged him to copy the data from her mother's pin drive onto the new one she bought from him, and plugged it into his machine. A few anxious moments passed before it consented to be read, but the data finally emerged. A hundred and twenty-three JPEGs. One Word document.

She tucked the new drive into her pocket, asked directions to the police station, and proceeded to understand absolutely nothing of the directions he gave her. She thanked him anyway, having gleaned from his body language the general direction in which she should drive.

She'd just look for signs for the *Polizia*. But as always, that was easier said than done. There was a huge *festa* in course, involving extensive illumination, a procession, marching bands, an open-air market, choking masses of people. Cars clogged all the streets that were not closed to traffic. She slowed to a crawl, twitching and cursing.

She found what she hoped was a legal parking spot, and spotted a place that dealt in cell phones and services. She could no longer afford to be incommunicado, not with a secret like hers.

She headed for it, footsteps quickening to a trot.

"Svetlana! Is that you?"

She shrieked and spun around. Hazlett leaned out of the back of his limo. He stared at her, horrified. "For the love of God, what happened to you? Were you in an accident? Did someone attack you?"

Oh, joy. Sveti looked down at herself, realizing just how filthy and disheveled she was. A day of hiking on broken rock, sliding on one's belly through a slimy cave, crawling out of a mass grave, and scrambling through a garbage dump could do that to a woman.

"No," she said stupidly. "Hi, Michael. I'm, ah . . . fine. What are you doing here? How did you find me?"

"Chance! We've been looking for you all day! That was a dirty trick, running off in the night! What on earth were you thinking? After what happened to you the other day?"

His scolding tone slid over her, not penetrating. She stared at him. Pure chance? "Why are you here?" she repeated.

He made an exasperated sound. "Who knows. Coincidence. Psychic magnetism. It's destiny that I should be drawn to you!"

Destiny, her ass. Her social functionality was at an all-time low. She could not chat with this guy right now. She had a list of crucial shit to do, and he was not on it. "Sorry, Michael. I have to go." She turned in the opposite direction from the one that his limo was pointed and started walking.

He got out and followed her. "Go where? Slow down, Svetlana!"

"To the police," she said.

He loped stubbornly after. "Why, for God's sake? To report a crime? Did someone hurt you? Rob you? Talk to me! Let me help!"

"Thanks, but only the police can help right now."

He danced out in front of her. "Let me give you a ride to the police station," he offered. "It will take you the better part of an hour to beat your way through this crowd, and I can get you there in twenty minutes. Frankly, you look like you could use the time off your feet."

Sveti looked around at the deepening night, the honking blare of traffic on the closest big avenue, the streets choked with people. She could wander until she collapsed. God, how she longed to get this done.

"Okay," she said. "But straight to the police station."

"Like a shot," he assured her, and opened the door of the limo for her, rattling off a string of instructions in swift Italian to his driver.

He got in after her. "Now, tell me. What on earth happened to you today? Excuse me for saying it, but you look like a train wreck."

This was the price she had to pay for this ride. Too late she had realized that it was too expensive. She sucked in a bracing breath, hung on to her patience with all her fingernails. "I found evidence of a terrible crime," she said. "I have to tell the police right away."

He looked shocked. "What crime? Has anyone been hurt?"

She cleared her thick, aching throat. "Many people," she said bleakly, thinking of the tiny skeleton, the toy bear. "It was hard to tell the number."

"Many? Good God, Svetlana, do we need to call ambulances?"

"It's not a recent crime," she said. "They're long past help. I can't explain right now, Michael. Please, give me some space."

"Certainly," he murmured. "I'm sorry. You've been through something terrible. Just rest, please."

She leaned back, covering her eyes with her hands to block him out. Michael made a call on his smartphone and talked into it with great urgency, in Italian. She felt so strange, jumpy. As tired as she was, she was jangling like an alarm bell.

As soon as he finished talking, she'd borrow his phone and call Tenente Morelli. She had to tell someone, anyone. Correction. Anyone who was not Michael Hazlett. Maybe telling someone would make her feel less like doom was breathing down her neck. As it so often was.

The limo slowed just as he hung up. She looked out. It was not a police station. It was the façade of a luxury hotel.

"Michael?" she said sharply. "What the hell? I said the police!"

"I have a better idea," he said smoothly. "Hear me out." He held up his hand to forestall her protests. "I keep a suite here the entire season. They have an excellent chef. The police commissioner, Zabretti, is a personal friend of mine and Renato's. I've dined with him many times. He speaks fluent English. I called him to tell him about you. As soon as he finishes his current business, he'll be right over. In the meantime, you can sit down someplace safe and comfortable, have a cup of tea, maybe even shower and change your—"

"I don't give a shit about my clothes! This is more important than my dinner fashion choices, Michael! This can't wait!"

"Certainly not, which is why it should be done right!" he retorted. "What's the point of going to the station, where you'll just wait for a long time in a hard plastic chair to talk to a series of thick, uncomprehending bureaucratic underlings before you even find someone capable of listening to you? Commissario Zabretti should come to you! You deserve it, after your ordeal! In the meantime, drink some tea or have a glass of wine and something to eat! I've ordered dinner. From the looks of you, you haven't eaten, am I right?"

She was staring straight at him, but she saw right through him, as if he were a ghost, or a fantasy. The skeletons in that hole, burned into her memory, were more vivid than he was. White flowers were twining around tiny rib bones, and he wanted her to sip some tea?

"I'm not hungry," she said.

He made an impatient sound. "Don't be ridiculous. It'll be very light. Steamed sea bass with lemon and herbs, salad, grilled vegetables, a nice chilled Pinot. You must eat. I'm sure even your pit bull would agree with me. Much as he thinks I'm opportunistic scum."

She flinched. "Don't, please."

Michael got out of the car and held out his hand.

She stared at it, still frozen. It was true. She was being hysterical and childish, spitefully refusing him just because she'd had the mother of all bad days. And because he was not Sam. That was not his fault.

She got out of the car, but she did not take his hand.

The suite he kept on the fifth floor was large and very beautiful. A table was set for two. White tapers twinkled. A wine bucket had a bottle chilling in it. A tea tray on a sideboard. Cream, sugar, lemon. Chocolate-dipped butter cookies. It was surreal.

"Ah, that's better." Hazlett shrugged off his jacket. "Wine or tea?"

She struggled with the question for a moment. "Tea," she croaked.

"Sit," he said briskly. "Zabretti should be here soon."

She collapsed into a chair. He poured her tea and stirred a heaping teaspoonful of sugar into it. "You look like you're about to go into shock," he scolded. "You don't take good enough care of your-self."

If only he knew. The tea was too sweet, but her wiped-out brain could use the fuel. She needed to be cogent, for Zabretti.

After her tea was drained, he poured and sugared another. "So tell me, now," Hazlett said. "What happened?"

"I found out why my mother was murdered," she said. "She'd been investigating a crime. Hundreds of boat people from Africa killed in illegal medical experiments and buried in a cave."

Hazlett's jaw dangled. "My God. I . . . I don't know what to say."

She shrugged. There was nothing he could say that would be pertinent, so he might as well shut up. But no such luck. He rat-tled on.

"You have proof? In there?" He indicated the plastic envelope.

Her hand tightened on the plastic envelope as she gulped more tea. She was afraid to let go of it, even for a second. It could disap-pear in a puff of smoke. She felt like she'd been chasing the damn thing half her life.

"Tell me more," he urged. "How on earth did you figure it out? It's amazing, Svetlana. Not that I'm surprised, having seen you in action."

She wished he'd stop kissing her ass, since she really didn't want him that close to it. "I have to tell the commissario all about it," she hedged. "Please, don't make me say it twice."

"Of course not," he murmured hastily. "You must be so tired."

"May I use your phone?" she asked suddenly. "I lost mine."

"Certainly." He pulled it out. "Who do you want to call?"

"The detective I talked to yesterday," she said.

Michael looked worried. "Don't you think you should let Zabretti handle this? The detective you talked to yesterday won't be investi-gating a crime that took place in another jurisdiction anyway—"

"I don't give a shit about the politics of jurisdiction," she said sharply. "I just want everyone to know about this. As soon as pos-sible."

"I know," he soothed. "Please, just talk to Zabretti first. He'll be here any minute, and, and he—ah! Here's dinner! Let's discuss it after."

Time dragged like a ball and chain. Her stomach was perplexed by food. The very small quantity that she managed to swallow seemed a lump of some alien substance that it had never encountered before, and had no idea what to do with. The luxurious place felt so fake. A façade.

She felt that way a lot, since the organ traffickers. As if she alone knew the dark truth, while everyone else inhabited a shiny dream world. Only Sam had made her feel fully rooted in the world around her. He made her feel like she inhabited it completely. Like she owned it.

Without him, she drifted, lost and transparent. Like a ghost.

Hazlett poured her wine. As she watched pale liquid glug into the glass, she thought of stories she'd read to Rachel about fairy mounds. People who visited the hall of the Mountain King. *Neither shall ye eat nor drink in the land of faerie, lest ye never again return to the world of men.*

The random, nasty stab of irrational fear put an end to dinner. She put down her fork and looked at the clock on the marble mantel.

"Where is Zabretti?" she asked. "It's been over an hour."

"He's a busy man," Hazlett said, dabbing at the corner of his mouth with a napkin. "And he understands it's not a time-sensitive emergency. This is Italy, after all. Nothing happens quickly."

"Not time sensitive? You told him that?" She leaped to her feet. "I should have gone straight to the police. I'll get a cab right now!"

"I did not say it wasn't important! I simply let him know that it was not a crime that was currently in progress! Do not get hysterical, Svetlana. I did not diminish how terrible this situation is. Don't panic!"

Panic was rising anyway. She trembled violently. Oh, please, please, let her keep her shit together just a little while longer. Until she could pass this torch on to someone she trusted. When no one needed her, when it no longer mattered, *then* she could fall apart. Not before.

She pictured the little girl, holding her bear. Her tiny bare bones.

"Let me make a suggestion, now that you have some food inside you," Hazlett said. "Let me help you organize what you're going to say to Zabretti. Just run through it for me, exactly the way you plan to say it to him. Let me ask all the questions that he will ask. It will save you time and energy, and it will give you more credibility. Please, Svetlana. I want so badly to help you. Come. Let's run through it."

The plastic envelope warped in her hands, sharp corners cutting into her palms. Her heart thudded. She was clammy with cold sweat.

"Let's start," he prompted. "First, tell me how you found this cave. And how on earth did you manage to climb down into it?"

Her mind froze into crystalline clarity. Her heart stopped beating. Time stopped, as she stared at his ruggedly handsome face, his expression of concern. His eyes, glittering. Knife-sharp. So focused.

She cleared her throat. "Who said I climbed down into the cave?"

Hazlett's frown was puzzled. "Oh, I just assumed, I suppose. The area has so many natural wells and cavities. It seemed obvious that—"

"What area? How do you know where I went? I was gone all day. I could have gone hundreds of miles and come back in that amount of time."

He took a meditative sip of his wine. "Svetlana," he said. "The intensity of your day is getting to you. The tone of your voice is bordering on offensive. Take a breath."

They gazed at each other. He was offering her a choice. She could laugh, abashed. Apologize for being a crazy, nervous hag. Smile, simper. Make nice while she frantically planned her escape.

She waited an instant too long.

Hazlett lifted a pistol and pointed it at her face. Still smiling.

"Oops," he murmured. "My bad."

CHAPTER 26

"Go on to the hotel. Get some rest, Dad. Both of you," Sam said to his father and sister. *So I can get some, too,* was the pleading subtext, but he could tell neither of them was listening to that.

"We don't want to leave you alone, in this place." His father's voice was rough with exhaustion. He was past seventy, with a triple bypass and heart valve surgery behind him. His eyes were red, his face puffy and blurred with weariness. Sam found it uncomfortable. He preferred feeling angry at his father to feeling sorry for him. Or worse, worried for him. Enough wrenching revelations about his feelings. He was fried.

"You shouldn't be alone," his father said. "What happened to that young lady whose honor you were defending so fiercely last week? Did she have no further use for you, now that you're an invalid?"

"She had some pressing personal business," he said stiffly.

"More personal than bullet wounds?" Connie jumped in fiercely. "She shouldn't have left you alone here! It's just common decency!"

"There's hospital staff to help me. And I'm feeling much better already. I really am. I'll be fine alone," Sam assured them.

"Fine? You've got contusions, torn muscle tissue, a bullet that almost severed your femoral artery and came within inches of your

genitals, too! What are you trying to tell us? If you'd fucking verbalize it, instead of coding it in bullet wounds, I swear we'd listen!"

Sam closed his eyes. "I did not do all this to myself to upset
you," he said. "And I can't deal with the histrionics."

"Histrionics?" She snorted. "As if getting yourself regularly shot
up by mobsters isn't attention-getting behavior!"

"Lower your voice," his father hissed. "Don't make a scene!"

"He always gets to," Connie yelled. "When's my turn? What insane lengths do I have to go to? A sex scandal, a psychotic break?"

"That is enough!" Dad thundered.

Connie's mouth quivered. "Yes, it is." She grabbed the wheeled
suitcases that leaned against the wall and turned toward the door.

"Hey!" Sam called. "The suitcase you brought for me. You're
not taking it with you, are you?"

She frowned. "Of course I am. It's much safer at our hotel. What
use do you have for it now? I'll bring it when they release you."
Her eyes swept the small, grotty room. "Or when we have you
transferred."

"I want it. It has toiletries, right? Shaving cream, toothpaste,
dental floss, fresh underwear? Leave it."

"But you can't even get out of bed!" she protested.

"I still want it," he repeated stubbornly.

"Oh, whatever." She gave it a shove, back against the wall, and
turned to her dad. "Shall I tell the car to wait?"

His father looked grimly reluctant.

"A night's sleep will help all of us," Sam urged. "I'm just going to
sleep. There's no point sitting in that hard chair watching me do it."

His father grunted and got to his feet. "Trying to get rid of me,
as usual," he muttered. "Fine. Tomorrow, then."

Ten teeth-grinding minutes of lecturing and scolding before
they were out the door. When it shut behind them, he almost wept
in relief.

He'd been lying, when he said he felt better. Pain was a meat-
mallet, hammering with each heartbeat. Face, head, ribs, thigh,
balls. Add being dumped by your girlfriend to that, plus a day-long
session of scolding familial disapproval, and you had the recipe for

exquisitely calibrated pain on every level of the self. A symphony of discomfort. He'd never been so angry, or so hurt, or so scared. Other than the other day, when Sveti had been clamped under the goon's arm, in imminent danger of dismemberment. A caustic stress cocktail zinged through him every time that image flashed through his mind, making him twitch and writhe on his bed. This could drive a guy right over the edge.

But hey. He'd left the edge behind a long while back. Ever since he saw that girl years ago, and promptly lost his mind. Inappropriately young, problematic, complicated, hostile, unattainable. And yet, he'd started courting her. Bugging her.

Stalking her. Call it what it was.

His eyes rested on her phone, which he had found in his tangled sheets in the night. A gift from a mischievous trickster god, intent on messing him up. A perfect opportunity for an obsessed, irrational ex-boyfriend. Hack into her phone, snoop into her life. Torture himself by listening in on her future love affairs. Feed the beast of his sickness, until it grew and grew, became more feral, more twisted. Less human.

Until they locked him up. That was the trajectory of a man's life, once he picked up the cell phone of a woman who had dumped him and started fucking with it. So why was he still holding on to the thing?

The locked screen wanted a six-digit code. He tried all the obvious ones: her birth date, Rachel's birth date, Irina's. He tried all the kids' names, one after the other, the ones who hung all over her and called her Auntie Sveti. None worked. He tried her parents' names, too.

He moved on to all the adults in the McCloud Crowd, starting with Tam and Val, Nick and Becca. He tried the ass-bite's name, too, just to torture himself, and was relieved when none of the "joshua" or "jcattre" or "cattrell" combos worked, either.

He hesitated for a long time, but since he was on the self-torture kick, why not? He tried PETRIE. Nothing, of course. Then he punched in SAMUEL. The device accepted the code and opened itself to him.

He started to shake. His vision blurred.

He sat there for a long time, unmoving. Pathetically grateful to be alone in the room.

It passed through him. He sponged off his face with a wad of sheet and flung himself into the contents of her phone, ass over head.

Her calendar had no surprises for him. Her contacts were all known to him, and the ones he did not personally know, he'd already investigated. She hadn't posted to her Facebook page, Twitter account, or v-log since before Nina and Aaro's wedding. Busy, busy.

He dug in to the photos. McCloud Crowd kids, all over the place. Rachel, Irina, and Sofia were featured most, but all the Mc-Cloud brood were represented extensively. Adults, too. Nick and Becca. Tam and Val, kissing on their veranda with the sunset behind them, Seth and Raine laughing on their yacht. Connor and Erin carving a ham. Davy and Margot, Sean and Liv, Kev and a pregnant, very happy-looking Edie. Lily and Bruno, Aaro and Nina, Miles and Lara. Zia Rosa. Hundreds of photos, from weddings and christenings, birthdays and barbecues.

She had a good eye. People looked good in her photos.

He found a batch that were all from the housewarming party of Lara and Miles. Their beautiful house in the mountains. Cedar paneled, thirty-five-foot vaulted solarium windows, panoramic views. Shots of the newly landscaped patio out back embraced by massive pines and firs, a big barbecue grill loaded with steaks, a big tub of ice full of beers. There was the beautiful waterfall, with a bunch of the kids swimming in the pool under Sean's and Davy's watchful eyes.

There were two more folders, one marked "Mama," one marked "Misc." He clicked on the latter.

The picture was out of focus, taken from behind a sliding glass door. Miles and Lara's housewarming party, where she'd never let him talk to her. She'd run away whenever he tried. The picture was Sam talking to Sean, holding a beer. The next one was the same photo, but enlarged, cropped. Everything trimmed out except his face.

He clicked the next one, which was of Kev and Edie's baby Jon's first birthday party, a clan-wide bash. Kev held little Jon up proudly, fat legs waving. Sam laughed at both of them. Next shot, just his own enlarged face, laughing, and a blurred flash of Jon's bare, dimpled foot.

The next one was from Lily and Bruno's wedding, years ago. There were several from that party. Him talking. Him smiling. Him drinking. Him staring moodily into the ballroom at the dancers. All pairs, first the original, then the enlarged, cropped version. On, and on, and on.

He scrolled down. Counted. One hundred and sixty-eight originals, one hundred and sixty-eight edited versions. Three hundred and thirty-six photos. Bigger than his own stalker stash of Sveti photos.

She had him beat. By a country mile.

It should be a balm for his ego, but his ego was past soothing. It was six feet under. All that was left was raw meat, exposed nerves. Pain.

Three hundred and thirty-six fucking jolts of it.

He had to close his eyes and just try to breathe. He was tempted to call the nurse and make a noisy, agitated fuss, until she put him down with some powerful opiate or other. Bring on the cosh.

But that made him think of Sasha. He'd given his life for Sam's. Sasha had done the hard thing, the brave thing. Out of respect, he'd do the same. No more morphine derivatives were going into his veins today.

He clicked on the folder "Mama." Childhood photos of Sveti and her parents. Sveti got the cheekbones and the dark coloring from her father. Sergei Ardova had been a severe-looking man. A sharp, measuring look in his eyes. He'd have been an ass-kicking, terror-inducing father-in-law, in some happy parallel universe.

Baby pics of Sveti were hard to look at, and equally impossible to look away from. It hurt, to imagine her that small, that defenseless. Pictures of her as a beautiful six- or eight- or ten-year-old had the same effect. He shrank from looking at that hopeful, delicate face, those big, innocent eyes, knowing what was in store for her.

Oh, fuck this. He was indulging in pure, distilled masochism, but he just couldn't stop himself. His crush on Sveti was his first experience of helplessly compulsive behavior. He was strung out on her scent, her touch, her glance. The caress of her breath against his chest, her slender limbs twined around his body. Warm and relaxed and trusting.

He covered his eyes for a while. Then clicked onward into the "Mama" file, just for something to do. Anything at all.

There it was, the fateful photo of her mom that had started all this. Her eyes were so compelling. They gazed out of the photo at him with haunting urgency. Begging him to do something, now, please, fast.

He was working himself into a state. Stress hormones messing with his head. He clicked off Sonia's silent plea. Opened another.

This one wasn't much better. It was that shot of Sergei, complete with Zhoglo's smirk behind his shoulder. About which he'd made those arrogant, butthead pronouncements about choosing your thoughts, choosing who got into the frame. Trimming out the undesirable.

Like he knew what the fuck he was talking about. Like he had even the most basic, elemental clue how to choose his own thoughts.

He recognized Sveti's heart-stopping smile in her father's grin. He was raising his glass, toasting that scum Zhoglo, and the other guy, the mystery dude, who—

What the *fuck?*

He stared at the phone, looked closer. He rubbed his eyes. Blinked furiously. No way. Oh, no fucking way. Not possible.

He used the camera's zoom function, clicked in closer.

The third man was Hazlett. Much younger, hair darker, but it was him, no question, complete with the dimples, the whitened teeth, the charming smile. He was not aware that he was being photographed. The picture had been taken from an interior, focusing out the window to where the three men stood on an outdoor veranda.

He had no idea what the hell this meant, but Sveti was in danger, more than he'd ever dreamed. And he'd ordered her to walk away from him and straight out into it, just because she wouldn't be a good little girl and toe his line. He couldn't even call and warn her. She was naked, incommunicado, in the mouth of the beast. Holy flipping *shit.*

He searched through Sveti's phone until he found a number for the Villa Rosalba, the one Renato had given her the day of the gala. Renato Torregrossa was probably dirty, too, but whatever. He had to try.

He dialed the number, waited while it rang. *"Pronto?"* a man said.

"Have I reached the Villa Rosalba?" he asked in Italian.

"Si. E lei chi è?" Yes, and you are?

"I'm Sam Petrie. I'm looking for Svetlana Ardova. Is she there?"

"Mi dispiace, but the Signorina Ardova left late last night and has not been back."

His heart thumped, hard. "Did she leave alone?"

"I do not know, signore."

"Do you know where she—"

"No, I do not. No one knows. *Buona sera,* signore—"

"No! Wait! How about Hazlett? Is he there? Or Torregrossa?"

"Neither of them are here." The voice was frigid with distrust. *"Buona sera, signore."* The connection broke.

Sam cursed viciously into the dead phone. It could be true, or it could be a brush-off. He tried the hotel where they were still checked in. They informed him she hadn't been back.

If only she'd taken one of Simone's minions with her to Villa Rosalba. If only he'd had the presence of mind to give her back her phone. He could have warned her, or even traced her, with the help of her family. No way would that crowd send off their precious damsel fair to Europe without a trace in her phone. They protected what they loved.

Unlike himself. He ripped out the surgical tape and the IV needle, letting the tube dangle and fluid drip forlornly out onto the floor.

He struggled to sit up. Had to roll to his side, strangling a groan. Fiery bolts of pain ripped through him with every hitching breath. His groin was swollen like someone had stomped his balls with a giant boot.

He was in no shape to pull off a grand rescue, even if he had the faintest idea where she was. He shoved his legs off the bed so that their dead weight would give him some ballast for the push—and sat up.

He almost passed out. Blood spotted his bandages. Thigh, ribs.

The suitcase Connie had brought taunted him from across the room. Fresh clothes, shoes. Twelve feet of floor. It looked like a fucking mile.

And where did he think he was going, once he dressed himself? The only people who might know where she was were Renato and Hazlett. It could take days to track them down. Sveti was all out of days. They were closing in on her. Like they had at the foundry.

That had been bugging him. A puzzle needing to be solved, when he had the time, and the bandwidth. How the fuck had Cherchenko and his mafiya hit squad followed them, after the complicated evasive moves he'd pulled? Someone must have planted a trace, but how, when, and on whom? Simone had bug-swept the car and hadn't detected anything. To be absolutely sure, they would have to dismantle the vehicle to its smallest component parts. Who had the time?

Pavel was dead, and the others. There was no asking a dead man. But what about Misha? Sveti had said he was a tech geek.

Of course, Misha might well have been the one who sold his brother out in the first place, by spilling the info about the *gelateria*. But Sam couldn't blame a fourteen-year-old for being intimidated by a dad who would cheerfully disembowel people. Misha was orphaned, brotherless, maybe stricken with remorse. Nervous about his future. Scared shitless.

Misha might know something useful. And this vague, formless plan was the only possible course of action Sam could think of.

One did not find a mafiya vor in the White Pages, but there were those silent calls Sveti had been convinced were from Misha. He'd chalked that notion up to wishful fantasy. Sveti wanted so badly to save the world, sweeten the bitterness. He'd been such an arrogant prick to rag on her about that. It made him squirm to think of it.

But maybe it wasn't a wishful fantasy. Maybe Sveti had insights from sources he couldn't imagine. Maybe he should have listened more carefully. Been more respectful of her feelings, hunches. In retrospect, it was a marvel she hadn't blown him off sooner, as dickish as he'd been.

He pulled up Sveti's call log. The first silent call had been, what, the day before yesterday? It felt like weeks. He dialed it. It rang four times. The line clicked open. There was a heavy, attentive silence.

Sam clenched his fist. "Misha?"

The line clicked, went dead.

Shit. Needles of pain stabbed through his temples, jabbing every which way. He opened a message and swiftly texted.

pls pls I need your help Sveti in danger.

He sent it and sat there waiting. A minute went by. Then two. The phone burped softly in his hand.

He thumbed the message open with a trembling hand

y do u have svetis fone

He texted back, getting the letters wrong with his swollen fingers. His thumb so goddamn thick and shaking violently.

she left it with me by mistake

Misha's response was swift and succinct.

u r both stupid

True to form, arrogant little shithead. But Sam could not afford to get his back up about Misha's manners today. He sucked it up, and texted again.

pls. talk 2 me. pls.

Another minute passed. Two more. Seconds measured by the thud of his heart in his torn, stitched, bruised, or otherwise fucked-up tissue. The smartphone buzzed. He clicked open the line. "Misha?"

No answer. For the love of God. He hung on to his temper. The kid had just lost his entire existing family in a gun massacre. "Misha," he said. "This is not going to work if you're just going to breathe into the phone."

"I am here," Misha said. His voice was clipped, robotic.

"Good." Sam groped awkwardly for something to say to the kid. "I know it's a hell of a time to ask for favors. I'm sorry about your father—"

"Don't be," Misha said. "He was a monster, and I am glad that he is dead. I would have killed him myself, if I had a chance."

Wow. That was cold. But it was better that they were both on the same page about his father. "Your brother, then. I'm sorry about him."

"Are you? I was told he died jumping out in front of you. To save you." Misha's voice had an accusing tone. As if he considered it a poor trade.

"I couldn't stop him," Sam said. "I would've saved him if I could."

Misha made a sharp, pained sound in his throat and didn't reply.

Sam was all out of segues. "I've lost Sveti," he said. "I can't call her, because she left the phone. She's in danger. I think she's with the guy who had her parents killed, but she doesn't know what he did."

"So why are you calling me?" Misha's voice was utterly remote.

"Because someone must have planted a trace on us, at some point," Sam pressed on. "Maybe your father. They caught up with us and Sasha at that old foundry, and I can't see how he could have followed us otherwise. Unless he already knew where Sasha was."

Misha was sullenly silent.

Sam's knuckles were white. "Did he know? Did she have a trace?"

"He did not know," Misha said heavily. "And, yes, she did."

His heart thudded, like a horse galloping downstairs. "Where? Shoes, purse? Where?" His voice was getting louder.

"Not in her clothes," Misha said. "On her body."

His control snapped. "What the fuck are you talking about?

How could it have been on her body? No one's touched her body but me!"

"On her head," Misha said.

Sam gaped. "Huh? Her head? How . . . ?"

"They put a trace under her scalp, day before yesterday," Misha said. "I listened in on a phone conversation. Seems strange to me that she did not notice. Such a thing should be painful, no? The incision?"

"Wha . . . but who? Who?"

"I do not know his name. He is a man who has worked with my father for many years. The client and my father both wanted something that they thought Sveti could find. My father wanted Sasha, and The Sword of Cain. They put a trace so they could follow as she searched for these things. Perhaps she is out finding them right now."

It smashed into him, head-on. So fucking obvious. "That fall, in the atrium. They said she fainted. Bumped her head. They drugged her and tagged her. Those fucking bastards. I'm ripping their arms off."

Misha grunted his approval. "Do something more permanent."

"I'm on it," Sam promised. "Do you have her frequency?"

"I could have found it for you," Misha said. "But not anymore."

"Why not?" he bellowed. "You have to!"

"I am bolted inside a basement room in my father's house," Misha said. "Papa locked me in before they came after you and Sveti. Josef came to tell me Papa was shot through the heart, and Sasha ripped apart by bullets. All Papa's men have gone. He said I would die of thirst, unless the police found me. If I had the strength left to call out when they arrive. Then he left. I yelled for help. But it's true. I am alone."

"Wow," Sam said inanely. "They let you have a phone in there?"

Misha snorted. "No, fool. I keep my SIM card taped to my leg. I hid a charged phone in this room. I knew I might end up here. He's locked me in before. Sasha spent months in here sometimes."

One life-threatening disaster at a time, for the love of Christ. "So why haven't you called someone to let you out? You're just sitting there? Doing what, Misha? Sulking? When you have a phone on you?"

Misha was maddeningly silent.

"Damn it, Misha!" he yelled. "Talk to me!"

"I do not have anyone to call," Misha said. "Only Sasha and Mama would have cared enough to come and let me out, and they are both dead. There's no one left. They're all gone."

Sam felt it settling over him, like a smothering blanket. The unwelcome load of fresh responsibility. He could not field this right now. He had Sveti to worry about. Lord knew, she was enough of a job.

"Not possible," he snarled. "No one?"

"No one that will risk it." Misha's voice was eerily tranquil. "Knowing my father's men, what they are capable of. I called Sveti, but I did not talk to her. She could not help me, I know. She has problems of her own. I just called to hear a voice in the dark. She said nice things."

He was being jerked around, big time. And he knew just exactly where this was going. "So call the cops! They'll get you out!"

"They don't give a shit about me," Misha said.

"They're bound by oath and law to protect the citizenry, no matter who their father is! And it's better than starving to death in a closet!"

Misha made a noncommittal sound, clearly not convinced of this.

"You're going to sit there in a cage with the charge on your phone dying because the world hurt your fucking feelings?" Sam bellowed.

Misha's stubborn silence made him frantic.

"Call the cops!" he urged. "I'll make a deal with you. Ask for their help, and I promise, I will personally make it my business to make sure that from now on you will always have someone to call if you're locked in a hole."

"Bullshit," Misha said. "No one can make such a promise."

"Kid, I just did. And I meant it."

"You are a cop," Misha said. "You come and get me."

"Jesus, Misha! Right now? You catch me at a bad time!"

"Hah, do not talk to me about bad time. Forget Sveti's trace if you cannot be bothered. Besides, I cannot call them now anyway. The charge on my phone has finished, and I cannot—"

Suddenly, he was gone. His phone's battery was dead.

Sam wanted to howl. He could call the cops for Misha himself, but everything in Cherchenko's house, most particularly the computers, was possible evidence in any number of crimes. He could explain the situation, get the local cops' help, but it would take time to straighten things out, get an all clear. He didn't have time. The only way to keep Sveti absolute top priority was to collect Misha and the trace himself.

He made a guttural, barely human sound as he lurched to his feet. Agony made everything go black . . . then the lights flickered back on in his mind, just in time to catch himself from falling. He launched himself toward the suitcase. So far away. The pain was sickening.

But the fear was worse.

CHAPTER 27

Michael Hazlett's smile was no different than it had ever been. It was her vision that had changed. A filter had been lifted. Now she saw him with the stark, torn-open clarity of the twelve-year-old girl she had once been back when they were about to tear out her heart.

It seemed impossible, that she had not seen the ice in his eyes.

She ignored the gun pointed at her face, intensely conscious of the Micro-Glock, pressing against her hip inside her jeans.

"It was you," she said. "You had my mama killed. You built that lab. You murdered all those people."

He kissed his fingertips in a mocking salute. "You clever, beautiful thing. I have been struggling with this all day."

"Struggling with what?"

"Letting you go," he said. "I've become so attached. That doesn't happen to me often. I don't bond easily, you see."

Bond? She would have laughed if she hadn't been frozen in stark horror. A leech or a louse did not bond with its host. It just fed.

But there was no point in saying it. He only heard his own voice.

"Renato and I have been arguing," he said. "He's put out with me, letting base animal desires stand in the way of business. But reason has prevailed."

"And just in time, too, I see!"

Sveti turned as Renato strode into the room, and gazed at his scowling face for a long moment. "I always thought you were a prick."

Renato's eyes flashed. "As I thought you were just like your lying cunt of a mother. But are you as good in bed? Shall we find out?"

"Renato." Hazlett looked pained. "Such language. Please."

"I knew you were a human bloodhound, just like her. Willing to lie and cheat and fuck your way in a straight line toward whatever you wanted. So she told you about the lab somehow? We monitored every scrap of paper she sent, but she coded it for you, eh? Slippery *bitch*."

"So you saw her last letter," Sveti said softly.

"Of course," Renato said. "We were still waiting and watching at that point, trying to see what she was up to. We waited too long. I didn't want to make the same mistake with you. I wanted you killed years ago, but Michael said no, Sonia's daughter is just a sad, insignificant little twat who will waft along into some unremarkable, mediocre life and not give us any trouble. But no." Renato shot a furious look at Hazlett. "Why risk it, you said! But I was right this time! We waited just long enough for her to come stab us to the heart!"

"We had also been informed that running afoul of your American protectors could be problematic. Calm down, Renato." Hazlett's apologetic smile was weirdly incongruous behind the pistol. "You'll have to forgive Renato his venom. Your mother had him fooled for some time while she gathered information about our project. He never saw or met her in the Ukraine, you see, so she targeted him when she began snooping in Italy. She introduced herself using her maiden name. She was very charming, very beautiful. Very seductive. It was months before I put it all together and told Renato what she was really up to. He's still upset with me. He got his feelings very deeply hurt."

"Whore," Renato said through his teeth. "Lying whore cunt. You look like her. You whore like her. You'll die like her, too."

"Yes, yes, Renato. Not now." Hazlett sounded bored. "We were fortunate that the lab was already closed when she discovered it. None of our research was compromised, like last time. It was just a matter of silencing her, making sure she hadn't told anyone." He shrugged. "I thought it was handled. But she slipped something past us evidently."

"We should have killed her sooner," Renato snarled. "And you just had to lure the daughter here, dangling the bait. Self-indulgent fool."

Hazlett looked wistful. "I was so glad, back in the day, when your fierce protectors gave us an excuse to wait to kill you. You were such a lovely little cream puff. They say, keep your friends close, but your enemies closer, right? You're an enemy I wanted to keep oh, so close."

"I would never have had sex with you," she said.

Hazlett did not appear to hear her. "I was disappointed when you soiled yourself with your pit bull. It compromised your virginal glow. But girls will be girls. Everyone needs a range of sexual experiences. That way, they can appreciate true skill when they finally encounter it."

She hated the turn the conversation was taking. The speculative way both men were looking at her body made her stomach flop.

"Lift your arms into the air," Hazlett said, getting up and walking slowly around her. She could smell the sharp citrus perfume of his aftershave, then the cold, hard circle of the gun barrel against the nape of her neck. "And do not think for one instant that I am not capable of putting a bullet into your brainstem if you move."

"I do not think that," she said, thinking of the lake of bones.

"Renato, take the gun from her waist holster. And search her for other weapons. I know you've been itching to put your hands on her."

"Certainly." Renato's voice was an oily ooze. He stuck his hands into her waistband and took out the gun, but left his hand under her shirt, stroking her belly, sliding up to cup her breast. "So warm and soft. *Bellissima.*" He ran his hands greedily over her chest, squeezing and probing. Sveti clenched her jaw, swallowed. Stayed motionless.

"Renato, stop fondling her and get that envelope she's holding," Hazlett said impatiently. "It holds what remains of Sonia's photos."

Renato snatched it out of her hands and shook the pictures into his hand. He shuffled through them, making angry, petulant little noises, then grabbed the silver bucket that the white wine had chilled in. He dumped the ice into the small sink in the bar, placed the bucket on the table, then grabbed one of the tapers out of the candelabra.

He set the sheaf of photographs on fire and held them in front of her as they burned. When the flame threatened his hand, he dropped the charred, blackened scraps into the bucket, darting Sveti a spiteful look. "She looks a bit the worse for wear today, Michael. Her glow has dulled. It happens to them all, my friend. Sad, but true. Beauty fades."

"She'd shine right up again, if not for those pesky moral principles," Hazlett complained. "Those are what dull her. Just like both her parents. It must be genetic. Such a pain in the ass."

"Both parents?" It jolted her like a cattle prod. "You knew my father, too?"

"Of course," Hazlett said. "That's where it all began, back in my impatient youth. I was looking for shortcuts to fame, riches, and glory."

It all crashed together in her mind. "The lab my father blew up, in Nadvirna," she said. "It was yours. Zhoglo was supplying you with test subjects. The orphans and mental patients."

He sketched a theatrical bow. "*Mea culpa*. It started decades ago late one night over a bottle of wine. Renato was researching a compound that blocked a certain molecule from binding to its cell surface receptor. If pretreated, the compound completely protected tissue, skin, muscle, bone marrow, from lethal doses of radiation. The implications were stunning. So that night we came up with a plan."

She felt as though she could see right through the flesh of his face. She saw his naked skull, with that wild, pale blue light blazing out of his eye sockets. A death's head, babbling cheerfully on.

"We went with a two-pronged approach. On the one side, Illuxit Transnational would set up random controlled medical trials for cancer patients undergoing radiotherapy, in Brazil, India, the Ukraine.

In the Ukraine, I started considering Vadim Zhoglo as a possible partner for the second prong of our plan. He saw the possibilities right away. An intelligent man, Zhoglo. I was sorry when he died."

"I wasn't," Sveti said woodenly.

"Well, of course, you wouldn't be," he said vaguely. "Anyway, we went ahead with the legitimate, slow and plodding development of the Milandra line of cancer treatment drugs, and they're a big cash cow for TorreStark, I'm proud to say. Zhoglo organized our shadow lab, where we conducted our more . . . well, aggressive research, you might say. He provided materials, and we—"

"Materials? That's what you call the people you murdered?"

"Don't be self-indulgent," he scolded. "You know how the world works. He provided test subjects—until your father stopped him."

"Papa," she whispered. For the first time, she saw the nature of this monster her father and mother had battled so bravely. She finally saw why they had felt so driven, so compelled to stop him at all costs.

They'd been willing to sacrifice themselves, and ultimately, her too. It didn't make it less painful, but she understood them now.

"Sergei had us fooled, right up to the end," Hazlett said. "He cost me years of research. I wouldn't have been forced to open the lab in Italy at all, if not for his meddling. All those lives could have been spared. But as it was, we built again and developed our secret compound. We piloted the legitimate research right where it needed to go, too. It's all legal and aboveboard now. One injection of ABR2B-88 before total body radiation completely protects the subject from both gastrointestinal and hematopoietic acute radiation syndrome. The possible applications for the military, for industry—"

"And the black market," Sveti said.

Hazlett shrugged. "We'll see. We haven't launched it yet. Renato, get the cuffs from my briefcase and bind her hands, so I can relax."

Renato complied, opening the case that lay on a table. He jerked her hands together, and Hazlett pressed the gun under her ear.

"Bitch," Renato muttered, as he ratcheted it brutally tight.

"I was there when your father died," Hazlett said. "A memorable anatomy lesson. He deserved it, for inconveniencing us. But in the end, Cherchenko's solution was better than Zhoglo's."

"The boats from Africa," Sveti said.

"Exactly. Perfect test subjects. Undocumented, illegal, invisible. Through Pavel's Italian mafia contacts, he could broker hundreds of them at a time. All sizes, all ages. So efficient, so smooth. No one noticed, no one talked. The Camorra had the local people well trained."

"They gave everything they had in the world to get their families away from war and genocide," Sveti said. "And they found you."

"Yes, I know their stories are heart wrenching, taken individually. But I console myself by the fact that the Milandra product line will improve cancer outcomes for hundreds of thousands of people, and our compound could pull the teeth of terrorism's most vicious threat against civilization. That's worth something, don't you think?"

"Don't," Sveti said faintly. "It's grotesque when you try to justify it. Be honest about your sadism."

Hazlett looked affronted. "I'm not sadistic! I simply don't suffer from the awful torment of empathy, like you do, and thank God for it. You're a slave to it, Svetlana. It's just agonizing to watch you suffer. It's so much simpler to be me. I don't actively enjoy anyone's suffering. I simply don't waste my time on guilt or remorse. I get on with it, see?"

"So you're a sociopath, then," she said.

Hazlett made a face. "I don't like labels," he replied with distaste. "They're limiting. Don't put me in a box. I won't fit."

"You're not even human," Sveti said. "Not if you can't feel."

"Don't be melodramatic," he scoffed. "I feel many things! I'm feeling disappointed right now, for instance. Cheated out of what's rightfully mine. That's a perfectly valid feeling!"

"Cheated of what?"

His eyes turned soulful. "You. If only you hadn't made the connections. If you'd been less stubborn, less obsessive, I would have taken you for my lover. Maybe even my wife."

Renato snorted and rolled his eyes.

Sveti suppressed a burst of bitter laughter. If there was a path through this experience that did not terminate in her grisly death, making this man angry and offended was definitely not on it.

"But I was stubborn," she said. "I was obsessive. And so?"

"It's not the first time I've suffered this way," Hazlett confided. "I'm not married, and not because I didn't want to be. I like intelligent, fascinating women as much as any man, but after a time, they start complaining. They want something that I can't give them. I could make do with stupid, unperceptive women, or gold diggers, but they bore me. I can't bear their presence for more than the time it takes to fulfill my biological needs. Then I want them escorted back to wherever they came from. But you would have been different, Svetlana. For you, I could have felt real feelings. We could have had something special."

He looked like he expected her to mourn what might have been. But she was incapable of playing along with his fantasy, even to save her own skin. "So it's all about you," she said. "All the time."

He looked politely blank. "Who else?"

A pointless discussion if there ever was one, so she abandoned it. "What are the dirty bomb materials for?"

"Oh, that." Hazlett chuckled. "That was random. Isn't that funny? This Sword of Cain was not my doing. That was Pavel Cherchenko's bright idea, foiled by your mother. She certainly got around, I give her that. We knew nothing about it until Pavel told us a few days ago."

"But . . . then why was he—"

"Presumptuous idiot," Renato said coldly.

"His plan was to proof his people against radiation with our drug, then set off a dirty bomb and have freedom and leisure to loot and pillage," Hazlett said. "The idea has merit, in a bestial sort of way."

"Ridiculous." Renato spat the words out. "Criminal scum."

"As you see, Renato does not approve of my plans, but I'm going forward with Pavel's idea anyway," Hazlett said. "But a new and improved version, of course. We noticed yesterday as we followed your RF signal that you lingered in the garbage dump in the canyon for over thirty minutes. So we told Josef to pay particular attention to that area. And lo and behold, there was The Sword of Cain. Josef is quite a discovery, by the way. He was the one who told us what happened in Sant' Orsola. Bold ideas, nerves of steel. A good replacement for Pavel. And thank goodness for someone who can make that bomb for us."

Sveti's mouth dangled open. "You're setting off the bomb? *Why?*"

He lifted his arms. "Because I can."

Her mouth worked. "But . . . but that's crazy!"

"Not at all," he said calmly. "Anarchic, yes, but Pavel's unhinged thinking process took him to places that mine had never dared to go. The more I thought about it, the more attractive the idea became. Remember at the gala, when I spoke of my passion for finding those pressure points? This is a nerve center so tender, it will make the whole world jump six feet into the air. It'll be so entertaining."

"You're doing this because you are *bored?*"

He looked irritated. "You're missing my point. You just handed me a once-in-a-lifetime opportunity. It's not exactly the gift I was longing for, but I'll be a good sport and take it. This bomb can never be traced to me. I did not purchase the material, nor build it, nor pay to have it built. Nor did I have contact with anyone who did, except for a few untraceable calls from burner phones. The only point of contact is you, Svetlana. With you gone, I can detonate this bomb and cause mass mayhem with absolute impunity. How could I possibly resist?"

The question was so foreign to the way her mind was wired, it left her stupid and stammering. Hazlett sailed smoothly on past.

"Renato and I were sure when we planted the trace on you that Pavel and his goons would just kill you. But you killed him instead. Who'd have thought you were such a virago, to look at you. So delicate. So feminine." His eyes raked her hungrily, up and down.

"Sasha." Her voice caught on his name. "Sasha killed him."

Hazlett shrugged. "Whatever. Last man standing takes the credit. I was astonished you survived. I hated the thought of Pavel doing something grisly to your lovely, delicate person, but it was such a simple way to solve our problem."

"Like with Mama," she said. "You let them execute her."

"True. But you survived long enough to deliver the long-lost radioactive materials into my hands. There's really only one thing to do with such an item, right? Josef is hard at work right now, making us a huge, awful bomb. Alas for poor Rome. So rich in history and culture. My heart bleeds for the Sistine Chapel, and Michelangelo's *Pietà*. Rome will be uninhabitable for God alone knows how long."

"Rome? But . . . but . . ." She looked frantically from one man to the other. "You can't mean to blow up a dirty bomb in Rome!"

Renato and Hazlett exchanged glances. "I've weighed the pros and cons, and I'm willing to sacrifice Rome," Hazlett said. "Though you'll be leaving this earthly plane tonight, so it hardly concerns you."

That was too obvious to deserve comment. "But a war could start!" she protested. "So many people killed!"

"Not really," Hazlett soothed. "Several hundred tourists are likely to die in the initial blast, yes, but it won't level the city like a nuclear bomb would. It's the lingering radioactivity that will be the problem. And the panic that will convulse the entire planet, of course. It's like a needle, and I can jab it at the nerve center of the global economy, stand back, and see what twitches. What a rush. Josef will go ahead with his looting, which will be profitable enough to content him. And there will be a tremendous surge in interest for our new compound. An anti-radiation sickness med from TorreStark. Imagine the possibilities."

Sveti's gorge rose. "You're doing this to drive up *stock value?*"

Hazlett shrugged. "I sounds so banal when you put it that way. It's not that I need the money. After a few hundred millions, one wouldn't even notice a tenfold increase. But once one starts making money at that level, it's a habit that's very hard to break."

She had to keep him talking. "Why Rome?"

"I personally would have preferred another city, or another country altogether. I'm fond of Italy, and I'd rather target a place where I don't own valuable property, where the disarray will not impact industries in which I am heavily invested, and where my favorite vacation spots will not become radioactive wastelands. But there are other considerations that lead me to choose Rome."

He waited for her prompt, his eyes glittering.

She was unable to wait him out. "And these are?"

Hazlett's smile was smug. "The people arriving at the airport this morning. Tamara Steel, Valery Janos, Nick Ward, Rebecca Cattrell."

Fresh panic scattered what was left of her composure. "But how did you . . . I didn't even know they—"

"We've been monitoring your e-mail, Svetlana. Ever since you were old enough to have your own accounts. They sent you their travel details. They have rooms at the historic Hassler Hotel, right next to the Trinità dei Monti church, overlooking the Spanish Steps. I'm very fond of the Hassler myself, and I regret blowing up a precious chunk of Roman history. But if it's necessary . . ."

"No! Think this through!" she begged.

"I've thought of everything. With one push of a button, all the angry, irritating people who would have searched for you disappear, in a puff of radioactive dust. Of course, there's your pit bull, but one of my people will pay him a visit, let's see"—he glanced at his watch—"any minute now. A few drops into his IV and goodbye, Sam Petrie."

"No! You don't have to hurt Sam! Call your man off! He won't look for me! We broke up, understand? Badly! He hates me now!"

"It's probably already taken care of by now, Svetlana. Resign yourself." Hazlett's eyes were gloating. "And don't lie. I saw the way he looked at you. You excite violent feelings, as you did in me. Renato, too. Even Josef. He wants to do the honors himself, when the time comes. You have panting admirers right and left." He patted her cheek with the hand not holding the gun. She twisted, tried to bite him.

He yanked his hand free and whacked her in the face with the hand that held the gun. "Snotty bitch," he hissed. "You never learn."

She reeled for a second, head ringing, but lunged to spit in his face as soon as she could see straight. He punched her in the belly.

She pitched off her chair and thudded to the floor on her side, gasping for air. Hazlett's flushed face hung over hers, the sour tang of wine heavy on his breath. "We're going for a drive. What Josef has in mind for you requires soundproof walls. Lucky you're so tiny. You'll fit perfectly in my rolling suitcase. Like a helpless little rag doll."

She struggled frantically, kicking and flailing. Hazlett pinned her while Renato knelt down by her, grinning. He brandished a spray bottle.

"I love it when they go limp," he said, with relish.

He squirted. She gasped, sputtered. His hideous face swelled like a balloon, distorting until it filled her entire field of vision.

Huge wings, beating. The harsh shriek of a raptor rending her ears, as it swooped down to rip and gouge and feed on fresh hot flesh.

And then, nothing.

The shotgun blast from the Saiga 12 that knocked out the lock on Pavel Cherchenko's back door was deeply satisfying.

Sam swung open the ruined door. Grateful to the departed mafiya asshole Sveti had gut-shot yesterday for posthumously donating his shotgun and his sintered breaching rounds to the cause. Thank God he'd urged Sveti to take the new car. The old one was waiting for him, right where Sveti had left it, with its bloodstained arsenal still in the trunk. The shotgun really should have been part of the evidence collection.

Tough shit. He needed it more right now.

The house was dimly lit. No alarm went off, no one challenged him. He was almost disappointed. Putting a slug into someone's chest would suit his mood. But the rats had abandoned the burning ship. After years in police work, he knew just how cruel people could be to one another, and it still chilled him to think of them leaving a kid locked in a basement to die alone in the dark. That was unfathomably cold.

He kept the gun at the ready as he kicked doors open, calling out, making lots of noise. He found a staircase leading down, and finally heard the kid's muffled voice through the walls and doors.

"Here! I'm here!" Misha yelled.

At the foot of the stairs was a long corridor. The doors that opened off it led to storage rooms, a huge garage with multiple vehicles cloaked in canvas, and what appeared to be a data center full of computer equipment. At the end of the corridor was a door with a barred steel gate mounted on it. A jail cell for rebellious sons.

To think how he'd whined about his own tragic daddy issues.

"I'm here! In here!" The kid's voice was high and trembling. The door rattled as he pounded on it.

"Stand back," Sam instructed. "Way back. As far as you can."

He heard scrambling footsteps. "I'm against the back wall now!"

Sam slid the last sintered metal breaching round into the shotgun, slid back the bolt. *Boom.*

There was a twisted hole where the lock had been. The door inside had a knob lock that yielded to a single violent kick, which ripped the stitches in his inner thigh. A flash of agony, and blood flowed, staining his pants. *Fuck.* Onward. He staggered forward into the dark hole.

The light did not go on when he flicked it. It was a storage closet, pitch-dark, with no ventilation. The stench of urine made his eyes water. What father would do this to his own child? It defied biology.

"Misha?" he called out.

The boy shuffled into the light, squinting. There were some bottles of water, a few packages of junk food lying on the floor. Nothing else.

"Are you okay?" he asked. "It's Sam. It's all right now."

Misha covered his eyes with his arm to block out the light. "I did not think you would really come." His voice quavered.

"Come on," Sam urged. "We have to get out of here. Fast. Move it."

Misha could not move faster than that dreamy shuffle. He flinched when Sam seized his upper arm. He was so thin. Nothing to him but bones and skin. As he lurched out into the corridor, Sam saw that he'd been badly beaten. Nose broken, both eyes blackened.

"Misha," he said more gently. "You've been through hell and

you're all messed up, but I need your help, and I don't have much time. Can you pull it together? Can you help me find that signal, for Sveti?"

Misha nodded. "I can do it," he said hoarsely. "I'll find her."

"Then let's get to it." Sam got behind him, nudging him along.

Misha led the way, shaking off Sam's helping hand.

"Where are we going?" Sam asked, as they climbed the stairs.

"My father's study," Misha said.

The study was a big, wood-paneled room with a huge desk of polished mahogany. A slim laptop sat upon it. Misha sat down in front of it and punched the keys, his pallid, discolored face eerily lit with the computer's glow. His fingers were a chattering blur. Sam stared over his shoulder and ground his teeth, until he saw the map. An icon, blipping.

"She's moving," Misha said. "The Autostrada. Near Salerno."

She could be in the trunk. Or joyriding with Hazlett in his fucking Ferrari, scarf fluttering behind her, no clue about her mortal peril. "Here's how this is going to work," he told Misha. "Charge up that phone and sit down, because we'll be on it nonstop until Sveti is with me. You don't take your eye off that icon until I tell you that you can."

"No, I am coming with you, with the *chiavetta*." He held up a router. "We will get coverage on the way with this."

Sam's blood roared in his ears. "You aren't going anywhere," he said. "You're staying right here, where it's safe. You are a kid."

"Kid?" Misha's voice dripped with irony. "Me? Safe? Where?"

Sam hissed through his teeth. "Okay, so you're not a normal kid, that I'll concede. But you're still fourteen, and I'm responsible for you."

"I've been responsible for myself since before my mother died."

"I don't give a fuck who you think is responsible for you. I let you out of that room, so I'm responsible now. And I say you stay here."

Misha's fingers clicked. The screen went dark. He snapped the laptop closed. "Okay," he said. "Take the laptop. Guess my father's password. Figure out how to use the program. Find the code for the RF frequency of Sveti's tag, all by yourself."

Sam's jaw dropped. "You manipulative little shithead."

Misha crossed his arms over his thin chest. His eyes blazed defiantly from his pallid face. "I have been called worse."

"I'm sure you deserved it. Do you want to help Sveti or not?"

"Of course I want to help Sveti," Misha said haughtily. "Sasha would want that. But if you want my data, you cannot leave me here."

Sam pulled out the Glock and pointed it at Misha's thigh. "Not happening, kid. Sorry."

Misha stared at the gun, then at Sam's face.

"I won't kill you," Sam said. "But I will turn your quadricep into red paste. And trust me. It will never be the same again, no matter what they do to it. You have ten seconds to pull that icon up again."

Misha gazed at him for a long moment, his face expressionless. "Do you remember the man who was with me when you and Sveti came to the house a few days ago?" he asked.

Sam did not lower the gun. "Yeah," he growled. "Why do you ask?"

"That was Andrei," Misha said. "He was the closest thing I had to a friend. Of course, he would have put a gun in my mouth if my father had told him to. But I do not blame him for that."

"That's big of you," Sam said grimly. "What about him?"

"My father was angry when he found you had been here. Andrei was just a warm body, not very smart. No one told him anything. But I knew. Papa had Andrei beaten to death in front of me. To punish me."

"Jesus," Sam muttered. "And you're telling me this exactly why?"

A smile flashed over Misha's face. He opened a drawer in the desk, pulled out a dagger with a jeweled handle, and laid it down. Then he took out a Walther PPK and a full magazine. He slid it into the gun, locking it in place. As if he didn't give a fuck whether Sam shot him or not.

"Put that down," Sam scolded. "You're fourteen, for Christ's sake."

"I would like to reach fifteen," Misha said. "I grew up around men who would shoot me in the leg if it was convenient for them. I know these men. You are not one of them. You cannot shoot my leg, Sam Petrie. Do not tell me that you can. It makes you look stupid. We are wasting time, and Sveti is in danger. This argument is finished."

Sam lowered the Glock. Christ, his groin hurt. His jeans were blood soaked to the knee, starting to dry stiff. "Fuck," he muttered.

"It is not a bad thing," Misha said, by way of consolation. "I did not mean it as an insult."

"That makes me feel so much better," he growled.

CHAPTER 28

The heavy drone in her head hummed beneath the images of blood and bones. Not until the drone lowered in pitch and she began to bump and lurch did she pull it together consciously. She was in the trunk of a car, and they'd turned off the highway, onto a smaller road, with stomach-churning twists and dips. She was folded up, arms still bound. Her shoulders hyperextended. Her hands were almost numb.

Liv's ring. She struggled to get the little blade snapped out, but no matter how she twisted and strained, she could not get her forefinger positioned so that she could get the blade near the plastic ratchet tie.

She snapped the blade back into position as the car slowed and finally rolled to a jolting stop. Car doors popped open. She heard the rumble of masculine voices. They were arguing. What a surprise.

The lock mechanism rattled. The trunk popped open.

Hazlett and Renato gazed down. The look on their faces reminded her of the hot glow that had always been in Yuri's eyes after beating her. To think she'd scolded Sam for playing dominating power games in bed. With what breath she had left, between one screaming orgasm and the next. But she'd scolded Sam out of sheer habit. To keep him at a distance. To keep her feelings for him in a little locked box that she could open or close at will. Embarrassed by her desire for him, ashamed of his power over her body. Now she could see Sam's passionate generosity so clearly. It shone in her memory like a star, compared to the less-than-human emptiness that squirmed in these two men's eyes.

She closed her eyes against it. She had no one to blame but herself. She'd fucked up colossally. She'd failed everyone: Mama, Papa. Her Seattle family. They were flying blind into a death trap, just because they loved her. The little girl in the cave, flowers twining around her rib cage, abandoned and unavenged. The entire goddamned city of Rome, for fuck's sake. She'd failed them all.

And Sam. She wondered if the killer had gotten to him yet. If Sam were sedated, or even aware enough to defend himself. He would have no reason to suspect someone in a lab coat, handling his IV.

Oh, please, Sam. Stay sharp.

"Awake already, I see," Renato said. "I gave you less than a half dose. I want you awake when we detonate the bomb."

"Fuck you," Sveti croaked hoarsely.

"Oh, please. A young lady of culture can do better than that. Josef, take her inside."

Josef sauntered up between them. The distilled malevolence on his scratched, swollen face made her shudder. One of his eyes was bandaged. "I am going to make your death last a long time, cunt," he said in Ukrainian. "And I will pay special attention to your eyes."

She looked up at Hazlett. "Sam?"

Hazlett frowned. "Your pit bull does nothing but give me trouble. When my person stopped by, he'd already left the hospital. And in his condition! The man is deranged!"

Tears sprang to her eyes. It made her dizzy. Hope, fear, in equal measure. The more hope roared up, the more fear tried to quench it.

If Sam was on his feet and moving, he had a chance. Oh, please.

"I will find that son of a bitch," Josef rasped. "I will do things to him that you could not even imagine."

Unfortunately, with her background, her imagination was unusually fertile. But that was a road she didn't want to go down.

Josef stuck his enormous hand between her legs and got a painfully tight grip on her crotch. He hoisted her over his shoulder.

Her face bumped Josef's massive back. She twisted and strained to get a sense of her surroundings. They were at the coast. She smelled salt in the air. She caught glimpses of a house. More modern and more modest than the Villa Rosalba. She heard the dull, faraway roar of waves crashing before she was carried indoors.

Lights flicked on, assaulting her eyes. She was tossed onto the floor, smacking her skull against the tiles so hard, she almost fainted.

Josef knelt next to her. "I don't think you're tied tight enough, bitch," he said. "Let's turn you inside out. Make those pretty tits pop."

He seized her feet and cuffed them with one of the plastic ties, ratcheting it tight. He jerked her ankles up and fastened them to the bindings at her wrists, bending her backward into a bow. She couldn't curl up to protect herself if he kicked or stabbed her. He sat back on his heels and pulled out a knife. Held her shirt out taut, slicing the fabric. Buttons popped and rattled on the floor.

"This is just the beginning, you sneaky whore," he whispered as he spread her shirt open. "I can't wait to play with you."

The tile was so cold against her bare skin. It burned, like ice.

He cupped her breast. Pinched her nipple until she cried out.

"Not now, Josef," Renato snapped from somewhere across the room. "You'll have all the time in the world to play later, but you have to set up this video equipment for us! Stay focused!"

Josef snorted in annoyance. One final, horrible pinch that made her writhe and flop, and he left her, shuddering with horror.

Facing away from them, she couldn't see what they were doing. All she could do was stare out through glass doors that opened onto a veranda. Some minutes later, Renato and Hazlett strolled over to look down at her twisted, exposed body. Both were sipping brandies.

Hazlett clucked his tongue. "Josef, Josef. What have you done," he chided. "Embarrassing the poor girl."

"What a bad, bad boy," Renato said.

The two men exchanged glances and sniggered.

"Nothing like a pair of lovely breasts to greet the day, hmm?" Hazlett offered.

"*A chi lo dici.*" Renato lifted his glass. *Clink*. They laughed.

Sveti had never hated them more violently than in that moment.

"It is finished," Josef said, from the other side of the room.

"Excellent. Josef, lift Svetlana up, so we can all see the setup."

Josef's hard fingernails dug into her armpits. He hoisted her up, giving her a swift glimpse of the terrace before she was turned to face the rest of the room. It was large, extending out onto a rocky headland. Beyond that, nothing. The sky had lightened, from black to deep blue.

The place had the air of an abandoned vacation house, deeply chilly, with the faint hint of damp and mold. A large monitor was set up, connected to a laptop on a nearby table. It had a split screen. On one was a view of the Spanish Steps, and the Trinità dei Monti church at the top. Near it was a handsome flesh-toned building, presumably the Hassler. The other screen's vantage point was from an angle. It zoomed in on the hotel's elegant but understated lobby entrance on the street.

"We'll know the minute they arrive," Hazlett said, sounding pleased with himself. "That will be our cue."

Sveti coughed to loosen her throat. "Where's the camera located?"

"An apartment owned by Cherchenko," Renato said. "Conveniently located to give us this visual. Isn't that handy?"

"Do you see that white Telecom Italia van parked by the gate?" Hazlett asked. "That's our bomb. Josef assures us it will take out the entire hotel and a good bit of the buildings around it. It's wired to a phone inside the van. All I do is dial a number, and ka-boom."

"All that death and destruction, just to entertain you." Her voice cracked with loathing. "You sick, perverted son of a bitch."

"Not at all," he said. "I'm as clear as a bell. Destruction is not necessarily a bad thing, my dear. It's always good for someone. I'm just careful to make sure that someone is invariably me." He sipped at his brandy and glanced at his watch. "Almost time. It'll be so stimulating to watch this with you, Svetlana. You have the biggest stake."

"And me?" Renato asked sourly. "I have a beautiful apartment and two priceless Picassos that will be worthless in a half an hour!"

"I said I'd compensate you, Renato. Don't nag and carp, please."

"You can't compensate the loss of a Picasso!" Renato bitched. "You have no soul, Michael. You cannot possibly understand that kind of loss."

Hazlett waved that away and turned back to her. "Although I don't feel emotions the way you do, I enjoy watching them. The dread, the terror, the buildup." He chuckled. "Rather sexual, come to think of it."

"You call the destruction of irreplaceable property and priceless artwork sexual? I call it stupid and wasteful!"

Josef tossed her to the ground with a bone-rattling thud. The other two men were too busy with their bickering to notice. She'd fallen facing them this time, so they wouldn't see what she did behind her back. If they saw her move, they'd probably focus on her breasts.

She had no hope of living through this. All she hoped was to hurt one of them, and maybe earn herself a quicker, cleaner death.

She worked Liv's ring open again. She couldn't get her hands free, but she could pick at the plastic strip that bound her ankles. With one hand, she seized the hem of her jeans, so that her bowed position would not snap suddenly loose and draw attention to her when the plastic finally gave way. She sawed away at it, heart thudding heavily.

They had forgotten about her for the moment, though Josef turned often to leer and grab his crotch. He started toward her just as the binding that held her legs together gave way. She clutched the hem of her jeans with all her strength, willing him away, away, away.

"Feeling lonely, bitch?" he crooned. "Want some attention?"

"Don't get distracted," Hazlett snapped. "Did you set up the other TV? I want to hear the live news coverage, too. Hurry, please."

Josef turned to obey. Tears of relief sprang to her eyes. If she got her moment, it could only be when someone was bending over her, thinking her still trussed. But not Josef. She'd have a better shot with the complacent Renato or Hazlett, rather than a feral, twisted creature like Josef. She had to just blow on that tiny, secret flame of rebellion. Keep it alive until she could burn out, all at once, with everything she had. Until then, she'd concentrate on looking helpless and terrified.

The role came to her very naturally, under the circumstances.

"She's in that house at the top of the drive," Misha said. "There are no other houses near."

"Great. Thanks for your help," Sam said. "This is the part where you tell me you'll be good and stay far away."

Misha just looked at him.

Sam sagged, exhausted. "Goddamnit, Misha," he said. "I can't protect you up there! I don't even know what I'll be facing."

"Josef is there. I tagged his car," Misha said. "He followed Sveti to the middle of nowhere yesterday and stayed for hours after she left. Now he is here. I think Sveti led him to The Sword of Cain."

"So the charming Josef now has nuclear capability," Sam said. "What a stimulating thought. And you want a reunion with him?"

"No," Misha said. "I want to kill him."

A sharp groan of dismay hissed from between Sam's teeth.

"Josef has been back in Rome all day, at one of my father's properties. A storage facility with large supplies of ordnance. Josef is good with explosives. He might have already built a bomb."

"Not my problem," Sam said curtly. "Only Sveti is my problem."

"I am coming," Misha said. "This is my problem, too."

Fuck. Sam let out a slow breath. "I will tie you down."

"If you die, they will find me tied, and they will kill me slowly."

Sam counted down from five. "Listen to me," he said. "If I go in and I don't come out, and you're not out here watching, there's no one to warn the world about the bomb, and no one to help Sveti. Sasha will have died for nothing. You're my only hope if it all goes to shit. This is the best way to help Sveti. Do this for her, and for Sasha. Stay back."

Misha considered this, and pulled out his Walther. "But I must come closer," he persisted. "How can I bear witness if I do not see?"

Goddamn stubborn butthead. It made it that much worse that he was actually starting to like the weird little freak.

He gestured at Misha's pistol. "Watch it with that thing. All I have is surprise. Play it too soon and we're done for."

They got out of the car. Light glowed from the large windows of the boxlike modern structure far above them on the ridge.

"We hike up this hill and circle around the back," Sam said.

Misha followed gamely behind him. The kid made a lot of noise, stumbling in the dark. The sky was lightening, and it was chilly and damp. Sweat had cooled on Sam's back. The bandage was leaking. He felt wet warmth, on his chest, his groin. Waves of nausea. He was running a fever. The scarring in his lungs from his old bullet wound made him struggle not to cough.

He pressed on, stopping periodically to wait for the panting, stumbling Misha, until the house came into view again from above. There was an outbuilding up the hill for the landscaper. Gardening tools leaned against it. He almost knocked a shovel over in the darkness. Caught it, just in time, as the door of the house opened.

He sank down, silently waving for Misha to get behind the building. Josef came out, walked to a black SUV parked in the driveway beside a sleek silver Porsche. He opened the back, hefted a big box and hauled it into the house, leaving the hatchback open. Other equipment was visible inside. It looked like he intended to come right back out again.

Sam gestured to Misha, whose eyes were big and scared in the shadows. He pointed fiercely at the ground. *Stay put, goddamnit.* He grabbed the shovel, darted across the driveway. Crouched behind the Porsche. If he took Josef down silently, his odds would be better.

Light spilled out the front door. Heavy boots crunched the gravel as Josef went to the back of the SUV again. Sam moved as silently as he could in the fucking noisy gravel alongside the SUV.

He leaped up, swung the shovel down.

Josef jerked up and to the side just in time, and grabbed the shovel, whip quick, wrenching Sam off balance. Sam stumbled back, gasping as white-hot pain stabbed through his groin.

Josef took in the fresh blood on Sam's pants, the spreading splotch on his shirt under the jacket, his sweaty pallor. He grinned. "Idiot goat-fucker scum," he hissed. "You look like shit. I'm going to break this handle to a knifepoint and fuck you with it."

He came on like a freight train, swinging the shovel. Sam jerked to the side. The shovel crunched against the frame of the car.

Sam darted in closer, jabbing an uppercut to the guy's huge lantern jaw that rocked his head back, but Josef came roaring back unfazed, kicking and punching. Sam ducked, blocked, and spun. Got in a good one to the arm that he'd shot, back in Portland, but the guy was big and fast, with long arms like an ape, and he seemed to feel no pain at all. Sam skittered back to miss a kick to the ribs and found himself pinned against the Porsche.

He tried to hook his legs to take the guy down to the ground, but the weakened muscles in his injured groin wouldn't respond. He parried a flurry of blows to the face, jerked up his knee to protect his groin—

Not fast enough. A punch to the balls, a sick wave of black—

He came to when the gravel smacked the air out of his lungs like a huge, pissed-off hand. That stinking behemoth landed on him, *oof.*

Smash sandwich. Should've shot the bastard. Brain-dead asshole, thinking he could take on a killer like that, as fucked up as he was. He couldn't see, or breathe. Josef's body had blocked the light.

Then Josef jerked, in a strange, vibrating shudder—and sagged on top of him, inert. His dead weight was smothering. Hot blood flooded over Sam's face, his neck, half-drowning him.

Sam tried to shove him off. Josef thudded limply onto his side.

Misha stood over him. The jeweled dagger he'd taken from his father's desk protruded from beneath Josef's ear, at the point of his jaw.

"I did not use the gun," Misha whispered. "Like you said."

"Stay out," he muttered, as he staggered to his feet. Not that he had any hope the kid would do as he directed, but what the fuck.

Showtime.

* * *

"Where the hell is Josef? Her people should arrive any minute!" Hazlett fussed. "Oh, look! A car's pulling up, and . . . yes! It's them!"

Sveti struggled onto her elbow, straining to see. She saw Val, stepping out of a big SUV, his long hair blowing loose in the breeze, his handsome face dark with beard shadow. Nick emerged from the other side, looking pissed off at Rome for harboring criminals that had threatened her. Tam was a ninja vision in tight-fitting black. Becca looked pale and worried. Four of the five people she loved most in the world, fifteen feet away from that lethal Telecom Italia van.

Then another dark, curly head bobbed at the vehicle door. Oh, no, no, *no*. Rachel. Her darling sister, her cellmate, her precious love.

She must have made a sound. Hazlett glanced at the screen and clucked his tongue. "That's a shame. They should have known better than to bring the child, with the adventures you've been having. But they had no way to know how out of hand the situation has become."

"Please, Michael," she begged. "You don't need this. Turn the bomb in, to the authorities. Be the hero. The world will love you for it."

"I don't need the world's love, or to be a hero. That kind of reward gratifies a different kind of person. Well, Renato? Shall we?"

"I still think we should choose a different city," Renato said sulkily.

"It's too late to change our plans. Call Josef in. I don't want him blundering in at the crucial moment. Did he set up the other TV?"

"I hate dealing with the technology," Renato fretted. "Josef will handle that. Josef!" he bellowed. "Ah, here he comes."

The door flew open.

Sam burst through.

CHAPTER 29

He took it in, with crystal clarity; Sveti half-naked and tied on the floor. She was calling out, but her voice was drowned out by Hazlett and Renato's yelling. *Bam*, he shot at Hazlett, but Hazlett was already diving for the ground, jerking Sveti up so that she covered his kneeling body. His arm clamped her bare torso, fingers digging into smooth white skin, the barrel of his gun stabbing beneath her chin, biting deep.

". . . bomb!" Sveti coughed against the pressure of the gun barrel.

"Bomb?" Sam looked wildly around the room. "Where?"

"Not here," Hazlett said. "Far, far away. And you can't stop it."

"Rome!" Sveti choked out. "Dirty bomb! White Telecom van! My family is right there! His phone! Stop . . . his phone!"

"Put down the gun," Hazlett said. "If you shoot me, my finger will contract, and the top of her head will come right off."

"Shoot him!" Sveti croaked. "Stop the bomb! His phone!"

A triumphant smile spread over Hazlett's face as he stared at Sam. "You're wasting your breath, silly bitch," he said to Sveti. "He can't risk hurting you." He nuzzled the side of her face and licked her neck.

Sam saw in his peripheral vision that Misha was holding his gun on Renato, and Renato was frozen, hands up.

"Put the guns down, both of you," Hazlett said. "Or she dies."

Sam stared at Sveti's eyes. It hurt, like staring at the sun. The intensity of her burned a hole in him. Light would blaze through it forever. He crouched and laid the gun down.

"Kick it away." Hazlett's voice quivered with excitement.

Sam did so. The gun twirled as it slid away on the mosaic tile. Hazlett reached out with his foot, nudging it toward himself.

"You too," Hazlett said to Misha. "Put it down."

"Do as he says," Sam said.

Misha muttered something disgusted in Ukrainian and dropped his gun, but he kicked it out of Renato's reach.

They were all frozen for a moment, as Sam stared into Hazlett's glittering eyes. Wondering how long he could spin this out, playing this guy's huge vanity. Hazlett was not going to kill them until he was done gloating, and this scumbag loved a good gloat.

Hazlett held up his phone. "I'm going to shoot you, as I am sure you know. But first, I'll let you watch the show. Should have had Josef put the number on speed-dial. Who knew I'd have to dial it one-handed?"

He started punching in the number.

Sveti looked at Sam. The words came out, strangled but comprehensible, in spite of the gun barrel pressing her throat.

"I love you," she said.

"Aw! How sweet," Hazlett crooned. "That's all that was missing. Now, scoot over so we can see the screen." He shifted, pulling her.

Sveti jackknifed. Hazlett tumbled backward onto his ass as his center of gravity abruptly shifted, and dropped the phone. Sveti's legs shot out, sending Sam's Glock skittering toward him.

Sam lunged for it. *Bam, bam, bam.* The picture window shattered. Splinters and shards rained down, glinting in the thin morning light.

A cold breeze swirled in, and the huge murmur of the sea.

Sveti lurched to her feet, overbalanced, and fell to her knees again. She dove to the ground, rolled. Kicked the phone out of Hazlett's scrabbling grasp, out the shattered window onto the veranda. It slid on the smooth terra cotta tiles and onto the rocky ground beyond. She barely noticed broken glass crackling beneath her body.

Hazlett bellowed with rage and charged after it, glass crunching beneath his shoes. She rolled to her feet and pelted after him, barefoot.

Bam. Bam. Sam shouted behind her, but she couldn't hear him. She wanted that fucking phone. Hazlett was ahead, trotting down the steps with frantic haste. She hurled herself off the veranda, hit the ground rolling up again. She got to the phone before he did. Kicked it off the path, onto the jagged rocks by the edge of the eighty-foot cliff. *Bam, bam.* Hazlett was shooting, but the shots went wild. He wasn't pausing to take aim.

This time Hazlett got to the phone first. He dove for it, howling in triumph, but Sveti was possessed with white-hot avenging fury. She ran headlong, screaming like a bloody maenad. He glanced up from the keypad, eyes widening as she hurtled toward him.

She smacked into him head-on before he could lift the gun.

He tottered. His costly, gleaming shoes slid on the slippery rocks. They rolled, tumbled. She smashed her shoulder on a rock, and pitched into the open air. The world spun, whirled. Down, down, endlessly down. He was below her, mouth open, screaming, arms and legs wide and flailing as he fell. The phone fell, too. Turning, over and over.

She sliced deep into the churning foam. A slap of freezing cold, salt stinging. No up, no down, just an airless, milky, roaring blur of cold, pounding wet. Her legs pumped frantically, but without her arms, she had no control over how the churning maelstrom tossed her.

She fought her way up for a gulp of air, and a fresh wave pounded her down into the bubbling darkness again, legs pumping.

They started circling her. Mama was there. Sad, but proud. *Tato,* too. Sasha. The little girl clutching a toy bear, smiling shyly. A crowd of angels to lead her home.

Ow. Fresh pain blazed through her hyperextended shoulder, making her twist and writhe. A strong hand on her upper arm. Pulling.

She broke the surface, choking. Astonished at the air.

Sam popped up, hair slicked back, bobbing in the churning foam.

"Do you want to live?" he yelled.

She nodded. A wave broke over them, but his grip was relentless. He towed her, backstroking. Everything hurt. Death had seemed so soft, gentle. Living hurt. It burned and pinched and kicked and stung.

She tried to kick, to move them through the water, but her legs didn't even feel like they were hers. Her crowd of angels had gone away.

All except for Sam, but he was enough. Her fierce, angry angel.

Sveti seemed barely alive when Sam finally maneuvered them to a place where the waves crashing onto the jagged rocks wouldn't batter them to jelly. This devil's cauldron might have drowned him even if he hadn't been full of holes, and down to one arm, and struggling to keep Sveti in such a position that she had a hope in hell of an occasional gulp of air.

He dragged her up onto the rocks. Her arms were still bound. He dug his pocketknife from his jeans, surprised that it was still there, and sliced the plastic ties. He turned her over, pounded on her back.

She choked, coughed. Vomited water. All her cuts and slices from the broken glass started to bleed, mixing with the water until there was a pinkish, salty slick over her skin. It was hard to get a grip on her.

He hoisted her up, let her head dangle over his back, and clutched her jeans-clad bottom half. Wet denim was easier to hang on to.

It was slow going. Pink tinted water dripped over his hands. At some point in his climb, he saw Hazlett sprawled on some sharp rocks, the ones he and Sveti had just barely cleared. He was on his back, eyes and mouth wide open, as if he'd gotten an unpleasant surprise. Sam crossed the guy off his list of current problems. No energy for triumph.

The easiest route up the cliffs also happened to be the longest, winding across the steep mountainside, but finally he made it back to the scrubby trees behind the house, nearly crawling with exhaustion.

He peered in the window, saw Misha on his feet. A good sign. Of course, he could be at gunpoint, so Sam approached as cautiously as he could, but he staggered with Sveti's weight loaded on his shoulder, slight though it was. Too tired for a tiptoe ninja walk.

Misha heard him and gave him a thumbs-up. Thank God. He had no fight left. It was not too cold, but the wind on his wet clothes made him shudder, and Sveti was shaking violently. She needed blankets.

He kicked the door open. Was greeted with the sight of Misha, holding his gun on Renato, who was on the floor, sobbing. His knee was a bloody pulp. "He tried to call himself, to detonate the bomb," Misha explained. "I shot him. And smashed his phone."

Sam glanced at the broken pieces of the phone scattered across the floor. "Try not to look so smug about it," he said.

"I did not shoot him in the face," Misha pointed out, affronted.

"What do you want, a medal?" Sam looked at the monitors. The image had not changed. A street scene, in Rome. An entrance to a hotel lobby. The white Telecom van that Sveti had told him about was parked there, in clear view, completely intact. Cars drove by. No smoking rubble, no sirens, no bodies.

He turned to Misha. "You have a phone still, right?"

"Yes. I charged it in the car. Why?"

"All the others are trashed, smashed, or drowned. Give it to me."

Misha dug it out of his pocket. Sam dialed in Val's number with Sveti still draped over his shoulder.

Val answered. *"Pronto? Con chi parlo?"*

"Val. It's Sam."

"Sam! We have been trying to call! Where is Sveti and—"

"Listen up. There's a white Telecom van parked outside your hotel that has a dirty bomb in it. Pulverized strontium-90. Rigged to blow with a flip phone. Call a bomb squad and deal with it."

"Cazzo," Val muttered. "Sveti?"

"Banged up, sliced up, and half-drowned, but still alive. We're a couple hundred kilometers from you, on the coast. When I know where the ambulance takes her, I'll call you again."

"Sam—"

He hung up and handed the phone to Misha. "You talk to him

when he calls back," he said. "Tell him to get on that bomb. But first call the ambulance. Sveti's going into shock. I'm looking for blankets."

There was a bedroom down the hall. The mattress was covered with plastic, but there were down comforters in the standing wardrobe.

He laid Sveti on the bed, jerked out two comforters, and rolled her onto one. His fingers were so stiff, he could barely undo her wet jeans. She shook. Dead white. Lips blue. He tossed the other comforter on top of her and went back to the front room. Renato was curled up, whimpering. Sam ignored him. "Ambulance on the way?"

"I told them there was a beautiful, wet, naked girl going into shock from the cold," Misha said. "They will be here soon, I promise."

"If they don't decide it's a prank. You're a manipulative bastard after my own heart, kid."

He headed back to Sveti and lay down. He'd do skin-to-skin, but he was so cold, he had no warmth to give her. Blood was seeping through the swaddling of white cotton. If only they could just stop. No picking through the wreckage. He just wanted to flip a switch. Go dark.

They'd won. He should be happy, but he just shivered, numb and blank. So alone. She was so far away. Always behind her steel-reinforced walls. Her tower was so fucking high. She would never let him in.

Med techs bustled in some time later, chattering in Italian. Sveti's eyes fluttered open as they began to peel the comforter away.

"Sam?" she whispered groggily.

"Congratulations," he said. "You won."

"Bomb?" she croaked.

"It never went off," he said. "I talked to Val. He's on it."

Tears welled into her eyes. "Rachel? Tam, Nick, Becca?"

"Fine," he assured her. "They're fine. You did it, babe."

She blinked furiously, eyes overflowing. "I love you," she said.

He flinched. Turn the fucking knife in the wound, why didn't she. He pulled away. "You thought you were about to die when you said that," he said. "It's like saying it when you come. It doesn't count."

"Sam—"

"Don't. Please. Don't sweat it. I'm not holding you to it."

One of the med techs tried to push him back down onto the bed. He shoved the guy away so hard, he bounced off the far wall.

The rest of the medics swiftly gave way as he made for the door.

CHAPTER 30

"Sveti?"

Sveti turned from the window overlooking the beach. She spent a lot of time there, staring at the waves receding, leaving gleaming sand, stranded foam. Something about the slow, muscular surge of the water was, well, not soothing. She was too tense to be soothed. But if she timed her breaths to coincide with the waves, she got a little more air.

Her lungs felt clenched. Pain, from her wrenched shoulder and the broken ribs. She'd gotten used to shallow, pain-avoiding pants. And to holding her breath as if a bullet was about to punch into her.

The doctors assured her that it was normal, that it would pass.

"Sveti?"

Rachel's voice sounded timid. She'd been doing too much jumping and gasping lately. Everyone was tiptoeing around her.

It made her want to snarl, which was bitchy and ungrateful. She was lucky to have people who gave a shit, including her precious Rachel. She grabbed the girl and squeezed. "What is it, sweetheart?"

"Kev and Edie just showed up," Rachel said. "With Jon. They brought Misha with them."

"Great," she said. "You must be happy."

"Oh, yeah. We'll have a blast."

Rachel's eyes sparkled. Misha was the latest addition to this crowd of misfits she'd come to love so much. They made space for him immediately, as they had done for Sveti; first because of the help he'd given Sam, but soon enough just for his own quirky, compelling self.

Misha had landed on his feet. Sam had pressured his family into sponsoring Misha to come to America, and the kid was now enrolled in an elite, tech-oriented boarding school for the talented and gifted that had recently opened in Seattle. He started after Christmas. In the meantime, he shuttled between various elements of the McCloud Crowd, assured of many places to go for school breaks and vacations.

Lately, he'd been with Kev, Edie, and little Jon. He'd spent time with Sam, too. They'd bonded, on their bloody adventure.

Lucky Misha.

Rachel and Misha had hit it off, too. They would sneak off to the game room now, and destroy each other all evening with inappropriately violent video games. With Tam and Val checking on them at ten-minute intervals, of course. Typical nervous parents of a pretty, budding girl.

"Edie wanted you," Rachel said. "Can you go down and say hi?"

Everyone must think she was a cowering invalid. "Of course I'll come down," she said. "It's my party, isn't it?"

"You deserve it," Rachel said solemnly.

Truth was, Sveti had only consented to this party to show everyone she was not as fucked up as they all seemed to think she was. Ostensibly, they were celebrating the book deal she'd recently signed. Three point five million dollars for her story, including the book she'd been writing before, plus the added story of what had happened six weeks ago. All of which had gotten massive news coverage.

She should be glad. The media buzz had sparked a big auction between publishing houses, and driven the offer way up. But the constant attention had been hard for her ragged nerves to bear.

That money would launch the Soul Rescue foundation. Something good would come of it in the end. She had that at least.

They would all be arriving soon. She was going to be hugged

and squeezed. Kids would crawl all over her. She'd chat, laugh, drink champagne, show them that she was okay. No worries at all.

She followed Rachel down the stairs and into the living room. Misha saw her and granted her a rare smile. She hugged him, and he stiffened, suppressing the urge to break free. His previous life had not included training in receiving hugs. It was time he got used to it.

Jon toddled over to show her a small robot with slitted eyes that lit red when a button was pressed. She exclaimed over its awesomeness.

Edie caught sight of her and pulled her into a long, tight, I'm-so-glad-you're-still-alive hug. "We came up a little early because I wanted to see you without a crowd," Edie said. "Hope you don't mind."

"Of course not," Sveti said. "I'm glad you did."

"I was wondering if you would like me to . . . well, don't feel obligated," Edie said. "But would you like me to draw for you?"

Sveti blinked. Wow. Edie's drawings were a phenomenon that no one could explain. Often when she drew, a channel opened, and she produced what she called a "charged" drawing, tapping into some issue in the person's life. Clarifying or illuminating, or warning of danger.

Edie's drawings frightened people. Sveti's threshold for fright was pretty high, but the drawings tended to shine a bright light on places that were usually left dark. A nerve-tingling prospect right now.

"Ah," Sveti said inanely. "Sure. I guess. Um . . . why?"

"I suggested it," Tam said. "Edie's drawings help people get out of a mind rut. They can give a girl a friendly nudge in the right direction."

Sveti let out a sigh. "I know you want me to call Sam. But it's not so simple. I know what you're hoping. Stop hoping it. Please."

"We're all hoping," Tam snapped. "He's hoping, too."

"You don't know that," Sveti said.

"Bullshit. He'd jump six feet in the air if you whistled."

Sveti held up her hand. For once, Tam had the sense to shut up. All those hours swathed in gauze and watching an IV drip were

conducive to agonized self-reflection about everything she'd done wrong.

She'd done just what her father did. He'd gotten himself killed, but his punishment had encompassed them all. Her mother did the same, putting her daughter aside to pursue her quest for truth. Both times, Sveti paid. And she'd been ready to pass that exact punishment on to Sam. To treat him as she'd been treated. Always put last on the list of priorities. Always deemed a sad but necessary sacrifice.

Her mother and father had done the hard thing, and so had she, good little girl that she was. Just as she'd been taught.

Not Sam, though. He'd put her first, always. He'd made her his top priority, and she hadn't known how to accept it. She just didn't know how to be that important to someone. She'd flinched away from it, as if from a too-bright light.

She respected Sam for drawing the line. He'd cut off all contact with her, and was avoiding the rest of them, except for Kev and Bruno. And Misha, of course. She'd heard that Sam's house was up for sale. He probably wanted to put as much distance between them as possible.

God, it hurt, to breathe, to smile. Not like the formless shadow of despair she'd battled before. This was sharper, deeper. More defined.

". . . Edie to do the drawing? Or what? Decide!" Tam demanded.

Sveti looked at Edie and forced a smile. "I'd be glad to have you do one of your drawings for me." She shot Tam a warning look. "Just don't breathe down my neck. And I repeat, do not get your hopes up."

"Rachel, take Irina and Jon up to the game room and keep them occupied," Tam said. She waved a hand at Val and Kev. "You two guys, go drink beer in the kitchen or something. Give us some space."

The two men glanced at each other and melted away.

Sveti sat down in one of the big fat armchairs, slipped off her ballerina flats, and tucked her legs up, facing the seaward windows.

Edie sharpened her charcoals and opened her sketchpad.

Tam sat next to her and Edie shot her a warning look. "Forget it."

With an exasperated eye roll, Tam scooted to the edge of the couch until the sketchpad was out of her line of vision.

Sveti and Edie gazed at each other. A look of complete absorption came over Edie's face. She was a tuner, searching for a frequency.

Edie's pencil began to scratch. Tam huddled on the couch, hugging her knees, staring down. Her feet were bare, her toenails painted black. Sveti looked out at the whitecaps on the ocean.

She drifted into a strange, dreamlike state. Time no longer marched in a straight line. She was breathing more deeply. Her belly hurt less than usual. Her heart felt hot and soft and aching. She looked down at her hands, covered with marks, though the red had faded and the marks were turning silvery. Noise came from the entrance hall, voices talking at once. Children burst through into the room but were swiftly hustled out again. Someone explained what was taking place.

She did not turn to look. They could all wait.

Finally, Edie rested her sketchbook on her lap. She brushed the back of her hand across her eyes. Her face was wet.

Tam unfolded herself with catlike grace. "So? What is it?"

Edie whipped the sketchbook away with mock sternness. "Sveti looks first. It's her drawing." She handed it to Sveti.

A keen, ethereal pain sliced through her when she saw it.

It was her little friend, from the cave. Same blouse, same bare feet, same embroidered pants. Her toy bear dangled by one arm. With her other hand, she held out a handful of flowers. The white ones that had been growing through her bones. She held the ragged bouquet out like an offering. The look on her face was one of total love and trust.

Sveti laid the sketchpad beside her and doubled over.

People came into the room. Speculative murmurs rose. Someone snatched up the sketchpad to take a look.

The cushions shifted as Tam sat down next to her. "What the hell?" Tam murmured. "Who's this? Her future kid? Doesn't look like it. Unless she ends up with a guy from Ethiopia."

"Don't be so literal," Edie chided. "It's messier than that."

"Spookier, you mean," Tam said. "So, past, present, future? Someone not yet born, someone already dead? Someone who hasn't—"

"Someone who's already dead," Sveti broke in.

"Oh, great. That's just peachy," Tam said sourly. "A ghost. And not just any ghost. A child's ghost. A flower-bearing, teddy-bear-carrying child's ghost. Very cheering. Just what she needed to perk her up and put her in a party mood. Thanks so much, Edie."

"Sorry," Edie said meekly.

Sveti started to laugh. It took less than a second for the laughter to morph into tears. She turned to Tam and grabbed her. Tam was tense, nervy, not the hugging type, but Sveti just hung on. Tam had put herself in the line of fire, and she could take the goddamn consequences. "You crazy bitch," Sveti whispered. "I love you."

Tam snorted. "I take it as a badge of honor." She added, after an awkward pause, "And, ahem. I love you, too."

When it became evident that Sveti wasn't letting go, Tam's arms circled her and she patted Sveti's back. Gingerly.

When the spasm had eased off, Edie was ready with tissues. People had filed into the room and were passing the sketchpad around. Miles and Lara were there, and Becca and Nick. Connor and Erin, too. Nina and Aaro were each holding a squirming baby girl. At the door, she heard Bruno and Lily's rambunctious twins, Tonio and Magda, and two-year-old, Marco, having some sort of loud snit fit at the door.

"Who is this kid in the picture, anyway?" Nick asked.

"She's one of the trafficked boat people murdered at Hazlett's lab," Sveti explained. "The flowers were growing up through her skeleton. She led me through the cave. I'd found her teddy bear in the dump outside the hole where they dropped the bodies. And I brought it back to her."

Nick looked pained. "Jesus. Rip my heart out and stomp on it."

"That's so fucked up," Seth said, staring down at the sketchpad. Raine, his wife, joined him and gazed at it, her eyes shiny.

"What a beautiful smile," she whispered.

The hug fest began, and after seeing the drawing, the hugs got very intense, but in some odd way, the comfort they offered could now find its way in. Her little ghost friend had cleared the way, with her open-hearted gift of flowers.

Tam's sharp voice cut through the babble. "How interesting! Look who just parked out behind everyone else, carefully positioning his car for a quick getaway. Did someone invite him? I certainly didn't."

Sveti's body went rigid. "Who?"

"Your cop," Tam said. "He's here."

Sveti cleared her throat. "He's not mine," she whispered.

"You greet him," Tam said. "I don't have anything nice to say to him. He drags you out of the sea half-dead, then walks away and leaves you alone and bleeding in a hospital bed? Ice-cold bastard."

"I recall someone I know doing something rather similar, long ago." Val shot Tam a cautious sidelong glance. "Glass houses, my love."

"That was different!" Tam snapped.

"Of course. I just had a bullet wound," Val murmured. "It was a trifle, yes. That I will concede."

"I was poisoned!" Tam yelled, outraged.

"Of course you were, my pet. Absolutely toxic."

"You condescending bastard. I'm going to the game room to check on the status of our daughter's virtue." She flounced out of the room.

Everyone looked at Sveti, expectantly.

"Well?" Edie said.

"Well, what?" Sveti hedged. "I didn't ask him to come."

"He didn't come here to see any of us," Nina said. "Want to go out and greet him alone? Without an audience?"

She pulled her ballerina flats on, with fingers that trembled. "No, I'll just, ah . . . go out on the terrace for a while."

The wind was nippy, and she only had a light knit wrap. But she wasn't getting near the entrance hall where her jacket hung. Not with Sam about to walk through it.

The terrace had two levels—the one opening off the living room, where the outdoor furniture and the barbecue were located. Wooden stairs descended from there over the rocks, leading to another landing about four meters below, smaller, but with an entirely different view. The stairway zigzagged down to the beach, which was accessible only in that way, except by sea. The cliffs, the drop-off, the smell of saltwater gave her a nauseating wave of discomfort as she remembered that awful morning. That desperate, screaming leap into the sea.

She dragged in deep, shuddering breaths and opened her heart to the stark beauty of the place. She knew how a heart felt when it was awake now. She could call the feeling forth at will. It was scary, painful. But bearable.

And full of hope. Like holding out a handful of wildflowers.

Sam stared at the parking area below Tam and Val's house, dismayed. There were ten different vehicles parked there, and the space in front of the garage was full, too. Years back they'd engineered a parking area, after bitter complaints from the McCloud Crowd who were sick of parking on the narrow, inhospitable road. All were cars he knew. There were the massive family cars of the four McCloud guys; Nick and Becca's sedan; Miles and Lara's truck; Aaro and Nina's car, with matching baby seats in the back; Bruno and Lily's seven-seater van; Seth and Raine's SUV. People he was specifically avoiding.

A wooden stairway led up from the parking area and zigzagged through rainforest foliage, around huge cedars. Vidcams were mounted on the trees, observing every leg of the journey. Tam and Val liked their guests to arrive on foot, single file and observed from every angle.

He would have saved this suicidal exercise for another day but for the vidcams. He'd been buzzed in at the gate and eyeballed at intervals during the drive. If he rabbited, thirty-odd people would watch him do it. More to the point, those people would watch Sveti watch him do it.

He started up the walkway, half expecting a bullet to take him down. Tam hated his guts, he'd heard. An unhealthy state of affairs, but whatever. A quick death would end his torment, too.

He didn't even know what he was going to say to her. This imperative welled from a part of him that was not particularly verbal.

But it knew what it wanted, and went after it, hairy knuckles dragging.

He didn't have the strength to fight it anymore.

The wound in his rib pulled. His thigh spasmed. He did not allow himself to limp. The front porch was full of people when he reached the top of the walkway. Val was in the forefront, his handsome face a grim mask. Nick frowned beside him. Those two men were Sveti's principal adoptive fathers, though all of those guys felt fiercely paternal toward her. Becca stood behind Nick, looking worried. Miles loomed in the back, his face guardedly sympathetic.

Sam stopped at the foot of the porch stairs in front of the human shield. Rachel wove her way between the taller adults, followed by Misha, who was the only welcoming face in the crowd.

"Hey," Misha said. "What took you so long?"

Only the most unanswerable question in the history of mankind.

His tongue felt as unresponsive as a rock. "What's the occasion?"

"Don't you remember?" Misha said impatiently. "They're here to celebrate Sveti's book deal!"

He groped for the memory. "Oh, yeah. Good for her. I didn't know the party was today."

"She has millions of dollars now," Rachel announced. "Guess that's why you're here, right? Probably all you care about. Jerk."

His chest jolted in a mirthless laugh. As if he gave a fuck. He was glad for her, sure, but he hadn't cared about money even before he'd gotten his balls tickled by the icy breath of Death.

He chose a random entry point in the mass of bodies and made for it. They gave way for him. Tam blocked his way, clad in her trademark black, red hair loose around her shoulders. Her topaz eyes blazed. "You sadistic son of a bitch," she hissed. "How could you run out on her when she was hurt? You *prick!*"

He looked past her, searching for Sveti. "She shut the door on me," he said.

"Bullshit! You're just punishing her for some stupid argument that was probably all your fault! What do you want from her?"

"I'm here to knock on the door again," he said simply.

"Oh, shut the fuck up," Tam snarled. "You make me sick. Putting it all on her. Go find your balls before you show your face again!"

He shook his head. It was now or it was never. "Where is she?"

Tam stomped out toward the kitchen without answering. Sam turned to the others. "Where is she?" he demanded again.

Miles finally took pity on him. "Front terrace," he said. "She bolted when she heard you were coming."

Great. *Fuck.* He headed for the sliding doors and stepped outside. This was his first cliff seascape after their adventure, and it evoked a sickening déjà vu rush. His scream of denial when he'd seen Sveti fall had damaged his vocal folds. His voice was still hoarse, after six weeks.

His heart rate spiked, sweat slicked his back. His belly churned. He fought it. Vomiting all over Tam's terrace would not help matters.

Sveti wasn't on the first terrace. He peered down the stairs and saw her a level down. Hair whipping out like a flag, ramrod straight. His eyes drank up the sight. She did not turn.

He couldn't fight this ceaseless pull anymore. It was like living on the end of a bungee cord. He might as well throw himself at her feet one last time. God knows, he had the choreography down.

He gripped the wooden railing as he descended. He thudded clumsily with his bum leg to announce himself, but she didn't turn.

He leaned on the railing next to her. The cove opened before them, flanked by the arms of two ridges slanting down into the ocean, thick with conifers. The wind whipped Sveti's hair around her face. Her profile was so delicate. The shadows under her cheekbones were prominent.

"Hey." His brain was wiped clean. He was a stammering idiot.

Her silence said so much. He stood there and took it for as long as he could stand. "You hanging in there okay?" he tried again, finally.

She shrugged. "It rolls over me sometimes, like a tank," she said softly, twisting her hands together. "But I think I've turned a corner."

"With the book deal?" he guessed. "Congratulations, by the way. Misha told me. I didn't know you were celebrating today."

She smiled, briefly. "Bet you weren't expecting the crowd."

"Yeah, it was special," he said. "Lots of hairy eyeballs."

She frowned. "They shouldn't blame you. They weren't there."

He braced himself against the delicate thrill of hope. "Sounds like you're defending me," he said carefully.

She laid her cool, slender hand on his. Excitement jabbed, hot and bright, like lightning lancing through the far reaches of his being.

"Nothing you did needs defending," she said. "You almost died for me. Your instincts were always right. I was such an idiot. All I ever did was fight you. I can't believe you hung around as long as you did."

"Well." He stared at the marks that marred her hand. "We didn't always fight. There were . . . memorable interludes. Here and there."

She cleared her throat. "I'm glad it wasn't all pure hell on earth."

The wind shifted. Voices filtered down from above. A glance over his shoulder revealed that the terrace was crowded with spectators of every age hanging over the railing, all suddenly fascinated by the view.

"They are chaperoning the living shit out of us," he said.

"Do you want to go down to the beach?" she asked. "They'll still stare, but at least we won't be overheard."

His heart thudded, but he played it cool. "Sounds good to me."

She led the way. He could not stop staring, not even to watch where he put his feet. She sat on the bottom step and slid off her shoes. He did the same, but held her arm as she started to get up.

He grasped her ankle, bending her leg so he could get a look at the sole of her foot. She let him study the scars. The glass had sliced her feet to ribbons, and the rest of her hadn't fared so well, either. She'd rolled all over the fucking stuff, shirtless. She'd been bleeding from more cuts than he could count the last time he saw her. But she'd healed. She walked fine on those feet. He inhaled the biggest chestful of air he'd had in weeks and followed her onto the sand.

It was cold, the sun long gone, due to the shape of the coastline, though it still lit Tam and Val's terrace and its load of onlookers. Sveti walked out to where the foam lapped up over the gleaming sand. Whoa. Toe-freezing sensory agony, to root him in reality. So much colder than the Mediterranean, in which they had so recently dunked themselves.

A wave swept in. He danced back and rolled up his jeans. Sveti laughed at him, which was well worth the soggy cuffs.

They fell into step together as they moved across the sand. A seagull strutted in front of them and gave them an insolent once-over before marching away. It left a spidery, twisting trail of tracks. He noticed these random details while he groped for an entry point into this life-altering conversation. He wished she'd just hand him one. Like, *Sam, why are you here?* or *Sam, what do you want?* Anything at all.

But no. She walked quietly, eyes downcast, letting him flail.

"I thought you were done with me," she said. "I'm surprised to see you here."

He grasped at the rope. "Oh, no. I'm not done. Not by a mile."

Her eyes flicked up, questioning. "No?"

"I want more," he blurted, then hissed through his teeth. "Damn, that sounds all wrong. What I mean is, I'll take what I can get. Aw shit, that sounds all wrong, too. I don't even know how to say it."

Her eyes looked huge and startled. "Oh, Sam—"

"I know, we've been through it. How you can't go there with me. No love, romance, or eternal devotion. You've got your big, hairy issues. Fine. I'll take what I can get. Whatever you've got, I'll take it."

She opened her mouth, but he hurried on. "I mean it. Wherever you go. Europe, New York, Brazil, Turkmenistan, I don't give a shit, I want to be there, too. I'll be your lover when you want one, and I'll be your friend forever. I think you're fucking awesome, and I need to be close to that. Wherever you are, whatever way I can. I'm not fussy."

She looked bewildered. "And that would be enough for you?"

"No, probably not, but who cares?" he said. "I've never felt so alive as I did when you were making me miserable. I'll take that, hands down, over any other alternative on earth."

"Oh, Sam," she whispered. "I don't even know where to start."

He held up a warning hand. "One thing, up front. I may be just a boy toy, but I'll be a jealous one. Whatever perverse arrangement we come up with, it has to be exclusive, or we'll have big problems."

"Sam. Stop."

The sharpness of her voice cut through his rant. "What?" he demanded. "No deal? It skeeves you out? Say it quick, if that's your answer. So I can start swimming to Japan."

"You deserve better than crumbs," she said.

Dread gripped his insides and squeezed. "That sounds like the classic 'it's not you, it's me.' Which you've been saying from the start."

"No! I just mean that you're the one who is awesome. You deserve everything, Sam. Not just crumbs. You deserve the whole cake."

"What I deserve is not the issue. The issue is what I can actually have." He paused. "Besides, crumbs from you were yummier than all the other whole cakes I've ever tasted. So? Lay it on me. Make me suffer."

"I don't want you to suffer," she whispered.

Good luck with that. He was born to it. He tightened his belly into impervious steel and forced himself to say it. "I take it that's a no."

"You don't understand!" she said fiercely. "I'm the one who wants more! I'm the one who wants it all!"

He frowned at her, perplexed. "What 'all' are you referring to, Sveti? Sex? Servitude? My heart's blood? It's yours already. So what?"

"Love," she said softly.

Heat welled up from someplace very deep, racing through the secret channels inside him like sap through a plant. "Love," he repeated stupidly. "You lost me. I'm dizzy. I've got whiplash. Help me out here."

She reached out and seized his hand, and pressed it over her heart. "Love," she repeated more loudly.

The edges of his hand pressed the lush swell of her breasts. Her skin was so warm, though she had goose bumps. She wore no bra, just clingy, drapey layers. A few inches to the left or right, and he'd be stroking one of her taut dark nipples.

"That was never an issue," he said. "You want it, you got it. Hell, you always had it. You're the one who needs to talk about love, Sveti."

"So let's talk." She placed her hands on his, pressing it to her chest. Her heart thudded against his palm. Steady, rapid, and strong. As if she were offering it to him. The heat, the strength. The certainty.

He didn't dare breathe. She clasped his hand to herself, as if she received some mysterious message in the contact. Who knew, maybe she did. He had a hard time swallowing the mind-reading hoo-ha the others talked about—Edie's drawings, Miles and Lara's wild tales. But Sveti was an ambassador from the Land of Weird who had absolute credibility for him. He'd believe any crazy thing she told him. Just please God, if she would just tell him the one thing he burned to hear.

"Do you feel it?" she murmured.

He laughed. "I feel a whole lot of things. Be specific."

"My love," she said. "I feel it coming out of me, like one of those high-power search beams. The kind you can see from space. Blazing straight at you. It feels so hot. So soft."

"What . . ." He stopped. He couldn't talk. His throat was vibrating.

Sveti touched his face, stroking her fingertips over his cheek and jaw.

"So. What, ah . . . what changed, for you?" he finally forced out.

She cupped his cheek. "Almost dying makes you see things so clearly. So did all that time in the hospital. I saw how selfish I'd been."

"Selfish?" His voice cracked. "You? The sacrificial virgin, out to save the world at any costs?"

"Yes, exactly. At any cost. That was the heart of the problem," she said. "The cost was too high, and I didn't get that until it was too late. I was so stupid, Sam. Always insisting on my own agenda.

Using your feelings for me for my own purposes. It wasn't right, and I'm sorry."

"Oh. Okay. You're, uh, forgiven." He discarded several vapid follow-ups to that and shook his head, defeated. "It was complicated."

"Maybe it was," she said. "But it isn't anymore."

He covered her hand with his own. "Just tell me what you want. Keep it really simple. I don't have a lot of brain cells left."

"Okay." Her fingers twined with his. "I don't want a boy toy, or a friend with benefits. I want you. Always, and forever. I want you in my bed, all night, every night of my life. I don't want crumbs. I want the whole cake. I want to gorge on cake every day. I want—oh!"

His kiss lifted her off her feet. Their combined weight sank his feet deep into the soggy sand. The surf lapped below his knees, but his legs were braced against the sucking pull of ice water. She made a surprised sound that swiftly turned into a sweet moan, a boneless yielding. She molded her body to his, twining her legs around his thighs.

He felt rooted, connected down to the center of the earth.

They drank each other in. Her crotch rubbed against the bulge in his jeans. Her lips were so soft. Her slender limbs so strong, around his.

With her perched on his thighs, his hands were free to move all over her as he sought to convince himself that this was not a fantasy or a dream. He splayed his fingers under her shirt to feel the pansy-like softness of her skin. Her spine felt prominent. Ribs, too. She needed feeding up. "You're so thin," he said accusingly. "What's with that?"

"Missing you," she said. "It was awful. Kills my appetite."

"We'll fix that quick," he said. "With lots of cake."

She laughed. He captured the happy sound in his hungry kiss.

Time dissolved, swirled, measured by the rhythm of the surf. He was wet to his thighs, but he barely noticed. At some length, he noticed flashes of light out of the corner of his eye. He turned to look.

Fireworks, shot off from Tam's terrace. Oh, for the love of Christ.

Sveti laughed, delighted. "How sweet! They're celebrating for us!"

"And probably monitoring me with a rifle scope, too," he growled.

"Don't be silly. Oh, look! I love pinwheels."

Colored sparks twinkled and glittered as they drifted down toward the beach, winking out on their way.

"I guess it's better than shooting me where I stand," he observed.

"No one's really mad at you," she scoffed. "They were a little miffed about you staying away when I was laid up, but they all love you."

He grunted eloquently. "Yeah, whatever. Tonight, we light out of here, find a hotel. Turn off our phones. Stay in bed. For about a week."

She rubbed her cheek against his. "Sounds perfect. But first, we toast with the champagne that Val ordered specially from France."

Sam sighed, resigned. "We're doing the family dance? Then we might as well make it official."

"Official how?"

"Like this," he said, digging in his jacket. "I brought it along. Just in case, you know, my wildest dreams should come true."

He pulled out a small hinged box covered with black ribbed silk and tied with a ribbon bow. Held it out to her.

Sveti slid from her perch on his thigh into knee-deep swirling foam, her smile fading to wonderment. She opened the box.

The ring was part of the set that had been on display at the Hotel Aurelio. Rounded rubies, sapphires, and emeralds embedded in a complicated tangle of burnished coils of gold. It glowed in the dimness, as if it had trapped some of the sunset light and held it for them.

"Oh, Sam." Her whisper sounded lost.

"I've got the earrings for you, too. I've been hungry for my cake for a long time." He waited as long as he could stand before prompting her. "Will you wear it?"

Her nod sent tears flashing down her cheeks.

He paused long enough to kiss them away. Her heat, her salt, her wet. All his to claim, to protect and cherish and treasure.

He pulled the ring out of the box. Managed to slide it onto her ring finger without dropping it into the foaming surf. It glowed on her hand, a perfect fit. Not worthy of her beauty, but fuck it. Nothing on earth could be. He gathered her close, kissed her wet face. It cracked his heart open, the trusting way she rested her head in his hand.

The surf continued its thundering hum of approval. Stars were coming out. Fireworks exploded from the terrace on the mountainside. The warm yellow squares of lit-up windows signaled approval and welcome, urging them to come in from the cold, which was well and good, but not quite yet. It was too soon to share. It was so sweet, so fine and rare. Vulnerable as a newborn child, powerful as a bonfire.

They could only cling and sway, cradled in the arms of the cove, lapped by foam, ruffled by the wind. Awed and humbled by the vast, unfathomable grace of it. They had found their hearts' home at last.

And they were welcomed in.

EPILOGUE

Six months later . . .

Rachel gazed morosely through the balcony railing. The party was in full swing, and from her perch on the walkway above, she had a perfect view of the dance floor. Sveti and Sam were lip-locked, swaying to an old ballad about crazy love. The plunging back of Sveti's ivory bridal gown made her look half-naked, the effect enhanced by the fact that her front was plastered to Sam's chest. Which was more or less where it had been since they got engaged. On the beach, in front of everyone. Flipping exhibitionists. Like, get a room. Please.

Of course, she was happy for Sveti. And Sam was great. Brave, smart, handsome, blah blah blah.

Misha sank down beside her, having sneaked up on her. Which was creepy-sneaky, but also kinda cool. She was glad to see him. He suited her mood. He had his pissy moments, but he was a good guy.

"You look sad," he observed.

She shrugged, rebelliously. "I hate how everything has to change," she said. "Why San Francisco? It's so far away."

"Better than Cambodia, or India," Misha pointed out philosophically. "It could have been anywhere. It still might. Soul Rescue will grow fast, with those two working together. Lots of money, lots of power." His cool voice had a tone of measured approval.

"Please." She echoed Tam's world-weary tone. "It's not about Soul Rescue. All she can talk about is Sam."

"That will pass," Misha observed.

"Yeah, and she'll be thousands of miles away when it does, saving the lost children. What are you doing here? You were supposed to play video games with Sam's pinheaded nephew. Weren't we supposed to be the friendly ambassadors to Sam's tight-assed family?"

"I tried." Misha's voice was long-suffering. "He is afraid of me. He thinks I will stab him if he wins. Not that he ever would. Kev is almost as good as you, but he and Jeannie are herding the little kids out of trouble downstairs. They did something terrible to the cake. The caterers are trying to fix the structural damage with sugar glaze."

Rachel snorted. That gang could be counted on to make trouble. Kev and Jeannie tried to cover for them, with limited success. But Sveti and Sam weren't concerned about their wedding cake. They swayed, blissed out. In fact, there was a lot of rapt romantic contemplation happening on that dance floor. Weddings brought it out in this crowd, though Mama could usually be counted on not to get mushy. Seth and Raine were twined together, Seth's nose buried in her silver-blond hair. Aaro and Nina swayed as close as they could get, with sleeping baby girls draped over their shoulders. Miles swayed with Lara, his big hand cupping her pregnant belly. Little Eamon, Uncle Sean's oldest, danced with Sofia, undaunted by the fact that she was a head taller than he. Nick and Becca snickered at some private joke and kissed, passionately. Yikes. Way too much PDA out there. Eeeuw.

Sam's father and sister were trapped in a corner by the decimated dessert buffet, hemmed in by Zia Rosa, who gesticulated wildly as she talked. God knew what story Zia was telling the Petries about them, but it hardly mattered. Any story that Zia might pick out of a hat would scare the piss out of a mere mortal man. Her weirdo family rocked.

Liv sat in a corner, nursing Caroline. Sean sat behind her, his cheek resting on her shoulder. Davy and Margot were in a clinch on the dance floor. Lily's head was on Bruno's shoulder—Marco was in the stroller next to Zia, blocking the Petries' escape route. Edie and Kev danced, Kev's hand splayed over her butt. Even Mama and Papa danced, though Mama glanced up, eyes narrowing when she saw Misha, who had not slunk into the shadows fast enough.

"Shit," Misha muttered. "Now she will come check on us. She hates me. She thinks I am a psycho killer."

"She does not," Rachel soothed. "She's just nervous."

"We should go, before she comes. I found a way to the tower on the fourth floor. Want to see?"

"The guy said it was off-limits, for insurance reasons! Locked off!"

"Locked?" Misha gave her a crooked smile. "With whom do you think you are speaking?"

She grinned, delighted. "You mean, you picked the lock?"

"Shhh, do not spoil it. Do you want to see? Or not?"

"Of course I do."

"Then come."

She followed as he padded down the staircase and skirted the ballroom, wending between tables and strollers. Liv smiled at them as she laid Caroline down. Liv and Sean rejoined the dancers as the ballad pulsed on. Zia Rosa hailed them as they slipped by. They pretended not to hear and darted into the corridor that led toward the kitchen.

Children spilled out of a bathroom. Kevvie was scolding. ". . . going to clobber us all! God, Tonio! Do you have rocks in your heads?"

"We just thought those pink roses would look cool in Lena's hair, because her dress is the same pink! I didn't know they were made of sugar, and I didn't mean to knock off the top tier! It just happened!"

Lena slunk out the bathroom door, her shiny black ringlets still gummed with flakes of pink sugar. Jamie followed, his freckled face dripping, frosting traces lingering under his square chin.

Kevvie caught sight of her. "Are they after us? Have they heard?"

"Nope," Rachel assured him. "You're good. They're all out on the dance floor, hypnotized by sappy old-time music."

"Good," Jeannie said, relieved. "We'll be okay until the caterers rat us out, and they're too busy rebuilding the cake, so scatter, everyone! Try not to look guilty! Hey, where are you guys going?"

"Tell you after!" Rachel called. Misha pulled her around the corner. He pulled a couple of metal tools from his pocket and jiggled them in the lock, an abstracted look in his eyes. The lock clicked open.

They slipped inside just as someone rounded the corner.

". . . a discount for the cake, since it's a tier short now, but the boss is gonna shit bricks. Who let those kids in there, anyhow?"

"The bride and groom aren't gonna notice," another voice said. "They can't detach their mouths from each other."

"Maybe not, but that old Italian lady is gonna be all over our asses. She'll come down like a ton of broken rock. . . ."

Rachel and Misha fought to muffle their snorts of laughter.

The locked-off stairway smelled different from the lived-in part of the house, older, dustier, colder. The lightbulbs were a lower wattage, the wallpaper darkened with age, and abandoned furniture covered with drop cloths loomed eerily in the corridor. This section of the building was not renovated. It was dusty and forgotten.

Misha led her through it as if he'd lived there all his life. They climbed stairs, higher and higher until they got to a twisting spiral ladder in a wooden tower. Rachel followed Misha up, feeling her way. He pushed a trapdoor in the ceiling upward. Moonlight spilled down onto them.

They crawled out, onto the floor of a gothic tower. Eight arches, open to the night. They saw everything: the grounds where the party had begun that afternoon, the rose garden, the fountain.

In the other direction, the tower looked out over the massive Columbia River Gorge. Moonlight had washed out the stars and lit the river into a pale, snaking ribbon that disappeared into the mountains.

They stood side by side, staring at the sky. The old mansion hummed beneath them, full of music, talk, light, and life. Above, the wind sighed and rustled, tossing the limbs of big, ancient trees. Whispering something she could almost understand, but only with a part of her heart that struggled under some heavy weight.

She stared up at the moon and felt that weight lessen.

"I feel like we could just take off from here, like birds," she said. "Fly out over the canyon. Follow the river all the way to the ocean."

"You are crying," he said, alarmed. "Is it because Sveti is leaving?"

"No." She flapped that wrong assessment away with her hand. "Well, maybe. A little. It's just that I think . . . I think I get it now."

"Get what?"

Rachel struggled to put it into words. "The point of Soul Rescue. It started with us. Sveti and I would have died if they hadn't rescued us."

"And me," Misha said, his voice flat.

"You too," she agreed. "Everybody's been rescued, one way or another. We have a safe, strong place now. To take off from, to come back to. She just wants that, for everyone. It's a good thing to want."

Misha made a low, wordless sound and nodded.

They were standing a little closer now. So close, their hands just barely brushed . . . and then clasped. Neither dared to speak.

They stood for a long time, barely breathing. Gazing at a world full of moonlight and shadow, magic and mystery.

And endless possibilities.